The Quality of Life Report

ALSO BY MEGHAN DAUM

My Misspent Youth

Meghan Daum

The Quality of Life Report

· · · · · · · · · · · · · · · ·

Viking

VIKING
Published by the Penguin Group
Penguin Group (USA) Inc., 375 Hudson Street,
New York, New York 10014, U.S.A.
Penguin Books Ltd, 80 Strand,
London WC2R 0RL, England
Penguin Books Australia Ltd, 250 Camberwell Road, Camberwell,
Victoria 3124, Australia
Penguin Books Canada Ltd, 10 Alcorn Avenue,
Toronto, Ontario, Canada M4V 3B2
Penguin Books India (P) Ltd, 11 Community Centre, Panchsheel Park,
New Delhi – 110 017, India
Penguin Books (N.Z.) Ltd, Cnr Rosedale and Airborne Roads, Albany,
Auckland, New Zealand
Penguin Books (South Africa) (Pty) Ltd, 24 Sturdee Avenue,
Rosebank, Johannesburg 2196, South Africa

Penguin Books Ltd, Registered Offices:
80 Strand, London WC2R 0RL, England

First published in 2003 by Viking Penguin,
a member of Penguin Group (USA) Inc.

1   3   5   7   9   10   8   6   4   2

Copyright © Meghan Daum, 2003
All rights reserved

Publisher's Note
This is a work of fiction. Names, characters, places, and incidents are
either the product of the author's imagination or are used fictitiously,
and any resemblance to actual persons, living or dead, business es-
tablishments, events, or locales is entirely coincidental.

LIBRARY OF CONGRESS CATALOGING-IN-PUBLICATION DATA
Daum, Meghan, 1970–
The quality of life report / Meghan Daum.
p.   cm.
ISBN 0-670-03213-1
1. Middle West—Fiction. I. Title.
PS3604.A93Q25   2003
813'.54—dc21   2002044859

This book is printed on acid-free paper. ∞

Printed in the United States of America
Set in Bauer Bodoni
Designed by Francesca Belanger

ACKNOWLEDGMENTS

For their comments, moral support, inspiration, and professionalism, the author wishes to acknowledge the following: Lara Shapiro, Sara Eckel, Alison Manheim, Thomas Beller, Ron Orth, Karen Murphy, Svetlana Katz, and the Corporation of Yaddo. Special thanks to Tina Bennett for her incomparable dedication to this novel and to Carole DeSanti for her extraordinary editorial wisdom and her appreciation for old farmhouses.

The Quality of Life Report

Open Arms, Open Minds

For the sake of those involved, I will say only this: my moral, ethical, and, if not spiritual, let's say existential coming-of-age took place in a more or less rectangular-shaped state in the Midwest—closer to the West Coast than the east by maybe one hundred miles, closer to Canada than Mexico by maybe one hundred—in a town populated by approximately ninety thousand government employees, farmers, academics, insurance salesmen, assembly-line workers, antique dealers, real estate agents, rape crisis counselors, certified massage therapists, girls volleyball coaches, and a whole lot of other people who, as they would tell it, just wanted to live in a peaceful place where movies cost six dollars and the children's zoo was free, and where library fines, even if you kept the book for a year, even if you dropped the book in the bathtub and returned it looking like it had been rescued by search divers, were rarely known to exceed five dollars. The state, dogged neither by oppressive Pentecostal leanings nor a preponderance of Teva-shod rafting guide types, was neither in the Bible Belt nor the Rocky Mountains. It had few lakes, only a handful of rivers, and none of the kind of topography that might attract Japanese tourists or inspire bumper stickers of the THIS CAR CLIMBED . . . variety.

There was very little to climb on this terrain. It was flat and treeless and cliffless. Even so, Prairie City had made the most of itself. It housed a state college, a public television station, and an independent movie theater that had screened *The Last Temptation of Christ* when the commercial cinemas had dropped the film because of picketers, most of whom were a small but vocal group of Seventh-day Adventists and a few of whom were Lutherans looking for a diversion. Generally speaking, though, all points of view were welcome. For years, Prairie City's welcome sign had read A GREAT PLACE TO LIVE until, under an initiative to promote diversity, the city council voted to change the motto to OPEN ARMS, OPEN MINDS. It was a fitting kickoff to the other placards in town. For every billboard reminding passing drivers that DURING AN ABORTION, SOMETHING DIES INSIDE there was another encouraging HIV testing, pet spay and neutering, or two-dollar mai tais at the Thirteenth Street TGI Friday's, which, though not all citizens realized it, was a major hangout for the community's sizable gay and lesbian population. For seven years running, the town had ranked in the top twenty in *U.S. News & World Report*'s Most Livable Cities. In addition to its low rate of violent crime, good public school system, and four meticulously maintained municipal pools, Prairie City had the good fortune to have been hit by only six tornadoes during the entire period of the Clinton administration, just three of which killed anybody, all in trailer parks.

In Prairie City, trailer parks rubbed right up against elementary schools, public playgrounds, and houses of worship. Train tracks crisscrossed the city like lattice work, leaving little room for right sides or wrong sides. At Effie's Tavern on Highway 36, assembly-line workers from the Firestone tire plant gathered after their shifts and downed Leinenkugels alongside insurance agents in short-sleeved dress shirts and choir directors in Birkenstocks and attorneys and social service case workers and even local politicians, most of whom got off work at 3:30 on Friday afternoons and began drinking around 3:54. Prairie City was a good-hearted place, not so much in the sense that moral aberrations never occurred but more in that when something did go wrong—a paleontology professor got caught downloading child pornography from the Web, an elected official was discovered freebasing coke in the public restroom behind the band shell—community head shaking took the form of bemusement rather than scorn. Everyone understood that everyone screwed up once in a while. What mattered was that you showed some class about it. What mattered was that you still helped your neighbor build his back deck. You still sat on the symphony board or at least volunteered to pick trash off the median of Highway 36 once a year. You accepted both your co-worker's gender reassignment surgery and the possibility that, during any given summer, golf-ball–sized hail could give your dog a concussion.

The concept of acceptance was vital to Prairie City. It stemmed from the legacy of its first residents, most of whom, in the mid-1800s, were bound for the West Coast on the Oregon Trail. Since Prairie City marked a point where the trail often became impassable in winter, the pioneers used it as a stopover until spring. Except that many never left. As legend has it, Prairie City was imbued with a mysterious force that kept its supposedly temporary residents from resuming their journeys. Of those who did leave, countless numbers found themselves coming back after just a few years on the coast. It was hard for them to explain what had brought them. The tug of that land was as strong and invisible as gravity. The wind, though it shrieked in every season, soon lulled even the most restless souls into contentment. The people stopped thinking about gold and started building schoolhouses. They had more children. They joined sewing circles. They told themselves so many times that they were going to leave that, as generations died and were born, the Plan to Leave became as much a part of community life as agriculture itself. It was all a matter of holding off until the right time, of getting through the winter and then the summer and then winter again. Long before Effie's Tavern ever served its first draft, the citizens of Prairie City had perfected the art of waiting things out.

Of course, I didn't know much about waiting things out before I came to Prairie City. I knew next to nothing about anything, unless you count a deeply ingrained knowledge of the latest sociocultural great truths about the twenty- and thirtysomethings of America, which I discussed with my friends over drinks on at least a twice-weekly basis. Some examples of our areas of inquiry:

A) No one wears gold anymore. It just went away. Remember how in the 1980s everyone wore gold? Like a gold tennis bracelet? Now it's silver. Nothing but silver. Wedding bands are platinum or white gold. When is the last time you saw a gold wedding band? Seriously? But you're not, like, *friends* with that person?

B) More and more women are feeling pressure to not get married until they're at least twenty-eight. But at the same time there's pressure to marry before you're thirty-four. That leaves a very small window. Six years to find a husband. Consider the latest census data that there are seven hundred thousand more single women than single men in New York (not even counting gay people, of which there are more men than lesbians). Ergo, limited window of opportunity plus disproportionate gender ratio equals . . . imminent spinsterhood for thousands of women. What to call this? The New Spinster? The Spinsterization of America?

C) Yogurt. What happened? It just went away.

D) Is thirty-seven the new twenty-six?

E) Lucinda's apartment lease. Loss of. What is she going to do?

Lucinda was me. Is me. Except the Lucinda who lost her apartment lease on Broadway and Ninety-fourth Street in Manhattan was a person of such a long time ago that I have difficulty even associating that face—pale, unlined, dabbed with Chanel makeup that I never knew how to apply right—with the one who now tells this story. Like so many people in Prairie City, my face has been subjected to a kind of wind that blows in so hard from the north that you find yourself reaching for a tree in order to stay on the ground, only to realize there are no trees, just an ocean of grass. This is the kind of place that makes you wonder if wind can render gravity irrelevant, if weather itself can make you crazy. You lie in bed and wonder if the Apocalypse has come or if it's just another night in June. The early settlers had a name for this; they called it prairie madness. Pioneers who had migrated from the east literally went insane from the shrieking wind. It seemed to affect the women disproportionately, maybe because the men were insane to begin with. But I'm getting ahead of myself.

When I was twenty-nine and a regular participant in conversations (if we were going to hand in the receipts to our office accounting departments we called them "brainstorming sessions") about What's Happening in America Today, I was an associate producer at a local television magazine show called *New York Up Early*. Despite not being on a major network, it had two million viewers in the metropolitan area. Hosted by Bonnie Crawley and Samantha Frank, a pair of thirtyish women positioned to "complement" each other (one was perky, the other, who wore nerd-chic glasses, quirky), the program dealt with a variety of New York issues: mob-related crime, the Bryant Park fashion shows, the rooftop gardens of rich people. I was the Lifestyle correspondent, a position I'd achieved after five years of fetching espressos and making restaurant reservations for *Up Early*'s bipolar, metabolically freakish senior producer, Faye Figaro (at five foot eleven, she weighed 119; she also threw staplers at people). Though my annual salary had been raised to a mere $31,900 (this made tolerable only by my rent-stabilized one-windowed cell on West Ninety-fourth Street), I enjoyed the privileges of a minor celebrity in that I appeared on camera and interviewed people about What New Yorkers Are Thinking About Today, which, in most cases, was what Faye, Bonnie, Samantha, I and the rest of the staff (all female except one gay guy) were thinking about.

Some examples of my journalistic endeavors:

- Lucinda Trout on takeout sushi and how it has replaced the soup and sandwich for the midtown office worker's lunch of choice.
- Lucinda Trout on thong underwear: can you learn to live with a permanent wedgie?
- Lucinda Trout on bridal registry etiquette: is it fair to expect your friend to spend eighty dollars on a single piece of flatware (especially when your friend has no marriage prospects!)?
- Lucinda Trout on adopted babies from China: the Upper West Side is overrun with them. What are the implications for the future mating patterns of this generation? In 2015, there will be seven teenage girls for every teenage boy on the Upper West Side. Are we not simply creating an equal and opposite paradigm of the unbalanced gender ratio in China? Will these girls have to move to Beijing to find a husband? Will Manhattan become a playground for men with Asian fetishes?

The Chinese baby story didn't delve as deeply as I would have liked. It ended up essentially being a plug for a store on Columbus Avenue called Asian Infant Accessories, which sold teething rings and mobiles in Asian designs so that the children wouldn't lose touch with their heritage. I almost quit over that. But I almost quit over half the stories I did. I had a degree in nineteenth-century American literature from Smith. My goal was to work for PBS or National Public Radio. And somehow I'd ended up holding a microphone in one hand and sliding a finger of the other hand under the thong underwear of a willing clerk at a SoHo underwear boutique to show "how roomy a thong can really be."

The day I decided not to quit over the Chinese baby story was the day my landlord slipped a note under my door saying the building management was changing hands and that starting September 1, my rent would be raised to twenty-one hundred dollars a month. It was June 1. I needed to ask Faye for a raise, though it was unlikely I could get her to triple my salary, which is what would have been required to stay.

Faye wanted to see me in her office anyway. Though it was muggy and 87 degrees outside she was wearing her usual getup—skintight black leather pants, a sleeveless (apparently wool) turtle-neck sweater, and Jimmy Choo mules with three-inch heels. Her black hair was tied in a severe French twist that appeared to be pulling back the skin on her temples (a do-it-yourself face-lift tech-nique? This itself was a possible story idea . . .). Faye's background was in the art world—she was rumored to have been, in the 1960s, the lover of either Gerard Malanga or Cookie Mueller, depending upon who you asked. From there she had migrated into the fashion world and eventually into television and she was as out of place in the business as I was, though in the completely opposite way. While she looked like a fifty-year-old version of Lara Flynn Boyle (though every year that I'd worked for her she'd claimed to be thirty-seven) I looked like a graduate student who sprang for good haircuts but wouldn't shell out for an iron. I was perpetually rumpled. Faye, for her part, was practically illiterate. She had been hired for her celebrity connections; I for my ability to write all of her memos and anticipate the fluctuations of her volatile brain chemistry.

Faye was looking particularly reptilian that day. Her eyes were reduced to mere slits underneath a puffiness that suggested her weekend at Donatella Versace's South Beach villa had involved some kind of head-on collision that activated a set of air bags be-neath the sockets. She leaned back in her chair and draped a lamp-postlike leg over her desk, knocking over an ashtray and a stack of videotapes and causing her shoe to fall off and reveal a set of con-torted blackened toenails.

"Lucinda!" Faye screamed, though I was three feet away. "I have received a memo from upstairs."

"Are they firing you?" I asked. We had this sort of relationship. Sparring, playful. Though there was always the possibility that she would lunge unexpectedly, like a big cat.

"They want to move the show in a new direction," she said. "They think it's too provincial, too New York centric. They want us to cover issues of concern to average Americans. Maybe even humanitarian issues. Of course, I find that profoundly uninteresting. But I have no doubt that you can tap into the psyches of fat housewives in trailer parks."

"Actually I've always thought the show was too limited," I said. "Are we going in a more, like, *Frontline*-ish direction?"

"Don't get uppity," Faye said.

I caught her noticing my shoes, which were scuffed and from Banana Republic and utterly beneath her standards.

"I'm sending you to the Midwest," she said. "There's a very dangerous drug there that women are doing to help them lose weight and clean the house. Basically it's coke for the Payless shoes set. It sounds disgusting and I'm sure you can find a bunch of disgusting people who will talk on camera and give the show a dose of realness."

She handed me a story memo.

> To: Up Early Exeuctives
> From: Faye Figaro, Senoir Producer
> Re: Methanfettymean
>
> Meth: Its Cheep, Its a Quick High, and Its Endangering Womans Lives
> Had lunch with Roseanne (Barr? Arnold? whatever) the other day to brainstorm about shows new direction and she told me about a new drug that is priminont in the midwest United Stats. It's called methenfetimyne and it is basicly a much, much more potant form of the "mothers little helper' upper that was previlant in the

1960s. It is made in labs that are often in farm houses
and then sold to averge, normal women who want to
lose wieght or just have more engery to do housewrk
or care for the kids. The main thing here is that it is
very, very common and extremley dangerous and
people die from it. I would like to send Lucinda Trout,
who has been doing a good job as Lifstyle Correp-
sondent, to invesigate this alaming trend.

"You had lunch with Roseanne?" I asked.

"They set it up," Faye said, lighting a cigarette and snaking her
foot around under her desk in search of her lost mule. "She's actually quite brilliant in her way, given her cultural context."

"Where would I have to go?"

"Hello?" Faye yelled. "That's your job. Figure it out! You're going on Friday."

"For how long?"

"I don't know, a week. Make it in depth. They're serious about
this getting serious thing. But no fat people, please. I'm not throwing all our standards out the window."

Faye softened as the nicotine worked its way through her nervous system. She slid her foot into her shoe and returned her leg to
the desk.

"So how are you, Lucinda?" she asked, turning suddenly em-
pathic. "Are you well?"

"My rent is being raised to twenty-one hundred a month," I said.

"Can't you ask your parents for money?"

"Faye, you know my parents are retired schoolteachers."

"Well, then I guess you'll have to move to Queens," she said.
"Can you redo this memo for me?"

I took the memo and got up to leave.

"Can you pick up my ashtray?" Faye asked.

"Faye, I'm not your assistant anymore."

Faye was on her fifth temp in fourteen months, a sweet woman who had made the mistake of wearing a plastic tortoise-shell head-band to her first day of work.

"I don't want that girl coming in here," Faye whispered, an inch-long ash breaking off her cigarette and landing on her Palm Pilot. "I'm serious. It messes up the feng shui thing in here."

The prospect of the show's moving in a serious, more humanitarian direction slightly abated my dismay over the hopelessness of getting a raise. I went to my desk and did an Internet search on drug rehab facilities in the Midwest. I then left messages with twelve clinic receptionists in places like Missouri, South Dakota, and Kansas, seven of whom were themselves in recovery and wanted to discuss their drug abuse at length. These discussions effectively completed my preliminary research. I rewrote Faye's memo and then typed up my own.

> To: Up Early staff
> From: Lucinda Trout
> Re: Methamphetamine: It's Cheap, It's a Quick High, and It's Endangering Women's Lives
>
> Methamphetamine, also known as crank, speed, ice, amp, blue belly, white cross, white crunch, albino poo, al tweakened long, beegokes, and bikerdope, among other slang terms, is a powerful psychostimulant that causes increased energy, appetite suppression, insomnia, and, when used over a long period of time, permanent brain damage and possibly death. Once associated with railroad construction and factory workers, meth is now the only drug in the United States that is abused more readily by women than by men. Today it has reached a purity level that makes it up to 80 times more powerful than the crystal meth of the 1960s and 70s. Labs are often set up in abandoned

farmhouses, where the putrid odor of the chemicals (which include common household products and agricultural fertilizers) can go undetected. This story will contain in-depth interviews with articulate, wholesome-looking women who found themselves sucked into the vortex of drug abuse and despair. I also envision long shots of cornfields and big sky (evocative of the paintings of Andrew Wyeth) with slow pans (underscored by Aaron Coplandesque music) across rustic farmhouses that belie the illicit debauchery festering inside.

The first person to call me back was Sue Lugenbeel. She was from some place called Prairie City and ran something called the Prairie City Recovery Center for Women. She said she had subjects for me. They would talk and appear on camera. She really wanted to help get the message out.

If only I had been away from my desk when Sue Lugenbeel called. If only the first clinic director to return my call had been some no-personality lout from some shabby town that I'd actually heard of and was therefore less exotic. But no. It was Sue. In Prairie City. I was on a plane with a cameraman the next morning. And from there began the end of my life as I'd known it.

Alternative Lifestyle Alert

My first impression of Prairie City was that it seemed not to be there at all. The "city," which, as Sue Lugenbeel had assured me, truly was a city with crime and drugs and "plenty of night life," wasn't visible from the air. We descended into wide patches of brown and green fields. Only two airlines served the place and despite the smallness of the airport and the relatively few number of people getting off the plane, I had never seen so many friends and family members waiting at the gate. At least half of the women had babies on their hips. They gave us curious looks as we pulled the video equipment off the carousel, or maybe it was just that I was wearing a leather jacket even though it was close to 100 degrees. Everyone else had on shorts and tank tops. The camera-man, Ray (Faye frequently called him Roy, and sometimes even Raoul, which incensed him), was close to retirement and consider-ably put out at having to make the road trip. "I'd like to see some of these chicks in thongs," he mumbled.

We rented a car and drove into town. Nearly every radio station played classic rock exclusively. Peter Frampton's "Do You Feel Like We Do" came on twice. We passed the welcome sign that said OPEN ARMS, OPEN MINDS and pictured a group of racially diverse individu-als holding hands. Along the highway, stretches of land gave way to factories and big concrete silos with train tracks running alongside them. Billboards seemed to stand in for trees and the vehicles on the street, most of them mammoth pickup trucks or SUVs, rolled to careful stops at intersections, even when the lights were yellow. Ray, who was driving, barreled through all the yellow lights until we reached the Ramada Inn, a slablike building in downtown Prairie City. At fifteen stories, it looked to be the tallest structure in town. We checked into our rooms and I called Sue Lugenbeel. Outside my ninth-floor window, the town looked so lifeless and depressing I wanted nothing more than to do the interviews in under two days and go home.

"Lucinda!" Sue Lugenbeel chirped. "Welcome to P.C.! I have seventeen fabulous women who are dying to be interviewed."

Prairie City, it seemed, was one of those towns that went by its initials, like D.C. or L.A.

After surveying the women, I selected the five thinnest ones and conducted on-camera interviews with them for the next two days. During this time, on odd sensation crept upon me. Though "fabulous" may have been an overstatement, the women proved themselves far worthier interview subjects than any of the boutique owners, dietitians, Pilates trainers, bagel makers, and relationship experts on whom I had cut my teeth as a journalist. Despite my plan to talk to them for no more than ten minutes each (and despite *Up Early*'s unofficial interview edict: "make 'em cry, say good-bye") I let the women talk for hours and hours. I loved them. I couldn't get enough of them. When Ray went back to New York I called Faye from my room at the Ramada Inn and told her I needed to stay and do additional research. Then I got out my microcassette recorder and passed another three days interviewing the remaining twelve women by myself. Something almost mystical had happened to me. Even though Prairie City was hot and dreary and the food, at least at the restaurants near the Ramada, tasted like lunch at a school cafeteria, something about the blandness of the town and the flat land that surrounded it were making me feel alive and exotic. Almost like another person.

This was, after all, serious country. The real heartland, the
plains. Not necessarily Prairie City itself, which, at most intersections, could have passed for Long Island, but the land surrounding
it, *that* was serious country. It was Willa Cather-novel serious. It
was Sissy Spacek-movie serious and documentary-film-about-poor-
conditions-in-meat-packing-plants serious. It was a place where,
according to my early observations, not only did substance trump
style but a very nuanced and therefore quietly sophisticated style
was born out of the substance itself. What I meant by this I wasn't
sure. All I knew was that observing the people of Prairie City, particularly the beleaguered women at the recovery center and the
careworn case workers who pressed empowering novels by women
writers into their hands and encouraged them to eat soy products,
made me feel for the first time like it might be possible to become a
good person. Not that there weren't plenty of opportunities to be a
good person in New York. I'd just never bothered to take them. I
had never worked with homeless kids, never adopted a stray animal, never volunteered to rake leaves in the park, never even, come
to think of it, attended a church service. No one I knew had ever
done any of these things, either. Was it laziness, busyness, distress
over not having the right outfit for such activities? What did it matter? It was shameful. Not that adopting animals or going to church
automatically makes you a good person, of course. And not that I
was necessarily a bad person. It was just that I had come to view my
moral status as a quantifiable entity that was measured solely
against one person. That person was Faye. And the fact that I did
not start fires and throw things at people had always firmly positioned me, if not in the "good" zone, at least in the "not remotely as
bad as Faye" zone. But now, as I drove past the cornfields along the
outer stretches of Highway 36, fresh from an interview with a
woman who worked on an assembly line at the Firestone tire plant,
an interview during which we'd *really bonded*, during which she'd
told me her troubles, and I, treating her as an equal, had told her
some of mine, like the rent increase ("you poor thing," she'd said) I

felt I was more than just not remotely as bad as Faye but actually *good*, at least potentially. And goodness, I realized, not only felt good, it felt *cool*. It *was* cool. The substance became style, the kind you can't fake. Any truly stylish person will tell you that's the only way it works.

It's possible, however (and looking back, it's not only possible but true, and it makes me wince), that I just felt superior. As I interviewed the methamphetamine-addicted women, listening to stories of bad boyfriends and accidental pregnancies and cars repossessed by the bank, smugness coursed through my veins like a narcotic. Of course, I didn't see it as smugness. I was merely *interested*. I was engrossed by the stories of other people's screwups, mostly because, though I didn't realize it at the time, they made my own screwups seem minor in comparison. After years covering the toe ring craze and announcing to New Yorkers that "scones are the new muffin," I felt that I'd finally found my niche. I was a socially conscious reporter passionately committed to the true-life health crises that affect thousands of women nationwide. With every press of my record button, feelings of righteousness released themselves in me like an Alka-Seltzer tab in water. And when it came to feeling not only righteous but heroic, there was nothing like ordering a room-service breakfast at the Ramada and then navigating the rental car to a trailer park with a name like Shadowland Estates for hours of heart to heart with some woman whose misfortune—husband got her hooked on methamphetamine and left her destitute with three kids and two minimum-wage retail jobs—was about to be rectified by what this woman believed would be a heartwarming, nonexploitive segment on *New York Up Early*.

Besides, methamphetamine was an easy story. Given the constraints of your average *Up Early* segment, there wasn't much more to say about the drug other than that it was a very bad thing and that even though it might help you lose weight (a fundamental concern of the show) it might also rot your teeth and/or land you in jail. Later, the promos for the segment would scream "The party may never end, but your life just might. Find out about the dangerous drug that's sweeping the not-so-innocent heartland and heading straight for New York!"

Of course, there was already as much meth in New York as there were opportunities to do good in New York. It's just that no one I knew had anything to do with either. That was another reason the story appealed to me so much: it was guaranteed to lead me in the opposite direction of my actual life. There was little chance of encountering a publicist, plus I noticed that people in recovery had a way of telling you everything, including things they really shouldn't tell you (like that they're high this very moment), which produced, in addition to the previously established feelings of superiority and righteousness, a tertiary sensation of omniscience. Thanks to the interviewees' own stupidity (and my disarming interview technique—what a pro!) dozens of disadvantaged waifs with no concept of the term "on the record" were putting themselves at the mercy of my compassion. And I would not let them down. They were safe. I would not quote the things they said about smuggling. I was Mother Teresa, a credit to my despicable profession and the snide, backstabbing metropolis I called home. Suddenly, I loved my job.

I also loved Sue Lugenbeel. She was the executive director of the Prairie City Recovery Center for Women and she wore batik harem pants and dangling silver earrings and had spiky, bleached blond hair that she claimed to have cut herself. She said she lived on a farm outside of town. I suspected she was around fifty. I also suspected she was a lesbian, which, given the farm, I found fascinating in terms of, as Faye would have said, her "cultural context." In addition to setting me up with seventeen recovering addicts, Sue also assumed the role of ambassador for Prairie City. The first night after Ray returned to New York, Sue met me at the Ramada and drove me in her Saab to a Japanese restaurant in a strip mall, where we met two of her colleagues and discussed women's issues. Generally I wasn't up for discussions of women's issues, having filled my quota in college, but there was something thrilling about the juxta-position of the vaguely 1970s-sounding rhetoric—the word "empow-erment" kept coming up—and the decor of the restaurant, which had a huge freestanding fish tank and was carpeted a deep red to connote "an Asian flair." I liked the warm, self-deprecating nature of the other two women. I liked the way the piped-in Kenny G mu-sic weaved in and out of their conversation. They segued flawlessly from sanctimony to cattiness, from the subject of rampant meth use among women in their community to gossip about who had slept with whom in the county health department. After dinner, we re-treated to a modular sofa in the bar area, where Sue smoked a cig-arette, a gesture I found admirably rebellious in light of her work as a health advocate.

After my third day of further research—there had been a red-headed truck stop waitress whose teeth had rotted from drugs, a nineteen-year-old mother who'd lost both her children to the state, a dental hygienist who, having tired of prescription drugs stolen from her office, had resorted to smoking meth in the basement every night while her husband watched *Jeopardy!*—Sue invited me for cocktails out at her farm.

I got lost on the way to Sue's place. Off the highway, there was one gravel road after another, roads with names like Little Mud Creek Road and Northwest 317th Street. Finally I found a farmhouse with a Saab in the driveway. It was old and rambling like something out of a Hallmark Hall of Fame movie except it had an aboveground swimming pool with rainbow wind socks on the deck and a rainbow beach umbrella on the patio table. Acres of tilled cornfields spread out in every direction. Tractors hummed in the distance. kd lang played on the stereo inside the house. Sue ran out to greet me, fol-lowed by three large dogs with rainbow collars.

"Welcome, Lucinda!" she cried, hugging me even though she'd seen me two hours earlier. "This is the old homestead."

There was an END HATRED sticker on the front door. The dogs were jumping all over me, covering my J. Crew capri pants with drool.

"Stop that, Willa! Stop that, Chloe!" Sue yelled at the dogs. The third one, an ancient-looking black Lab, cowered behind her legs. "This one's Isaiah. He's a little shy. He was abused by his old owner."

Another woman emerged from the house. She was wearing Birkenstocks with the same harem pants I'd seen on Sue. She had long, slightly frizzy, dirty blond hair that she'd tied up on her head and pierced with chopsticks.

"This is my partner, Teri," Sue said. "She has to take off, unfortunately. She's taking a Chinese medicine class at the college."

Teri gave a quick wave and climbed in the Saab and drove off, kicking up a trail of dust on the road.

"Wine?" Sue asked. "I just went to Shop 'N Save. I have some Triscuits, too."

Sue and I drank approximately two and a half bottles of wine that night. Because I was in interview mode, I asked her a lot of questions. And because what little inhibitions she had were erased by the wine and at least half a pack of Merit filters, she told me what seemed like everything about herself. Her life story read like an entry in *Our Bodies, Ourselves.* She had turned fifty-two that year. She was in the process of planning a menopause shower for herself and a number of other women—"it's like a baby shower except you get calcium supplements instead of teething rings!" Sue had grown up in Prairie City, taught health at Prairie City High School for several years, and, upon realizing she was a lesbian, attempted to open a gay cocktail lounge, which had ultimately failed because of competition from the more established queer hangout, the Thirteenth Street TGI Friday's. Given her interest in women's issues, she began working at the Prairie City Recovery Center for Women and was eventually promoted to executive director. She'd met Teri at TGI Friday's and, a few years later, they'd bought the farm, where they'd recently installed track lighting and a subzero refrigerator. Sue had twice received the League of Women Voters' Antonia H. Kubicek Award for excellence in community service in the interests of women. She was on intimate terms with all of the city's left-leaning elite. The liberal county commissioner and his wife, a former all-state women's softball champion, were her best friends. She was also very close with her brother, Leonard, who drove a garbage truck for the Prairie City Department of Sanitation. He was Native American by blood but had been adopted into Sue's family as a toddler.

"He took back his Indian name," Sue said. "So now he's Leonard Running Feather. You can imagine how my mom felt about that. It made my being a lesbian seem about as big a deal as getting a D in math! But they got over it."

"Do you ever get, like, harassed?" I asked, now a probing journalist in the Katie Couric vein, unafraid of raising the tough questions. "I mean, being openly gay and living out in the country and everything."

Sue looked bewildered. "No."

She said this as if I had asked whether coyotes ever came near the house, opened the door, and sprawled out on the couch to watch *Friends.*

In the adjacent field, a farmer drove by on a John Deere tractor, a bright headlight guiding him through the dark. He extended his arm in a giant wave.

"Hi, Joe!" Sue called out.

So why was it that everytime Sue went inside the house for more wine or Triscuits I could do nothing but look out at all that farmland and, with the mixture of fear and exhilaration that accompanies a dare, wonder if the solution to my problems, the problems that began with my apartment lease and ended somewhere around my growing feelings of shallowness and moral worthlessness, was to move to Prairie City? Why was I so stirred by the selection of magazines in Sue's bathroom: *Country Living, Travel & Leisure,*

Mother Jones? Was it merely amazement that someone living on a farm in the Midwest would subscribe to *Mother Jones?* Or was there truth to my mounting suspicion that I had discovered a secret pocket of American society, a place farmers waved at semibutch lesbians, a place where women threw menopause showers and the sky—I'd noticed this even from my hotel room—seemed to eclipse the Earth itself. It could have been another planet. It was certainly a cheaper planet. As I scanned the classified section of the local newspaper I picked up at the airport on my way home, I noticed that houses rented for as little as four hundred dollars per month. Prairie City was, if not an obvious paradise, a bizarre and intriguing idea.

My one-room, one-window apartment in New York had mice and hardly any kitchen. Though I'd never even attempted to entertain more than two guests at a time, I was considered an obstreperous tenant, mostly by my downstairs neighbor, Bob, the longtime lover of my upstairs neighbor, Yuri. They'd lived there at least twenty years and both of their apartments were rent controlled. Neither paid more than three hundred dollars a month, so instead of getting a place together they moved between the first and third floors as if they had one apartment, padding up and down the stairwell in their robes and slippers like college lovers in a dormitory. It was as if my existence on the second floor was that of a guest who would not leave a dinner party. My apartment itself seemed an infringement on their rights as private citizens. Bob was forever shoving notes under my door. "You walk so heavily on the floor. Could you please remove your shoes upon entering your apartment?" "Would it be possible to lower the ringer on your phone?" "Your overnight company is, shall we say, a bit vocal. Have you any idea what I can hear?"

This last was so mortifying I vowed never to run into Bob or Yuri again. I scampered down to the lobby to fetch *The New York Times* and the mail, terrified of the sound of Bob's unlocking door at the foot of the stairs. I lingered on the sidewalk if either of them happened to be walking ahead of me into the building, Yuri holding the door for Bob like a patient grandfather, his jet black toupee sweeping across his deeply creased forehead, his imitation silk ascot tucked in his shirt like a Russian lounge singer, which he may well have been at one time. I would watch them from the entrance of the Korean grocery a few doors down, counting the seconds until I could walk toward my building without their seeing me, clutching my plastic container of deli salad and wondering exactly how a person gets to be twenty-nine and still finds herself hiding from her neighbors before going to her apartment and eating tricolored pasta salad in front of a TV with barely any reception. I experienced this sequence of thoughts almost weekly.

On the evening I flew back from Prairie City, I dropped my luggage off in my apartment (a glance in the darkened kitchen area revealed two dead mice in overturned traps) and took the subway downtown to meet my friend Daphne at our favorite cocktail lounge, Bar Barella. Daphne was usually my favorite friend, though not necessarily my best friend (my best friend was Elena Fein, with whom I was usually angry or vice versa). Part of Daphne's appeal, part of the reason I was willing to come home from a long trip and meet her in a bar that was forty-five minutes from my apartment and one block away from hers was that she was notoriously unavailable. She would disappear for months at a time. She would retreat to Maine, staying in some cottage owned by her relatives, and not call anyone. She would go to Africa for six months as a relief worker, then slink back to New York, sublet an apartment, and wait weeks before letting anyone know she was around. Her dominant characteristic was her lightness, her lack of rules, her ability to perceive individual stupidity as a natural response to global stupidity. During a time several years earlier, when I was briefly dating a guy who netted hundreds of thousands of dollars a year running a high-end escort service that catered to Wall Street brokers, Daphne was the only person I told. Years later, when Daphne dated a guy who netted

hundreds of thousands of dollars a year selling high-grade marijuana to rock stars, I was one of many people she told. That was the
difference between us. She could do stupid things and actually
come off looking cooler for it. For this I worshiped her.

When I arrived at Bar Barella, Daphne was sitting on a Victorian sofa in a dark corner. A flickering candle on the table reflected
in her Armani glasses, for which she'd paid four hundred dollars
despite difficulty making her rent. I wanted to tell her about Prairie
City, about Sue and the farm, and my thought of moving there,
which, by the time I picked my bags off the carousel at LaGuardia,
had evolved from a thought to a full-fledged, terrifying plan. But
she needed to talk first.

"Oh my God," she said.

"What?"

"My fucking life."

It seemed that in the week I'd been gone, Daphne had managed
to sleep with two different men. This was after a year and a half
without sex.

"Rock on," I said, which isn't the kind of thing I usually say.
But it seemed a less offensive cliché than "You go, girl." Given the
census data, the seven hundred thousand surplus of single women,
two men in one week was less an act of sluttishness than of stock-
piling. We hardly ever got laid. My "vocal" overnight guest had
been an anomaly. As for Daphne, two men in one week, especially
two men taller than she, merited a glass of Champagne.

But no. One of them was an ex-boyfriend, a struggling actor
who'd dumped her long ago for an actress with a trust fund and a
SoHo loft. The other was her ostensibly platonic friend Ira, who had
been in love with her for years and to whom she wasn't attracted.
Somehow she'd gotten drunk and spent the night in his apartment
because she didn't feel like taking the scary D train all the way
home from Brooklyn. Neither had called her since.

"Fuckheads," she said. "I have to move."

"Move to the Midwest," I said.

"Really?"

"Oh, sorry," I said. "We're not done with you. Keep going."

"No, I'm finished," Daphne said, sucking down her last bit of Pinot. Her eyes darted around for the waitress. "And even more disgustingly," she continued, "Ira has a single bed. He's too cheap to get a grownup bed. And I can't believe I'm even admitting this but he has *Smurf sheets*, like a child's sheets. Like it's ironic or something. Like we're still in college. I mean, he's fucking thirty-three."

"I met these lesbians in the Midwest," I said.

"There are lesbians in the Midwest?"

"They live on a farm and drink wine and read *Mother Jones*," I told Daphne. "You can rent a house for four hundred dollars. I don't know. Something's happened inside my mind."

"I thought *Mother Jones* went out of business."

"And," I said, "the town is called Prairie City. How cute is that?"

"No fucking way!"

"Way," I said. "I think I might have to move there. I think the train has left the station. I have the idea. I can't not do it."

"Uh oh," she said. "Alternative Lifestyle Alert."

When my friends and I were not discussing the lack of available men, we were usually discussing moving out of New York. Again, the subjects were related, though not entirely. Someone was always coming up with an escape plan, a way to lower the cost of living, a way to increase the odds of meeting a guy who actually knew how to hammer a nail into a piece of plywood. The plans varied according to the books we'd recently read, the movies we'd recently seen, the city most recently featured on *The Real World*. We'd say Austin, Seattle, Paris, New Delhi. When somebody came home from an unusual location—a wedding in Nova Scotia or a snorkeling trip in Australia—and spent two weeks obsessing about moving into a yurt on the Bay of Fundy we called it an Alternative Lifestyle Alert. The guiding principle of the Alternative Lifestyle Alert was that it was never acted upon.

Until now. No, I thought as I rode the subway back to my verminous apartment, this time it would be different. I, Lucinda Trout, would break the pattern of Alternative Lifestyle Alert inertia and actually alter my lifestyle. That night, as I unpacked my clothes, which still smelled like the country air and cigarette smoke of Sue's farm, I entered a kind of trance. It was an intensified version of the kind of trance I'd occasionally enter on nights when I'd catch some kind of heartland movie on TV, *Country*, for example, which starred Jessica Lange and an especially scrumptious Sam Shepard, and, despite the fact that it was produced by Disney, had always been a secret favorite of mine. Out of this trance would always arise the same question, a question that asked what would be left of me if I uprooted myself completely. What would happen if I removed myself from the crowds and the money and the constant talk of who had been featured in articles in *New York Magazine* with titles like "Under 35 and Over the Moon: Gen-X Internet Moguls Cash in and Take the Real Estate Market by Storm"?

I bring this up because in the stack of mail by my door was that very magazine with that very article. And one of the underthirty-fives was a woman I'd known in college who had taken what basically amounted to a personal Web page chronicling her sexual exploits and sold it to Time Warner. Then she'd purchased a seven-hundred-thousand-dollar loft in TriBeCa. A full-page color photo showed her reclining on a leopard-print Victorian sofa. The caption read "Haley Bopp (née Alice Sterngold), creator of the cyberdiary *This Broad's Sheets*, might have given up creative control of her Web site, but she now seeks artistic expression in her 1500-square-foot loft, which she's decorated with the help of the red hot design firm Home Planet, known for its innovative approach to feng shui."

My trance was briefly interrupted by an outburst of envy and disgust. I considered calling Elena, who was an early riser and might have taken a 3:00 A.M. phone call as an opportunity to get a head start on her workout. But then, like a light breeze, the trance returned, bringing with it the realization that no amount of leopard-print Victorian sofas or feng shui consultation from Home Planet could justify fifteen hundred square feet going for more than ten times the amount of Haley's and my tuition at Smith College, a place where we had been required to take courses with names like "Gender, Power, and Commerce," courses from which I, who was still paying off my student loans, had obviously garnered fewer benefits than she. It occurred to me that Sue and Teri's farmhouse, purchased in 1991 for sixty thousand dollars, would probably sell for close to a million were it located within a seventy-five-mile radius of New York City. It then occurred to me that the *2 BR, 1.5 BA, c/a, fenced yd, w/d hookups, gar, gorg. woodwork, $475/mo* listing I'd spotted in the *Prairie City Daily Dispatch* would not only reveal what would be left of me if I uprooted myself but would leave me with enough extra funds to fly home and have drinks with Daphne at Bar Barella every month if I felt like it.

But there was more to it than the cost of living, more to it than the male-to-female ratio and lack of chivalry from men who had Smurf sheets. Though I couldn't put my finger on it (and, indeed, would never be able to articulate whatever "it" was, even years later) my reasons for wanting to go to Prairie City, for *needing*, as I was now convinced, to go to Prairie City, had something to do with my relationship to what I could only describe as "real life." Even in childhood, which I'd spent in a middle-class suburb of Philadelphia, I'd had the distinct feeling that nothing that surrounded me, not the boxy Cape Cod houses of my street, not the multiplex at the mall where my friends and I had skulked around on weekends, certainly not the chemically maintained grass of my parents' small backyard, was ever quite the stuff of "real life." There was a neither-here-nor-there quality to my existence. We were neither rich nor poor, neither city dwellers nor country dwellers, neither athletes nor intellectuals (we played a bit of tennis, but not enough to ever join a racket club). My parents had been old when they'd had me, my sister already at Penn State by the time I was three. Though they'd never have admitted it, I was an accident and, as if rising to the occasion, they delayed their retirements until I got through Smith, after which they promptly moved to Florida. After that, I'd scarcely seen my family again. In keeping with the overall impermeability of my life, this was neither a loss nor a relief, just the way things were. My sister got married and then eventually divorced somewhere near Pittsburgh. My parents retreated into a world of halfhearted tennis and early cocktails. And I had moved to New York, a world that, despite its endless opportunities to experience "real life," I had managed to make as trivial and petty as the social politics of my own high school. As hard as I'd tried to enter the "real world," I was still eating from plastic containers and reporting on thong underwear. Though I considered myself semiintellectual, I was also semiattractive, semisuccessful, and semihappy. Not a bad state of affairs, when you thought about it. But in Prairie City (though I still hadn't fully admitted this to myself) there seemed the possibility of being (or at least appearing) very intellectual, very attractive, very successful, and, if not very happy, at least in possession of a bigger apartment. And if it didn't work out that way—and no doubt it wouldn't—I could always come back. Except for the small matter of my job.

I looked out my window at the building across the alleyway. Though it was just past 4:00 A.M., the sounds of shouting and the occasional ring of a telephone still punctuated the night. In one apartment, where the lights were on, a couple was unfolding a futon in their one-room apartment. I watched them throw books on the floor, pull out the frame to where it rammed up against their dining table. The air was muggy and they took their clothes off with the curtains open; it was too hot to bother with privacy this time of year. I watched them shut down the computer and climb into bed. There was a tiny television set on their night table and on top of it a towering stack of papers. The man reached up to turn off the light and the papers fell to the floor. I heard the echo of his "shit" across the courtyard as the window went dark.

Then it all came to me. The key to what I wanted, the way to get out without really leaving. Like a math formula passed under the desk by a much smarter student, I now had everything I needed, and it was so much simpler than I'd ever imagined. I turned on the computer and began to type.

To: Faye Figaro
From: Lucinda Trout
Re: Idea for Segment Series

My trip to the midwestern town of Prairie City, where I conducted a number of probing interviews with methamphetamine addicts, proved useful in more ways than just producing the meth story (which, btw, I have no doubt will be emotionally resonant and really groundbreaking). While in Prairie City, which is a town of just under 100,000, smack in the middle of the country, where the flat prairie stretches out to meet an endless sky, I had a startling and potentially ratings-boosting revelation: this place represents the American Dream. Far from the cramped quarters and moral compromises of New York, a town like Prairie City, with its surprisingly diverse population and plethora of old farmhouses that sit on acres of natural grassland, is precisely the kind of setting New Yorkers imagine when they think about "escaping New York."

So, in keeping with *Up Early*'s new initiative to expand coverage into national issues, I propose a yearlong series that allows New Yorkers to live out this fantasy without actually having to do it themselves. I propose that I, as Lifestyle correspondent, move to Prairie City for one year and produce weekly dispatches that show New Yorkers exactly what it's like to trade apartment life for a farmhouse, Chinese takeout for steak flanks, and rude drivers for friendly farmers on tractors who wave as they drive past. I could also feature interviews with quirky locals, such as, for example, a farmer who is a champion ballroom dancer, a ranch hand who writes poetry, or a garbage man whose larger goal in life is to conserve energy by installing (for free) solar panels in people's houses. Slice of life stories aside, however, the real essence of this series is that it taps directly into New Yorkers' concerns over the idea of "quality of life." New Yorkers think they don't have it (or must pay a lot for it). In Prairie City, quality of life flows like water. What does "quality of life" really mean? What does it say about our identity as New Yorkers? Our identity as Americans? After all, more and more people are leaving the big city for places like Prairie City. Is it a trend?

I will be the one to bring Prairie City into the homes of New Yorkers. I will be the guinea pig for their escape fantasies. And they'll be able to see it only on *Up Early.* If this doesn't appeal to you, I'd be happy to pursue the cell phone rage story we discussed at last week's meeting.

So jazzed now by my trance that I could feel actual sparks in my body, I skimmed my memo, found it to be frighteningly brilliant, and e-mailed it to Faye, even though she wouldn't get it until she arrived at the office, which was never before 11:00 A.M. I didn't bother unpacking the rest of my clothes.

At noon the next day, Faye called me into her office. Two grande cappuccinos were sitting on her desk and her temporary assistant was trying to pour packets of Equal in them without knocking anything off.

"Is this your resignation?" Faye asked.

"Faye," I said, "you may think I'm kidding but this is potentially huge. There is a wide, wide market for this kind of thing. Because what I'm tapping into is not only a fantasy; it's an anxiety, a crisis. It's a conflict. And because so many people feel it, it's a trend."

"It's a trend to move to some backwater shit hole?" Faye said. "Where everyone's a drug addict? Plus they're fat. I saw the footage from the meth story."

"Those were average-sized women!" I said. "Besides, that was just one marginalized group. But get this, there are just as many men as women there. Not like here. And I met some cool lesbians."

"There are lesbians in the Midwest?" Faye asked. Her eyebrow, tweezed to the width of an extrafine pen, arched slightly. She picked up one of her cappuccinos and the lid fell off. Foam rolled onto her hand and dribbled on her desk. "Fuck!" she yelled.

"Look, just try it," I said. "Send the memo upstairs to see what they say."

"They'll never go for it," she said. "We're supposed to pay you to do a couple stories a month about fat people? There's no way it's a weekly thing, Lucinda. There's a reason Roseanne's show got canceled, although in talking to her I see she had a real vision. It was quite scatological really. She's coming out to the Hamptons this weekend."

"Well," I said—was it time to resort to begging?—"you could keep me on, like, as a freelancer. You wouldn't have to pay me quite as much. The cost of living there being, you know, lower."

Faye looked startled. "Well, obviously we'd pay you less," she said. "Obviously."

"I mean, not that much less," I said. "I mean, I'd be constantly researching stories."

"I'll send this upstairs," Faye said. "But you really do appear to be having some sort of crisis. And I would encourage you to get into therapy rather than working it out on company time. In the meantime I want you to do a story on jungle gym safety. John McEnroe's kid fell off some climbing thing in Central Park. He's pissed. I think he might talk. And can you bring me a paper towel?"

Four hours later, fate stepped in. Because fate is what steps in when you take charge of your fate. Or something like that.

"*Lucinda!*"

When I walked into Faye's office, Bonnie Crawley and Samantha Frank were sitting on the love seat drinking bottled water and looking vaguely disgusted. They shushed each other when I came in.

"Well, you got your wish," Faye said. "They accepted your resignation. I mean your proposal."

"Are you serious?" I yelped.

"What? Now you changed your mind?" Faye said.

"No!" I said. "No, I think this is great. This is going to be a great series. And of course I'll still come back for meetings whenever possible."

"Don't bet on it," said Faye. "They want to do it, but the budget is tight. Now, Samantha had an idea for the name of the series and Upstairs likes it so we're going to go with it."

"I thought it should be called 'The Quality of Life Report,'" said Samantha. "It's sort of the lifestyle equivalent to barometric pressure. It goes up and down. You've got good days and bad days. Except here, 'quality of life' refers to the larger concept of the good life, the life New Yorkers feel deprived of. As Faye pointed out in her memo."

"That was my memo," I said.

"You're brave, Lucinda," Bonnie said. "But that's the whole point, right? Courage. Risk taking. Kudos, I say! At any rate it'll be great to have you stationed in a remote."

"'Cause it will add some freshness," Samantha said. "Not that we won't totally miss you and be sad."

"I have to meet my trainer," said Bonnie.

The hosts departed. Faye sat back in her chair. "Okay, here's the thing, Lucinda," she said. "If you want to do this, you're going to have to, like, give a little."

"Yes."

"I mean, like cooperate."

"With?"

"The budget," she said. "We're going to have to pay for editing facilities and a cameraman from a local station out there. Your salary is going to be, like, cut back a little."

"To what?"

"To adjust to your lowered living expenses."

"Well, sure, of course. But I still have student loans and everything."

"Is that my problem?" Faye hissed.

"What am I going to be paid?" I asked.

"You're going to be paid by the segment," Faye said. "Per segment. But look at it this way, if you do forty-five segments you get paid for all forty-five. It's ipso facto."

"Do you mean quid pro quo?"

"Don't be uppity."

"And what do I get paid per segment?" I asked.

"A thousand dollars," Faye said. "But we're going to cover an HMO. So that's really a pretty good deal when you think about it."

"A thousand dollars?" I said. I felt sick. "Well, then, I'm going to do a story a week, right?"

"Whatever we work out," she said. "Come on, what does it cost to rent an apartment there, a couple hundred a month?"

"Well . . ."

"I have a doctor's appointment," Faye said, looking at her watch. "Or a lunch. I have something. You should be happy. You got your way. They want you on site by the end of the month."

"Wow, okay."

"Just don't get fat!"

*   *   *

So the American Dream began. At least my version of it, which didn't stir up a lot of envy.

"I'll come visit you," said Samantha Frank, who had never even come to my apartment when I lived ten blocks away from her on the Upper West Side.

"I'll come visit you," said Daphne. "Maybe, anyway."

"I'll come visit you," said Elena, who, since turning thirty a few years earlier, had gotten LASIK eye surgery and braces put on the backs of her teeth, which caused her to lisp. "But not until you get indoor plumbing."

Elena and I were having coffee at The One, a café near Elena's yoga studio whose main attraction was that it had binders filled with profiles of single people looking for dates. Elena was sweaty from a yoga class and her curly black hair was springing out from under a floppy hat she'd purchased in an effort to copy Jennifer Aniston on *Friends*. She'd bought one for me, too, but it just gave me a kind of Peppermint Patty appearance, which Elena had pointed out and suggested I use to land a well-heeled lesbian who might give me room and board for a while. Elena was usually looking for a boyfriend, but since she felt she was above actually filling out a form she went to The One only to scrutinize the bios of the other women. "Just sizing up the competition," she always said.

"Look, this twit thinks it's worth mentioning that she prefers Hatha yoga over Ashtanga," Elena said, slurping her soy latte through the rubber bands behind her molars. "Translation: lard ass!"

"I find it interesting that you only ever read the women's profiles when you come here," I said.

"The men have atrocious handwriting," she said. "And if I hear of one more software consultant who aspires to write for *The Simpsons* I'll buy him a one-way ticket to L.A. Why won't they grow up?"

"That's exactly why I'm moving to Prairie City!" I said. "I mean, not exactly. But it'll be a perk. Not having to deal with the backward baseball cap set."

"Yeah, you'll just have to deal with the chewing tobacco set. You'll have to deal with wannabe truck drivers," Elena lisped. "Can you imagine? Single male, age thirty, works as bricklayer but dreams of long-haul trucking career and possible membership in North American Man Boy Love Association!"

"Maybe I can date one of my movers," I said.

"Lucinda," Elena said, "you better tell your movers to wait in front of your house for the first night. Because that's how long it's going to take you to realize you're coming right back to New York! I mean, it's one thing to go to Nepal, like Daphne. But this is beyond the third world. I mean, they don't even do Backroads Adventure trips there!"

My parents, for their part, thought I was going to graduate school. Since their associations with the Midwest were almost completely limited to Big Ten universities, they could not imagine anyone moving there for any other purpose.

"I'm doing an extended assignment for the show," I said to my mother on the phone. "It has nothing to do with getting a master's degree."

"But maybe you could at least take some classes," she said. "It will give you something to do. It's also a good way to meet people."

My mother had a long-held belief that the reason I was relegated to the thong underwear beat was that I lacked a postcollegiate education. She was under the impression that senior-level news anchors—even those on *Entertainment Tonight*—held Ph.D.s. She also felt that the reason I was never able to upgrade beyond a studio apartment was that I couldn't type sixty words per minute.

"If I have to take a class it'll be a driving class," I said. "I haven't driven a car in eight years."

"Well, honey, I wish we hadn't sold the station wagon."

On the eve of my departure, I lay in a sleeping bag on the floor of my studio and cried for exactly seventeen minutes. Small apartments have a way of looking so much better when they're completely empty and something about the echoing space that now surrounded me, the white walls with marks where the pictures had been, the naked oak floors, the curtainless window that now offered a direct view to the apartment across the courtyard, where a woman was stirring something on the stove while talking on the telephone, knocked the wind out of me like I'd fallen hard off a bicycle. During the month that I'd spent preparing to move to Prairie City, I'd maintained an alarming composure, not allowing myself to second-guess a decision that the whole world was waiting for me to second-guess and then, with my tail between my legs and a few self-deprecating comments to save face, totally renege on. Now, the tears came like a train that was creeping into the station weeks behind schedule. As sincere as they were, they were also perfunctory and I gasped through the sobs until I began to feel like I was wasting time. The movers had come only that day, the last possible day they could come. There had been a delay because my furniture, being a partial load, needed to go on a truck with several other loads and they couldn't find a truck that was going anywhere near Prairie City. When they finally found a truck they claimed it was too big to turn the corner from Broadway to West Ninety-fourth Street and they had to bring in a smaller truck and then transfer my stuff to the bigger truck. Though I barely had twelve hours left, I still had to take everything out of the medicine cabinet and either throw it away or pack it into one of the three duffel bags I was carrying with me. I still had to take a bunch of canned foods out of the cupboards and put them on the steps of the church down the street. It was already getting dark. So I stopped crying. The nighttime summer air sat motionless outside the window; there was no breeze to bring it in. Car alarms and sirens hummed outside as they had every night of the last nine years. Yuri's phone rang upstairs. The elevator clanked through the building. Doors slammed shut. Someone outside yelled an obscenity. Someone else laughed. A garbage truck went by. The apartment looked so big without the furniture. It occurred to me that maybe I just should have lived in it unfurnished.

The next morning, as planned, I got up before 5:00 A.M., stuffed my sleeping bag into one of the duffel bags, brushed my teeth, got dressed, walked out of the apartment, and took the bus to La-Guardia. *Up Early* had not even sprung for car service. Dawn broke as the bus ambled through Harlem and over the Triborough Bridge. Looking back toward Manhattan, the sun glinted off the redbrick housing projects that bordered the East Side. Behind the projects, the skyscrapers where earlier in my career I'd worked more temp jobs than I could remember jutted out into the sky just like they do in the opening credits of movies about people who come to the city and suffer a million knocks before something happens to them that is so spectacular, so redeeming, and so much a testament to their unrelenting passion and hard work that it's like the knocks never happened, it's like they sailed in and the city greeted them as though it were heaven and they had died trying to rescue someone who'd fallen onto the subway tracks.

Though it wasn't yet 7:00 A.M., planes were climbing and landing from every direction. The terminal was packed. I waited in line for half an hour and checked my bags. I got coffee at the Starbucks stand. To calm my nerves, I pretended I was going on a business trip. I pretended that *Up Early* had sent me off on a story, a story concerning, perhaps, women who had been fondled by their gynecologists. I got on the plane, we took off, and the island of Manhattan shrank away behind the clouds. Four hours and one airport connection later, we descended into a patchy prairie. From the plane I could see tiny boxlike farmhouses, sectioned-off fields of crops, the occasional factory flanked by a huge parking lot, which was flanked by acres of cornfields, then acres of prairie grass, then a highway with barely any cars on it.

What was I doing in this place? Then I slapped my wrist with the plastic coffee stirrer. I wasn't allowed to ask. That had been the pact, no getting upset for six months, no breaking down, no admission of error. Besides, it was beautiful down there. Land and sky and nothing in between. This place seemed less a place than a huge amount of space, enough space to see what you'd do with yourself when given so much room, enough space, I later realized, after it was much, much too late, to get yourself in a whole lot of trouble.

A Serious, More Humanitarian Direction

The truly remarkable thing about a person like Sue was that you could call her up on a summer evening, having met her only briefly a month earlier, and announce that you were taking a drastic pay cut to move to her town and she would respond as if a) she'd known you for ten years, b) you were making the best decision of your life, and c) moving from New York to Prairie City was not only understandable but obvious, a crucial step everyone reached eventually, as integral to the maturity process as moving out of your parents' house. When I'd called Sue from New York to tell her about my plans, under the guise of fact checking my methamphetamine story, I'd feared she'd think I was some kind of stalker or, at the very least, a total loser. Was this not, after all, the equivalent of someone from Paris visiting my nondescript suburban hometown in Pennsylvania and deciding, upon returning to her seventeenth-century flat in the 21st arrondissement, that all those sunny afternoons picnicking on fresh bread and jam in the place des Vosges were wearing her down and she felt she'd be better off shopping for super-sized Velveeta at the Union Avenue Safeway? Sue didn't see it that way. Instead, she let out a little shriek, which I was 99 percent convinced connoted delight rather than horror, and immediately began to list all the different landlords she knew who could rent me a *2 BR, 1.5 BA, c/a, fenced yd, w/d hookups, gar, gorg. woodwork $475/mo.*

"But you can stay on the farm as long as you want," she'd said. "And you can buy our old Saab. I'm buying an Isuzu Trooper. Or just use the Saab as long as you want until you find a car."

And so I was met at Prairie City Municipal Airport by Sue, who drove me to her farm, showed me to the luxuriously appointed guest room, handed me the keys to her 1989 mint green Saab 900, and then had no fewer than twenty friends over for a welcoming party.

"Too bad you missed the menopause shower," Sue told me. "I haven't been that stoned since my early forties. But this party will be fun, too."

The party *was* fun. I was greeted the way I imagined Olympians were welcomed home when they returned triumphantly, or even less than triumphantly, from the games. People handed me drinks and fistfuls of Triscuits. They came up to me and threw their arms around me. "Lucinda! I have to actually touch you to believe you," said a fiftyish woman named Brenda Schwan, who had newscaster hair and perfectly white teeth despite her cigarette voice. "No one *ever* moves here."

Sue's brother, Leonard Running Feather, spent much of the afternoon playing water polo in the aboveground pool with Teri and the county commissioner, whose name was Phil and who looked more like Peter Fonda than any man I'd ever seen, including, in a strange way, Peter Fonda himself. Lacking an appropriate ball, they used a beach ball for their polo match. When a sudden wind gust blew it into the adjacent cornfield, they attempted to play with a giant inflatable chair.

Maybe it was because my own parents were so old that I didn't think of Sue and her friends as being that much older than me. They laughed and poked each other and rolled out of their lawn chairs like college students—not students at my college, I thought regretfully, but the students at the kinds of colleges where people have tailgate parties and play pranks on the president by putting his office furniture on the roof. Over the ensuing months I would see that there was an enviable ease to everything Sue and her friends did, an effect of the overall uncomplicatedness of life in Prairie City and the fact that, like a huge family, they seemed utterly without personal boundaries. They walked inside one another's houses without knocking. They all knew where everyone kept her silverware. If someone needed to make a run for beer or cigarettes, he or she simply hopped in whoever's SUV was at the end of the driveway. Everyone left his keys in the cars or, if not, everyone knew which pockets or purses from which to retrieve them. Unlike my friends in my world, I couldn't imagine them ever sitting in restaurants dividing up checks. They didn't go through the social kissing routine. For this I admired them. For this, I wanted to *be* them. At least in some ways. Nearly all of them wore Birkenstocks and, every once in a while, someone's cultural or political reference would serve as a jolting reminder that most of them were at least twenty years older than me. Sue had graduated from high school two years before I was born. The Peter Fonda county commissioner had barely avoided the Vietnam War draft. Leonard was a huge Three Dog Night fan. It was hard to believe that they were actually Faye's age, especially given her insistence that she was thirty-seven.

The day after my welcome party, I drove all over Prairie City in Sue's Saab looking for an apartment. Memo to New Yorkers: this is what I found: a twelve-hundred-square-foot, five-room apartment that took up the entire ground floor of a Craftsman-style house. It had oak floors, gorgeous oak woodwork, built-in glass china cabinets carved in the style of the Sullivan school, French doors, a perfectly restored 1930s-era Hotpoint stove, a claw-foot bathtub, and central air conditioning that was paid entirely by the landlord. In Manhattan the place would have gone for five thousand dollars a month. The rent in Prairie City: five hundred dollars.

I called Daphne and Elena and told them.

"That much?" they both said.

Sue's friends, to my astonishment, also thought the place was overpriced. They also thought the neighborhood was "marginal." I disagreed. With the exception of one house whose porch was sinking into the ground, probably because of the sofas and large kitchen appliances that had been placed on it, the neighborhood exuded an aura of neither deprivation nor pretension, merely solid citizenship and, judging from the bumper stickers on most of the cars, some serious pro-union leanings. Though there were tenants in both the basement and on the second floor of my house, I entered through the front door and was sole proprietor of a large porch that was just crying out for a swing. My furniture arrived and filled up maybe a fifth of the place. I got a Pier One charge card and bought a camel-colored sofa and two olive green velvet pillows. I ordered an INN-KEEPERS ARE NOT STUPID hotel shower curtain from the Restoration Hardware catalog and purchased some sheer eggplant-colored fabric from Target and made panels for the French doors. I set up my office in the larger of the two bedrooms. I unpacked my CDs, put on the soundtrack from *The Buena Vista Social Club*, which, though I wasn't in fact crazy about it, was something I figured would be unavailable in Prairie City and best purchased in advance. I danced around the house, admiring my flawless design sense. Even if tomorrow I become miserable, I thought, even if I get into an accident with the Saab and the whole venture turned out to be a disaster, my house was a goddamned showplace.

My upstairs neighbor was a thirtyish heavy metal fan named Toby Vodacek. He worked the night shift at the Firestone tire plant and spent his days tinkering with several vehicles he kept in the driveway and on the street. At all times, Metallica or Judas Priest blared from the stereo of one of the cars. Given his apparent auto mechanic credentials, I let him convince me not to buy Sue's Saab. Replacing a part that on most cars would cost two hundred dollars would run upward of eight hundred on a Saab, he said. He told me not to be a slave to fashion and to buy a solid American car. So after thinking that I couldn't possibly drive anything other than a Honda or a Toyota I gave in and bought a 1990 Pontiac Sunbird from one of Toby's co-workers. It was white and looked like a rental car and I was soothed by its air of impermanence, as if I could return it at any moment and be on the next plane back home.

But I had no real urge to go home. I was, quite possibly, a new woman. With my car, my apartment, my new membership to the YMCA, which cost just thirty-nine dollars a month and had an Olympic-size pool, I felt like the most privileged person in the world. Compared to New York, everything in Prairie City seemed like it was free. As the weeks went by and I absorbed the various symbols of the town's commitment to safe and easy living—the three-bedroom colonials with list prices of eighty thousand dollars, the ribbons of public bike paths on which parents rode with helmeted babies strapped in behind them, the endless telephone directory pages devoted to free services for every possible variation of the less fortunate (ESL classes for new immigrants, safe houses for battered women, food pantries and clothing dropoff sites, and, to my count, more support groups than there were people with the last name Schmidt)—I found it increasingly hard to understand why anyone lived in places like New York or Boston or San Francisco at all.

"The Quality of Life Report" was to be produced using the facilities of KPCR, Prairie City's public television station. It seemed the station manager was an ex-New Yorker named Joel Lipinsky. He was the cousin of the brother of someone who married the ex-wife of some friend of Faye's in the Hamptons. When I called him to arrange a meeting to discuss the series, he invited me to a barbecue at his house the following weekend.

"Come on over," he said. "Meet my wife, meet my friends. There will be a lot of interesting people there."

Joel's house was a split level ranch with solar panels over the den, a Brady Bunch sort of house, which was why I was surprised to find that Joel was a short man with a goatee, a diamond stud in his ear, and shoulder-length silver hair that was tied back in a tiny ponytail. Even though it was at least 85 degrees on his back deck, where people who looked exactly like Sue's friends were grilling burgers

and eating potato salad out of giant containers, Joel was wearing
Doc Martens, black pants, a black jacket, a black shirt buttoned all
the way up to the top, and a string tie. When I introduced myself,
he hugged me.

"The famous Lucinda Trout," he said.

"I'm really eager to talk to you about this series," I said.

"Whoa there," he said. "Relax, this is a party."

He dragged out a couple of lawn chairs and made me sit down.
I noticed that Brenda Schwan, the woman who'd had "to actually
touch you to believe you" at Sue's, was at the other end of the deck.

"I've really been eager to meet you," Joel continued. "Especially
because, you know, I totally relate to what you're going through.
When I came out here I was like this guy from Brooklyn. I had no
clue about the Midwest. I was like, man, where can I get a decent
bagel? I'm telling you, I asked for lox at the supermarket and they
sent me to the hardware section. I kid you not!"

"When did you come out here?" I asked.

"'73."

"1973?"

"Yeah, but man I tell you, sometimes I still forget the news
comes on at ten."

Joel was interrupted by his wife, who introduced herself as
Valdette Svoboda-Lipinksy. She leaned over the lawn chair and
hugged me, spilling drops of margarita on my lap.

"Get up so I can talk to her," Valdette said to Joel, nudging him
out of the lawn chair. "I think your foie gras is ready."

"You're serving foie gras?" I asked.

"No, it's just nachos," Valdette said. "It's a little joke we have.
We call everything foie gras. Joel has attended cooking seminars in
France. He's quite a Renaissance man."

Valdette had long silver hair—she seemed to match her husband; they had his and hers hair—and wore a zebra-print blouse
and black leggings. She wore earrings shaped like frogs and a Star
of David around her neck. Though she eschewed the Fritos for ap-

ple crisps, which she told me could be purchased in bulk at the health-food store, she chain smoked Virginia Slims and knocked back two margaritas in under twenty minutes. Her speech had a curling, almost Southern drawl to it. She was a rape crisis counselor for the Prairie City Domestic Violence Commission. She was also a member of the Prairie City Coalition of Women, through which she knew Sue.

Brenda Schwan noticed me from across the deck and blew me a little kiss. Then I noticed another familiar figure walking across the yard. It was Sue's brother, Leonard Running Feather.

"You know Leonard?" I asked Valdette.

"He's our neighbor," she said. She raised her arm, a mess of silver bangles sliding down her wrist as she called to him. "Hi neighbor!"

In the few weeks I'd been in Prairie City, I'd seen Leonard a number of times, not only at Sue's farm, where he went nearly every weekend to swim, but also driving the garbage truck around town, where he would sometimes pull up next to me at an intersection and give a little wave. According to Sue, he'd gotten divorced a few years earlier, after his wife ran off with a car salesman she'd met on the Internet. Though she'd returned two weeks later, begging Leonard's forgiveness, Leonard had found himself rather enjoying his time off from the streaming criticism of Josephine Hornbach Running Feather and decided his authentic self was that of a bachelor. Given his wife's indiscretions, he was awarded primary custody of their two children, which mitigated his child support obligations and generally left his weekends free. Given the kids' Native American blood, federal grants would surely pay for their college educations, if things ever got to that point. Life was sweet for Leonard.

Valdette leaned close to me and whispered in my ear.

"You know he's really Sue's *adopted* brother, right?" she said.

Leonard was exactly Sue's age. He wore tinted aviator glasses and kept his receding hair pulled into a ponytail. Other than his name and his hairless face, there was nothing palpably Native American about him. A cigarette hung from his mouth as he stepped over the bedding plants in the yard. He'd brought his own beer, one he'd already opened and another tucked under his arm.

"You're already on the party circuit," he said to me. "It's all downhill from here."

I couldn't tell whether or not he was being sarcastic. Joel, though his wardrobe distinguished him from the other members of the crowd, who wore T-shirts and shorts and the ubiquitous Birkenstocks, had begun to sing show tunes with a small group at the grill. Brenda Schwan wanted to sing "Maria," but Joel was saying that was "too obvious."

"Don't you guys know any of the songs from *Rent?*" I heard him ask.

Dripping with sweat, slapping at the mosquitoes that were landing on my face and neck, I explained to everyone I met how "The Quality of Life Report" series was designed to tap into New Yorkers' fantasies about the good life. Most reacted with shock. A few hugged me and said they were sure I'd meet plenty of interesting people, especially if I hung out at The Grinder, Prairie City's most popular coffee shop.

"So if you know any farmers who are champion ballroom dancers I'd love to hear about it," I said. "Or any other kind of quirky local thing."

"You should do a story about my book club!" said Brenda Schwan. "We're a really interesting group."

"That *would* be interesting," I said, even though it sounded so uninteresting the very thought of it made me want to go back to thong underwear reporting. Book clubs, Faye once said, were "so middle brow they're unibrow." She held the same opinion about bachelorette parties and women's investment clubs, though we'd done stories about both.

I needed to stop drinking, otherwise I wouldn't be able to drive home. And since I didn't think I could stay at the party without consuming more alcohol, I got up to leave. The air-conditioning inside the house caused the last vestiges of sweat to break through my pores. In the living room, as I approached the front door, Leonard appeared out of nowhere.

"You're leaving already?" he asked.

"I can't keep drinking."

"Just stay off the main roads," he said. "The cops hardly ever stop anyone on side streets. Hey, want a tour of the house?"

"This house?"

"No, my house," he said. "I need to grab some more beers anyway."

Leonard led me across Joel's yard to his house, which looked almost exactly like Joel's minus the solar panels. He took us to his back door, requiring a trip through the side yard so everyone on Joel's deck could see me going inside.

"Just showing her the old hacienda!" Leonard shouted.

The kitchen sink was piled with dirty dishes and an overflowing laundry basket sat on the floor.

"My ex-wife has the kids on weekends," Leonard said. "Which means I have two whole days to clean up after them. Wanna see the upstairs?"

"Sure," I said, although I had no idea what the point was. We padded up the carpeted steps, where Leonard opened a door marked with a NO TRESPASSING sign. It was the kind of sign I'd seen only in television shows featuring thirteen-year-old boys.

"This is Kyle's room," Leonard said.

"Maybe he wouldn't want me going in here," I said.

"Ah, screw him," Leonard said. "I told him to dismantle the meth lab."

The room, relatively large and covered with dingy beige wall-to-wall carpet, was plastered with rock posters, including one for a musician named Papa Roach who apparently had an album called *Infest*. There was a desk with some textbooks and a globe. There was a terrarium with a toad in it. There were piles of clothes everywhere. The bed was unmade and I saw that it was covered with

Smurf sheets. I thought of Daphne and her platonic friend Ira. Leonard looked suddenly embarrassed. "Tomorrow's laundry day," he said.

He showed me Danielle's room, a feminized, preteen version of the same teeny-bopper consumer syndrome. There was an *NSYNC poster on the wall and several bottles of blue and purple nail polish on the bureau. I couldn't remember how old he'd said she was. Eleven? Leonard showed me his bedroom, a tribute to the minimalist aesthetic of the divorced male. An overturned cardboard box served as a bedside table. I recognized the pseudo Indian-style bedspread from Target. A John Grisham book and a copy of *Newsweek* lay on the cardboard box.

Leonard now seemed to realize that it was silly to give me a tour of his house. He walked me out the front door and onto the street, where my Sunbird was squeezed between two Jeep Grand Cherokees.

"So this is the Sunbird," he said.

"That'd be her."

"You were smart not to get the Saab," he said. "Replacing a simple Saab part costs twice as much as on a normal car. So would you want to go out sometime?"

"Oh!"

"Like to a movie or something?"

"Oh . . . Yeah, that'd be great."

"Maybe sometime next week," he said. "I figure you probably don't have much to do yet, don't know that many people."

"Well, when I get started on my reporting series I'm going to be really, really busy," I said. "But I'm not so busy now."

"Great."

"Great."

He gave a little wave, the same kind he gave in the garbage truck, and I got in the Sunbird.

It was nice of Leonard to invite me to a movie, I thought, struggling with the ignition key, which had a way of locking. It really was. Because he was clearly aware that he was far too old for me and therefore didn't mean it as a date. And he was secure enough and with-it enough to be able to ask me to a movie without worrying that I would interpret it as anything more than that.

The car finally started. A Peter Frampton song erupted from the classic rock station and I turned down the volume and lowered the window. From Joel's deck, where the trunks of nearby elm trees reflected the flickering citronella candles and the smell of grilled chicken kabobs hung in the humid air, came the sound of an adult chorus singing "Nathan Detroit."

My first "Quality of Life Report" was going to be a sort of introductory piece to the whole series, a summing-up of the reasons I—and many New Yorkers—might choose to abandon the rat race for greener pastures. As I'd left his party, Joel had told me he was going to find me a cameraman who could capture some sweeping prairie footage, some peaceful shots of Prairie City's many parks and recreational areas, and then shoot me sitting on my front porch. Most of the segment would be a voice-over. One day before the script needed to be e-mailed to Faye, I still hadn't started it. I sat in my office and admired the sheer eggplant-colored panels that covered the French doors. I flipped through the *Prairie City Daily Dispatch* and read a column called "Family Matters," in which a woman named Loni Heibel-Budicek humorously pondered the challenges of going to the supermarket with four kids under ten, all of whom still wanted to ride in the shopping cart. I tried to write a first line.

Sometimes choices are right in front of you. Sometimes you have to search for them.

I decided to call Daphne. She wasn't home. I called Elena at her office. She worked at a publicity firm that specialized in promoting gym equipment. The person who answered the phone said she was working from home that day. I called her at home and she was about to leave for a yoga class.

"All I can say is that I've set a stopwatch to see how long it takes you to pack up and come home," Elena said.

I went back to my script.

The sun rises over the prairie like a silent alarm clock, much like the alarm that woke me to new possibilities, new frontiers, new ways of thinking about myself.

The word "prairie" fascinated me. It was a childlike word, something that had a legitimate meaning but was hard to say out loud without sounding like you were talking baby talk. "Tundra" and "muff" were similar words. But I lived on the prairie now, or so I intimated to the *Up Early* staff, who pictured me living in a shanty amid acres of cow pastures and wheat fields, an illusion I made no effort to dispel since the chances of getting Faye to approve segments about the spiritual benefits of living on a street with refrigerators on front porches were slim.

Incidentally, the apartment, despite being a showplace, was infested with fleas. Having remained dormant in the time that elapsed between my arrival and the departure of the previous tenant, who I later learned kept a ferret—and this explained the pungent uriney smell of the house—the insects found new life in my flesh. It had taken me an egregiously long time to figure out what was happening. For weeks, the itching kept me awake at night and in the mornings I'd find my sheets bloody from scratching in my sleep. Even after setting off a flea bomb, they still hadn't all gone away. I planned to do another one that night. My legs looked like they had shrapnel wounds. I could only imagine what Faye would say if she saw me.

The phone rang. Daphne?

It was Samantha Frank. "How's it going out there, Little Miss

Anne of Green Acres?" she said. "Did you see the show this morning?"

"Samantha, *Up Early* doesn't air here," I said.

"Oh, right. *Hello!*" she said. "Anyway, there's a particular, like,
line of inquiry I'd like to just chat about with you. It's certainly not
foreign territory to you. But everyone's wondering about it. Have
you met a man yet?"

"I've met many men," I said.

"Are any of them cowboys?"

"No," I said. "But, uh, I suppose I could run into one."

"Try to," she said. "Because we want to do a spot on this new
book called *The Good Girl's Guide to Bad Boys* and were thinking
we could do a tie-in with your, uh, you know, thing you're doing."

"You want me to find a bad boy? Are cowboys bad?"

"Well, you know what I mean," said Samantha. "They're not,
like, investment analysts. They probably smoke, what's that stuff?
Chew? Can you smoke chew? Chewing tobacco? Or maybe you just
chew it. Like baseball players. You know, whatever. All I'm saying
is maybe you could brainstorm on that. Oh, I gotta take this call.
But how are you otherwise?"

"Fine," I said.

"That's awesome. Well, bye."

All the women I knew in New York were dying for me to find a
boyfriend, preferably in less than a month, because it would con-
firm the very syndrome that we spent nearly every moment discussing: that there were no men in New York and if any one of us
stepped as far outside Manhattan as, say, Stamford, Connecticut,
we'd have more propositions from high school guidance counselors
and auto mechanics in ten minutes than we'd had from actors and
Wall Street brokers in ten years. Not that most of my friends were
willing to date guidance counselors or auto mechanics, which is why
they kept fighting over the same handful of architects and *Men's
Journal* editors. But the hypothesis among my friends was that

within three weeks of being in the Midwest, Lucinda Trout, who hadn't had a boyfriend in two years, would find herself a veterinarian who looked like Sam Shepard, a younger Sam Shepard, Sam Shepard circa 1983. It was as if I were on a space walk and all the women of New York were gathered around a snowy television screen waiting for me to tell them whether or not there was life on other planets. I wasn't particularly in the market for a man, but it seemed there was more at stake in that area than just my need to adjust at my own pace and have a time of solitude before embarking on a relationship, or even a date, with some unsuspecting Prairie City male.

The ratio of men to women in the twenty-five to forty-five age group in Prairie City was, according to the census data I'd looked up on the Internet, approximately 51 percent to 49 percent. Considering the number of men I saw at the Hinky Dinky supermarket, the post office, and the YMCA, these statistics appeared fairly accurate. It was just that a lot of these men, if they were not wearing Joe Camel baseball caps with wraparound sunglasses perched on the brims, were wearing short-sleeved dress shirts, Dockers, and wedding bands. From what I'd seen so far, there seemed no middle ground between the kind of guys I saw buying filterless Winstons at the Gas 'N Stop and the kind of guys who kept framed portraits of their families on the walls of their cubicles at the bank and said things like "Lucinda, we at P.C. Union and Times are committed to making your banking experience a positive one."

Not that a Sam Shepard veterinarian wouldn't have been nice. Back in those last weeks in New York, during that terrifying time when I'd sit in my apartment and nearly shake with fear about what I was about to do, I'd allowed myself to dabble in hyperbolic fantasy. It was both a distraction and a defense mechanism. I'd inflated it to the point of caricature so as not to get my hopes up by actually believing it. In the fantasy, Sam Shepard would live next door. My house would be on the outskirts of Prairie City, conveniently located near both a Starbucks and a cornfield so vast that when I strolled through it in a 1940s-style floral print dress, my hair blowing in the prairie wind, my mind calm and contemplative, my soul clean and pure and good, my hands calloused from some sort of manual labor (clothes hanging? corn husking?) that you'd swear I was an extra in a Sam Shepard movie. Make that the star of a Sam Shepard movie. Make that the costar, playing opposite Sam, who was really my neighbor and not literally Sam Shepard but a rancher or an organic farmer or, yes, a veterinarian, a large animal veterinarian. He'd start coming over for coffee in the mornings and we'd discover each other's inner goodness and things would just take off from there. Everyone I'd meet in Prairie City would be both interesting and kind, every conversation meaningful, every gesture sincere, every woman nonanorectic, every man tall and able to fix cars. I would not be an anxiety-prone, epicurally challenged bad driver but a woman of heart and mind who possessed the kind of sexual appeal that comes not merely from regular exercise or a good bikini wax but from some innate quality that, were she to have any religious background whatsoever, might be characterized as God-fearing. I would be a home slice of a woman, the kind of woman Lyle Lovett might write a song about, the kind of woman Willa Cather might have lusted after. I would officially qualify as decent folk, a good person living among good people.

It was already past noon. I had less than twenty-eight hours to finish my script. That didn't count the four hours I was going to need to be out of the house to set off another flea bomb, which I'd planned to do that evening while I went to a movie by myself and then perhaps sat in The Grinder and attempted to finish my script.

The sun that rises over the prairie is the same sun that rises over the city, but somehow the light is different. In the city, dawn marks the end of the evening. On the prairie, it means a new day.

The phone rang. Daphne?

"Lucinda!" a male voice said. "Joel Lipinksy. How's it going?"

"Just great."

"Hey, I know this is really last minute," Joel said, "but I was wondering if you had plans tonight."

"I'm setting off a flea bomb," I said, which turned out to be one of the stupider things I said during my first month in Prairie City.

"Valdette has her class at the synagogue tonight," Joel said. "And I don't know if you're familiar with the Heidi Vidlak Memorial Film Theater here in P.C. but they show art films, like, you know, foreign flicks and stuff other than the commercial crap that plays in the regular theaters. And tonight's the last night of a film called *Julian Donkey-Boy*. I'd really like to catch it."

"Oh," I said.

"I thought you might need a dose of culture by now," he said. "Because I know what that's like. I mean, man, it can get bleak around here."

Because I had essentially announced that I had no specific plans and had to be out of the house for at least four hours, I had no choice. Besides, I needed to foster a good working relationship with him.

Joel picked me up and helped me set off the flea bombs. He made a big show of running out of the house as if we were ducking out of a sudden rainstorm, though he also seemed concerned about getting chemicals on his suit, which was an army green version of the black one he'd worn the night before. When he started up his SUV, the soundtrack to *The Buena Vista Social Club* blared from the speakers.

"*The Buena Vista Social Club!*" I chirped.

"Oh yeah," Joel said. "I really dig this. I have Ibrahim Ferrer's solo album, too. Really great stuff."

During my last year in New York, my aspirations to be a more serious journalist had led me to work as a film critic. It was an unpaid position at a free newspaper that pretended to be neighborhood based and therefore had different names according to where it was distributed, though the content was the same in each edition. It was called *The Upper West Side Eye, The Chelsea Ear, The Flatiron Focus, Greenwich Village Accent,* and, most perplexingly, *The Upper East Side Top Hat,* which seemed a misguided effort to evoke an Edith Wharton-flavored aura of old Manhattan society. Every week I delivered lengthy essays on the films that the senior critic, a second-tier socialite who was married to a real estate mogul, couldn't be bothered to cover. I would review a documentary about highway rest stops or the latest movie from Iceland. Often the film had ended its brief run by the time the review was published. As it happened, I had reviewed *The Buena Vista Social Club.* It was a Wim Wenders documentary about a group of legendary Cuban *son* musicians who, thanks to the American slide guitarist Ry Cooder, were reunited after decades of cultural repression under Castro. Though the film was earnest and stylish—so much so that, in a weak moment, I'd bought the soundtrack in the hopes of impressing the Prairie Cityites—I'd also thought it smacked of cultural imperialism, especially the finale, which showed the band playing a sold-out show at Carnegie Hall and saying they owed it all to Ry Cooder, whose atmospheric steel pedal guitar chords were about as organic to the music as a John Bonham drum solo at the Ice Capades. I said as much to Joel.

"Really?" he said, pulling into a parking garage near the theater. "I didn't think so. I found it really interesting."

Julian Donkey-Boy, I quickly discerned, was the latest atrocity from independent cinema's enfant terrible Harmonie Korine, who was best known for writing the (in this critic's opinion) facile and exploitive docudrama *Kids* and then went on to make the horrifying *Gummo,* wherein a prepubescent, trailer trash punk systematically kills neighborhood cats and a retarded girl is gang-raped. In *Julian Donkey-Boy,* a schizophrenic nudist with a fascistic German father impregnates his adolescent sister, who then has a miscarriage at a skating rink. The film appeared to have been shot by a seventh grader with a handheld camera and most of the dialogue was unintelligible. The audience at the Heidi Vidlak Memorial Film Theater was comprised of a combination of college professors, students, and middle-aged women wearing batik sundresses. When the screen faded to black after no particular dramatic conclusion, the crowd let out a collective *mmm.* As we left the theater, people were saying things like "It really makes you think."

Joel wanted to get a drink. Since I had almost two hours left before I could enter my house, I agreed. We went to a place called Cosmo Club, which he said was much "classier and hipper" than the usual dive bars downtown.

"That was really interesting," he said as we sat down in the bar. It was dark and had couches with low tables and candles. It was sort of like Bar Barella, except the clientele appeared to be exclusively Prairie City State College students. A ponytailed guy in an army jacket was scribbling in a notebook while drinking Scotch and smoking a cigarette.

I made the mistake of telling Joel that after three years minoring in cinema studies in college and two years of reviewing the debuts of every film school grad who ever had a rich uncle, my patience for high art had waned.

"That's one of the reasons I moved here," I added, suddenly feeling the oddness of my presence in a midwestern cocktail lounge with a fifty-year-old married man. "I wanted to see what it was like to be normal. It's really, you know, just an experiment. I know I probably seem very strange to everyone. And everyone's been so nice. But, you know, I'm still doing my job. *Up Early* is very behind this project. It was practically their idea."

"Well, I for one am just totally psyched that you've chosen to live here and do this documentary project," Joel said. "Partly because we're all looking forward to getting to know you more as a person and partly for selfish reasons. I mean, it's great to have someone who can talk about culture, who knows what's going on in the world, who can think outside the box."

"You mean like telling you I thought that movie was gratuitous, pretentious shit?" I said. Suddenly I felt like I'd crossed the line. He

had, after all, paid for my ticket. So I added, "Other than Chloe Se-
vigny's performance, which was quite good despite the material."

"See, I love this," Joel said. "You just tell it like it is. That's how
we used to do it back in Brooklyn. Something's *meshuggeneh*, then
it's *meshuggeneh*. No B.S. You're really refreshing, Lucinda."

He leaned toward me slightly. Or maybe he didn't. I wasn't sure.
But something became awkward. We were silent for a moment and
I looked around the bar and pretended to survey the scene.

"Where did you say Valdette was tonight?" I asked. "At the synagogue?"

"She takes a class," he said. "Jewish cultural studies. She enjoys
it. She's really open to other cultures."

"She's not Jewish?"

"Oh no, she was raised Lutheran. She's from Kansas."

Joel ordered me another drink even though I hadn't finished the
first one. I wondered what would happen if I went in my house before the allotted four hours for the flea bomb. Would I die of gas poi-
soning in my sleep, not to be found for days until Toby smelled
something strange?

"What initially brought you to Prairie City?" I asked Joel.

"Couldn't turn down the job offer," he said. "KPCR is a serious
station, a well-regarded station. Granted, I was just an office clerk.
But I knew there was room for movement. And here I am more than
twenty years later. Station manager. Making good money. Producing quality programming."

"Yeah, I caught that thing on the native grasses," I said. "I
thought that was really well done."

"Actually that's a Canadian production," he said. "We just aired
it here. Did you ever see *Parent Talk* with Loni Heibel-Budicek?
That's ours."

"Hmm."

"You know, it's funny," Joel said. "The way life goes by. You
grow up in the sixties. You think you're going to change the world.
I mean, I went to marches. I smoked pot. I still smoke pot. I mean,

sometimes, you know, occasionally. Not, like, all the time or anything. But you grow up. You get married, you live in a place thinking you're not going to live there forever. Valdette and I had a farm
outside of town. We lived off the land. We baked bread. But then the
commute got to be too much, so we moved into town. We lived in a
kind of rough section. There were gangs."

"There are gangs in Prairie City?" I asked.

"Oh yeah," he said. "Big time. Especially back then. Not that it
bothered me, being from Brooklyn and all. Growing up I got beaten
up by the blacks and the Italians on a regular basis. But after a
while we sold out and moved to a better neighborhood. I got promoted to station manager. We go to Europe, the whole fucking
bourgeois scenario. Sometimes I think about packing up a tent and
living in the desert." He gestured to the street outside, which was
completely empty except for a hippie-looking kid unlocking his bicycle from a parking meter. "Away from all this."

"Everyone has his alternative lifestyle fantasy," I said. I wished
I was at Bar Barella with Daphne. Or that she was here. She would
be so impressed with my apartment.

"You know, Lucinda," Joel said, "I don't mean to be out of line
but there's something I want to say. And I say it because I'm a firm
believer in saying what I mean. No B.S. I know you're the same way.
So do you mind if I say it?"

"I guess not," I said. My stomach lurched.

"What I want to say," Joel said, "is that I think you're really,
really interesting."

"Oh," I said. "Thanks."

"And I think you're really brave to do what you've done and I
want you to know that if you ever want to talk, if you ever feel like
being with someone who, you know, is on the same wavelength, I'm
here."

"Oh, thanks." This was quickly turning hideous.

"And I also, forgive me if this is out of line," he said, "I think
that you're really sexy."

I don't know how long Joel stared at me because after making eye contact for no more than two seconds I laughed and looked away and blushed, which he probably interpreted as giddy excitement but was in fact an involuntary reaction to the complete horror I felt about the immediate situation and the creeping feelings of regret I felt about the general situation of having left New York, where the one thing you could usually count on was not being told you were really sexy, at least by married men with tiny silver ponytails. And because I was incapable of confrontation, because I could spend hours by myself working up long, bitingly eloquent speeches designed to chew someone out but had never actually implemented one of these speeches, I said, "Oh, thanks. That's nice of you." Then, after a long pause, I said, "I'm wiped. I should get home."

I'm wiped? Who uses that word?

Joel seemed to realize he had stepped over the boundary. But on the other hand, perhaps he didn't. He was now sitting so close to me that he could have easily attempted some sort of kiss, but I reached for my wallet as if to pay for the drinks, which he didn't allow, and put on my jacket. Inside out.

On the drive home I chattered nonstop. I asked Joel about the weather patterns in that part of the state, about the percentage of nonwhites in Prairie City, about gang-related activities in his old neighborhood, and about whether or not the local public radio station aired *Talk of the Nation.* He answered but also seemed to be pouting. When we reached my house, Joel offered to go inside before I did to make sure the flea bombs were finished.

"I'll be a canary in your coal mine," he said.

"Oh no, no, no, no," I said. "That's fine. Really. I'm fine. Thanks."

"Thanks for coming out," he said.

"Thank you," I said. And then something awful happened. Because I was from New York, where everyone kisses everyone on the cheek when they say good-bye, usually not even touching the skin but kissing the air next to the skin, I sort of moved toward Joel like

I was going to do just that. I did this because I literally did not know what else to do. In New York, not kissing someone on the cheek when you say good-bye is tantamount to not saying "hello" when you answer the phone. You have not met a basic requirement of social discourse, you have drunk the tequila but forgotten the lime. Joel, also being from New York, moved toward me similarly, except we ended up not kissing the air or even each other's cheeks but actually touching lips, which is a common fumble in all social kisses but, given the circumstances, a grave misfortune.

"Good night, Lucinda," he said. He looked at me as if something had transpired between us, as if we'd shared a moment. I jumped out of the SUV and ran into my house, pretending I could hear the phone ringing.

There were two messages on my answering machine. I pushed the button, praying for Daphne or Elena. The first was from my mother, asking me what time zone Prairie City was in. The second was Leonard inviting me to go to the Bruce Willis movie the following weekend.

The air reeked from the flea bomb and yet somehow the ferret urine smell was still seeping through. The minute I got in bed, Toby Vodacek tromped up the stairs outside, shaking the entire house. I heard his door slam, then the screech of his computer modem, then a blast of heavy metal from his stereo. I put in my ear plugs and tried to fall asleep but my legs were itching again. I turned on the light and found a flea on my pillow, then another on the sheet.

The Lay of the Land

The next day, my twenty-third day in Prairie City, was the worst day yet. I felt so bad that I did not call any of my friends. I couldn't let them see me like this. I sat at my computer and tried to write my script. I wrote two sentences. Around noon, I e-mailed Faye and said that I was very close to finishing but would need an extra day to polish it. By the late afternoon, I was feeling so sorry for myself and disgusted about the Joel situation that I decided I had to exercise. I'd gone swimming at the YMCA once but had been asked not to return until the open sores on my legs had healed. The only thing left was to go jogging, though I had no idea where. I took out my map of Prairie City and looked for the nearest recreational area. There was a place called Nemaha Park a few miles from my house, so I put on the Reebok running gear I'd purchased for seventy-five dollars in my last days in New York and got in the Sunbird.

After several wrong turns, I found a wooded area on the other side of the highway that appeared to have some running paths. There was a small parking area with one beat-up pickup truck taking up two spaces. I got out of the car and was spraying myself with insect repellent when a man emerged from the wooded area. He was wearing nothing but cut-off shorts and flip-flops. He carried a tank top in his hand and had a beard and wore small round glasses. My first instinct was to be frightened. But then he waved hello nonchalantly and I noticed that he looked like Brad Pitt might have looked if Brad Pitt had lived during either the Civil War times or the late 1960s. I realize this is an odd mixing of genres, but this guy had them perfectly mixed. He was a sort of Jeremiah Johnson meets Brad Pitt. His blond hair had a strawlike quality. The glasses were more like spectacles. He had a tattoo of an eagle on his arm—not a Budweiser kind of eagle but an actual eagle-in-the-wilderness kind of eagle. He walked over to the beat-up pickup, took out what appeared to be a library book, and headed back toward the wooded area. There didn't seem to be any jogging paths.

"Excuse me," I said to him. Was I actually speaking to this bearded stranger? "Do you know if there's anyplace to jog around here?"

"To jog?" He said this as if I'd asked him where the skating rink was.

"Or, you know, walk," I said. "I just don't want to get lost."

"Ah hell, you won't get lost," he said. He had a slight drawl, sort of like Valdette's, although his wardrobe changed the effect totally. "If you make a left through those trees up there you'll run into some water. I think there's a little path that follows the crick through there."

The *crick*. Had he actually said that? Crick. I assumed that meant creek. He had nice eyes. Blue and squinty with nice crow's feet. I thanked him and headed left through the trees. "Watch out for poison ivy!" he called after me.

"What?"

"Just stay on the path when you get to the crick. You should be fine. Other than the plethora of poisonous snakes."

"What!" I yelled.

"Just joking," he said. He walked back into the woods where he must have been before. I couldn't believe he'd used the word "plethora." He was sexy in a way, in a redneck, woodsy, serial killer sort of way. I hadn't seen a guy in flip-flops since the mid-1970s, when I was a preschooler. I tried to jog but the trail by the creek, which was nearly dried up and littered with beer cans, was covered with roots and twigs and I was afraid I'd fall. I walked for a half hour or so, thinking about the Jeremiah Johnson guy. He was interesting. Not necessarily interesting, since we'd barely spoken, but intriguing, largely due to the combination of "crick" and "plethora" and his squinty blue eyes. He seemed closer to the kind of guy I'd hoped to meet in Prairie City than anyone I'd met so far, even though I hadn't met many men other than Joel and Leonard and Toby and wasn't in the mood for meeting one anyway. But still, if I was to meet a guy, this guy represented a step in the direction of someone who might be a good candidate for a Prairie City boyfriend, not to mention what Samantha needed for the bad boy segment. Even though I'd never see him again and he seemed inappropriate anyway, it was heartening to know that at least there were people like him out there. But what was he doing in the woods in the middle of a weekday? I wondered. He could easily have been a rapist or murderer. In retrospect, it had been unwise to talk to him. A close call, really. On the other hand, though, maybe he was a wildlife biology professor or a fish and game warden. Maybe he'd traveled all over the world studying the migration patterns of cranes and was at that very moment supervising a bunch of students (far off in the bush, which was why I hadn't seen them) who were observing the mating patterns of the red-shafted flicker. More likely he worked at the Firestone tire plant, I thought. And it didn't matter because I'd never see him again.

Except that I did see him again. I saw him that very moment. As the creek circled back toward where I'd started, I smelled a campfire. Then I saw Jeremiah Johnson/Brad Pitt sitting on a log by the fire reading the library book. He waved at me.

"Nice run?" he asked.

"Not really," I said. And then I tried something. Even though the reference made little sense, I said, "It just looks like the set of *Deliverance* back there. I didn't want to go much farther."

"You ran into a mutant banjo player?" he said.

Unbelievable. He'd gotten it. Despite the hopelessly collegiate nature of this tactic, I'd somehow made it to age twenty-nine without figuring out a better acid test for cultural intelligence than dropping a reference to an obscure (or semiobscure) movie or book to see if the other person picked up on it. I still think I fell in love with my Last Serious Boyfriend the moment I said, "I want the truth" and he said, "You can't handle the truth!" Even though, in retrospect, *A Few Good Men* is hardly esoteric. Of course, the test often backfired, as in my pseudo rapport with Joel about *The Buena Vista Social Club*. But getting the *Deliverance* reference, while less than an astounding feat, was more than I expected from a guy in flip-flops sitting by a campfire on an already hot afternoon. I noticed his book was a collection of Gary Snyder poems. I was suddenly self-conscious about my scabby legs.

"How is it that you live here and don't know where to go jogging?" he asked, effectively opening the door for what in the last month had become the greatest conversation piece in the state's history: Lucinda Trout's Unlikely Presence in the Heartland and What Prompted It. I knew this would lead to his asking me on a date, though I was shocked by my sudden confidence that, after years in New York with nary a proposition, any random midwestern man would ask me out.

"I just moved here," I said.

"From where?"

"Manhattan," I said.

"Manhattan, Kansas?"

"No," I said. "New York. New York City."

"Why would anyone want to live in New York?" he asked.

"That's a narrow outlook," I said, smiling.

"So you want to go out sometime?" he said.

Lucinda Trout, girl psychic.

"That depends," I said. "Are you a serial killer or anything?"

"Other than that one time, no," he said.

"If it was just once, then it wouldn't be serial, I guess," I said. Such a wit.

"Good point," he said.

It went on like that for a while until he walked me back to the parking area and I gave him my phone number, which he wrote down on a matchbook he had on the dashboard that said JIM'S BAIT AND STEAKS. He said his name was Mason Clay. I'd always admired people who had last names for first names.

He was forty.

"And as long as you're asking so many questions, I'll tell you that I'm an Aries," he said. "And I hate Chinese food. It tastes like bugs."

"What were you doing out here anyway?" I asked.

"Reading," he said. "I got off early from work and I'm killing time before I go pick up one of my kids." He lowered his head and looked at me over the tops of his glasses as if to issue a warning. "I have three kids."

"Oh."

"So," he said.

"Okay," I said.

"So I'll call you," he said. "Do you like to camp?"

"Do I like to camp?" I said. "Not on first dates."

"We'll figure out something else, then," he said.

"What do you do?" I said, hoping against hope for wildlife biologist.

"For fun?"

"For a job."

"Oh shit, not much," he said. "I work in an elevator."

Not the ideal answer, but, then again, not the Firestone plant. I couldn't imagine a building in Prairie City tall enough to have an elevator operator. He must have been lying, although why would you make up a profession like that? Besides, he'd never call. Except that he would. As I watched him lie down on the log, holding the poetry book in front of his face to block the sun, I was certain I hadn't seen the last of him.

I didn't tell Daphne or Elena or anyone else that I'd given my phone number to a guy I met in the woods, a guy with three kids who worked in an elevator, made jokes about killing someone, and, come to think of it, hadn't said he wasn't married, which, in light of the Joel encounter, didn't appear in Prairie City to be a deterrent in asking women on dates. I didn't tell anyone that when Mason called a few days later—"Uh, hi I think we met in the park," he said when I answered, invoking neither his name nor mine—I agreed to meet him, albeit in a public place. He suggested we go to Effie's Tavern.

As I explained earlier, Effie's was legendary not just in Prairie City but also throughout the region for being an equalizing force among all socioeconomic and ethnic groups. Though some chalked this up to Effie's affable, low-key atmosphere (there was a pool table but no keno gambling) I soon learned what all the regulars knew—that the equalizing force had less to do with things like open arms and open minds than with the fact that Friday afternoon happy hour drafts at Effie's were $1.00 and at Applebee's, just a quarter mile down the road, they were $1.50.

It was a Tuesday evening when I met Mason at Effie's. There was hardly anyone in the place, just a handful of overweight white women with muscled black boyfriends, every single one of them with a shaved head. Mason was sitting at the bar wearing the same outfit he'd worn in the park, except his tank top was actually on his body. I had on my J. Crew pants, a linen Brooks Brothers shirt, and a strand of freshwater pearls.

"I didn't think you'd show up," Mason said.

"I always keep my appointments."

He surveyed my outfit. "I don't think they have wine spritzer here," he said.

"I'll just have a beer," I said. "I'll have a, uh, a Heineken."

"I don't think they have Heineken."

"What are you drinking?" I asked.

"Leinenkugel," he said.

"What's that?"

"It's kind of like urine," he said. "With a note of Heineken."

A gigantic woman with bleached blond, permed hair was leaning over the pool table, her two-sizes-too-small shorts riding up over the tops of her thighs. I noticed a small child clinging to her legs. Stevie Ray Vaughan was blasting through the speakers. Mason got up to get me a beer and came back with a Rolling Rock.

"Best in the house," he said.

"So," I said, "what building do you work in?"

"What building?" he said, perplexed.

"Where is your elevator?"

"On Highway 36."

"Is it an office building?"

"No," he said. "It's just an elevator. A grain elevator."

A grain elevator! He wasn't an elevator operator as in a guy with epaulets and a hat. He worked with grain. He worked in an agricultural capacity, which put him in the neighborhood of farmer.

"Did you think I worked in a regular elevator?" he asked.

"Oh, no," I said. "Well, maybe."

"And you still agreed to meet me?"

"I'm not sure what a grain elevator is," I said.

"It stores the grain," he said. "Farmers bring their crop in after they've harvested it, we put it in bins, sometimes dry it off if it's wet, and then load it onto trains."

"Why is it called an elevator?"

"Because an elevator lifts the grain up to the top of the bins," he said. "Ours is about seven stories high."

"So how do you spend most of your days there?" I asked.

"Most of the guys watch soap operas," he said. "I leave as much as possible. It's pretty slow except during harvest. The boss practices tai chi all day."

"And feng shui?" I said, thinking of Faye.

"What's that?" he asked.

In truth, I wasn't exactly sure all of what feng shui entailed. We were silent for a moment. Mason guzzled the last of his beer and signaled the waitress for another.

"So do you live near here?" I asked.

"I have a cabin by the river," he said.

"There's a river nearby?"

"It's about twenty-five miles from here," he said. "The Flatwater. I've had a little A-frame for about ten years. Wait 'til you see it. You'll love it."

"You mean you live there all the time?" I asked.

"Pretty much."

"So it must be, like, fully outfitted and everything."

"It has everything I need," he said.

"So it has heat and everything?" I asked.

"I have a woodstove," he said. "I have a really nice outhouse. You should see it."

"An outhouse?"

"I've got it all fixed up," he said.

"The cabin?"

"No, the outhouse," he said. "It's probably one of the nicest outhouses around here. I do abstract paintings. I put a really nice one in the outhouse. It's a Kandinsky kind of thing. "

"So how do you, like, take a shower?" I asked.

"I bathe in the river," he said.

The child of the gigantic woman suddenly started screaming. She picked him up in her giant arms, kissed his head, and lit a cigarette. I looked at Mason, who, again, was downing his last swig of beer.

"Are you making all this up?" I asked.

"No."

"So where do you bathe in the winter?"

"There's a truck stop on the way to the cabin," he said. "Sometimes I use the showers there. Though the clientele is a little . . . iffy."

"Uh huh," I said. "So . . . you said you have three children."

"Yup," he said.

"Do you see them often?"

"All the time."

"And how old are they?"

"Let's see," he said. "Sebastian is thirteen, Peter is nine, and Erin is, uh, four."

"That's quite an age range," I said. "So you're divorced?"

"Oh, well no."

"What?" I yelped.

"Give me a break," he said, rolling his eyes. "Of course I'm divorced. You think I'm some kind of scumbag?"

"Oh," I said. "Well, you must have not been divorced for long."

"Ten years," he said.

"But didn't you say you had a four-year-old?" I asked, forgetting about the nine-year-old. This sort of math wasn't my strength.

"She has a different mother," he said.

"So you have two from your ex-wife and one from this other woman?" I asked.

"Well," he said, "actually, the first is from my ex-wife and the second one is from my ex-girlfriend, and the third kind of just, you know, happened."

"Oh!"

Had this date been on one of those television shows where they follow the couple around and have pop-up cartoon bubbles saying things like "Nice tie" and "Guess his mother never taught him how to use a fork" this would have been the moment where a giant bubble, a bubble nearly the size of the screen, would pop up and say, simply:

"!*?#**!!!"

"Do you want another beer?" he asked.

Before I could answer, Mason got up to get me another beer. I wondered if I should just walk out and leave. If Elena had been on this date she would have shouted "Next!" and stridden right out of the bar. But Mason came back almost instantly. He plopped the beer on the table.

"So you're probably wondering what I'm doing in Prairie City," I said.

"Being glad you're not in New York, I assume," he said.

"I'm actually a television producer," I said. "I'm doing a series for a New York morning show about the quality of life."

The gigantic woman's child started screaming again and this time she swatted him on the head.

"Well, they sure don't have that in New York," Mason said.

"Have you ever been there?" I asked.

"Why would I want to go there?"

"Because it's great!" I said, sounding very much like Bonnie Crawley. "Great restaurants, amazing, smart people. It's just, you know, my rent was going up to twenty-one hundred dollars a month."

"Susannah took Sebastian there a couple years back," he said. "I was worried the whole time. Susannah being my ex-wife."

"And, uh, what does she do?" I asked.

"She's a professor at the Center for Great Plains Studies at P.C. State College," he said. "My ex-girlfriend's a nurse."

"And what does the third woman do?" I asked. "The other mother?"

"These days, your guess is as good as mine," he said. "But Erin's gonna grow up to be a professional outdoorswoman. I'm seeing to that."

He paused and looked at me.

"I know it looks bad," he continued. "But I love my kids. I see my kids all the time. I don't regret anything that's happened. As far as the kids go."

"I don't want kids," I said.

"Then don't have them," Mason said.

I drank three Rolling Rocks. Mason drank nine Leinenkugels. He didn't appear in the least bit affected by any of them. I asked him if he knew Sue, since everyone else in town seemed to. He said he didn't and I felt a short breath of fresh air rush inside me, as if I were being let out of a crowded house and allowed to walk down the street. I thought about Samantha and her bad boys story. This guy seemed qualified. He wasn't a cowboy, although he did say he'd owned a horse once, which he'd kept tied up in his yard on the edge of town when he was married to Susannah. I looked at his hands. His fingernails were encrusted with dirt. His skin looked as rough as tree bark.

"What are you doing on Thursday?" Mason asked me.

"On Thursday?" I said. "I don't know. Working." I'd managed to e-mail my script but I'd avoided calling Joel to assemble a crew for the shoot. I'd spent the weekend running speaker wire from the office to the living room, using a staple gun to attach it to the bases of the walls and around door frames so the speakers could be placed on opposite sides of the room for maximum sonic effect. Then I'd painted the wire white so it wouldn't look ugly on the walls.

"You should come out to the cabin," Mason said. "It's gonna be a full moon. We could spend the night out there. You'd love it."

"Spend the night?" I asked, trying to sound as incredulous as possible while at the same time worrying about his feelings, which suddenly seemed entirely capable of being hurt. And because I couldn't think of how to respond, because the only appropriate response to such an inappropriate suggestion was something hackneyed enough to sound like a joke, an aphorism in the vein of "You go, girl," I said, "I'm not that kind of a girl." (Lucinda Trout had, on one or two occasions in the past, been that kind of a girl. But neither occasion had involved cabins with outhouses.)

"I don't mean it that way," he said. "I'm sure!"

He said "sure" with the odd little drawl that crept up in a num-

ber of his words. I'd noticed that he'd pronounced "wash" like
"warsh." *I warsh my clothes in the crick,* he'd said.

"Then where would I sleep?" I asked.

"In the bed in the loft," he said. "I'd sleep on the couch. Or outside in the teepee."

"You have a teepee?"

"Of course," he said. "The boys sleep in it all the time."

I said I'd consider going to his cabin on Thursday but that I
wouldn't spend the night. Mason said that was fine but that I'd
probably change my mind and want to spend the night when I saw
how beautiful the river was. Outside in the parking lot, as I watched
him climb into his pickup, which was littered with power tools, library books, and Neil Young cassettes, I noticed on the floor a container of Muppet Babies diaper wipes.

I'd returned Leonard's call but I'd done it during business hours when
I knew he wouldn't be home and had purposefully screened the phone
calls in the evenings when I knew he'd call me back. He'd left two
messages saying the Bruce Willis movie was still playing but if I didn't
want to see it we could always see something else or skip the movie
and just have dinner or, if I felt like it, go for a bike ride. In the meantime, Joel had left a message making sure I was aware of a party being
thrown by the Peter Fonda county commissioner on Friday and asking me if I needed a ride. He didn't mention the *Up Early* shoot. I'd already known about the Peter Fonda county commissioner's party from
Sue and had decided to skip it. I'd also decided that the best way to de-
fuse the Joel situation was to actually do something with Leonard. By
not doing something with Leonard, Joel might think I was saving myself for him. By doing something platonic and innocuous with
Leonard, like going for a bike ride, I would establish a position of non-
romantic bipartisanship and therefore encourage both of them to give
up. For added protection against Leonard's developing any interest in
me, I wore shorts, which revealed the festering scabs on my legs.

Leonard said we could take a bike tour through his neighborhood and then he would cook dinner for me at his house. I didn't
have a bike, but he said I could use his daughter's. Though she was
just eleven she must have been quite a bit taller than I. Leonard had
to adjust the seat and the handlebars. We ended up riding over to a
huge public rose garden near the children's zoo. Leonard had us
park the bikes and wander along the paths. A young couple was
getting pictures taken by a professional photographer. The woman
wore what looked like a prom dress and the man wore a light col-
ored three-piece suit with a pink bow tie. The photographer kept
putting them in poses where the man was kneeling before the
woman as if proposing marriage. In another shot, the woman held
a rose in front of her face and cocked her head to the side. Leonard
picked a rose and gave it to me, which I accidentally dropped on the
way back to his house.

He made lasagna with Velveeta cheese for dinner. Apparently
the kids, whom I had yet to lay eyes on, had already eaten at their
mother's house and were watching TV in the basement.

"Kyle and Danielle, come up here, please," Leonard yelled. After several minutes, the kids emerged begrudgingly from the basement, the blare of a sitcom laugh track pouring through the open
door. Kyle was tall and scrawny and zitty and wore a RAGE AGAINST
THE MACHINE T-shirt and several hemp bracelets around his wrist.
Danielle looked like she was about thirty. She was at least five foot
eight and had olive skin and some of the darkest, glossiest hair I'd
ever seen. She wore bell-bottom jeans and a navel ring. She looked
a bit like Cher in the 1970s.

"I want you to meet my friend Lucinda," Leonard said.

The kids murmured something. Then Danielle said, "We're out
of pop."

"Then drink water," Leonard said. "And what is that on your
stomach?"

"It's a clip-on," Danielle said.

"A clip-on navel ring?" I asked. "They have such a thing?"

"I got about five of them," she said.

I wondered then if Leonard had invited me over to somehow get to know Danielle so I could be a positive influence on her. It seemed conceivable that Leonard was not interested in me romantically but instead saw me as an independent, professional young woman who might serve as a role model for his wayward daughter. I immediately warmed to him. He was a good father.

"Okay, you can go back downstairs now," Leonard said. He got us more beers and suggested we sit outside on the deck so he could smoke.

"So when did you change your name to Running Feather?" I asked after at least a minute had passed in silence.

"About twenty-five years ago," he said.

"When you were a kid?" I asked.

"I was twenty-five," he said.

"Oh, right," I said. "And had you always known your biological parents were named Running Feather? Did you have your adoption records opened up?"

"Oh, I never did that," Leonard said, blowing smoke rings as he spoke. "I was never interested in finding my parents."

"Oh!"

"My mom was probably your typical drunk Indian," he said.

"But did you suddenly become more interested in Native culture?" I asked.

"Not really," he said.

"Then why did you change your name?"

"I don't know." Leonard laughed. "I just wanted to be different somehow. I thought maybe it would impress women. I figured lots of people changed their names. Look at Cher."

"And she's part Cherokee, isn't she?" I said.

"Is she?" asked Leonard.

I looked at my watch. Though it was just past 9:30, it suddenly seemed very late. I told Leonard I had to get going and he politely walked me through the house and outside to the Sunbird. "How's the car?" he said.

"Great."

"It's a good thing you didn't buy that Saab," he said.

"Yeah."

" 'Cause replacing a Saab part costs a lot more than replacing a part on most other cars," he said.

"Yeah," I said. "Hey, you wouldn't know a guy named Mason Clay, would you?"

"Never heard of him," Leonard said.

"I thought everyone knew everyone in this town."

"We do," he said. "So this guy sounds suspicious."

I drove off and went several miles in the wrong direction. When I figured out where I was, I was seized with the urge to go home and drink wine while listening to Joni Mitchell's *Blue* album, so I stopped at the Hinky Dinky supermarket. I'd been to Hinky Dinky enough to know that there appeared to be an employee policy against visible body piercings. Almost every high school kid who worked there had a tiny Band-Aid on his or her eyebrow where there would normally be a ring. But it wasn't until now that I realized that every single adult who worked there—and this meant nearly every member of the night crew—had something wrong with them. One clerk, whom I'd seen before in passing, I now noticed was missing part of his ear. The woman working the express lane, punching the register with long, artificial pink finger nails, was a dwarf. When I went to the liquor area to pay for my $7.99 chardonnay, the clerk had a Band-Aid on her eyebrow and also a speech impediment. "I'm ga-need to thee thome I.D.," she said. As I walked away she called after me, "Wah happen to your legths?"

Safely in the Sunbird, I felt tears come to my eyes. This was in violation of my no-crying policy and I bit my cheek until I got back to the apartment, where I listened to half of "All I Want" before turning off the stereo and trying to fall asleep before the inevitable thunder of Toby's footsteps.

From: Faye Figaro
To: Lucinda Trout
Re: Were not paying you to do nothing

Lucnda, you better get your ass in geer. you've been there a month and not one segment have you filed. I gave you the number of the guy at KPCR. Call and get a crew together and shoot the fucking series itro piece. how busy can they be covering pta metings and hog auctions?

To: Joel Lipinsky
From: Lucinda Trout
Re: NY Up Early segment

Joel, I would very much like to proceed with the first *New York Up Early* segment, which revolves around the theme "Choices and Chances." All this requires from you is a videographer, a sound man (or woman), and no more than an hour of shooting on my front porch, 2321 S. Sunnyvale Av, Prairie City. Please let me know ASAP when we can set this up.

And thank you for taking me to the movie the other night. Hello to Valdette!

The day after the bike ride with Leonard was the date to go to Mason's cabin. He was picking me up at 4:00 in the afternoon, which seemed an odd time to start a date but perhaps would work to my advantage in that there would be less pressure to spend the night. I spent the day talking on the phone to Elena and Daphne. I told them I had met a guy who read Gary Snyder poetry and bathed in the river. I didn't mention the kids or the grain elevator. I told them he wanted me to go to his cabin but that I wasn't going to go until I knew him better. Daphne was all for it but said to wait until the fifth date to go the cabin. Elena said he sounded like the Unabomber and that I shouldn't go anywhere near his cabin or even see him again. She said there must be an architect or a professor of Great Plains studies who would make a more suitable boyfriend. As for Joel, she said he sounded like a cross between Alvy Singer and Humbert Humbert and was an embarrassment to the Jewish people, mostly for living in the Midwest. She said I was in danger of becoming a hussy.

"Get the lay of the land before you become the lay of the land!" Elena said. "Stick with the lesbians," she said.

"I'm going to have them over for dinner," I said. I would do this as soon as I got a ceramic Italian swirl-style salad bowl from Pier One.

"Good," she said. "And after you've done that you can come back to New York and resume the thong underwear beat. This is madness."

Mason showed up around 3:30. I could hear him coming from a block away. The engine in his pickup was competing for volume with the Neil Young tape. I watched him as he pulled up in front of the house and drove the left side of the truck onto the curb. The last few bars of "Down by the River" petered out as he idled for a minute and finally turned off the ignition. He was wearing the same tank top, cut-offs, and flip-flops he'd worn both in the park and in the bar. I let him in the house. He smelled like a campfire.

"Great woodwork," he said.

Mason suggested we get dinner first because we'd be hungry later and he didn't have much to eat at the cabin. It turned out this meant going to the drive-through at Jack in the Box and eating in the truck. When I couldn't finish my hamburger he took it from me, stuffed the wrapper in the ashtray, and threw the food out the window onto the country road.

"Some opossum or deer's gonna love that," he said.

We drove past grain silos and cornfields and acres of natural

prairie grasses. Mason pointed out red-tailed hawks and turkey vul-
tures. He told me that in December bald eagles gathered by the
dozens on the river in front of his cabin. An eagle feather on a
leather string dangled from his rearview mirror. "It's illegal to have
these," he said, "but I find them all over the place near the cabin.
Indians are allowed to have them. I always wished I was an Indian."

"I used to wish I was Jewish," I said.

"Huh?"

The cabin seemed much farther away than twenty miles. On the
other hand, Mason said he hated driving on the highway and only
took back roads and rarely went more than forty miles per hour. The
closer we got, the more I realized that if this guy tied me to a chair
and raped me before murdering me with the ax I noticed he had in
the back of the truck, no jury would convict on the basis of the victim's sheer stupidity. He turned off the main road onto a gravel road
and then a dirt road. Trees were closing in around us. We passed
ramshackle cabins and trailers onto which people had built shaky
screened-in porches. We reached a gate. Mason climbed out of the
truck, unlocked it, got back in and drove it forward a few feet, and
got out and locked it back up. I was surely going to be killed out
here, I thought. Except that I knew I wouldn't be. At least probably
not. Somehow he seemed implicitly trustworthy, despite growing
evidence to the contrary.

The evidence to the contrary grew further when I saw the cabin.
It was a tiny A-frame surrounded by huge driftwood sculptures under which he had placed fluorescent lights. Animal bones had been
placed strategically on several of the sculptures, deer skulls and
snake spines and coyote pelvises, all of which he claimed he'd found
over the course of twenty years of hiking around the Flatwater
River. Inside the cabin, giant paintings of herons and eagles and demonic, tortured human faces hung from the rafters. Indian relics
were everywhere. An entire wall was covered with feathers and
bird's nests and tattered brown photos of Indian chiefs and cowboys
and settlers standing in front of their homesteads. Books and cas-

settes were spilling from shelves. He had Hunter S. Thompson and Ken Kesey and no fewer than twenty paperbacks by Edward Abbey. There was an old cast-iron woodstove in one corner, a television, VCR, and small refrigerator in the other. He opened the refrigerator and took out two beers.

"So what do you think?" he asked.

"It's just like my apartment in New York!"

"Really?" he said.

"No," I said. "But it's about the same size."

"And you haven't even seen the outhouse yet," he said, handing me a beer. "How are you with heights?"

"Is the outhouse in a tree?"

"No, I want to take you on the bridge," he said. "There's an abandoned railroad trestle a little ways down the river," he said. "You'll love it."

He was going to push me off. But wouldn't he rape me first? I figured it was too early in the game for him to try to kill me. So I walked with him along the riverbank to the bridge. It must have been a mile long. It rose about twenty-five feet above the river, the ties splintered and worn down. The end had literally collapsed where it had once met the bank, so we had to climb up the side of one of the pilings, which was covered with tar.

"It's an advanced-level skill to do this with a beer in your hand," Mason said, pulling me up as I tried to avoid the tar and keep my shoes from falling off. "Even more so in the dark. Or during a storm."

"You come up here during storms?" I asked, crouching on all fours when I reached the top. There were huge gaps between many of the railroad ties. Looking down through them I could see large rocks, jagged pieces of driftwood, and broken beer bottles.

"Sure," he said. "I was nearly struck by lightning once. More than once actually."

The sun was going down and the sky was turning red. I had no choice but to hold on to Mason's arm as we walked along the bridge.

He pointed out a blue heron landing on a sandbar. He pointed out a beaver swimming in the river. I saw neither of them as I had to look directly at my feet to avoid falling through the holes between the railroad ties.

"You're going to miss everything if you're so worried about falling," Mason said.

We walked along the bridge for about half an hour, then we climbed off in the dark and went back to the cabin. I ventured into the outhouse. It had a blue light inside that illuminated a small painting of a crow encircled by yellow rings. A bottle of air freshener and a stack of *National Geographics* sat on the floor. Back in the cabin, Mason had put on a James Taylor tape and was shoving an old copy of *Rolling Stone* in the woodstove to get the fire lit.

"Do you smoke pot?" he asked.

I hadn't smoked pot in years and even then I could never get it to do anything for me. Lucinda Trout preferred the drink. Two glasses of wine and I was usually blitzed. This was an economic advantage.

"Well," I said, "if you're having some."

He took a small bag of pot out of a drawer and gingerly packed it into an intricately carved wooden pipe. He sang along to the James Taylor song about the cowboy living on the range. He took a hunk of smoked sausage out of the refrigerator and sliced off a few pieces. I couldn't believe he had smoked sausage, one of my top five favorite foods. I told him this and he seemed pleased.

"What else do you like?" he asked. "I make a tremendous meat loaf."

We sat around for another hour. I took two hits of the pot, which had no effect, and told him I didn't want to waste his stash and then immediately felt adolescent for using the word "stash." He talked about his kids and about camping and about Neil Young, his favorite musician of all time. He talked about his ex-wife, who was remarried and with whom he now got along better than he ever had. He talked about his ex-girlfriend, the mother of his second son, with whom he had a so-so relationship. He mentioned only in passing the mother of his daughter, saying, "Accidents happen, but sometimes they're happy accidents. For the most part."

I talked about my job at *Up Early* and how I did stories about thong underwear. I talked about Daphne and Elena and my old apartment with Bob downstairs and Yuri upstairs. Though Mason listened, I felt like I was describing a television show. Outside, there was a sudden cacophony of high shrieks, a yip yipping, like a siren in a European city.

"Coyotes," Mason said. He pronounced it "kie-oates."

"Do they attack?" I asked.

"Not unless you're a rabbit or a Maltese dog," he said.

I suddenly wanted him to kiss me. I'd never kissed a bearded man before.

"We'd better get you home," he said.

He put the pot and sausage away, tamped out the fire, and locked up the cabin. We got in the truck and drove through the small path between the trees, the leaves of which were now glistening and looked wet under the full moon.

"If we're lucky we might see an owl," Mason said. "Or a skunk."

For the first time in thirty days I felt the distance I was from home. There were no lights out here, no telephone wires, no pavement for at least ten miles. Mason hummed along to Neil Young. The eagle feather dangling from the mirror made a shadow on the dashboard, like a bird gesticulating to make a point. When we got to the gate, Mason got out of the truck to unlock it. In the glow of the headlights, as his plaid flannel shirt flapped in the breeze and his lanky body leaned over the padlock, I caught a glimpse of his profile and gasped. From that angle, framed by the rusty fence posts and the flat gravel road that stretched out behind him, I could have sworn he was Sam Shepard.

A Sociocultural Analysis of the Margin of Error

Here, briefly, is the history of Mason. He'd grown up in a small town in the opposite corner of the state, come to Prairie City ostensibly to attend school, and, upon dropping out almost immediately, insinuated himself into the community until he seemed to have been there all his life. Like a genuine local, Mason married the woman he happened to be dating when he was twenty-four. Susannah was smart but not yet ambitious, the kind of girl who baked bread and grew vegetables but also got stoned a little too often and sometimes got out of her car without turning off the ignition. Three years after the birth of Sebastian, she decided she wanted a life that extended beyond the boundaries of Effie's Tavern and the drafty farmhouse that she and Mason had bought with money loaned from her parents. On a cold Sunday just before the Christmas of 1988, right after Mason had quit his third job in six months—this time at the Firestone tire plant, where he claimed to be having hallucinations on the rubber hose line—Susannah announced that she was going back to school to get her degree, moving in with her sister, and divorcing him. She'd had hopes that Mason would also return to college to finish the art degree he'd abandoned after one semester; consequently she asked for no child support, merely an amicable parting and regular visits with Sebastian. Mason was devoted to his boy. When the child was born, Susannah worked at a used-book store and Mason stayed home and cared for him during the day, an arrangement he claimed made more economic sense than holding a job. Upon the divorce, despite Susannah's protestations, the court ordered that he pay child support. Mason managed to build his cabin using materials he'd collected from abandoned farmhouses. It was a veritable fort for his son and him. He made rafts and floated with Sebastian down the river. He cooked wieners for him on the woodstove. And a year or so later, while drinking at Effie's Tavern during the Friday afternoon happy hour, he met Jill and more or less repeated the whole scenario over again.

Jill, to her credit, had managed to steer Mason toward a job he could tolerate. Her third cousin, Frank Fussell, was the supervisor at a relatively low-traffic grain elevator. A borderline schizophrenic, Frank fancied himself a healer and spiritual guru. He liked the fact that Mason was an artist and, as he did with his four other employees, made fruitless attempts to convert Mason to his own form of mystical wellness. Frank practiced tai chi in the small office attached to the elevator. He also drank his own urine, a ritual he claimed prevented both cancer and hiccups. When a train did happen to pull into the elevator, which was infrequent except during harvest season, Frank stood by the tracks that ran underneath the head house and chanted commands to his staff like a yoga instructor. There was no way they could hear him. The farmers who came in to unload their grain all knew he was crazy, although rumor had it that Frank had once talked one of their wives into drinking her urine.

Despite Frank's eccentricities, this was a good job for Mason. Though he made little more than minimum wage, he managed to keep up with his child support payments and take both Jill and Sebastian on regular outdoor excursions. In fact, he was such an enthusiastic father that in the summer of 1990, Jill, who wanted a baby but did not want to get married, at least not to Mason, found herself pregnant in a not altogether accidental manner. By this time, Mason had moved in with her, keeping his cabin as a weekend getaway spot, and was ensconced in the renovation of Jill's kitchen.

When Peter was born the following spring, a time when the grain elevator's major concern was the storyline of *Days of Our Lives*, Mason again cared for the child during the day while Jill worked as a
nurse practitioner at a doctor's office. As Peter grew older, he found
a loyal older brother in Sebastian. On weekends Mason took them
both to his cabin, where they caught frogs and constructed the
teepee, sometimes with Jill, more often without her. It was in the fall
of 1995, when Peter was five, that Jill decided she wanted a life that
extended beyond the boundaries of Mason's cabin, Neil Young, and
the small house that had felt considerably smaller since Mason had
begun sleeping on the sofa in the den. On Halloween night, when
Mason returned from trick or treating with Peter, Jill asked him to
move out. Mason, stunned but also relieved, proceeded directly to
Effie's Tavern, where a woman in an elaborate cat costume bought
him no fewer than ten Leinenkugels, took him back to her condo
near the Homestead Mall, and, six months later, called him with the
news that his third child (*most likely* his child, anyway) would arrive in the summer.

Mason, because he couldn't think of what to say, had asked the
one-time wearer of the cat costume if she needed a Lamaze coach.
She had answered with a blunt "No, but you'll be hearing from
me." And despite Mason's efforts to call her back and say he in-
tended to be in the child's life, it wasn't until two days after Erin's
birth that Mason actually saw the woman, whose name was Julie,
without the cat costume. Other than the one phone call at the beginning of her third trimester, Mason had had no contact with Julie
other than a court order for a DNA test "upon the birth of the child
of the petitioner, Ms. Malacek." The court order had been delivered
to him at the grain elevator by the county sheriff and he'd studied
it in bewilderment for several minutes before realizing that he'd
never even learned Julie's last name. Like Jill, Julie had insisted that
the child take her last name instead of Mason's. The result was that
even three years later—a period during which Mason had seen the
child at least once a week (as soon as she stopped nursing, it was

three overnights a week)—Mason still had trouble remembering the precise spelling of his daughter's surname.

"Guess it's funny how things go," Mason had said when he finally got around to telling the whole story. We were at the cabin, where it was beginning to rain. Mason was mending a hole in my sock with a needle and thread.

"But I don't understand how she can just hand over the kid to you when she barely even knows you," I said. "That's just insane."

"I guess I have a reputation around Effie's as a good dad," he said. "It's better than being known as a drunk or a pervert."

In retrospect, I saw that Mason's life was the way it was largely because of the sheer amount of space that surrounded him. Prairie City was for him, as it was for many of its citizens, a place in which the margin for error was as wide as land and sky itself. The blitheness and lack of prescience that Mason carried with him was something I could only begin to understand during moments when I was a passenger on a plane making a final descent into Prairie City Municipal Airport. Normally, I was a nervous flier. I tapped the aluminum twice before boarding. Every variation in engine noise or change in altitude usually had me gripping the spine of a book I'd been pretending to read while monitoring the flight. But descending into Prairie City had a way of making me feel that there was virtually no chance of crashing. There was so much space, so many miles of flat, open fields that landing a plane seemed less a matter of hitting a target than of simply getting close enough.

In New York, this had not been the case. At LaGuardia, the smallest error—an extra few degrees of bank to the right, a misheard syllable from a rapid-fire controller—would land you in Flushing Bay. The same principle applied down on the ground. There, the margin for error was so narrow it was hardly there at all. In New York you looked to the left and the right and back again, your head spinning from fear and indecision. The wrong college, the wrong job, the wrong direction on the A train could overturn you. We were so careful in the city. We checked ourselves at every corner. We were careful whom we lent things to, whom we invited inside, whom we fell in love with. Like planes stacked up over the airports, we didn't make a move until we knew we were cleared. We dated for years before risking cohabitation. We didn't marry until we were sure we couldn't do better. We didn't have children until it was almost too late. To act sooner, to not agonize over every option until they all practically lost their appeal, would have been to risk disaster. We were packed so tightly and moving so rapidly that one misstep could knock us permanently off course. We always seemed an instant away from losing everything.

In Prairie City, it seemed nearly impossible to screw up significantly. You could get pretty far getting close enough. A pasture was as good as a runway. The runway at the airport was so long that it was an alternative landing site for the space shuttle (I learned this from Joel). In a sky like that you could swerve and skid and lose your vectors and still get on the ground safely. A house was affordable, a marriage reversible, a minimum wage sustainable. People married young—the wedding pages in the newspaper looked like a high school yearbook—and then divorced young and married young again. There were left turn lanes with arrows on the traffic lights so you wouldn't have to negotiate intersections on your own. The supermarket aisles were wide. The shopping carts were large enough to fit four children, which, by the way, were everywhere. Everyone seemed to have at least one kid, more likely three or four or five, a couple of kids for each marriage—or lack of marriage. This was what amazed me. Mason's situation, however aberrant in my mind, fell squarely within the norm. For every white-bread nuclear family I spotted in the cereal aisle at the Hinky Dinky, there seemed even more households that had been broken and reconfigured many times over. Everyone seemed to have embarked on various permutations of couplehood and cohabitation and custody. Never in my life had I seen such a mishmash of ex-spouses and new lovers and half siblings and stepparents. Just as I had never seen so much wedlock, I had never seen so much out of wedlock.

Hence Mason. And everything about him. He was like a piece of driftwood, carved and contorted by the river that carried him along, worn down by the natural elements, fractured by responsibility. He'd made a mess of his life. Either that or life had made a mess of him. Still, a lesser man wouldn't have carried it off as well as he did. He made fatherhood look like nothing more than the benevolent supervision of Huck Finnhood, grown manhood look like a chance to play hooky without getting caught. From certain angles he was stunning. Paddling a canoe, there was never someone so dazzling. Explaining the mating patterns of the sandhill cranes, the digestive system of a wild boar, the religious practices of the Pawnee Indians, he was as good as any lantern-jawed naturalist on the Discovery Channel. Like the river itself, he could take your breath away if the sun caught him just right.

But when it came to living in the actual world, to having a bank account and paying taxes and going to the doctor and having any idea what his kids were studying in school, Mason's attention wandered. As a boy, he explained to me, he'd prepared himself for a life as a full-time outdoorsman. Even as a teenager he'd had no plans to be anything other than a woodsman who made clothing from buckskin and ate deer meat he had cured in a smokehouse behind his log cabin. He had eschewed schoolwork in favor of multiple readings of every single nature book ever written and repeatedly run away from home to see how long he could last in the woods with nothing more than a Swiss Army knife and a sleeping bag. As he grew older, the woodsman fetish expanded to include a hippie fetish, which quickly grew to include hallucinogenic drugs as an extension of environmental awareness. Though he was born too late to experience the sixties as a communal movement that would eventually push its adherents toward a more staid form of capitalist expression—as had been the case for Sue and her friends—Mason held on to the peace and love aesthetic for as long as he could. He was a person who, as late as the early 1980s, drove a Volkswagen van with flowers painted on the side. He spent an entire summer in his early twenties (he couldn't remember the exact year) living in a school bus by the river and dropping acid every day for three months straight.

So how was it that Lucinda Trout, the girl who had once declared (admittedly under the influence of her mother) that she wouldn't date anyone not in possession of a master's degree and a subscription to *The Nation* (at age twenty-five, this requirement was loosened to *The New Yorker*), had become romantically involved with a guy who had never been in possession of a checkbook? To be sure, part of it was novelty. My life had taken an off-the-record quality since I'd left New York. Despite my protestations to the contrary, I harbored a sense that, like an affair with a cabana boy during a vacation, nothing I did in Prairie City quite counted. Like everyone else there, Mason was so out of my usual context, such an anomaly to my senses, that I felt a freedom—maybe even a mandate—to explore him without fear of repercussions. There were no Masons where I came from. In my former life, a person like him would have been homeless long ago. But in Prairie City, Mason resided in an error margin that was so wide and so accepted by the unblinking, laid-back community that it was hard to tell where the margin ended and the legitimate space began.

And at that stage in the game, I was convinced I lived, irrevocably, in the legitimate space.

"Good morning, New York! For all of you sitting in your cramped apartments catching a few minutes of *Up Early* before fighting the traffic and crowded subways to get to work, let me invite you to spend those minutes in a place far away from all that. I'm coming to you from my front porch on a quaint little street in a heartland town called Prairie City. For all of you who've ever toyed with the idea of trading the rat race for a quieter, simpler life—and don't pretend you haven't—I hope you'll tune in throughout the year as I share with you my thoughts, hopes, and revelations about my new life on the prairie. For starters, I have an actual porch swing!"

"We're having some sound problems," said Jeb the cameraman, a doughy guy in a pink polo shirt who Joel had assured me was "the best in the business." He was the head camera operator for *Parent Talk* with Loni Heibel-Budicek. "I'm gonna need you to do that again."

The first installment of "The Quality of Life Report" was taped on the swing Mason had swiped from an abandoned farmhouse and set up on my porch, though he warned me not to sit down on it all the way since it was unclear whether the ceiling could support it. We didn't have a TelePrompTer, so Mason had been enlisted to hold up pieces of paper on which I had printed out my script in twenty-four-point font. It was 6:45 A.M. Jeb had wanted to shoot early because the light was better, plus he had to be at work at the station at 8:00.

Mason, shirtless and wearing a torn pair of shorts with his flip-flops, lost his grip on the pages and they blew into the yard, which was mostly dirt with a few patches of dead grass. A couple of kids on bikes had stopped on the sidewalk and were staring at us.

"I can try to just wing it," I said as Jeb reached inside my shirt and adjusted the mike wire that ran up to my collar. Mason saw this and registered a proprietary little wince.

"Try it again," Jeb said.

"Good morning, New York! If you're wondering why I haven't been reporting from the familiar streets of Manhattan over the last month or so it's because I've embarked on an exciting new journey. Just a few weeks ago, I took a step so many of us talk about but never seem to go through with. I traded the rat race for the quiet life. I packed up my apartment and moved more than a thousand miles away to a town called Prairie City. Maybe you've never heard of Prairie City. But all that's going to change because over the next year I'm going to share with you my hopes, thoughts, and revelations about my new life on the prairie. To begin with, I have an actual porch swing! And as I sit here drinking my coffee and watching the sun come up, I think about how the sun rises over the prairie like a silent alarm clock, much like the alarm that woke me to new possibilities, new frontiers, new ways of thinking about myself—"

A huge, ancient Oldsmobile with a bad muffler pulled up to the curb in front of the house, forcing Jeb to stop filming. A large woman in a waitress uniform got out, her purse dangling from her arm. She charged toward us while fumbling to light a cigarette.

"What the hell is going on here?" she yelled. "Who the hell are you?"

Jeb turned toward her, the camera still on his shoulder. The woman slammed her hand against the lens.

"I live here," I said. "We're just shooting a segment for a New York morning show—"

"I live here," the woman said.

"Well, actually I live here," I said.

"I live in the downstairs apartment," she said. "Are you the new girl?"

"Oh!" I exclaimed. "Yes, I've been hoping to meet you!"

"We make the six o'clock news or something?" she asked, pulling on her cigarette. Her name tag was on her uniform. It said DAWN. Below it were the words "If I don't offer you dessert, it's on the house."

"Oh no!" I said. "No no! I'm a producer. I work for a show in New York. That's where I'm from. My name's Lucinda."

"You're from New York?"

"Yeah!" I said. "I know it seems weird. But, yes, I am."

"I gotta take off," Mason said. He handed me the script pages he'd picked out of the yard. He leaned toward me as if to kiss me. I flinched slightly and he patted me on the shoulder and walked toward his truck. I noticed Dawn looking at a script page. In huge block letters it said "Stay with me throughout the year as I discover the charms and challenges of—" There wasn't room for anything else on the page.

"Man," said Dawn. "I thought you were from *Cops* or some- thing. I'm like, 'I don't need that shit.'"

"Oh God, no," I said. "It's nothing like that. In fact, if you have any interesting stories about living here I'd love to hear them."

Dawn looked like she weighed about 250. Faye would never want her on camera.

"I mean, for research purposes," I added.

"'Cause if you were from *Cops*, I'd tell you to get the hell out of here," Dawn said. "I don't need any more of that."

I made a mental note to spend some time later thinking about *Cops*. Was it the primary liaison between ordinary people and the entertainment world? The *Candid Camera* of the millennium? I'd have to get more information from my neighbor.

I'd hoped that Jeb could shoot some B-roll footage of grain si- los, windmills, and cornfields for the *Up Early* segment, but he said he was only budgeted for the porch shoot and that I could find stock footage at the KPCR station.

Later, when I called Faye, she said they'd pull some outtakes from the meth story.

"You've seen one farmhouse, you've seen them all," said Faye. "Anyway, we need you to work on the bad boy story. Do you have a boyfriend yet?"

"Well, kind of," I said. "Sort of."

"Is he a cowboy?" she asked. "A ranch hand?"

"This isn't really ranch country. It's farm country."

"Is he a farmer?"

"He works in a grain elevator," I said.

"He's an elevator operator?" Faye gasped.

"He's in the agricultural business," I said. "He's kind of an artist, too."

"Does he show at a gallery?"

"He has his work up at his cabin," I said.

"He has a cabin?"

"He lives in a cabin," I said. "He bathes in the river."

"What?" Faye snorted. "Isn't that unsanitary?"

"He's fairly unconventional," I said. "He's sort of a woodsman."

"That's good, that's good," Faye said. I could hear the clicking of her keyboard as she hit random keys that she erroneously believed fit together to form words.

"Why don't you do a story on him?" she continued. "It'll tie in to the *Good Girl's Guide to Bad Boys*. It'll be a Little Red Riding Hood kind of thing. He lives in the woods, he's kind of scary. But deep down a sex god."

"Uh . . ."

"Hold on, I have another call," Faye said. She attempted to put me on hold but hung up instead. Later in the afternoon, she sent me an e-mail.

> To: Lucinda Trout
> From: Faye Figaro
> Re: bad boy
>
> do bad boy sex dog sotry asap. Focus on animal mangetism of him. Get footage of batheing in river.

I put off asking Mason about the story because we had big weekend plans. I was meeting his children. And their mothers. It was to be a three-part event, followed by a trip to the cabin for hiking, fishing, marshmallow roasting, and video watching.

"They are going to be traumatized," I said to Mason the night before we went. We had just finished the chicken I had roasted in the Hotpoint stove and served in the dining room. The table now had an antique lace runner Mason had given me and a constant supply of fresh flowers he picked from the pasture near the grain elevator. As we did most nights, we were watching *Antiques Roadshow* and eating bridge mix.

"They're going to see me as a threat," I continued. "They'll think I'm taking you away from them."

"I don't know where you get these ideas," he said. He was completely naked and drinking a beer. His skin was so tan it nearly matched my camel-colored Pier One sofa. On the television, an appraiser valued a Civil War-era sword at eighteen thousand dollars. The owner almost fainted.

"Whoa!" Mason said. "I used to have one like that. Can't remember what the hell I did with it."

"It just seems to me that introducing a new romantic partner into your children's lives is a delicate matter that would require a serious conversation with them," I said. "They need to know they're still the most important things in your life. They need to know they're your priority."

"They know that," he said. I was surprised by how the words stung.

The credits rolled on *Antiques Roadshow*. It was 9:00.

"Time to hit the hay," Mason said. He climbed out of the couch, his lanky body looking especially Brad Pittish except for the unruly beard and the way he clutched his hip and limped slightly—the result of falling down a grain shaft many years earlier. It occurred to me that I hadn't told Faye his age. But perhaps we could get around that. If thirty-seven was the new twenty-six, didn't that make forty the new twenty-nine?

> To: Lucinda Trout
> From: Samantha Frank
> Re: Bad Boys
>
> I'm thrilled to hear that you'll be doing a story on your new significant other. Since I'll be the one who's interviewing Courtney Rosenzweig, author of *The Good Girl's Guide to Bad Boys*, I want to suggest a few de-

tails you might want to touch on in your piece. As always, these are just suggestions. I don't want to impede your vision.

1. Talk about how he's so much different from the men you've dated before. (I don't really know your dating history, but, just guessing: actors, lawyers, Web designers?) How did you feel about dating someone a bit "outside the box"? Do you make more money than he does? Does that cause tensions?
2. What do your friends think of him?
3. Is the sex better (than with normal guys)?

Mason kept Erin's diaper bag in his truck. It was decorated with Winnie the Pooh characters and wedged behind the seat between a circular saw and an electric drill. On the day I was to meet the kids, Mason put the diaper bag in the Sunbird, which we would be taking to the cabin since we couldn't all fit in the truck.

With Mason behind the wheel, we retrieved the kids like a school bus on its route—Sebastian first, Peter second, and Erin third—a routine Mason obviously followed at least every other weekend and, from what I could see, must have appeared to him like the portrait of personal demise. It was clear he'd been off to a good start with Susannah, who, now remarried with stepchildren, lived in a huge Victorian house on the outskirts of Prairie City. Her hair hung down her back in a long braid and she wore turquoise earrings, a hand-knit sweater, jeans, and Birkenstocks with purple socks. She sipped coffee from a handmade pottery mug.

"Lucinda," she said, "welcome to the tribe. Coffee?"

"We can't stay," Mason said.

Her house was astonishing. So large it had required two furnaces, Susannah explained that she had bought it after selling the farm she'd had with Mason. She'd begun fixing it up herself, eventually hired a contractor, and then married him.

"It was a pit," Susannah said, taking me inside, where a giant staircase presided over a giant foyer. All the wood was restored and gleaming. Sunlight cascaded through the windows and ricocheted off the spotless pine floors. Early American antiques, handmade quilts, and plants in terra-cotta pots were everywhere. The kitchen had a pine floor, a butcher block table, and a Sierra Club calendar overflowing with scribbled notes like "Steve, dentist 2:45," "Sebastian, soccer practice," and "Susannah, eco-lit symposium presentation."

"We completely redid this place," Susannah continued. "I did the floors myself."

A patchwork quilt had been tossed over the sofa, where it curled around copies of *The New Yorker* and *Art in America.*

"This is beautiful," I said, touching the quilt. "Is it a family heirloom?"

"I made it, actually," Susannah said.

Sebastian came down the stairs with a sleeping bag and a roll of comic books. Tall and gangly and unassuming, he was the opposite of Leonard's son. In fact, he was a carbon copy of Mason. Mason tousled Sebastian's hair and pretended to box with him. The boy was at least a foot taller than me.

"The other two look just like Mason, too," Susannah said. "We wonder if he's just cloning himself."

She was right. Minus several inches, Peter was indistinguishable from Sebastian. When we pulled up to Jill's house, a good-sized bungalow with a pillared porch decorated for Halloween, Peter was raking leaves in the small front yard. Not recognizing the Sunbird, he didn't look up until we got out of the car, and Sebastian tackled him and wrestled him into a pile of leaves. Jill came out of the house carrying Peter's duffel bag. She was a nearly translucent redhead with closely cropped hair and wire-rimmed glasses. Like Susannah, she was small and pretty, though in a kind of icy way. Without really greeting us, she handed the duffel bag to Mason.

"You're going out to the cabin?" she asked.

"Yup," Mason said. "Just gotta get Erin and then stop at Hinky Dinky for some grub and we're outta here."

"It's supposed to rain," Jill said.

"It won't," Mason said.

"And we need to talk at some point about a few issues," Jill said.

"Like?"

"Like, for instance, his diet," Jill said. "He could use a little more nutrition than chips and hot dogs."

"You're the nurse," Mason said.

Jill smirked at him, then looked at me as though I were wearing a *Playboy* bunny outfit.

"I'm a nurse *practitioner*," she said to me. "And, I'm sorry. I'm not usually like this."

According to Mason, Jill usually was precisely like that, though I soon saw that Jill's way of being was preferable to Julie's way of being.

For the entire time that we were in her house, a prefab ranch with imitation brick face and a mailbox shaped like a dachshund, Julie talked on the phone. She had the kind of perm that leaves large ringlets of hair dangling like corkscrews. She also had extremely long fingernails, which she tapped on the kitchen counter while she talked. Though the 1980s were nearly twenty years past, she wore leggings with ankle boots. The house was teeming with knick-knacks, mostly related to dachshunds, and framed portrait studio photos of Erin in ruffled dresses posing with various dolls and stuffed animals. A real dachshund waddled into the living room and Mason pretended to kick it. Glancing up only momentarily, Julie waved us toward Erin's room, where a Pocahontas overnight bag was sitting by the door. Inside, a little blond girl, a four-year-old female version of Mason, was playing on the floor amid a mountain of toys. Every imaginable manifestation of consumerized girlhood sprawled out of drawers and toy bins. Most were Barbie-related. The Barbie Grand Hotel, a giant My Size Sugar Plum Fairy Barbie, a Barbie Jam 'N Glam Tour Bus, a Shop with Me Barbie cash register. There was a canopy bed with a pink comforter, a dressing table with a tiny Spice Girls hand mirror, a play makeup set, and something called the Polly Pocket Barbie Stylin' Mall.

"Dad!" Erin yelled. She got up and threw her arms around him. She was wearing a Little Mermaid T-shirt and had a plastic tiara on her head. In the girliness of the room, Mason looked like Sasquatch. He picked her up and kissed her head. Then he removed the tiara and tossed it on the floor. He did it so gently she seemed not to notice.

"This is my friend Lucinda," Mason said. "She's coming with us."

She hid her face. Then she got down and ran to Julie, who put the telephone receiver on the counter and said, "Bye-bye, sugar plum princess, be good" and then looked at Mason and said, "Try not to bring her back looking like she's had a mud bath this time." She looked at me, mumbled a faint hello, and resumed her phone conversation.

"She attended charm school at a feed lot," Mason whispered as we walked to the car. "Fortunately Erin takes after me."

We piled into the Sunbird and went to Hinky Dinky. Mason bought frozen pizzas, marshmallows, Doritos, and two giant bottles of Pepsi.

"Can I have Oreos?" Erin asked.

"No," said Mason.

"Can I have candy corn?"

"No."

"Can I have Fruit Roll-Ups?"

"No."

The little girl's chin started to quiver, then her whole body followed as if a wave of grief had come over her.

"We have Doritos," Mason said.

"I don't want Doritos!" Erin screamed.

"Don't start this," he said. Sebastian and Peter ambled on ahead in the snack aisle. Erin started sobbing and then wailing. I pretended to ignore her. People were staring. Did they think I was her mother, pretending to read the ingredients list on a package of Fritos while a four-year-old in a Little Mermaid shirt hyperventilated and threw herself down on the floor? I slinked off to the liquor department and bought a bottle of Fetzer.

After stopping in the video section, where they rented *Poké-mon II*, *The Haunted*, and *The Naked Gun*, we made our way through the checkout, where a teenager with not only a Band-Aid on her eyebrow but Band-Aids on her chin, cheek, and nostrils rang us up.

"That's $37.24," she said. Her tongue was pierced with a giant silver stud. Apparently the Band-Aid rule did not extend into the mouth. "Oh shit," Mason said, digging through his wallet. He turned to me. "Do you have five bucks?"

In the car, Erin tore open a package of Fruit Roll-Ups. Sebastian and Peter sat quietly. I asked them about school, what grades they were in, whether or not they played sports. They answered in mono-syllables. Erin fidgeted and whined about having sticky fingers. When we got about ten miles outside of town, lightning tore across an open field to the side of the highway, followed by the loudest clap of thunder I'd ever heard. It was like a truck had tipped over in front of us. Then the rain started falling so hard we couldn't see in front of us.

"Oh, this is just great," Mason said.

"It's raining, Dad," Erin whined.

"Duh," said one of the boys.

"Dad, it's raining!" she said again.

"I can see that, Erin," Mason said.

"Will it pass?" I asked Mason.

"Do I look like a weatherman?" he said. The kids were fighting in the back over what appeared to be the last Fruit Roll-Up in the box. The rain was pelting the windshield so hard we couldn't see the road. Mason pulled over to the shoulder.

"Dad, why are we stopping?" Erin asked.

"Just be quiet for a minute," Mason said. Tractor trailers were rushing by us, kicking up water and spraying the little Sunbird with mud from the side of the road.

"We won't be able to drive through that road near the cabin in this car," Mason said. "It'll be too muddy. If I had the truck we could do it."

"You want to go back?" I asked, thinking of what I might do alone at home that weekend. I could write some story proposals for *Up Early*. I could call Daphne or Elena.

"I suppose we could hang out at your place," Mason said.

"Oh!" I said.

"They could watch movies," he said. "I mean, if you don't mind."

"Oh, no, that's fine," I said. "And then you'd go back out in the truck later?"

"We can't all really fit in the truck," he said. "Besides, it'll be too late. And it'll be so muddy out there."

"Oh."

"They have their sleeping bags. They can sleep on the floor."

"Oh."

"Unless you don't want to do that," Mason said. He reached over and put his hand on my cheek. I flinched; the kids could see us. His eyes were tired-looking and lovely with those little lines around them. It occurred to me that if I was a trouper about this, then he might be a trouper about the bad boy story for *Up Early*.

"No, it's fine," I said. "As long as they don't mind."

"It'll be an adventure for them," he said. "And for you."

He turned the car around and drove back to town. When we entered my house, the urine smell seemed worse than usual. I could see the boys wrinkle their noses slightly, but they were too polite to say anything. Erin, hyper from the Fruit Roll-Ups, began tearing around the house. She ran into the dining-room table and knocked off the flower vase. Mason grabbed her by the collar of her Little Mermaid shirt and put her in a time-out in my bedroom. The telephone rang once and it took several seconds before I realized that Erin had grabbed the extension by my bed and attempted to carry on a conversation with the person on the other end, a person who turned out to be my mother. Even from the next room I could hear her piercing interrogation through the receiver.

"Who is this?" she demanded.

"Hello! Hello!" Erin chirped.

"Where is Lucinda?"

"Who's Lucinda?"

I yanked the phone out of the child's hands. My mother was now engaged in a conversation with my father about whether or not she'd dialed the wrong number.

"I'm here, Mom," I said.

"Who was that?"

"The neighbor's little girl," I said. "She lives next door. They just stopped by."

It amazed me how easy it was to lie to my mother when I could not so much as tell Joel that I was spending an evening doing something other than flea-bombing my apartment.

"We don't live next door," Erin said loudly.

"Lucinda," my mother said, "I want to tell you this. A very nice couple whom we know down here have a son who lives in Texas. He sells wireless service and he's very nice and he doesn't have a girlfriend. I thought that since you lived nearby maybe you'd let him take you out."

"I don't live near Texas!"

"Honey, you can't just limit yourself to people within walking distance. It's not New York."

"But Texas is hundreds of miles away!"

"There's such a thing as airplanes," she said. "They have some very good fares right now."

"Lucinda," my father said, taking the phone from my mother,

"your mom's afraid you're not aggressive enough in finding a boy-friend. The best guys are in graduate school."

"Actually, I am seeing someone," I said. Erin was now jumping on the bed and singing the *Little Mermaid* song.

"Really? What does he do?"

"He's an artist."

"An artist! Watch out, he'll get famous and become a heroin addict. We just rented *Basquiat.*"

Erin jumped up and landed on the bed so hard that she knocked the phone cord out of the wall. My father's voice was replaced by silence. Or so it seemed until I realized Erin had hit her head and was now bawling hysterically.

Rode Hard and Put Away Wet

To: Faye Figaro, Samantha Frank
From: Lucinda Trout
Re: Bad Boy story

My friend Mason has agreed to be filmed for the bad
boy story. However, I think it would be best if we presented it more like an "unconventional boy" story.
For reasons of personal privacy, I'd rather not go into
the specifics of my relationship with him, but we can
collect footage of him hiking around his cabin, working on his paintings, and walking along an abandoned
railroad trestle. Unfortunately, it's too cold now to
show him bathing in the river. But I think the segment
can focus on the "alternative lifestyle" nature of his
existence and show that there are lots of different
ways to be satisfied in life.

To: Lucinda Trout
From: Samantha Frank
Cc: Faye Figaro
Re: Re: Bad Boy story

I understand your need to protect your friend but, as I
said, the story is about Bad Boys and needs to at

least touch on the ways that his alternative lifestyle affects your relationship. Also, I really like the bathing in the river idea. Is there any way you could just get him in there quickly, just to get a few shots? Courtney Rosenzweig's book has a chapter called "The Baddest Boys Are Softies Inside." Perhaps your segment could touch on that issue. To help you organize your thoughts further I am adding a few more suggestions.

1. Is he much gentler in bed than you would have thought?
2. In spite of his overall rough and tumble demeanor, does he have a secret soft spot that really turns you on (he's super nice to his mother, he drinks herbal tea)?
3. Does he talk about having kids someday? Does he ever look in your eyes and say, "Honey, I know I seem a little rough around the edges, but nothing would make me happier than settling down and having a family with you"?

Later the next week, Valdette Svoboda-Lipinsky called to make sure I had a ticket to the annual fund-raiser for the Prairie City Recovery Center for Women, of which she was a newly elected board member.

"And if you've met anyone whom you'd like to bring," Valdette said, "you sure can do that."

"I have met someone," I said, hoping she'd immediately pass it on to Joel. "I'll have him check his schedule."

"We'd love to meet him," she said. "Is he a special guy?"

Let me digress for a moment and explain something about the mating patterns of Lucinda Trout. They had always been driven by a number of neuroses and proclivities, the saddest and least flattering of which was my chronic embarrassment about the social pre-

sentation (i.e., cocktail party banter and ability to discuss independent films) of whomever I happened to be dating. This was due
partly to narcissism and insecurity—the combination of an inflated
sense of my own social adroitness and a nagging fear that I had
some terrible personal trait, like body odor or a tendency to interrupt, that everyone talked about behind my back—and partly a
function of my ever-intensifying desire, possibly even need, to date
men so unlike myself or anyone I knew that introducing boyfriends
to my friends ended up seeming more like show-and-tell than a
normal social interaction. Such had been the case with my Last Serious Relationship, of which most of my friends, particularly Elena,
had roundly disapproved.

His name was Dave Davenport. He was an airline pilot. No
joke. I'd met him on an *Up Early* assignment about the caloric content of airline food (he'd been featured briefly in the segment as an
example of a crew member who packed his own lunches) and upon
our falling madly in love he had spent a year flying up from his
home base in Atlanta to visit me in New York. He would ride the
subway in his uniform and wonder why people were staring at him.
When he got disoriented while walking along Broadway he'd say "I
need to find my coordinates." When I'd bring him to parties people
would ask him what he did for a living and, when he'd answer,
they'd say "No, come on, what do you really do?" A pilot, like a
fireman or lighthouse keeper, was so removed from their orbit as to
almost be fake. A pilot was like the word "prairie." It was extreme,
foreign, and utterly its own thing. To date Dave was to not just date
a guy but to gain access into a world that had absolutely no rele-
vance to my own. It was to find things to talk about other than independent films and whether or not *A Perfect Day for Bananafish*
conveyed more nihilism than *Uncle Wiggly in Connecticut*. It was to
move past the fact that once, during dinner with some friends of
mine who were discussing a mutual acquaintance who had gotten
tenure, Dave started shaking his head and clucking his tongue be-

cause he apparently didn't know what "tenure" meant and inferred from the word "got" that it was a sexually transmitted disease.

But I actually found tons of knowledge about one thing and virtually none about anything else to be a huge turn-on. I loved Dave because he knew every circuit and fuse of the electrical system of a Boeing 727 and had never heard of Martin Scorsese. I loved Dave because everything about him was pilotish—his military-style haircut, his pastel golf shirts, even his name: *this is Captain Davenport speaking.* And because of the time I spent with Dave, I knew quite a lot about flaps and spoilers and light chop and yaw, which is the term for the back-and-forth rocking motion that is caused by opposing aerodynamic forces on the rudder. These were things I'd never know if I'd spent a year with someone who knew about Martin Scorsese and *A Perfect Day for Bananafish.* I already knew about those things. There seemed little point in going over all of it again.

A similar principle applied with Mason. Despite knowing the meaning of "plethora," he did not, for instance, know the meaning of "conducive." He tended to say "orientated" instead of "oriented" and favored sentences with dangling prepositions, such as "where's my hammer at," which I was able to overlook out of the sheer novelty of being with a man who actually used a hammer. Mason did not eat sushi or much fish in general because "it was like eating bait." Mason was extreme.

All of this is to say that "is he a special guy?" was among my least favorite questions in the English language. And because I had not yet figured out a way to finesse a response that neither insulted the guy in question nor expressed the kind of commitment that would elicit a lecture—and they always came—about my "judgment" or my "choices" I said to Valdette the thing I always said to everyone. I said, "It's fun for now." Then I changed the subject.

"I should be getting a tape soon of the *Up Early* segment I did on methamphetamine," I continued.

"Wonderful," Valdette said.

"I hope Sue will be pleased with it," I said. "You just have to re-member that I have very little control over how they edit it."

"So what does your friend do?" she asked.

"He's . . . an artist."

"Really? Does he have a gallery?"

"Sort of," I said.

"Wonderful!"

Mason owned only one pair of shoes other than his flip-flops and they happened to be shoes that he'd made himself. They were moc-casins that he'd sewn out of deer hide and thick thread. They were at least ten years old and curling out at the sides and so worn down that they did not so much look like shoes as hooves. It was these hooves that he wore to the benefit for the Prairie City Recovery Cen-ter for Women, which was held in the special events room at the Lasagna Factory restaurant.

All of Prairie City's left-leaning elite (that's to say, all of Sue's friends) were in attendance. The Peter Fonda county commissioner and his wife stood behind a long table serving cocktail wieners and baked ziti from aluminum trays being heated by small propane burners. Since the proceeds from this twenty-dollar-per-ticket event were on behalf of substance abuse treatment, alcohol was not in-cluded in the package, which meant that almost everyone was gath-ered around the Lasagna Factory bar buying their own drinks and smoking cigarettes and, as Mason and I approached, staring at us and looking aghast. I had taken the opportunity to wear my little black cocktail dress and my Cynthia Rowley stiletto heels, which had pointed toes that all but eliminated my ability to walk, there-fore requiring me to cling to Mason's arm and, I realized after it was too late, making me appear dependent upon him and therefore unfeminist, which was as good as a slap in the face of the recovery center, whose motto was EMBRACE, EMPATHIZE, EMPOWER. Sue looked radiant in a floor-length batik dress and a red blazer that she ap-

peared to have thrown on in order to connote her position as executive director. Teri wore a tuxedo suit. Joel was there, too, wearing
his standard all-black ensemble with a red string tie and, oddly, a
red AIDS awareness ribbon on the lapel. Valdette wore purple velour
leggings, a black velvet jacket with a fur collar, and earrings in the
shape of turn-of-the-century telephones. Mason wore jeans and a
Hawaiian shirt. Everyone was staring at his hoof shoes.

"Those are some earrings, Valdette," I said.

"Ring ring," Valdette cooed, holding the tiny dangling receiver
to her ear. "I got them on eBay. Couldn't resist. Introduce us to your
friend, Lucinda."

"This is Mason Clay," I said, avoiding eye contact with Joel. I
noticed Leonard wasn't there.

"Jason?" Joel said.

"Mason," Mason mumbled. He extended a hand to Valdette and
Joel and then Sue and Teri. He looked directly at none of them.

"Nice to meet you, Jason," Sue said.

"It's Mason," I said.

"Oh sorry!" Sue said.

Sue and Teri were interrupted by the director of the Office of
Native American Affairs and Valdette said she had to go check the
wiener inventory. This left us alone with Joel.

"Why the AIDS ribbon on this occasion?" I asked.

"I think it's important to show support for the cause when you
make a public appearance," Joel said. "There's so much hatred
these days."

Without saying anything, Mason walked away and went to the
end of the bar, where he sat with his back turned to everyone.

"What did you say your friend's name was again?" Joel asked.

The entertainment at the benefit was a lesbian folksinging duo
called Estrogen Therapy. Their names, as far as I could make out,
were M.J. and Dee Dee. The one who played the guitar and sang
lead on most of the songs wore a purple tent dress and huge silver
earrings with silver fringe hanging from them like wind chimes. The

other one played the tambourine and gazed adoringly at the other one, who prefaced all of her songs with lengthy ruminations about the inspiration behind the songs, most of which dealt with silent flirtations in places like the bank and the library and, to my astonishment, the Hinky Dinky supermarket.

"You know how sometimes you can feel like you know everything about a person, even though you've never talked to them," M.J. (or maybe Dee Dee) said, strumming and checking her tunings as she spoke. " 'Cause it's funny, for years I've been buying my groceries at the Hinky Dinky and, well, you folks know about the Hinky Dinky—"

The audience laughed knowingly yet respectfully, unsure whether or not it was okay to titter about dwarves and people with speech impediments. Mason, whom I'd persuaded to sit with me at a table that included Joel and Valdette and a cluster of rough-hewn, chain-smoking women who had graduated from the recovery center, let out a loud "hah."

"But there's one woman there," the singer continued, "who, I don't know, seems like she's going someplace. There's a spark in her eye. You can feel her spirit. And so this song is about not only her but all of us whose spirits come through even when we're doing things like, you know, weighing a head of lettuce. It's called 'Jane at the Register.' "

I thought I knew who she was talking about. There was a clerk at the Hinky Dinky who, other than the Band-Aid on her eyebrow, appeared to have no physical or mental defect and looked like she might one day advance beyond the sideshow ranks of the other employees. Her name was not Jane but Clara. Her name tag said CLARA: AN EMPLOYEE/OWNER FOR 2 YEARS. The "2" was written in with a red Magic Marker. Some of the other employees, like the woman with the forked tongue, had name tags that said AN EMPLOYEE/OWNER FOR 12 YEARS. Clara looked like she was in high school and she looked like she could have been on the field hockey or speech team if she didn't have to earn extra money working what appeared to be twenty or more hours a week at Hinky Dinky. Though she did sport a Band-Aid on her eyebrow, she was trim and pretty and well groomed and laid off the makeup. Her regulation blue oxford shirt was always tucked into her regulation khaki pants and I had often found myself imagining that she was a good student who, given the proper channels, could probably get a scholarship to a place like Smith, which would be likely to favor someone from Prairie City and give her all sorts of financial assistance. I was so impressed with Clara that I sometimes avoided getting in her line if I was embarrassed about what I was buying. Since I still clung to the Manhattan habit of never buying more than one bag of supermarket items per trip, I'd often go to the Hinky Dinky three days in a row and buy prepackaged deviled eggs every time. I didn't want Clara to take note of something like that. She was alert. She seemed capable of making an observation and then a judgment. If only she knew that Estrogen Therapy had written a song about her. She could go anywhere from there.

Jane, you're a flower, don't let them call you a weed.
Jane, it's your hour, don't be afrai-aid to need.

"Jesus fucking Christ," Mason said under his breath, although I think Valdette, who was seated to his right, heard him. Her eyes shifted toward him and then to Joel, whom I caught looking across the table at the cleavage of several of the recovery center graduates. Valdette lit a cigarette. Mason was fidgeting. He whispered to me that he was getting up and going to the bar.

"But we're closed in," I said. "If you get up, everyone else will have to get up. You can't squeeze through."

"I can't sit here anymore," he said.

"You can't get past all those women," I said. "You'll make a scene."

"Which women?" he asked.

"The detox graduates," I said.

"You mean the ones that are rode hard and put away wet?" he asked.

"What?"

It's your special time, now you've got to shine.
The planets are aligned, now make them your shri-hi-hine.

"Rode hard and put away wet," Mason said. "Horse terminology."

"You can't get up now."

"They look like they've spent thirty years smoking filterless cigarettes in a tanning bed somewhere in the Arctic," Mason said. "It won't kill them to stand up for a second."

Mason stood up. The whole table looked at him. Then he gestured for everyone on our side of the table to get up and let him out. Since the tables were packed so tightly everyone at the adjacent table had to get up, too. He ducked through the tables and walked out of the room. The singer watched him leave the room and then shook her head and smiled as if to say "there goes one more man who just doesn't get it."

After the last tune, which was called "Lady and Her Loom," the audience broke into thunderous applause and rose from their seats. In an effort to make up for Mason's conspicuous departure, I clapped my hands madly.

"That was very moving," I said to Valdette.

"They have a CD, you know," Valdette told me. "You can buy it at The Grinder."

"I'll get it tomorrow," I said.

We filed back out to the bar. Mason was sitting by himself smoking a cigar.

"We can go now," I said.

"We don't have to," Mason said. "If you want to stay, that's fine."

"But you don't seem to be having a very good time."

"I'm having a fine time," he said.

I went to say good-bye to Sue and Teri but Joel caught me by the arm and pulled me aside. My heart began pounding.

"Lucinda," he said. "I'm sensing a little awkwardness between us tonight."

There were two ways to go here. I could be straightforward (i.e., empowered) and tell him his behavior in his SUV had been inappropriate and that it was in both of our interests to maintain a strictly professional relationship or I could do the thing I'd always done in this kind of situation and pretend like nothing happened. The choice was clear.

"What do you mean?" I asked.

"I sense you're avoiding me," he said. "You haven't made eye contact with me all night. And so I just want to say something. Let's just get this out on the table. I like you as a person. I think you're really fun and interesting. And as flattered as I am that you seem to have feelings for me, I'm a married man and just don't want to pursue something like that."

"What?" I gasped. There was a very real possibility that I would throw up.

"Don't get defensive," Joel said. "I know no one likes to hear these things."

"Uh," I said. "I don't think . . . I think you've misinterpreted . . . I think you know . . . uh . . ."

"Don't feel like you have to say anything," Joel said, suddenly casual. "Hey, I've been there."

By now, the crowd at the Lasagna Factory looked like an aquarium of shoulder-padded blazer-wearing goldfish smoking Virginia Slims 100s. I pushed through them in my stiletto heels, hating at that moment the town of Prairie City more than I'd hated anything in my life, except perhaps Bonnie Crawley when she remarked, after meeting Dave Davenport at the *Up Early* Christmas party, that I was lucky to find a man who appreciated a more disheveled woman.

When I finally found Mason he was on the other side of the restaurant looking out the window. It was beginning to sleet, so I

had to grab his arm as we stepped outside. The blast of cold air al-
leviated my nausea, except now I felt like I was going to cry.

"Fun time," Mason said.

"You obviously didn't have a good time," I said.

"I had a fine time."

"Then how come you didn't talk to anyone?"

"I didn't feel like it," he said.

"Well, it doesn't work like that," I said. "You have to talk to
people!"

"Why would I want to talk to any of those people?"

"Because you're at a fucking party!"

"Settle down, bootsy," he said. This was his pet name for me,
established only over the past few weeks. I didn't dislike it.

"You don't have to keep trying so hard to get them to like you,"
Mason continued. "They already seem to like you enough."

"But you can't just sit there with your back to everyone," I said.
I was choking back tears. "It's creepy to people."

"Sorry, babe," he said. "It's that Nam syndrome. I wasn't there
but I have it anyway."

And I think, right then, I fell in love with him. Or at least felt a
wave of affection wash up over my anger as I clung to his arm on
the slick sidewalk. The din of the party noise faded into silence as
we walked to the car. I'd never tried to get Mason to like me, and yet
he liked me more than anyone else in Prairie City did—and ever
would.

A few days after the recovery center benefit, I had Sue and Teri to
my house for dinner. This was to thank them for everything they
had done for me—the lending of the Saab, the automatic entry into
Prairie City's power crowd—as well as show them the tape of the
Up Early segment on women and methamphetamine. I was a little
worried about what they'd think of the segment, although by *Up
Early* standards it was pretty hard hitting. The evening had been
planned for months but Sue and Teri's schedules were so tight with

parties and fund-raisers and their lesbian poker club that by the time they came over there was a dusting of snow on the ground. To accommodate Teri's vegetarian diet, I had prepared penne with pesto sauce and oven-dried tomatoes, a dish I'd practiced a few weeks earlier but that Mason had insisted upon eating with a hot dog because he couldn't have a dinner that didn't include meat. I had purchased the ceramic Italian swirl-style salad bowl from Pier One along with heavy pewter salad servers, white embroidered placemats, and eggplant-colored napkins that matched the sheer eggplant-colored panels that hung over the French doors. I put on Joni Mitchell's *Ladies of the Canyon* and waited for Sue and Teri to arrive. Sue had seen the house once, but that was before it was fixed up—well before the dried roses and sheer eggplant-colored panels. They would be blown away.

They showed up, I took their coats. I poured them each a glass of $11.99 chardonnay.

"Lucinda," Sue said, "that guy you brought to the benefit looked like the Unabomber. You can't date him!"

"He was creepy," Teri said.

I didn't know Teri all that well. I wanted to like her, although, looking back on things, Mason had been right: I was so interested in making sure people in Prairie City liked me that I barely got a chance to decide whether or not I liked them. But now Teri had said this to me, not really said anything to me but echoed what Sue had said. I did not like it one bit. I supposed Sue had a few more rights in this area. I knew her better. She'd told me she was taking hormone replacement. I'd told her about my lesbian affair in college, which had lasted approximately five days. But telling someone you had had a lesbian affair at Smith is like telling them that you took an introductory English course. It did not give one license to criticize someone's boyfriend. They obviously didn't understand the mating patterns of Lucinda Trout. I was furious. But as the seconds ticked by, as I set down a baguette and a tray of olives and goat cheese and grasped for an answer—do I explain my theory of ex-

treme men? Do I tell them that Mason's IQ was tested at 130
(granted this was in eighth grade and predated years of drug use).
Do I tell them I dumped him?—I realized I was furious at Mason.
Because, of course, Sue and Teri were right about him. And had
they known about the three kids by three different women they
would have been even more right. I shouldn't have been dating him.
Except that I was and except for the incident at the Estrogen Therapy concert and one other time when we'd been at his cabin and I
looked at those paintings of anguished, screaming human heads
and thought that perhaps I had entered a zone that was fraught
with more demons than I could take on, I was happy with Mason. I
loved him. Probably, anyway.

"It's not serious with him," I said.

"Just a boy toy?" Sue said.

"Fun for now," I said. "You know. He takes me to see eagles.
He brings me flowers. He polished my floors once while I was at
the gym."

"You let him in your house alone?" Teri asked, although she
was interrupted by Sue, who said "You go, girl" and Teri stopped
talking.

We moved on to other topics— a political scandal involving the
city health commissioner, the growing influence of the Prairie City
Coalition for Diversity, the nutritional benefits of free-range
chicken—and ate the pasta, which they didn't say much about, nor
did they remark on the salad bowl. For decaf and dessert, we went
back to the living room to view the *Up Early* tape.

"Now remember, it's not as in depth as I would have liked," I
said. "Such are the limits of television."

"Oh I can't wait," said Sue, who was pouring Kahlúa into her
coffee. "Because I'd really like to show this to the city council when
it comes time to ask for more money."

I put the tape in. Bonnie Crawley, with her giant head and tiny
body, sat in a director's chair on the *Up Early* sound stage. The set
was designed to look like a loft apartment, with a kitchen area for

cooking demonstrations, an overstuffed Victorian sofa for interviews and Bonnie and Samantha's "rap sessions," and a "work station" with a desk and a laptop computer that was supposed to look
like it was constantly posting wire stories that the hosts would announce throughout the broadcast. In fact, it permanently displayed
a screensaver picture of a kitten peering into a fish bowl. Bonnie
took a sip from her *Up Early* coffee mug, opened her enormous
mouth, and delivered the introduction I had written.

"Turning to women's health this morning, *Up Early* has discovered a shocking trend involving a dangerous new drug affecting
thousands of women in, of all places, our nation's heartland. And it
may be coming east. Lifestyle correspondent Lucinda Trout traveled to the land of cornfields and found that there's a lot more to
country living than Sunday picnics and apple pie."

"The women you interviewed don't live in the country," Teri
said. She was leaning toward the TV with her elbows on her knees
like a baseball manager in a dugout.

"I know," I said. "It's really reductive. I don't have much control over the intros."

A wide shot of a cornfield appeared on the screen, followed by a
dilapidated farmhouse, and then the shadowy figure of one of the
women from Sue's clinic.

"I lost my kids," the woman said. "I lost my house, my marriage, my car. This drug destroyed me."

My voice came on.

"The gently rolling plains of America's heartland may look
peaceful, the kind of quiet place where women still get together to
sew quilts and compare potato salad recipes, but, more and more, a
terrifying plague is gripping these once-innocent people. It's called
methamphetamine."

Another woman appeared in shadow. She was sitting on the
front porch of the Victorian house that functioned as the clinic's
"therapeutic neighborhood." A title appeared beneath her that read
"Jenny, age 20."

"I have three kids," Jenny said. "And I got to where I didn't care nothing about them. All I cared about was chasing my next fix. My weight went down to 104 pounds. People told me I looked good. I had so much energy. I stayed up all night and cleaned the house. I tweaked so hard I scraped the pattern off the kitchen counter. But I was spending five hundred dollars a week on meth."

" 'Tweaking' refers to the compulsive, sometimes frenetic behavior that results from excessive methamphetamine use," continued my voice as footage of police-confiscated meth appeared on screen, vials of white powder and the small rocks from which the stuff was broken off and snorted like coke. "Some women say they started using meth because it allowed them to do more housework. Others were in it for the weight loss. And still others, like Karen, who didn't want her real name used, found it helped in not only tearing up the kitchen but tearing up the sheets."

"We got into the craziest sexual positions," said Karen, who wasn't from Sue's clinic but a friend of the bartender at the Ramada Inn whom I'd tracked down thanks to my intrepid investigative journalism skills. Though she wanted her name changed, she wasn't in shadow. Gaunt and smoking, we'd filmed her in her trailer home.

"I'd be hanging from the ceiling, tied to the bedpost," Karen continued. "I'd dress up in a maid's uniform and scrub the bathroom floor while he, you know . . . Sometimes I'd get distracted and want to keep scrubbing. And I was so thin that it really added to the experience."

"Oh my God!" Teri said. Sue poured herself another glass of wine.

The segment continued for another minute and forty-five seconds. I interviewed a police officer, a doctor, and another woman, who rolled up her sleeve and showed her track marks from injecting the stuff. There were a few more cornfields, then a shot of me standing in front of a barn holding a microphone.

"Experts say that if the trend continues, meth will claim more and more victims in the Midwest and then make its way east. And although New York might not have the abandoned farmhouses that are the labs of choice in these parts, anyone with access to the simple household products that make up the ingredients of this deadly drug can find the recipe on the Internet and make a small fortune off innocent victims. A scary thought, because, as these women have told us, meth can make you lose a lot more than a few extra pounds. You can lose your life. Back to you in the studio."

Bonnie, now on the Victorian sofa, clutched her coffee mug and shook her head. "Thanks for that sobering report, Lucinda," she said.

"Scary stuff," said Samantha.

"Although I gotta say, I wouldn't mind weighing 104," Bonnie said.

"Wouldn't we all," said Samantha.

Sue's jaw dropped. "Jesus Christ!" she said.

On the videotape, Samantha's face registered chagrin as the director glowered at her. "Not that that's the way to go, of course," she added.

"No, of course not," Bonnie said.

"Of course not," Samantha said. She turned to the camera. "Well, stay tuned because up next we have fitness trainer Jaycee Chung here to show us the latest moves in our favorite new workout, tai-bo! Stay with us!"

I stopped the tape. Teri wouldn't look directly at me. Sue slung back the rest of her wine.

"Well, that's show biz," Sue said.

"That's really a lot of the reason I moved here," I said. "To get away from that kind of reporting. Believe me, I plan to handle things much more in depth from now on."

"I hear ya," Sue said.

"Boy, we gotta go," said Teri. "It's late."

It was 9:30, the Prairie City equivalent of 12:30 in New York. A terrible feeling was coming over me, a feeling not unlike the one I'd experienced while accidentally kissing Joel in his SUV. It suddenly seemed idiotic to have invited Sue and Teri to dinner, mostly be-

cause it seemed idiotic to be in Prairie City in the first place. I was
a one-woman army of cultural imperialism—that was a pretty good
line, I thought, momentarily distracted from this new wave of mis-
ery. It was kind of clever, especially for having consumed so much
wine.

"I know I seem like a one-woman army of cultural imperialism," I said as I got their coats.

"What?" said Teri.

"Oh hush," said Sue. "We all survived when they built that giant shopping mall on the south edge of town. We can survive you."

"Oh yeah." I laughed, though it was more like panting. "Thanks.
And thanks for everything you've done for me, with, you know, the
car. And letting me stay with you. And inviting me to all your
parties."

"You don't have to thank us," Sue said. "That's just what
people do."

"Right," I said.

They bundled up. Sue handed Teri the car keys and they both
hugged me good night.

"You're okay," Sue said to me.

"Thanks," I said.

"And you'll be okay," she said. "It's all going to be okay here."

Sue said this in a way that managed to sound neither condescending nor new agey, which to me seemed like an impossible feat.
She was like the bionic woman in that sense.

They opened the door, letting in an arc of cold air. The temperature must have dropped 20 degrees since they'd arrived.

"Oh, not too bad out yet," Teri said.

Without bothering to zip up their coats they walked down the
porch steps to the Isuzu Trooper on the street. I closed the door behind them and picked the half-eaten baguette off the coffee table. I
couldn't believe I'd said that thing about cultural imperialism. It
smacked of such self-importance and was the kind of line that only
worked on Faye because she wouldn't really be listening.

Through the air vent, I could hear Dawn screaming downstairs. Her boyfriend, who she said had lived with her in the basement apartment for seven years, was now serving a three-year prison sentence for dealing crack. I'd seen Dawn only twice after meeting her during the *Up Early* porch shoot, once when she'd locked herself out of her apartment and another time when she gave me her keys in case she locked herself out again. She'd been matter-of-fact about her boyfriend, explaining the crack dealing like someone might explain an illegal right turn. I'd told her how sorry I was, which I actually was. She seemed nice enough. She called me "hon." She thought Toby was "weird" and that the landlord was "a shit" and the house was "a pit," mostly because the paint was almost entirely flaked off and the ferret urine smell emanated throughout all three apartments. I kept telling her to come up for coffee or a glass of wine whenever she felt like it. She'd never come. Her key ring sat on my kitchen windowsill. It had a plastic decoy that said I'M NOT A BITCH, I'M *THE* BITCH.

"I fucking do *everything* for you," Dawn's voice rose through the vent. It seemed she was on the phone. "I sit here. I *wait* here. I visit your fucking *mother!*"

Then Toby stomped up the staircase outside, causing the dishes in the drying rack to rattle. I heard him unlock his door and slam it shut. A wine cork rolled off the kitchen table to the floor. Metallica started playing upstairs.

"What am I to you?" Dawn continued. "Just another one of your bitches? A fucking ho? We were supposed to get *married!*"

I picked up the phone and dialed Mason's cell phone number. He was at the cabin with Erin. He answered on the first ring, whispering so as not to wake her.

"So how was your evening?" he asked. There was so much static I could barely hear him.

"I wish you were here," I said.

"What?"

"I wish you were here," I repeated. Then the signal was lost. I

called back three times and finally got through, though the static
was even worse.

"I wish I was there, too," Mason said.

He started to say something else but the phone disconnected
again and I hung up. I went to bed and listened to the end of Dawn's
conversation. She screamed and cursed some more. She said something about Christmas. Then she slammed down the phone and
wept.

Mason had agreed to be filmed for the Bad Boy story as long as I
promised to get some footage of his artwork. I hadn't exactly told
him the subject was "bad boys," just that it was a companion piece
to an interview with an author who had written about "transcend-
ing your type."

In preparation for the bad boy shoot, Mason smoked a joint. It
was a raw day in early November. Jeb met us at the cabin, where the
river was gray and choppy; 10 degrees cooler and there would have
been a glaze of ice on the banks.

"I'm really sorry that you have to get in the river," I said.

"That makes two of us," Mason said. It occurred to me he'd
been at my house nearly every night since we'd met. He hadn't
showered at the truck stop.

"But it's gonna be great for the story," I said. "Remember,
you're doing this for the sake of your art!"

"Let's do that part last," Jeb said, hoisting his camera over his
shoulder. "For now, why don't we get you chopping wood or something."

We filmed Mason chopping wood. We filmed him stoking a fire
in the woodstove. I had him pretend to mend his hoof shoes, sweep
the cabin floor, and pour himself a cup of coffee and sit contempla-
tively on the deck. To show Mason's and my togetherness, Jeb
filmed us holding hands while hiking around in the woods. To touch
on the bad boy aspect, I had Jeb get close-ups of the animal skulls
mounted on the walls. The cabin reeked of pot smoke.

"You wanna move that crib out of the way?" Jeb said.

I scooted Erin's portable crib across the floor. Mason finished his third beer and Jeb followed him out of the cabin and filmed him tossing the bottle into a recycling bin overflowing with Leinenkugel bottles.

"You got some shots of the paintings, right?" Mason said.

"Oh sure," said Jeb. He looked at his watch. "Interesting work."

A wind was blowing in from the north. If I didn't get some shots of Mason's bathing in the river Faye would kill the whole segment.

"Are you sure you don't mind doing this?" I asked Mason. "You won't have to be in there for very long."

"Whatever," he said. I got several towels and a scrub brush out of the car and found Mason's bottle of Pert Plus in the cabin.

"Just get in the river, suds up your hair, and use this scrubber on your back," I said.

"I don't use a scrub brush," he said.

"I know, but it looks better on TV," I said. "I'm sorry. Just . . . it'll be better that way."

Jeb, who had put on a pair of gloves, looked like he felt genuinely sorry for Mason, who was pulling his clothes off and dropping them on the ground. His shirt started to blow away in the wind.

"I told you you could wear a swimsuit," I said.

"I don't bathe in a swimsuit," Mason said.

He was completely naked except for his flip-flops. Still tan except for his white buttocks, he faced Jeb and the camera, holding the shampoo bottle in one hand and the scrub brush in the other.

"You can turn around," Jeb said.

Mason ambled to the riverbank, kicked off his flip-flops, and jumped in. When he resurfaced he let out a loud holler, "Woo-ee!" Sort of like a cowboy, I thought, which was good. Except that he was already turning purple. I pantomimed for him to start shampooing himself. He sudsed himself up and began scrubbing his armpits.

"Shit," Jeb said. "I'm out of tape."

"What?" I said. "Can you reload really fast? So he doesn't notice."

"He's gonna notice," Jeb said. "Unless he's blind, which he may be by now."

Jeb sifted through his camera bag for another tape. Mason was jumping up and down in the water and singing.

"Don't rinse your hair out yet!" I yelled.

"What?"

"Keep doing what you're doing. It looks fabulous!"

Mason was hooting and hollering and shaking his arms around. Even from thirty feet away I swore I could see goose bumps forming on his back like welts. I imagined how perfect it would be if a bald eagle came and landed on a nearby branch as he was washing himself. For that, I would receive an Emmy.

"Getting a little chilly out here, bootsy!" he yelled.

"I know," I yelled. "Hang in there!"

Jeb was finally reloaded and I continued to mime my directions. Wash hair. Scrub back. Lather up the beard. Rinse.

"Can we do one more take?" I yelled. "I'm really sorry."

After fifteen minutes we let Mason get out. I told him I would treat him to dinner anywhere he wanted and he said he wanted to go to the all-you-can-eat buffet at USA Steaks. He had four helpings of prime rib. I told him I loved him. He said he'd loved me from the moment I'd walked in the door of Effie's Tavern on our first date.

"I couldn't believe you actually showed up," he said. "I'm sure you'll leave me one day for a long-distance trucker with a very large tool box. But I'll have my way with you as long as I can."

What was it about that sparse, windy place that made big steps seem so small? Was it the great distance between things, the way all that land and sky could make a human trajectory seem so tiny, so irrelevant, so much like a blade of grass that could break from its stem, blow in any direction, and then land in another pasture where it lay until the next gust, indistinguishable from the rest of the field, untraceable by even the keenest animal nose, and no worse for the wear? Why was I able to get in deeper with Mason, someone at once so scattered and so inert, than I ever had with anyone else? Even years later, after Mason and I had damaged each other beyond what we thought was possible, I would still see that land as a place I had only just come to, as a space too wide to truly inhabit. Time passed on the plains the way clouds often do; you couldn't sense the motion but in the time it took to turn your head the formations would be different, something would have blown in and then blown out, something else would have edged in sideways, slipped just above the horizon line and left so many streaks in the sky that it was like one hundred planes had passed over in the time it took to eat your dinner. Change was not so much a tangible entity as it was something you realized had already taken place.

Winter never really happened that year in Prairie City. Snow fell in January and March, melting, on both occasions, within a week of the first flake. The pastures turned green earlier than expected. The bald eagles flew past Mason's cabin on their way back to Alaska. I turned thirty. Dawn married her boyfriend in prison. She showed me her ring one day in the basement laundry room. She had purchased it herself at Wal-Mart. He'd be out in a year, she said. Now all this waiting for him actually meant something.

Something else happened that spring. This is how it didn't happen.

One Sunday morning, as Mason and I drank coffee in bed, snuggling and listening to the drip of melting snow outside my window, he turned to me and looked deeply into my eyes.

"I think we should get a place in the country," he said. "I'd like nothing better than for us to evenly split the rent of a charming yet modernly outfitted farmstead. I have the financial stability to take

on such a responsibility and I hope that we can talk through the various issues of this obviously serious decision and make a smart and well-considered choice."

"I agree," I said, nuzzling my honey around the ear and taking another sip of coffee. "The runaway success of my series for Up Early *has given me lots of financial stability as well. And though I've never lived with anyone before, I feel confident that we can co-exist peacefully under one roof and solve domestic conflicts in a mature and thoughtful way. But let's give ourselves a few more months to continue talking about it until we're absolutely sure we're making the right decision."*

"I completely agree," Mason said. Then we made passionate love.

This was the way it happened.

One Tuesday afternoon, as Toby's stereo was blasting upstairs and I was sitting at my desk panicking over the fact that in the course of seven months *Up Early* had used only three of my "Quality of Life Report" segments, thereby forcing me to live off my rapidly dwindling savings, Mason called me from the grain elevator.

"Did you see the *Dispatch* classifieds today?" he asked. "Look on the second page of the rental listings under "acreages."

The acreage listings were typically the second thing Mason and I turned to in the *Prairie City Daily Dispatch*, right after the horoscopes. We had never actually discussed the ramifications of living together, just of living on a farm, presumably together. Over time this talk expanded into the actual act of looking through the classifieds and then, once or twice, going out to an acreage (and this meant any domicile situated on more than one acre of land) and actually looking at it. Most of these turned out to be trailers or houses that appeared to have been designed to look like trailers. But every once in a while there was a real house with a real barn for rent. Since these properties got snatched up as quickly as Manhattan apartments, we were always too late and had never been faced with an actual decision.

"You see the one I mean?" Mason said.

The listing read like this: *4 BR on 12 acres, barn w/stable, new water heater, $800/mo.*

Mason called the landlord, came back to my house, and we drove the Sunbird out to the place immediately. The road, which had the uninspired name of County Road F, was gravel but the driveway, marked by a rusty mailbox, was just dirt with tire ruts. It sloped up a gentle incline for about a quarter mile until it reached the house, a large turn-of-the-century farmhouse not so much of the Hallmark Hall of Fame variety but the PBS-documentary-about-struggling-farmers variety. It was three stories, if you counted the attic, and had the small, south-facing windows typical of farm-houses in the region. Large windows, Mason had told me, let in too much cold air, plus they could break during storms. The foundation appeared to have shifted at some point over the years, leaving the porch lopsided. The paint had flaked almost entirely off the clap-board siding and the shingles were sliding off the roof; a few had entangled themselves in an elm tree, one of just a handful of trees on the entire twelve acres.

The back door opened into a mud room with painted floor-boards and a wall of windows that bore cracks from the strain of the wind. The kitchen walls were covered with dark, old-fashioned wall-paper and glass cupboards that were similarly cracked in places. The living room and dining room were empty other than a ratty sofa and an elaborate TV and stereo system. In the den, which must have been built later as an addition, a king-sized waterbed took up most of the room. Throughout the house, blankets covered the win-dows. Cumbersome security lights were mounted to the pillars of the porch. Inside the front door, a motion detection system sounded an alarm whenever anyone pulled into the driveway.

"We had a little trouble with these people," the landlord said. He looked like an old farmer. He was missing part of a finger. "Real nice couple. But somehow the husband got into some trouble and he's doing some prison time and the wife couldn't make the rent payments. We let her slide for six months or so but, you know, sometimes you have to say enough is enough. A shame."

Dozens of cars were coming up the driveway to see the house, each one setting off the alarm. It was the only nontrailer or trailer look-alike rental that had been in the paper in weeks. People were milling around in the yard and the barn. I had brought tax returns, bank statements, landlord references from New York, and, just in case, a videotape of my first "Quality of Life Report" segment. The label said *Quality of Life Part 1: Choices and Chances: How I Went to the Heartland in Search of My Soul.* I heard the back door open as another prospective tenant came inside. I offered to write the landlord a check right then and there. We hadn't even looked upstairs.

We got the acreage. Actually, I got the acreage. Mason, who sacrificed half of his paycheck to child support, had no money, no tax returns, no references. My name was on the lease. But Mason was ecstatic about the whole thing because, as he whispered to me while the landlord went to his truck to get a copy of the lease, "I can board horses here and make so much money I can quit the elevator!" The barn, nearly as big as the house, had seven horse stalls, cathedrallike rafters, and a tack room. According to the landlord, there was already a horse in the pasture, named Cupid, whose owner had paid the previous tenants $75 a month, technically bringing the rent down to $725. The landlord also said he'd reshingle the roof and pay for paint if we painted the house ourselves. I pulled back the blanket on the window and peered out onto an endless stretch of gently rolling hills. The sun was beginning to set and the sky was turning violet. A hawk circling the pasture landed on a cottonwood tree far in the distance.

"So what did the guy go to prison for?" Mason asked.

"Meth dealing," said the landlord, shaking his head. "His poor wife. She had no idea. One day they just showed up and dragged him out."

This guy knew how to pick them.

How to Throw a Barn Dance for Under $300

To: Faye Figaro
From: Lucinda Trout
Re: Exciting News!

Guess what? I am moving to a farm! Now "The Quality of Life Report" will really be able to take on more of a structure. I'll bring viewers along as I stroll through the fields in the early evening light as well as struggle with the harsh realities of farm life (brutal winters, possible animal invasions—grasshopper infestations). Think of it as *A Year in Provence* meets *Lake Wobegon Days.*

To: Lucinda Trout
From: Faye Figaro

I'm thikning of it as *Girl Interuptted* meets *Deliverance.*

There were cats all over the farm. At least seven. The meth addict previous tenants had fed them and now they were mangy and unvaccinated and apparently extremely pregnant by a lone tom cat that lurked in the rafters of the barn. Mason and I had asked the landlord to take the cats away but on the morning we showed up with the first load of furniture they were still there. By the time we returned with the second load, they'd all given birth. And they were the worst mothers I'd ever seen.

Kittens were strewn everywhere—in the yard, in the barn, underneath the porch. Most of them still had their eyes closed, their multicolored fur obscured by wetness and grass. The farm seemed to wheeze with their cries. The mother cats skulked around in complete indifference. Mason stared at them, cursing and breathing heavily.

"Why aren't the mothers taking care of them?" I asked.

"Because they're too young!" he yelled. "The mothers are probably six months old. That tom cat is probably *their* father, too. What the hell was the matter with those people? Everyone knows you don't feed stray cats."

"Maybe they'll get the hang of it," I said. I picked up one of the mother cats and set her down by two kittens. She sniffed them and walked away. I realized then that a sound I'd first thought to be the squawking of a bird was actually coming from a place closer to the ground. I followed the noise to the horse pasture and saw a white kitten, no bigger than a mouse, howling under a long stalk of prairie grass. Afterbirth was attached to its side.

"Oh God, come over here," I said.

Mason looked at the kitten. His breath grew even heavier.

"Go someplace else," he said.

"Maybe the mother just needs to find it," I said. "Come here, kitty! Come over here!"

"Walk away!" Mason yelled. "Go inside the house. Don't look out the window."

"Why?"

"Just let me handle it. You don't need to see this."

I went inside the house and up the stairs, which creaked so loudly you wondered if they'd cave in. The room that would be my office was the second largest of the four bedrooms. Sebastian and Peter would share the largest room when they visited on weekends and Erin, who would sleep over three times a week, would have the small maid's room, which had slanted ceilings and a tiny window seat and, were I four years old, would have been the coolest place imaginable given its similarity to the sleeping loft on *Little House on the Prairie*. Mason's and my bedroom had windows facing the west, where a plain of natural grasses that the Department of Land Management paid the landlord not to farm stretched for more than a mile. I stood in my office and pictured where my desk would go. I scanned the walls for a phone jack. There was none.

Through the window I watched Mason take a pair of gloves out of his truck. He looked up and saw me.

"Go to the other side of the house!" he yelled. "Go in the bathroom or something. Get away from the window!"

I went into the bathroom. There was only one in the house. It was on the second floor at the end of the hallway and there were happy face stickers all over the walls. The light switch cover was decorated with a picture of a sunrise and the words "AND GOD SAID 'LET THERE BE LIGHT.'" After about five minutes Mason called to me from the bottom of the stairs.

"Why don't you go back into town?"

"Why?"

"Just let me deal with this," he said.

"What did you do?"

"Never mind that," he said. "Why don't you go to the Y and go swimming or something?"

"My car has all my shit in it," I said. I'd stuffed the INNKEEPERS ARE NOT STUPID shower curtain and the eggplant-colored window panels and all the sheets and towels and clothes I could fit into the Sunbird.

"That doesn't mean you can't drive it," Mason said.

"But my stuff will get stolen."

"This isn't fucking New York!" he shouted. I noticed he had tears in his eyes.

I got in the car and drove into town. This was terrible. Was I wrong to let Mason do what I suspected he was doing? No one I knew from home would have allowed it. They'd take all the kittens in, feed them with eyedroppers, and then submit essays to the back page of *The New York Times Magazine* about how saving the lives of forty-two newborn kittens made them reconsider their position on abortion. Except that even I knew you couldn't save an hours-old kitten with an eyedropper. I knew from watching The Discovery Channel that there were certain nutrients they needed, certain things that couldn't be provided by humans. And *The New York Times Magazine* didn't accept unsolicited material anyway. I knew because I'd once tried to submit something about the deluge of Chinese baby girls on the Upper West Side and received a form reject letter.

I didn't know where I'd packed my swimsuit, so instead of going to the YMCA I went to The Grinder and sat in the outdoor section so I could keep an eye on the car. Mason had told me to come back in no less than two hours. This seemed an interminable amount of time. I flipped through a copy of the *Prairie City Daily Dispatch*. The lead story was about the latest statistics regarding playground safety. Then I did something I'd been dreading but absolutely had to do. I took out my cell phone and called my parents in Florida to tell them I was moving in with Mason. When I got the machine I left a message saying that I was moving to a farm "for job-related reasons" and could be reached at a new number. I decided to omit the part about Mason.

During my fourth cup of coffee, I saw Sue standing at the counter. She was talking on her cell phone and looking very businesslike in a blazer, tailored slacks, and Birkenstocks. She saw me and waved.

"Lucinda!" Sue cried, walking toward me as she attempted to balance her grande cappuccino with her cell phone and canvas EMBRACE, EMPATHIZE, EMPOWER tote bag. "It's been forever. Whatcha been up to?"

"Oh, this and that," I said.

"How's the TV stuff going?"

"Great!"

My heart began racing. I hadn't told Sue—or anyone in Prairie City—about moving to the farm with Mason. It seemed obvious that I had to tell her now, though, as if on reflex, my mind flipped through a list of alternate subjects toward which to veer the conversation.

"How's work?" I asked.

"Fine," she said, "which reminds me, I've been meaning to call you. I want you to meet a new friend of mine. She just started working at the recovery center and she's around your age. She's an African American woman named Christine and she's just terrific. A really interesting woman. I think you two would hit it off."

There were, from what I'd seen, perhaps 154 African Americans in Prairie City. Nine of them worked for the Prairie City Coalition for Diversity. The remaining 145 appeared to be men who dated and occasionally married overweight white women who bore their children and shouted things like "Wait until I tell your father"—always with enough volume to inform the other shoppers that there was, in fact, a father to tell—in the cereal aisle of Hinky Dinky. My impression was black women who grew up in Prairie City fled town at the first opportunity. Just as, according to my prophecy, by the year 2015 regular Jewish girls on Manhattan's Upper West Side would be unable to vie for men with the *Chinese* Jewish girls who had been adopted in the late 1990s, it seemed that no woman of color in Prairie City could be bothered to compete with the Caucasians their male counterparts seemed to prefer. Dawn's imprisoned husband, it turned out, was African American. In this regard, there was quite a bit of interracial coupling in Prairie City, surely a testament to the efforts of the Coalition for Diversity.

"We're having a little get-together this Saturday," Sue continued. "Sort of a women-only thing. I hope you can make it."

"Great!" I said.

"I'm not sure what time Teri will be home from work," Sue said. "So I'll call you and let you know when people are coming."

Sue was now looking at her watch and pulling her car keys out of her pocket. I couldn't believe I'd waited so long to break the news to her. It was clear I'd have to tell her now and that it would be totally weird and she'd look at me all concerned and want to have a longer conversation wherein we discussed my motives, Mason's and my level of commitment, and my ability to remain independent and empowered in the context of heterosexual cohabitation.

"Actually," I stammered, "I have a new phone number."

"Really?" said Sue.

"Actually, I'm moving to a farm."

"Really! Whereabouts?"

"About twenty miles west of town, on County Road F," I said.

"Wow, that's far," said Sue. "Are you going to be able to manage out there?"

"Actually," I said, "Mason is moving there, too."

I couldn't look directly at Sue, so I fixed my eyes on a couple of college students who were going from table to table with some kind of petition about the Green Party. I prayed they'd come over and interrupt us.

"I didn't realize you guys were that serious," she said.

"I know it seems weird," I said. "But I've really thought about it a lot and I'm prepared to take it on."

I waited for her to issue some warning about Mason or at least tell me that I could always stay with her and Teri if things didn't work out. Instead, she pulled her Palm Pilot out of her tote bag and asked for the new phone number.

"Well, how fun!" she said. "You'll have to have a housewarming."

"Oh definitely," I said.

"And I bet it'll give you a lot more material for your TV series."

"That's right," I said.

"And if it doesn't work out," Sue said, walking away, "you can always move back into town. Nothing's irreversible."

How true, I thought. Nothing was irreversible here. I made a mental note to explain to Daphne and Elena that moving onto a farm with a guy in Prairie City was equivalent to, say, giving a guy the extra keys to your apartment in New York. It was a convenience rather than monumental occasion. It was, simply, a passage. It had both an entrance and, if need be, an exit. In Prairie City, finding a new place to live was as easy as taking back your extra set of keys. This was what we meant by quality of life. So there you had it. No further explanation was required. Suddenly I felt lighter and, if not carefree, less burdened by the implications of the farm. What fun times surely lay ahead!

The Green Party petitioners, with their clipboards and righteous, steely eyes, were coming toward me. Bolting out of my chair, I ran toward the sidewalk, inadvertently throwing the newspaper in the trash can rather than the recycling bin.

Returning to the farm exactly two hours after I'd left it, I found Mason sitting on the porch drinking beer with his boss, Frank Fussell. Actually, only Mason was drinking a beer. Frank was drinking a bottle of iced chai. I'd met Frank only once before, when Mason had given me a tour of the elevator, and he was wearing the exact same thing he'd worn that day: a surgical scrub shirt, acid-washed jeans cut off just below the knees, and Jesus-style sandals that wrapped around his ankles.

As I walked up the porch steps, Frank came up to me and put both hands on my shoulders. Like Leonard, he wore aviator-style glasses that darkened in the sun. A ring of thick, graying hair encircled his bald head and hung past his earlobes. The kittens were gone, though a few mother cats were still ambling about.

"Lucinda," he said, "sometimes kindness must take the form of cruelty."

"That's pretty deep, Frank," Mason said. There were empty beer cans all over the porch.

"You know," Frank continued, "we tend to think of nature as a self-sufficient entity, as a force that ebbs and flows peacefully with-

out human interference or a lot of, you know, input from mortals
such as ourselves. But I hope you've learned today that that's not always the case. And it can be a karmic bummer."

They had killed the kittens. Mason never told me how, but considering there was no water around to drown them and it didn't
make much sense to shoot them I can only imagine Mason and
Frank had hit them with blunt objects. Actually it was Mason who
had done the killing; Frank mostly stood around and coached him.
Mason had needed to drink to do it, and even through the salve of
alcohol he seemed shaken up, discombobulated, and still pissed off
at the people who'd lived there before. He said he'd thought about
killing the mother cats, too, because chances were the humane society would put them to sleep anyway, but he couldn't bring himself
to do it.

I resisted making a smart-ass remark. I resisted saying "that was
big of you" or "you deserve a humanitarian award." Mason seemed
so upset and the situation seemed so much bigger than anything I
was in a position to judge—especially with what he would surely
call my "urban mentality"—that I didn't say anything. I went up to
my empty office and watched through the window as Frank drove
off in his truck. When I went downstairs, Mason was in the kitchen
opening another beer.

"Can't we keep the ones that are left?" I asked. "We can get
them spayed."

"You have seven hundred dollars?" he asked. He already owed
me upward of a thousand dollars for his share of the security deposit,
the first month's rent, the interior paint, new phone service, the electric bill, and the establishment of a propane account, which he insisted wouldn't be necessary if he could put in a wood-burning stove.

"Maybe we can find homes for them," I said.

"We won't," he said. "They're wild cats. They'll get pregnant
again immediately."

"We should take them to the humane society," I said.

"Like I'm sure we can get them in the car," he said.

"We can try."

I took the boxes of dishes and clothes out of the trunk of the Sun-bird. A plate fell out and shattered on the steps on the way through the back door and Mason cursed again. When the trunk was empty we both put on gloves and caught the cats, Mason two at a time, and threw them in. Mason got scratched on the face. I screamed and dropped one and it fled into the pasture. We drove back into town listening to the screams of the cats in the trunk. They were louder than the engine. Mason turned the radio on. He flipped past Garri-son Keillor and settled on a classic rock station. His cheek was bleeding. I started crying. Partly out of sorrow and disgust, partly because I wouldn't be able to tell any of my friends about it.

"I know you think I'm awful," he said.

"I don't think that," I said.

The sun was beginning to go down over the passing farmland. The sky was streaked with pink and a jetliner was arcing around for a landing at Prairie City Municipal. Grand Funk Railroad's "Amer-ican Band" played on the radio.

"Let's not mention this to the kids," Mason said. I had forgot-ten his kids existed.

When we reached the humane society I opened the trunk of the car, and the cats leaped out and tore across the parking lot. We stood there and watched them as they headed toward the highway. It was the last we saw of them.

"Well, that was a fine use of time," Mason said. "Now they can all get run over by cars. Does that make you feel better?"

From there, we went to Effie's Tavern and drank more beer. Then we went back to the house and, since the bed wasn't put to-gether, slept on the mattress. We had, at that point, officially lived on the farm for eleven hours.

The following Saturday, when I arrived at the women's party at Sue and Teri's, the first person I saw was Joel. He was in the kitchen making crab cakes. A towel was thrown over his shoulder and he wore an apron that said I'M COOKIN' WITH *THE FRUGAL GOURMET* ON PRAIRIE CITY PUBLIC TELEVISION.

"I thought this was a girls' party," I said.

"Why would you think that?" he asked.

Sue barreled into the kitchen, a margarita in one hand and a finger sandwich from the prepared-food section of Hinky Dinky in the other. She wore a beaded African necklace.

"Lucinda!" she said. "You made it."

"I thought this was an all-girl thing," I said. "An all-women thing."

Sue looked startled for a moment.

"Oh that was the original plan but these guys wanted to come," she said. "What can you do? Come in here, I want you to meet Christine."

Someone in the corner wore an Angela Davis-style dashiki and huge earrings. It was Valdette, sitting mesmerized on the couch next to a woman who looked like Vanessa Williams. Presumably, this was Christine. She wore a sleeveless, white cashmere sweater that showed off slim, hairless arms. Her long, straightened hair was pulled back in a headband and she wore tiny pearl earrings.

"Christine!" Sue said, dragging me over by the elbow. "This is Lucinda Trout. She moved here last year from New York."

Valdette appeared slightly peeved at the interruption. Christine extended a perfectly manicured hand.

"I hear you're new in town," I said.

"Yes," she said.

"Where did you move here from?" I asked.

"Des Moines," she said.

"Great town," said Valdette.

"How do you like P.C.?" I asked.

"It's nice," Christine said.

"Well, you're lucky you ran into Sue," I said. "She's the reason I ended up here. It's all her fault!"

"Yeah, she's really nice," Christine said.

"It must be difficult being a woman of color in P.C.," Valdette said.

"I haven't found that," said Christine.

"Really!" said Valdette. "How can that be? We're so white bread. A sea of Wonder bread. Pillsbury Doughboys."

Valdette was making swimminglike movements with her arms as she spoke, the sleeves of her dashiki becoming entangled with her wooden bangles. She lit a cigarette.

"Last Christmas I said to Joel, 'You're Jewish, I'm a lapsed Lutheran. Why don't we just call it even and celebrate Kwanza?'" Valdette said. "But he said, 'Screw that. I want a tree!' I said, 'You can get a tree as long as I ain't the one putting it up and taking it down.' That's why I like menorahs. Much easier to assemble."

"I hear ya," Sue said. "Lucinda, you might be interested in talking to Christine about some of the women in the clinic and their struggles with methamphetamine. She's an absolutely brilliant case-worker."

"Oh really?" I said. "Have you been getting a lot of meth cases?"

"Usually they're multiple substance abusers," she said.

"Do you find there's more meth here than in other places?" I asked.

"Not really."

"Because I lived for ten years in New York," I said. "And no one did meth."

Over the last year, I had upgraded myself from an eight-year resident of New York to a ten-year resident, having decided to factor in my summer internships during college.

Christine said nothing.

"Yeah, it's weird," I continued. "Just wild how common it is here."

"It's pretty common everywhere."

"Crazy," I said. "Wild."

I waited for Christine to say something, but again she just sat there, smiling affably with her mouth closed, cherry-red gloss cov-

ering her lips, the kd lang music filling the silence of the immediate
area. She was extremely attractive, but in an overly well-kept, almost droidlike way. She exuded an aura that hovered somewhere between Vanessa Williams and National Security Advisor Condoleezza
Rice. The white cashmere and the lip gloss gave her a Love's Baby
Soft quality. I found it hard to believe she was a drug counselor. Most
drug counselors were worn-down social work types, ex-addicts with
savior complexes, people with need-to-be-needed syndrome. Christine didn't appear to need anything, except, from what I could see,
a personality. Surely this job was a stepping-stone to a political office or cabinet position, which, if she hung out with this crowd long
enough, she'd obtain within six months.

Joel appeared with a plate of crab cakes.

"For you, madam," he said to Christine.

"Thanks," Christine said.

"Can I get you another drink?" he asked. My glass was nearly
empty, though he didn't look in my direction.

"I'm fine for now," she said.

Her Coach purse was lying next to her on the couch. She appeared not to have moved since the party started. Though the
women were actually waiting in line to talk to her, the men were
standing in huddles and sneaking glances from across the room. It
was a pity this wasn't a pool party.

In the dining room, Teri was holding court with a group of
concerned-looking women, gesticulating wildly, and saying something about soy products. Leonard stood on the periphery of the circle smoking a cigarette. Guests at Sue's house were supposed to go
outside to smoke but Leonard obviously had family privileges. He
tapped the ashes into an empty beer bottle and stood there serenely
while Teri nattered on.

"How much more evidence do we need?" I heard her say. "Milk
is snake venom. Bovine growth hormone. Recombinant somatotro-
pin. These girls hit puberty at age nine. Then we have unwanted

pregnancies up the wazoo. We have incest. We have gang rapes. And Monsanto's got the feds in its back pocket."

"So how's life on the farm?" Leonard finally said to me.

"Great!"

"It's supposed to be a bad winter," he said.

"Well, I've got the Sunbird," I said. "Built Chevy tough, you know."

"Isn't it a Pontiac?"

"That's what I mean, then," I said. "How are the kids?"

"They're in the car," he said.

"Good move."

"I'm not kidding," he said. "Josephine's out of town so I have them this weekend. And I told Danielle that if I couldn't trust her to watch her brother without sneaking out they'd both have to come with me."

"And they're in the car!"

"They're doing their homework. It's an SUV. There's room."

"Does Sue know that?" I asked. "I'm sure they could have come in and done their homework upstairs."

"Danielle would have just stolen the booze," he said.

"Well, it sounds like you're on top of the situation."

The kd lang had been turned off. *West Side Story* was on. The Peter Fonda county commissioner was singing "Maria." Christine was still sitting on the couch, squeezed between Sue and Valdette. It would take me forty-five minutes to get home, not that I was that eager. Mason had all the kids that night. They were planning to watch *Terminator 2* after Erin went to bed.

I said good-bye to Sue, who seemed disappointed that I was leaving so early.

"Is everything okay?" she asked.

"Everything's great," I said. "I just have a long drive."

"You can spend the night here, you know," she said.

"That's okay."

"How's everything going on the farm?" she asked. "Why didn't you bring Mason tonight?"

"Because I thought it was a girls' party," I said. "I mean, a women's party."

Why was it that I could never bring myself to call Sue's bluff in these kinds of situations? It was obvious that the reason she had told me the party was women-only was that she didn't want me to bring Mason. So why didn't I have the spine to confront her with it? If the situation had been reversed—though, barring my hosting of an "all meat-eaters party," I couldn't fathom a situation where I could discreetly exclude Teri—Sue would have been the first to take me aside and discuss the issue in a way that was straightforward and self-respectful without being petty. She would have said, *Lucinda, I'm sensing a little awkwardness here and I'd like to clear it up.* But then again she was the bionic woman, not a mere Lifestyle correspondent.

"I'm sorry about the confusion," Sue said. "I should have called you and told you that men were invited."

"Mason has the kids tonight anyway," I said.

"Good for him," Sue said. There was no trace of sarcasm in her tone and this somehow annoyed me, which in turn made me feel guilty for being annoyed.

Outside, where the SUVs lined the gravel driveway like cars in a cemetery, the air felt cooler than it had for weeks. I could hear the singing through the window screens, the frequent spasms of laughter, the buzz of the outdoor floodlight. As I walked to the Sunbird I passed an unfamiliar pickup truck at the end of the row of cars. There were sounds coming from it, a radio playing an old Dire Straits song, a creaking of seats. I turned toward it and saw Danielle, in nothing but a pink bra, engaged in heavy petting with an older-looking guy in the front seat. I could see his baseball cap and beaded choker, his hand sliding under the strap on her shoulder. Danielle's hair covered most of her face and as I passed by she saw me, lurched up, and caught my eye for a split second before I pretended not to see them. Her eyes were ringed with mascara. The boy looked like he could have been in college, though more likely he was a fifth- or sixth-year senior at Prairie City High. In the floodlight, Danielle's profile looked like those silhouette portraits they take of children at Sears, small nose, long eyelashes, lips red even after the lipstick had smeared off. Her breasts, tawny and sweaty and pinched by underwire, swelled out of proportion over her rib cage. The bra probably cost more than her shirt and shorts combined. Was she twelve now? Thirteen? How long had it been since I'd seen her that evening in Leonard's kitchen?

I looked for Leonard's SUV, virtually indistinguishable among the others. When I found it, the silver Grand Cherokee with a worn bumper sticker saying MY KID IS A SOCCER STAR AT MILTON ELEMENTARY I looked through the open window at Kyle, who was reading a comic book with a penlight.

"Whatcha reading?" I said.

"Batman," he said.

"I heard you were doing your homework."

"I finished it."

"That's good," I said. "You're not missing much in there."

"No kidding."

"Well, good night," I said. "Hope your battery holds up. Your dad says hi."

In the interests of public relations, I told everyone, especially the staff of *Up Early*, that the farm was paradise. This was partly because my one-year series on the quality of life was almost halfway up and I felt I needed an extension and partly because, in a way, the farm *was* paradise. I'd yanked the blankets off the windows immediately and peeled off the hideous kitchen wallpaper and painted the walls Lake Champlain, a dazzling shade of aqua blue. I'd put the cotton window panels in the windows and had a phone jack installed in my office. Susannah came by to drop off Sebastian and brought tomato plants she'd started in her garden.

"Don't let Mason tell you he can't cook," she said. "He's actually a great cook. He makes good meat loaf."

Susannah, somewhat unlike Jill and completely unlike Julie, who I didn't think knew my name, was unwaveringly friendly. She'd given me a Christmas present even before I'd moved in with Mason, a painted ceramic coffee mug she'd made herself. She frequently passed along books by regional writers that she thought would help me with my "Quality of Life" reports, although Faye, when I'd mentioned them, told me she "didn't need to hear any more 'hawk, you are my sister' crap." Susannah also told me to make sure Mason didn't let the farm get out of hand.

"He'll load the place up with animals and soon you'll have a petting zoo," she said. "Ever tried running a classified ad for five goats? I thought selling my 76 Buick was hard."

But suddenly, Mason was energized. It was as if a lightning bolt had hit the barn and pierced his psyche. He reshingled the roof and painted the outside of the house and the barn. He started a flower garden of daylilies and petunias. He'd made flyers advertising the horse-boarding operation and plastered them on bulletin boards in the farm co-op and the horse supply outlet, as well as The Grinder and Hinky Dinky. He believed the enterprise should have a name and wanted to call it Crazyhorse Stables or Harvest Moon. When I talked him out of both of those he said he thought Mason and Lucinda Stables sounded nice. I said that sounded like a designer shoe boutique on Columbus Avenue.

"Huh?" he said.

We were drinking margaritas in the stock tank. It was a hundred-gallon aluminum horse trough, rusted on the outside and just big enough for the two of us to sit in if we didn't move around much. Mason had found it among the discarded farm implements in the pasture, hauled it into the yard, and filled it with water. "We have a pool!" he'd said. We could only get in if we slid in at the same time and entwined our bodies around each other's waists like twins in a cold womb.

"Everything should have a name," Mason said. "Boats have names. Ranches have names."

"You're saying we should name the farm?" I asked. I looked at the buckling foundation under the mudroom. I looked at the chimney on the roof and saw that the bricks were coming loose.

"We should call it South Fork," he said. "But I guess we'd have to put in some chandeliers."

"We need an insurance policy if we're going to board horses," I said.

"Aw, don't worry about that right now."

"If one of them gets loose and damages something, we're up shit's creek," I said. "I didn't move here to get sued."

"Bootsy," Mason said, "this isn't New York. Don't make such a big deal out of everything."

"Then we'll just call it Shit's Creek Stables," I said.

He reached over the side of the tank to pick his drink up off the ground, sloshing water onto the grass.

"Shit's Creek Stables sounds kind of nice, actually," he said. He looked at his watch. "Uh oh, *Antiques Roadshow*'s on in five minutes."

Cupid, the lone, old horse already in the pasture, watched us as we climbed, naked, from the stock tank and darted into the house. Cars rarely drove down the road and Mason saw fit to walk around naked much of the time, even to feed Cupid or fill his tank, though he often wore a cowboy hat for such tasks. From the kitchen window I'd watch his bare buttocks as he walked—always in his flip-flops—from the barn to the pasture and back again. He'd feed Cupid an apple and talk to him as though he were a person.

"Do animals know when you're naked?" I asked, knowing it was an idiotic question.

"They know when you're high," Mason said. "But not when you're naked."

*   *   *

Up Early had liked the idea of my living on the farm—"it's like *Under the Tuscan Sun* without the language barrier," Samantha had said—but they wanted me to give the impression that I actually lived there alone. Promoting unmarried cohabitation would result in letters from right-winger zealots. Besides, the idea of me alone on the prairie, "pumping your own water" as Faye had written in an e-mail (although she had typed "pimping") and "maybe milking a cow," was more enticing to the average *Up Early* viewer, who, according to market research, was a single woman between twenty-two and forty-five with a bachelor's degree and a nine-to-five office job. The average viewer watched the show between the hours of 7:00 and 8:00 A.M. and listed marriage, career advancement, and weight loss as her top three goals. Living with a man would alienate this viewer, the show executives said. Faye had even suggested I go on a blind date in Prairie City to show what the dating pool was like in the Midwest.

"Because we all know you can't really date bad boys," she'd said. "And that guy bathing in the river was, you know, extreme."

"Faye, I'm living with Mason," I said. "I can't go on dates."

"Don't be unprofessional," she said. I heard a toilet flush. She was calling from her apartment and had taken the phone into the bathroom.

"Did you just go to the bathroom while talking to me?"

"It's called multitasking," Faye said. "Am I hearing cartoons in the background?"

"Mason's daughter is here," I said.

"God, how awful. Hold on, I have another call," she said. Then she hung up.

Erin, in a Pokémon haze, watched videos in Mason's and my bedroom on the three nights a week that she stayed with us. She was a cute kid in the typical sense, though not a terribly interesting one (at least compared to my notions of children, which came mostly from novels where precocious toddlers said things like "Mommy, does the moon have dreams?"). For all of Julie's apparent intellectual indifference to her daughter, she didn't skimp on the toys. Dolls and plastic toy telephones and tiny acrylic Barbie dresses seemed to dribble from the girl's hands onto the floor like mud sloughing off boots. It wasn't so much the mess I couldn't stand—Mason ordered her to throw everything in a bucket before going to bed—but the way the toys seemed physically connected to her body. Like her favorite plaything of all time, a repugnant, troll-like doll called Diva Starz Nikki, Erin was in perpetual need of some accessory—a handbag, a hairbrush, an AA battery. At any given moment, a piece of something seemed to have just broken off in her hand, fallen between the sofa cushions, permanently snapped out of joint. Such calamities always sent her running to Mason and since he was usually in the barn or the field or someplace she couldn't access without putting on her shoes (a task she couldn't yet perform solo) Erin would then proceed directly to my office.

The poor girl. Had she been just a few years older she might have caught on to the fact that when it came to fixing a toy there was probably no worse place to seek help than my office, particularly when that toy was the Diva Starz Nikki doll. Even in my limited knowledge of children's playthings, I couldn't imagine that any object had ever come closer to inducing psychosis than Diva Starz Nikki. Frightening enough when naked, the snap-on dresses activated a computerized voice that said, in a kind of valley speak, things like *Silly willy I look like a noodlehead* and *Today's word is "glamoricious"* (other days the word was "bodalicious," a term I was powerless to explain to Erin). On Nikki's shoes were buttons saying "yes" and "no" designed to let children converse with her. Erin pounded the buttons relentlessly, often so hard that the dress would get knocked slightly askew and then stuck and she would be forced to seek assistance.

"Lucindaaaa!" she'd cry, sliding off the bed and running toward my office. "Diva Starz Nikki stopped talking again."

I'd offered to let her type words on the computer in my office. I'd offered to buy her certain children's books I remembered from my own youth—*Where the Wild Things Are, Sylvester and the Magic Pebble.* She wanted none of it. Only Diva Starz Nikki and Barbie and the Little Mermaid and their attendant books, videos, and clothing accessories.

"You can't pound the buttons so hard," I'd always say. And then, because even after nearly a year in Prairie City I was still not the kind of woman Lyle Lovett would have written a song about, I'd take the doll, pretend to examine it, and while Erin wasn't looking, put the positive ends of the batteries together so the thing didn't work.

"The batteries are dead," I'd say. "We'll get new ones tomorrow."

In the meantime, I needed to do another meditative sort of segment that would introduce the farm. One Saturday afternoon, while Erin was watching *The Little Mermaid* downstairs and I was slightly hung over from the previous night's margaritas, I began to type.

> *As I sit on my porch swing, drinking lemonade and watching the cows moseying in the pasture across the road, I realize that my petty concerns are upstaged by the subtly dramatic scenery of the high plains. With miles of rolling hills to the north, the seven acres of horse pasture to the east, the five acres of natural grassland to the west, and the—*

I was only that far when Erin abruptly aborted her *Little Mermaid* watching and raced upstairs to the bathroom. "Dad!" she shouted. "Dad! Dad!"

> *indescribably huge, frequently biblical-looking sky that looms above it, the house is a vessel of tranquillity . . .*

"Dad!"
"He's outside, Erin!" I shouted, almost like a mother. Except a

mother might have risen from her chair. Though not necessarily Erin's mother.

"I think the children's Ex-Lax is working," she called from the bathroom. There was no hint of joke or irony in her voice. In fact, she brought to the statement the same intonation she might bring to *I have eighteen different Beanie Babies.*

Unlike her alter ego, Diva Starz Nikki, Erin had a problem with constipation. Tucked inside her Pocahontas knapsack were always squares of chocolate-flavored children's Ex-Lax wrapped in foil along with notes from Julie saying things like "Take one in late afternoon" and "Make sure she poops before you bring her home." Surely this malady was the result of being shuffled between two houses, plus the fact that Mason fed her Little Debbie's and microwavable dinners with fried chicken cutlets shaped like circus animals. Mason felt it was his prerogative as a father to feed his kids junk food, as if Oreos and root beer would endear him to them, as if his very presence connoted a holiday.

"I said, 'I think it's working!'" she called again.

I was also working. I was doing very important work. But because Mason was far out in the pasture mending a fence (did all the folks back in New York hear that? I thought, *mending a fence!*) I got up from my desk and went into the bathroom, the floor of which was covered in shit, as were Erin's buttocks and the backs of her legs.

I expected her to be crying—I would have been—but she was matter-of-fact about the situation.

"Do you want me to get your dad?" I asked.

"No. I want you to clean me up," she said. She had brought Diva Starz Nikki in with her. *Today's word is "glamoricious,"* the doll said.

"Get my clean clothes from my knapsack," Erin directed.

I got her underwear, which was decorated with tiny strawberries, and a pair of pants. When I went back in the bathroom I accidentally dropped the clean clothes on the soiled floor.

"Don't put them where the poo is!" Erin screamed.

I was gagging. I was also still thinking about my script. I felt so

terrible for Erin that I could not look her in the eye. When I was
four an incident like this would have humiliated me. I would have
wanted to go home to my mother immediately. But Julie had gone
to Kansas City for the weekend to attend a Madonna concert.

I accomplished the task. I cleaned Erin up. Later, when Mason
came in from mending the fence, I told him what had transpired.

"Way to go, bootsy," he said.

I'd expected a gush of praise. I'd expected effusive, guilt-ridden
declarations of his love for me, a teary recognition of the unde-
served good fortune he had to meet a woman such as me, a young
chippy who didn't want kids herself but was willing to interrupt her
very important work to wipe shit off someone else's kid. I expected
him to take a trip out to the Hinky Dinky and buy me a bunch of
carnations for $5.99.

But he didn't. Instead he sat down on the love seat in my office
and said, "I've decided to sell the cabin."

"What?" I said.

"I need the money," Mason said.

"Isn't that a little rash?"

"You don't like it out there anyway," he said.

"That's not true!" I said. It was true. I had enjoyed the cabin for
maybe the first two times. Then the bugs began bothering me. And
other than the *Sweet Baby James* tape he had no music out there
other than Neil Young.

"I don't like it as much as I used to," Mason said. "I can sell it
for ten thousand dollars."

"That's it?" I asked, even though I was actually surprised it was
worth that much.

Presumably, he needed the money to pay his share of the rent,
which he was not currently paying. Despite the flyers we'd plastered
all over town, no one had called about boarding a horse. Mason was
getting calls from creditors. Jill was demanding money for a private
tutor for Peter; Julie wanted ice skating lessons for Erin. For the two
months that we'd been on the farm, I had bought all the groceries,

paid all the utility bills, and lent Mason the Sunbird whenever his truck broke down, which was about every other week.

I'd also encouraged Mason to invite Frank Fussell over for dinner, partly to ingratiate ourselves to him so that he might consider giving Mason a raise. Mason said he had done so, though it wasn't until that moment, when I looked out the window and saw Frank's pickup coming up the driveway, that he told me when to expect him.

"Who is that?" I asked.

"What?"

"Someone's here."

"Oh shit," Mason said.

Though he worked in a dusty grain mill, Frank washed his truck at least every other day. Other than the debris it had collected en route to the farm, it was gleaming and spotless. Some kind of new age atmospheric music was blasting from the stereo. I watched as Frank actually put on his turn signal to pull around to the side of the house.

"Is today Saturday?" Mason asked.

"Is he here for dinner?"

"Is it Saturday?" he asked again.

"Well, you're not at work and you worked yesterday, so I would assume so," I said.

"Man," he said, running down the stairs. "Guess I lost track of time."

Frank, in yoga pants and a Little Feat T-shirt, was standing in the driveway doing a sun salute. When we came outside he hugged us. He smelled like patchouli oil.

"I come bearing carrots," he said, presenting a bunch of leafy carrots he must have grown in his garden. He handed them to me along with a bottle in a paper bag.

"Prune juice," he added. "The stuff is awesome."

"You kind of caught us off guard," Mason said.

"No you didn't!" I interrupted. "We're just running a little behind. We can get you a drink."

"We've got a specimen cup if you'd like some of your own urine," Mason said.

"I'm only drinking prune juice these days," Frank said. "I'd like to rinse off my truck if you don't mind. These gravel roads are a killer."

Mason showed Frank where the hose was and came into the kitchen as Frank sprayed his truck several times and then, astonishingly, dried it off with a rag. I opened all the cupboards and couldn't see anything that could be turned into a meal for a guest. I opened a bottle of wine and poured myself a glass.

"We don't have anything to eat!" I said. "How could you have forgotten to tell me?"

"Relax, boots," Mason said.

"I'm gonna have to go get a pizza or something."

Mason surveyed the cupboards, pulled a package of frozen hamburger out of the freezer and put it in the microwave to defrost.

"We don't have any hamburger buns," I said.

"I can make meat loaf," he said.

I hated meat loaf. This was the reason we had never had it, though Mason claimed to love it and be an expert in its preparation. I got out the Italian swirl-style ceramic bowl and dumped a bag of chips in it. I got the place mats and napkins out of a drawer, saw that they were filthy, and threw them in the washing machine.

"This is not the way I like to entertain," I said.

"This is not New York," Mason said. "Besides, it's Frank. We could serve him dirt and tell him it's organic and he'd be happy."

Erin padded downstairs, clutching Diva Starz Nikki, and announced that her movie was over.

"Go outside with Lucinda and talk to Frank," Mason told her. He was almost manic. He'd laid out every spice container in the cupboards and was mulling them over as if they were watercolors.

"Do we have any bread crumbs?" Mason asked.

"We have stale bread," I said.

Outside, Frank was picking rocks out of the yard, holding in-

nocuous little stones in front of his face, and inspecting them as
though he were a jeweler. He'd made a pile of rocks next to his truck
and when Erin scuffed through them with her pink sandals he
gasped.

"I had a project going there!" he said.

"It's just dumb rocks," Erin said.

"That is a very limited viewpoint," said Frank. "Every rock is a
bone fragment of the earth. Within them lies the marrow of life's
essence."

"We have Doritos inside," I said.

"I can't support corporate globalization," he said.

"Is this a bone?" Erin asked, handing Frank a rock.

"It is a sacred shard from the femur of Gaia," Frank told the
four-year-old.

Erin leaned against Frank's truck, causing Frank to grab the
dust rag out of the bed and wipe the spot she had touched. Then he
spit on his hand and wiped the dust left by the rag.

"Do you need any help in the kitchen?" Frank asked.

"I think Mason wants to be a solo act," I said.

"Good," he said. "Because I'm going to take this opportunity to
practice some tai chi. I'm getting a very intense vibe from this place."

I took Erin back in the house. Mason had actually broken apart
the stale bread into crumbs and was drying it out in the oven.
Somehow, in the wasteland of the refrigerator and cupboards, he
had managed to find Parmesan cheese, eggs, an onion, and even
some frozen bacon. He was mincing Frank's carrots like a veritable
television chef. I noticed that he'd picked some daylilies from the
side of the house and had put them in a vase on the table.

"I put the place mats in the dryer," he said. "I'm making soup
and a sandwich for Erin."

"Can I have some of this juice?" Erin asked, eyeing Frank's
prune juice.

"Absolutely not," I said.

*   *   *

Mason's meat loaf was tremendous. In about ten minutes, he'd managed to whip up something so edible, so not only edible but actually tasty, that I found myself hoping we could have meat loaf at least once a week. This was the charm in Mason, his ability to occasionally make his chronic lack of effort look like a magical effortlessness. He had a way of bringing a complete unselfconsciousness to tasks that I would have fretted over for days. If I had known Frank was coming over for dinner, I would have begun preparing for it a week earlier. As it was, Mason had taken less than an hour to make a meal, a flower arrangement, and fold the napkins into what he claimed was the shape of sandhill cranes. He popped open another bottle of wine and filled my glass.

"It may look like chardonnay, but it's actually Frank's piss," Mason said. "And a fine vintage at that."

"Have you been out to the cabin lately?" Frank asked.

"Not much use for it these days," Mason said. "I reckon I'm gonna sell it."

It amazed me how I now barely noticed Mason's hickish locutions. The "reckon"s and the sentences ending in "at." He stopped short at constructions like "don't got any" and had even corrected Erin when she'd said "I don't got any more ketchup for my fries." But still, his Texan-like drawl belied his midwestern upbringing. Frank, for his part, sounded like some new age life coach on cable television. Or maybe local access cable television.

"It sounds like you're in the midst of a life passage," said Frank. "You must respect your instincts."

"Actually I just need the cash," Mason said.

"How much would you want for it?" Frank asked.

"I reckon whatever I can get."

"I'll buy it," Frank said. "I've been thinking I need a country retreat."

I caught myself snorting. A country retreat. For Ted Kaczynski maybe.

"I've been thinking I'd like to hold some meditation workshops out by the river," Frank said. "You know George Andersen, that farmer who brings his soybeans to the elevator? His wife has expressed a real interest in studying transcendental meditation with me. These rural women get so isolated."

And there's nothing like a dilapidated cabin miles from any telephone lines to foster a sense of empowerment in a farm wife, I thought. Mason was gazing out the window and nodding his head. Frank was cutting his meat loaf into small pieces, arranging them in a circle on his plate, and eating them counterclockwise. He examined each forkful the way he'd examined the rocks outside.

"How does ten grand sound?" Mason asked.

Frank bought Mason's cabin. This gesture was, I supposed, in lieu of giving him a raise. Mason loaded his truck up with the giant paintings and the skulls and the photographs and drove it to the farm and put it all in the tack room. Except for the absence of the woodstove and the loft bed, the tack room looked just like the inside of the cabin had. He told me he'd stood in front of his cabin and cried before he drove away for the last time.

He gave me five hundred dollars. He made a few trips to the grocery store. He paid for a couple of dinners at Rib Ranch. He said he was going to pay off all his credit cards as well as get a vasectomy, which was not covered by his insurance. As the summer ebbed away we drank more margaritas in the stock tank. Erin, who had finally been won over by a children's book about a divaish little pig, began demanding bedtime stories from me every night she stayed over.

I had, during this time, a sense that when it came to living the kind of life that most people lived, I was as close as I was ever going to get. After all, the basic trappings were there—house, car, child, regular dinners eaten at home while seated. It was as if my previous life were a rare, poorly understood disease that had gone into remission. I felt I needed to make the most of things, explore every corner of this odd normalcy before I was yanked, like a weed in a manicured lawn, back into the mess from which I'd come. Of course, I now know my sense of things was already misguided. Though I was still running through the pastures yapping on my cell phone to Elena about how spiritually cleansed I was, the truth was that I was spreading a disease far worse than the one I'd whined about in my old life. It would be months before I would bring myself to admit (because admitting it would constitute not only personal failure but also professional failure, which despite all the bedtime stories and Stovetop stuffing preparation was still my primary concern) what was happening was that my problems weren't going away so much as they were changing. They were becoming more serious. My previous problems, which had mostly been problems of style (rumpled clothes, Chinese baby hypotheses) were rapidly converting to problems of substance. Actual Problems. And I was about as equipped to deal with actual problems as Faye would have been equipped to compete in a spelling bee.

Still, I'd received permission to extend the "Quality of Life Report" series through another year. Though Faye had canceled the meditative introduction-to-the-farm idea—"That's a snore, we've had enough with the coffee," she'd said—we were now proceeding with what was sure to be the most exciting segment yet: How to Throw a Barn Dance for Under $300.

> To: Lucinda Trout
> From: Faye Figaro
> Re: Barn Dance
>
> As part of Party Week series for early September we wood like you to throw a bran dance on your farm to show how this can be an ecomonical and fun way to entertane outdoors. Sense the other segments will featur a rootftop party on the Upper East side, a reception in the sculpture garden at the Museum of

Modurn Art and a loft part in the Tribeca Home of twenty-something internment diarist Haley Bopp, we thought it would make nice contrast to show a folksy event on your farm. Maybe you could corporate square dancing and roast a pig or somethng.

A stylist will be callling you to discuss what the guests should wear. Also please no fat people!

"How fun!" Valdette Svoboda-Lipinsky said. When Joel had told her about the barn dance shoot she immediately called to find out how she could help.

"We're all going to be famous!" she said.

"Only in New York," I said. I could hear her smoking on the other end of the phone. I imagined her telephone earrings dangling against the receiver. "And I'm embarrassed to say this, but there's kind of a dress code."

"Oh!"

"You're going to need to wear, like, certain kinds of clothes," I said.

"Like costumes?" Valdette said. "I've got a Cat Woman outfit."

"Like, uh, overalls," I said. "Or, uh, leather vests. Cowboy boots."

The stylist had sent me a fax listing the clothing options for the barn dance guests. It said:

1. a few people in overalls (but not too many), preferably with white shirts underneath but not plaid shirts underneath
2. plaid flannel shirts (again not too many), no mixing of plaid and overalls
3. boot-cut jeans
4. cowboy boots on men (maybe on one woman but not more than that)
5. suede—for example: long suede bias cut skirt ($248 at Ba-

nana Republic), suede vests ($190 at J. Crew) and suede
jodhpurs ($390 from J. Peterman) or just about anything
leather (soft leather though, brown not black)
6. no visible tattoos, piercings on men, strange hair colors
7. no black (too New York), no green, no polka dots, stripes, or
   animal prints
8. no smoking on camera

"I have the perfect thing to wear," Valdette said. "It's adorable.
It's like a poodle skirt from the fifties except instead of a poodle it
has a cow. And the cow's tail actually wraps around like a belt and
it has a little bell on it. It would be *so* in keeping with your theme."

"Hmm," I said. "Do you have anything suede?"

"I don't do suede," she said, exhaling abruptly on her cigarette.
"You know I'm an animal person."

Mason had reservations about the event, mostly because he couldn't
quite think of anyone to invite. He invited some of the people from
Effie's Tavern, though I was concerned about the tattoo element.
Frank would come and maybe Susannah and her husband and Sebastian but other than that we were reliant on the Sue contingent.

"I don't see why we have to do this," Mason said to me one
evening as I was making dinner—chicken breasts marinated in gin-
ger and lime juice, served over angel hair pasta in the painted ceramic bowl from Pier One—and drinking our requisite bottle of
$5.99 Fetzer.

"Because it will pay a month's rent," I said. "And the electric
bill. Consider your participation a way of paying your share."

Even after selling the cabin, Mason still hadn't paid me anything more than the initial five hundred dollars. Though he said he
was paying his credit card bills, the collection calls were still coming. He'd made an appointment with a urologist about the vasectomy but said he'd had to cancel it at the last minute because Jill
demanded his presence at a science fair at Peter's school.

In the middle of dinner, however, we got good news. We had a new horse boarder. "A stud!" Mason announced when he got off the phone with the owner, who, for some reason, had to bring over the horse right that very minute.

"A stallion," Mason said again. He was almost salivating. "He'll have to be kept separate from the other one. That means we can charge more."

"How much?" I asked. Possibly the amount of Mason's entire portion of the rent?

"We didn't go into that," he said.

"You didn't go into it!"

"I didn't want to scare him off," Mason said. He went to the refrigerator for another beer. "We need to generate business."

The horse was white and caked with mud and had a knotty, matted mane and odd pink circles around his eyes. His hooves were so badly in need of trimming that they had the effect of platform shoes, raising him at least an additional four inches off the ground. Slabs of muscle bulged from his legs. His neck rose from his body like a construction crane. He stood in the driveway, rearing and making that sound horses make—a whinny, I supposed, though that seemed an inadequate description for something that sounded like an eighteen-wheel truck skidding across a road.

I turned my head for what couldn't have been longer than a few seconds and when I looked at the horse again he had a new appendage, a beastly trunklike organ, pink with large black spots. It swung out from under him in a pendulumlike motion.

"Oh my God," I said.

"I think he likes you," Mason said.

The horse's name, evidently, was Lucky.

"Hope this doesn't change your feelings about me, bootsy," Mason said, winking.

Lucky tried to charge Cupid, who was running in circles in the pasture and crashing into the barbed-wire fence. He tried to charge the cottonwood tree, then the Sunbird. It took both Mason and the owner to get him in the barn. The horse would have a stall and a small corral, barely enough room to take five steps.

"He's paying us a hundred dollars a month," Mason said after the owner had left.

"That's it?"

"Hey, be glad," he said. "It'll add to your barn dance story to have a horse actually in the barn."

"That's true," I said. "But is he mean?"

"*Mean?* He's not mean; he's aggressive," Mason said. He got out the broom and began sweeping the kitchen floor. "Hell, I'm gonna ride him if that guy brings out a saddle. Or even if he doesn't bring one."

When he finished sweeping the floor, Mason pulled the toaster and the coffeemaker and the blender away from the wall and began scrubbing the counter.

"I already did that, you know," I said.

"You gotta stay on top of it," Mason said. "Especially given how you are about mice." We'd had one mouse. It scampered across my feet one afternoon in the summer as we were arguing about whether or not Mason would be able to make conversation if we went to a pool party at Sue's. I'd screamed and run outside. I'd nearly hyper-ventilated. The mouse never came back but Mason blamed its appearance on my shoddy housekeeping. We'd ended up going to Sue's and Mason spent the whole time floating in the pool without speaking to anyone. A few days later I received a note in the mail from Sue. On a piece of clinic stationery, with the slogan EMBRACE, EMPATHIZE, EMPOWER running across the top, she had written

Dear Lucinda,

I hope things are going well on the farm. Please know that you always have friends.

Peace, Sue.

"Not so long ago I thought you couldn't possibly throw a party—much less a dance—without spending a fortune on cocktails and caterers, not to mention renting a party space. But here I am on my farm in the Midwest putting the final touches on what promises to be *the* event of the fall season. I'm hosting a barn dance. And believe it or not, I've done it for under three hundred dollars!"

The evening of the barn dance, I stood before the camera and delivered my intro in a long suede skirt, a suede jacket, and a pair of too-large cowboy boots I'd borrowed from Susannah, who couldn't come because she'd had to give a lecture on "Greenhouse Effect Prophecies in the Work of Ralph Waldo Emerson." The skirt, which was not from Banana Republic but from some exclusive designer the stylist had chided me for not knowing about, had been FedExed by an *Up Early* stylist with explicit orders not to get it dirty or wet. But Faye had instructed me to give at least part of the report standing next to the horse and, ten seconds into the shoot, the nine-hundred-dollar skirt was splattered with mud. Standing next to Lucky had required getting into the corral, where he'd stomped his feet and licked the camera lens and, with the tape rolling, presented all eighteen inches of his male organ and swung it in and out of the frame. Jeb, who had experience filming livestock but couldn't tolerate the lens licking, moved us to the barn. It was looking almost cathedrallike. I'd decorated the rafters with old-fashioned outdoor Christmas lights I'd ordered from the Restoration Hardware catalog for seventy-five dollars. I'd spent another hundred dollars on a keg of beer. Valdette, in her commitment to accurate media portrayals of the Midwest and her role as wife of the KPCR station manager (who received a tiny end credit on *Up Early* every time a "Quality of Life Report" segment aired), had generously offered to provide the food. The back of her Volvo station wagon was packed tight with Tupperware trays. She'd also brought two bottles of vodka and several lawn chairs.

"So here's the menu," Valdette said. She'd worn the cow skirt,

though the tail had come loose from the belt and was dragging behind her. "Bratwurst, because that's traditional to the area. Regular
hot dogs for people who don't like bratwurst. Cold cuts and sand-
wiches. Deviled eggs. Jell-O and Rice Krispies treats for dessert.
And just to show that the Midwest isn't all white bread Christians,
matzoh balls!"

"Oh my goodness," I said.

"Joel makes fun of me but I *love* them," Valdette said conspira-
torially. She took a loaf of white bread out of a Hinky Dinky grocery
bag. "I'd love those people in New York to see us on TV square
dancing and eating matzoh balls."

Frank Fussell's truck pulled into the driveway. He was blasting
sitar music from the tape deck and when he climbed out I saw that
he was wearing yoga pants and a T-shirt that said MY KARMA RAN
OVER YOUR DOGMA. Clichés had a way of coming late to Prairie City.
It was possible that "Where's the beef?" had not taken hold until
the mid-1990s; "Don't go there," for its part, had recently become
a favorite mantra of Sue's and she used it on every possible occasion, including when her dogs wandered into the road. Frank stood
in front of his truck and stretched his arms to make sure everyone
could read his shirt. Then he walked over to Lucky and began whispering in the horse's ear.

Respectful of the call time—we needed to start shooting before
sundown—everyone showed up at once. Sue and Teri arrived wearing western-style shirts. The Peter Fonda county commissioner and
his wife wore Birkenstocks and Prairie City State College Women's
Softball sweatshirts. Leonard showed up in a T-shirt that said I DIG
BACKYARD FARMER ON PRAIRIE CITY PUBLIC TELEVISION.

In a caravan of SUVs and the occasional Volvo or Subaru station wagon, it seemed all of Prairie City was coming up the driveway at once, parking on the grass, and gawking at one another as
though they recognized the person from some earlier incarnation—
such as seventh grade—and couldn't believe how fat or mangy or
just generally old the other had become. Mason had handed out

party invitations at Effie's Tavern and a good portion of the Friday afternoon regulars were now milling around the farm, at least a third in violation of the "no visible tattoos" directive. Though he'd been drinking Leinenkugels at Effie's Friday afternoon happy hour for almost half his life, Mason was vague on many of their names and he greeted them with generic slaps on the back and, in the case of one biker-looking guy with a long, gray beard and bags under his eyes, a sort of mock stomach punch. Mason had gone to school with this guy, he explained to me.

By "school," Mason meant the semester he'd spent smoking pot in the makeshift art studios of Prairie City State College. Since then, more then twenty years had passed. And as the crowd separated into clusters—Frank Fussell and a few would-be disciples by the horse corral, the Effie's people in the tack room, Sue's gang in the house, where the women laid Triscuits out on plates and Joel managed to find my *Buena Vista Social Club* CD and was now adjusting the volume on "Chan Chan"—I had the startling realization that late adolescence, like the smell of wood smoke in Mason's clothes, would never leave them. This was an intentional condition. And it came not from a lack of maturity or ambition but a lack of need. Though their bodies might have pulled ahead into middle age—and it shocked me that anyone with a gray beard could have gone to school with Mason—they had had the same friends for thirty years. Since the 1960s, their guest lists had remained the same, their in-jokes never changing, their speed dials so permanently fixed they knew no one's phone number. Even as their configurations shifted over the years, even as couples divorced and remarried and new partners were brought, under the scrutiny that accompanies a sorority rush, into the clique, there was always a sense in these people that the reason they were there was because they'd always been there. When they said "We go way back" they meant it. They meant it in a way that I would probably never be able to mean anything in my life. And that was because in Prairie City "way back" meant way back and every month of every year in between. It

meant they never missed a New Year's Eve, a Fat Tuesday jamba-
laya party, or, for that matter, the Peter Fonda county commissioner's annual margarita mix-off in honor of Settler's Day, a day in
early June for which Prairie City Avenue was closed and barbecued
ribs and beer were sold on the street and anyone who wore an OPEN
ARMS, OPEN MINDS T-shirt got a free corn dog. It meant that even
when someone told a wholly unoriginal joke and they threw their
heads back and said things like "This gang, they're too much," you
had to forgive them because this was *their* gang. This was their
town, these were their in-jokes, their backyards and lawn furniture
and ice chests and they were the ones who had picked each other
out of the various abysses over the years, taking the phone calls late
at night when the marriages were dissolving or the kids were sick
and driving one another to the airport and the hospital and passing
around their favorite books with certain passages highlighted to
show how much they cared, how much they understood, how much
they believed in what Sue would call "what matters." And because
of all that they had shared, because, unlike me, *what mattered* was
to them a tangible and attainable state of being as opposed to an
alien, mockable concept, they had earned the right to say things like
"You go, girl." They could have stood on that fertile soil and recited
the recipe for beef stew if they'd wanted to, they could have elected
not to say anything relevant or interesting or even entertaining ever
again and it would have been fully within their prerogatives. It was
a privilege that came from having honored the legacy of their home-
steading ancestors, of having stuck it out through miserable weather
and late-night talk-show jokes at their expense and the low-grade
yet unyielding indignity of the fact that 65 percent of educated
American adults were unable to locate their state on a map. They
could leave themselves wide open for those jokes, fashion themselves into walking chestnuts, and no one, least of all someone like
me, could, with any degree of fair play, fault them. As I checked my
makeup in the bathroom mirror, listening to their explosions of
laughter downstairs, I understood for the first time that I was a

guest on their land. Even now, as they stuffed beers in my fridge and carefully wiped their shoes before coming inside, I was the guest and they were the hosts. And I hadn't once bothered to wipe my shoes.

Back in front of the barn, microphone in hand, I resumed my narration.

"As my friends and neighbors arrive, I imagine what it would have been like more than one hundred years ago during the Homestead Act. This very farm might have been the setting for barn dances held by the pioneers to commemorate the end of harvest, a final celebration before hunkering down for the long winter. In the 1800s, someone would surely have brought out a fiddle. But since it's the twenty-first century, we have the benefit of a stereo system."

Neil Young's "Mr. Soul" erupted from the tack room. A few feet away, by the horse, Frank Fussell was practicing tai chi moves.

"If they're gonna square dance they'd better do it soon," said Jeb from behind the camera. "We're losing the light."

When I went into the tack room to tell Mason to change the music he had already lit up a joint and was passing it among a circle of Effie's people.

"Listen," I said, "I just need to put on square dancing music for maybe half an hour."

Mason was leaned back in the reclining chair that had been left by the previous tenants. His eyes were glazed over. He looked like the proprietor of an opium den.

"Do what you need to do," he said.

I went to the cassette deck and put in the "barn dance" mixed tape that I'd made from some traditional folk music records I'd checked out of the Prairie City Public Library. Jeb had set up extra lights in the barn and when he turned them on it was as if the guests were jolted out of their conversations and reminded, with a certain dread, why they were there. The pressure to perform had suddenly eclipsed the novelty of appearing on television and several people slunk away toward the house. Sue and her gang, however, stood ready. The spirit of volunteerism was alive and well. Valdette took a compact out of her purse and touched up her makeup.

"Okay, you guys," I said, already hating the sound of my group-address voice and the seeming unavoidability of the high schoolish "you guys" (because I could not have brought myself to say "folks"). "I really appreciate your willingness to come out here and partici-pate in this segment of *New York Up Early*. I will let you know when it airs and make sure anyone who wants a videotape gets one."

"And what about those of us who want all copies destroyed?" said the Peter Fonda county commissioner. "Folks, we now know that I'll never be reelected."

They laughed. They clapped their hands. They shouted things like "Just don't let Linda Tripp get ahold of the tape." Mason was still in the tack room.

"Now, Lucinda," the Peter Fonda county commissioner contin-ued, "I heard you mention before that you didn't exactly know how to square dance. And despite you and your employer's insistence on portraying us as backward, inbred hicks without indoor plumb-ing—which is true of only half of us—I feel it's my duty to tell you that we don't know how to square dance, either."

"Only dirty dance!" someone shouted.

"Which is why," the Peter Fonda county commissioner contin-ued, taking another swig of beer, "we're going to do the funky chicken."

I began to say something witty, something that was only partly conceived when I opened my mouth, something I trusted (since they were so generous with their joke appreciation) would pass muster as it left my mouth, but they all broke out in applause and began whistling and cheering and, when I went to the tack room to turn up the music, avoiding looking at Mason as I did so, they stampeded into the barn and began to perform the most dazzling and corny ar-ray of dances I'd ever seen. Like auditioners for a local production of *Oklahoma!*, they stamped their feet and slapped their thighs. With beers in one hand, they twirled one another and bumped

butts, drinks spilling onto the dirt floor, faces turning red with ex-
ertion. They did the funky chicken and the twist. They broke into
small groups and did haphazard macarenas, hokey-pokeys with
huge gaps in the circles, old cheerleading routines from their days at
Prairie City High. They imitated Irish clog dancers. They grabbed
hands and attempted a Rockettes-style kick line, though most of
them couldn't get their legs beyond much more than a 90-degree
angle. Joel, who had taken tango lessons at L'Elegance Dance Studio above the P.C. Union and Times Bank on Prairie City Avenue,
grabbed me and attempted to propel me down the length of the
barn.

"I thought all New Yorkers knew how to tango," he whispered
in my ear as we glided (though it was more like galloping) past the
empty horse stalls to where Lucky, excited by the goings-on and apparently just having relieved himself of several pounds of fecal matter, was craning his massive neck over the gate of his stall.

"Where'd you get that idea?" I asked. His goateed cheek was
pressed hard against mine. His groin dangerously close to the folds
of my leather skirt.

"'Cause you're all gluttons for punishment," he said, and then
he dipped me. He dipped me so low I could hear my back crack. I
could feel the back of my head brush the dirt floor. Out of the corner of my eye I saw a mouse scurry into a stack of alfalfa horse feed.

And then I was back up. Joel could dance. I had to give him
that. And Jeb had gotten the whole thing. From behind the camera
he gave me a thumbs-up. Joel stretched my arm out, knelt before
me, and kissed my hand.

"I know how to get ratings," he said. Then he winked.

I will be forever indebted to them for this, I thought. Even as I
had forced them to perform like midwestern monkeys, even as I told
them what to wear, even as I privately mocked their provincialism
and then exploited their provincialism for the sake of my career
while insisting that my role was to debunk the myth of their provincialism, the Prairie Cityites were never less than perfectly gracious.

*   *   *

Even when the folk dance music was replaced by Neil Young and Frank Fussell tried to call attention to himself by jumping over the campfire and explaining that he had learned the technique from the Pawnee Indians, they stayed at the party. Even as Mason didn't once come out of the tack room and instead held court with anyone who came in to look at his paintings, which in the candlelight looked less like the work of a Picasso-influenced abstract expressionist and more like the product of a mental patient, the Prairie Cityites had the decorum to get drunk and stand around in their groups talking about the change in management of the health-food store and how disappointing the turnout was for the Prairie City March Against Intolerance this year and—despite the gnawing feeling I had that something was terribly wrong, despite my fear that they held it against me that I had not participated in the Prairie City March Against Intolerance—entertained the notion that I could entertain them.

Jeb wanted to make sure to get some shots of the stallion and so even in the darkness, as I held a small floodlight to supplement the light from the campfire, he filmed Lucky prancing around, bucking up against the fence, and letting forth loud whinnies. Lucky was as good a sport with the camera as the dancers had been, so much so that Jeb summoned the courage to move the camera inside the corral to get what he hoped would be an "artsy shot" of the horse's face.

"I'm thinking if I shoot from below, if I crouch in front of him and point the camera up, I'd get a really cool shot," Jeb said.

Suddenly Jeb was ambitious. Perhaps the success of the dancing scene had sent him dreaming of a regional Emmy (an honor Prairie City Public Television hadn't received since a long-ago documentary about ethanol production). And suddenly Mason was out of the tack room, delighted to act as Lucky's handler while Jeb set up the shot, which required floodlights that a number of the Effie's people, as well as Joel and Sue and Teri, had to hold up.

It must have been while they were preoccupied with the lighting (and I was preoccupied with gauging Mason's state of mind, which

had seemed to lurch from comatose to manic within five-second intervals) that the horse had brought out his giant penis and begun
slapping it against his belly. At first, the motion was little more than
a source of amusement.

"Good grief!" said Sue, who had consumed a number of margaritas. "And I thought that scene in *Boogie Nights* was intense."

"I think he likes you," Joel said to the Effie's woman.

"Better get thee to a nunnery," Mason said bizarrely. He was
holding Lucky's bridle and laughing. I was standing off to the side
in an effort not to get any more mud on my skirt.

"He's not going to do anything, is he?" I asked Mason. "I mean,
this isn't going to, like, *result* in anything, is it?"

"Ah, hell no," Mason said. He was snickering like an adolescent
boy.

Jeb seemed willing to ignore Lucky's behavior on account that
at least the horse was standing still. He got on his knees and tilted
the camera toward Lucky's face, motioning for no one to move
while he got the shot.

It must have been their midwestern work ethic, that Prairie City
respect for authority, that kept the makeshift production crew from
leaving their posts even as the sound of Lucky's fully engorged, one-
and-a-half-foot-long appendage hitting his chest and gaining mo-
mentum in both speed and volume caused nearly everyone at the
party to cease his conversation and turn toward the horse at the
very moment that he released, in the manner of a fire hydrant illegally unplugged, a spray of semen that traveled through his front
legs and onto both the camera lens and Sue's and Teri's western-
style shirts as well as one leg of Joel's pants.

The party fell silent except for Neil Young's "Ohio" playing
from the tack room. A few seconds went by and Joel threw down his
light and yelled "Jesus fucking Christ" and Sue dropped her light
and tried to examine her shirt but Teri screamed "Don't touch it! It
might get in your mouth!"

People swarmed into the kitchen, wetting paper towel and rubbing them with dish soap. I followed Mason into the tack room, where he claimed to be looking for a towel. He seemed for a moment like he didn't want me to come inside, and when I forced my way in there was a terrible stench, neither pot smoke nor cigarette smoke. More like something from a chemical explosion.

"What the hell is that smell?" I asked.

Mason, though he looked like he could barely stand, doubled over and started laughing so hard that tears fell straight from his eyes and onto the floor. There were beer cans everywhere. An ashtray brimmed with cigarette butts. The music was so loud that I couldn't hear him laugh and he appeared to shake silently, his head bobbing up and down as if he had an uncontrollable twitch.

"How could you let that happen?" I yelled.

"That was a money shot if I ever saw one," he said. His face was red from laughing. "Those people can't even tell when a horse is about to spray himself on them. They might as well be from New York!"

"You better get a towel," I said. "You better help me deal with this."

But then I knew that something worse was happening. Mason's paint brushes were spread all over the floor and tubes of acrylics with half the paint squirting out were on the rug. He had taken one of his finished pieces and begun painting over it. Stripes and polka dots now covered the demonic face and a new, even more demonic face was emerging where a perfectly rendered hawk had been.

"I gotta finish this painting first," Mason said.

As if to contain the damage—not the damage of the horse but of Mason, who, in the time it had taken him to return to the tack room, had apparently forgotten that we had guests at all—I closed the door behind me and went back to the campfire. Sue and Teri, wearing borrowed jackets, were walking toward their SUV carrying their shirts in a plastic Hinky Dinky bag.

Had the event occurred under the auspices of anyone other than me, it might have been admitted into the canon of Prairie City folklore. Surely if the offending animal had belonged to the Peter Fonda county commissioner or to Joel or even to Sue herself, the episode would have instantly been converted to an anecdote that would dominate their party talk for decades. The horse himself would become an in-joke. "Don't pull a Lucky on me," they'd say while lounging around Sue's pool. The phrase "Look, no hands" would be a constant refrain.

But the horse had been on my property. And the incident, whether or not they blamed me (and, after the initial shock, they all insisted it wasn't my fault), was forever tinged with a larger feeling of unrest. Though they didn't say it—not then anyway—Mason was a troubling specimen. The impression he made that night went beyond the adversarial note he'd sounded a year earlier at the Lasagna Factory fund-raiser. In his curious seclusion in the tack room, his insistence on Neil Young and nothing else, his affiliation with the regulars from Effie's (and not the once-a-week Effie's types, not the schoolteachers and secretaries who gave the place its populist cachet but the every-day-of-the-week Effie's types, the perennial holders of odd jobs, the welfare check collectors, the borderline and not-borderline drunks, the *bikers*) Mason's persona was no longer problematic, but an actual problem.

The Hidden Benefits of Tanning

The day after the barn dance, the Sunday when things officially began to unravel, Mason got up early to pick up Erin. The visit was at Julie's behest, to make up for the way the barn dance conflicted with Erin's prearranged Saturday stay. I was still in bed reading the *Prairie City Daily Dispatch* when they returned. Erin, as if there were a magnet drawing her to the television, immediately came upstairs and handed me a *Pokémon* video.

"Dad said to put this on for me," she said.

I put in the tape, then got dressed and went downstairs. Through the kitchen window I saw Mason sitting in the yard with his head in his hands. When I walked outside I could see he was crying.

It was a breathtaking day. Autumn was fleeting in that part of the country and the morning was edged with a crispness that probably only happened six or seven days every year. The few trees, though they didn't turn red like the maples and elms of the East Coast, had worked themselves into a respectable gold. The pasture gurgled with pheasants.

It was all working in his favor. The bucolic tableau. The Thornton Wilder backdrop that I used in my bullshit scripts, it was actually alive and real that day. Like it was mocking me. Like it knew the terrible thing that Mason was about to tell me. If only it had been a hot and miserable day. If only it had been anything other than a beautiful and miserable day.

"What is it?" I asked.

He continued sobbing. He couldn't speak for a moment. Then he said, "I never thought it would happen to me."

And he spilled it all. Mason, who had gone forty years never getting addicted to anything, who had swallowed more acid, more pills, done more lines, drunk more beer than the Rolling Stones collectively (well, maybe not that much, but if he had been able to afford it, who knows?), was now addicted to the cheapest, trashiest, smelliest, most chemical-laden (we're talking ammonia as a major ingredient) drug there was. He was addicted to meth. How it had ended up this way he just couldn't figure. After all, as he explained it, he'd never even really tried the stuff before. It just wasn't around his scene. But some guy from Effie's had some, a guy he'd known for years, whom he used to go to Grateful Dead concerts with in the eighties. This guy was getting it from his son, his twenty-year-old kid. It was a family thing. This guy was a respectable guy, he owned a hardware store, the kid went to junior college. So how bad could it have been? And it's not like they were making the stuff. We're not talking about labs that explode inside barns—that's for the Mexicans and the serious scumbags. And Mason, having some extra cash from selling his cabin, just happening to have ten thousand dollars in hundred dollar bills stashed in his night table, simply thought he'd partake a little. And the months went by. The months seemed to run together like a movie on cable TV; he was waiting for the commercial but it never came. He'd stop soon but somehow he didn't. And six months went by, six months of taking money every few days from the night table, and the ten thousand turned into six thousand and then three thousand and then twelve hundred dollars, and, suddenly, a day before I was having dozens of people who disliked him out to the farm so I could put them all on television in New York, he realized he had three hundred dollars left. And he hadn't paid off his creditors. He hadn't helped me with any of the bills. He hadn't gotten a vasectomy. He'd barely kept up with child support (though he never failed to pay it—he might have gotten behind, but it was always there, eventually it was paid, that's what separated him from the sleazeballs). So he took the three hundred dollars and scored half an ounce of the stuff. He'd told the guy who got it from his son that he wasn't doing it anymore. He'd told himself that even though he tried to stop back in August, tried to stop for two hideous days when he'd almost wanted to slap me after I freaked out over a mouse and he realized he couldn't stop, that he'd stop now. He had to stop now. Because he was out of money. The ten thousand dollars was gone. The cabin was gone. And I, if I had any common sense, would see to it that he was gone, too.

I'm paraphrasing, but that was the gist. It was not yet 8:30 A.M.

How to respond to information like this? Mason had resumed his sobbing and walked into the pasture. And as his plaid flannel shirt—the shirt that had, from a certain angle nearly a year earlier, as he had bent over to lock the gate near the cabin that he had sold for drug money, made him look like Sam Shepard—disappeared into the tall grass, suggesting *Days of Heaven*, a movie where Sam ended up tying Brooke Adams to a chair while the farm was engulfed in flames, my thoughts turned to where they invariably turned: myself.

Fucking moron. Self-destructive, naïve, blind victim not even on the Montel level but the Jerry Springer level. The filmed-in-shadow "I had a $300-a-day habit, I lost my kids, I lost my trailer" *Up Early* real-life-health-crisis-segment level. And I'd had the audacity, the gutlessness, the lack of imagination to sit there on the grass during his confession and say things like "What?" and "Oh my God." As if it were a shock. As if I hadn't suspected something was wrong, hadn't wondered where his money was going, hadn't noticed his leg jerking in his sleep (a common side effect of the drug; I'd even mentioned it in an early draft of the *Up Early* script).

In the house, in my office, I went through the closet looking for my notes from the segment. I'd dragged them all the way from New York to the apartment in Prairie City to the farm. You should always keep your notes for a few years. You never know when you might be sued. There was an entire box of them, downloaded data from the drug czar's office, graphs and pie charts and National Institutes of Health figures, brochures from the Prairie City Recovery Center for Women. EMBRACE, EMPATHIZE, EMPOWER. If nothing else, it was ironic. That was something to hold on to, the narrative value of the situation. Surely that was greater than if not equal to the trashiness of the situation. Lucinda Trout, the girl reporter who had nodded in faux sympathy as women who lacked her innate sense of dignity and judgment spilled their drug-addled guts into her microcassette recorder; Lucinda, the smug Smithie who woke two million New Yorkers up to the news that a terrifying plague was gripping these once-innocent heartlanders, now found herself seeking a purer and more moral existence with a guy who blew through ten thousand dollars of meth in three months.

And like a child's puzzle that takes the adult forever to put together, I suddenly realized why I'd turned my head all those times. It was the meat loaf. It was the flowers in the garden. It was the amazing enthusiasm he'd put into turning that heap of a house into a passable sound stage for a "Quality of Life Report." The act of articulating the truth to myself, of forcing myself to recollect every instance of pretending he was an intact man, of literally walking in the other direction when he walked toward the barn, felt like throwing up a year's worth of dinners. I sat on the love seat and made myself mouth the words. Here was the truth: Mason was better when he was high. He was funnier, nicer, and more sociable. Though, unlike the woman in the *Up Early* segment, "crazy sexual positions" hadn't exactly figured into his addiction, he was, in some ways, a better boyfriend on meth. Perhaps (and this was horrifying) I'd even been afraid he would stop doing whatever it was that made him that way. Certainly I'd been afraid that I would find out and then be forced to make him stop. I would have either had to make him stop or leave him. And despite everything, there was a spark in him that had addicted me to his bizarre, addled presence. I was addicted to his addiction. And now we both had to kick.

There was other stuff in the closet. Amazing what you just throw in there in the rush of moving into a new house. Winter coats in piles on the floor. Boots I'd forgotten about. A framed Tanglewood poster I'd felt exhibited too much class anxiety to hang up. There was a bathroom scale underneath a couple of sleeping bags and, out of a need for distraction, I stepped on it.

I'd gained six pounds. Five if I subtracted for clothing. Since when? I'd never been much for weighing myself. Bonnie Crawley actually had a doctor's scale in her office and periodically a staff member, as if seized by a self-dare, would dart in her office for a midday check. But not me, not the serious journalist Lucinda Trout who aspired to work for public television and was above such concerns. Now, however, as though I were being transported back to the offices of *Up Early*, back to that moment when my proposal to move to Prairie City had been approved and I stood on the threshold of a purer and more moral life, I could hear Faye Figaro's shrill forewarning: "Don't get fat."

And it had happened. Just like she said it would. I was a blimp. Okay, not a blimp, not even fat, just a little soft around the edges. A little heavy in the hip, a slight paunch in the belly, eyes embedded a fraction of an inch farther into the flesh. Still reasonably attractive but now by midwestern standards. With hot rollers and the proper application of Maybelline bright lash, I could have been in the running for Miss Swine Queen in the county parade, a hot number standing in line for tickets at the state fair; pretty enough, but no longer, by New York standards, a player. Instead—and here was the horror—I had assimilated into the culture of Prairie City and the whole Midwest. The Thousand Island dressing, the spreads of deviled eggs at the parties (though when was the last time I'd been to a party?), the nightly margaritas had fomented into the person who now stood in this closet, Little Mermaid sheets tumbling onto her head from the shelf where Mason had carelessly stuffed them, a bound copy of the Drug Enforcement Agency's Schedule One chemical substance list jammed between an old computer and a broken CD player. In that cluttered room of that creaking house, as a hastening breeze shook the elm tree outside and the sound of cartoons seeped out of the bedroom, I realized that at that moment, in fact not even at that moment but many moments, many months, perhaps even a year before, I had crossed over into the error margin.

"Dad!" Erin shouted from the bedroom. Suddenly she was in the doorway of my office. She clutched the news anchorwoman Barbie I'd bought for her birthday after she once again declared she had no interest in *Where the Wild Things Are.*

"He's outside, Erin."

"The show's over," she said.

"What's on after it?" I asked.

"Will you play Barbies with me?" she asked.

"Not right now," I said.

"Can I go outside?" she asked.

"Do you want to watch your movie?" I asked.

"No," she said.

I heard the back door open and slam shut. Mason came upstairs, looking relatively put together. He'd taken a liter bottle of Pepsi out of the refrigerator and was drinking straight out of it.

"Can I have some pop?" Erin whined.

"Why don't you watch your movie?" Mason said.

"I don't want to," she said.

"Well, then go play outside. Or read a book."

"I can't read," she said.

"Then look at the pictures," Mason said.

"I'll watch the movie," she said.

I went downstairs to the kitchen. I wanted very much to have a glass of wine. But it was 9:45 in the morning. Mason came down and began sobbing again.

"I'm a terrible person," he said. He hugged me, his body shaking.

"You're a good person," I said. I could hear the theme music of *The Little Mermaid* coming from the bedroom.

"I wouldn't blame you if you left me," he said.

"I'm not going to leave you."

"I'm going to stop," he said. "I'll just stop. I have to. I have no more money."

"That's a good reason."

"Peter almost caught me once," he said. "Last weekend. You know how he always follows me around. I thought he was in the front yard. I thought he was playing with Erin. He was in the barn. He was messing around with the lawn mower. He must have smelled the smoke. Jesus Christ."

"What smoke?" I asked. I pulled away from him. There was only so much conversation that could take place, outside of a soap opera, while hugging a crying person.

He looked at me, his eyebrows raised, like I was some kind of imbecile.

"What do you think?" he said.

"What smoke?"

"How do you think I was doing the stuff?"

"I don't know," I said. "Snorting it."

"The first few times, maybe," he said. "But then it doesn't work as well. You have to smoke it." He wet down a sponge and began wiping the counter.

Interesting, the prescriptive nature of this. *You have to smoke it.*

"And no, I never injected the stuff," Mason said. "If that's what you're thinking."

"Are you sure?" I asked. I hadn't been thinking it. But now that he mentioned it, the ramifications piled up in my mind. A junkie. Needle sharing. AIDS.

"Jesus, what do you think I am?" he asked.

For the moment, he was wiping the side of the toaster with Windex. I recalled one of the women from the *Up Early* segment. *I tweaked so hard I scraped the pattern off the kitchen counter.* And all this time I'd just thought he was an enlightened male. Now I'd have to do my share of housework. I truly hated to clean.

The next day, the day after I didn't kick Mason out but told him I would if he ever did meth again, he came home with a present for me. He told me to stand in the yard with my eyes closed.

"Hold out your arms," he said. "Don't drop it."

It was warm and furry. It looked like something out of a Disney movie. It was a wonder he hadn't put a bow around its neck. It was brown with white markings and exceptionally fuzzy. Blue eyes. The pinkest little tongue and the whitest, pointiest little teeth. There is no way to describe a puppy without sounding like you're talking baby talk. Which is what I did.

"Hello!" I cooed. "Sweet little thing!"

"You can't have a farm without a dog," Mason said.

"Where did you get him?" I asked. "Is it a him?"

"There was a farm outside of town with a litter," Mason said. "It was in the paper. He was the nicest one in the bunch. His mom was a Samoyed. His dad was an Australian shepherd."

All I could do was hold him to my cheek, smell his puppy scent, and pet his impossibly soft fur. All I could think was that now Mason *had me.* He might as well have tied me to the fence post with a rope. He might as well have gotten me pregnant with twins.

I immediately went out to PetSmart and bought a three-hundred-dollar wooden dog house in the shape of a Victorian mansion. The store had cheaper ones but I didn't want anything tacky in the yard. Mason said he'd grow to be at least seventy-five pounds, so I got the extra-large dog house. I put it in the yard and the puppy began chewing the side of it.

"What are we going to name him?" Mason asked. "Nothing too silly. A dog needs his dignity."

We were sitting in the yard in the very spot we'd been in when he'd told me about his meth addiction. It seemed like ages ago, though it had only been two days.

"Max?" I said.

"Too typical," Mason said.

"Jack?"

"Too boring."

"Spiro Agnew?" I said.

"Huh?"

"Faye Figaro? Rudy Giuliani? Lex Luthor? Martin Luther? Martin Amis? Famous Amos?"

"Neil?" Mason said.

I looked at the dog. Even at eight weeks, he was handsome. He had the blue eyes of a seducer. Half Samoyed, half Australian shepherd. Suddenly his name was clear to me.

"Sam Shepard," I said.

"Oh Jesus," said Mason.

"That's his name," I said. "It's perfect."

"No."

"He's my dog," I said. "You said he was my dog."

"Why don't you just name him Fabio?"

"You're not really in a position to tell me what to name my dog," I said.

And that was how I came to live out my original fantasy. That's how I came to live on a farm with Sam Shepard.

> To: Lucinda Trout
> From: Carol and Richard Trout
> Re: We've Got E-mail!
>
> Dear Lucinda,
>
> It's Mom and Dad. We have electronic mail now and will be able to communicate with you in this very modern way. Your sister said that since we finally got an answering machine we can take another step forward and join the information freeway. Please write back if

you got this. Also, did you say you were living on a
farm? Do you have crops?

Love,
Mom and Dad

Mason said sugar helped him get through the meth cravings. I
bought bags of Hershey's kisses, candy corn, Jolly Ranchers. They
sat in a bowl on the dining-room table like treats at a grandmother's
house. Erin tried to grab a handful everytime she passed and Mason
would yell at her like he did at me for just about anything, including not having anything ready for dinner when he came home from
work, which was usually around 4:30.

It was difficult to devote a lot of time to developing "Quality of
Life Report" projects because I had been seized by a sudden urge to
improve my appearance. I went to the YMCA every morning and
when I discovered that a full set of remarkably natural-looking artificial nails could be obtained for twenty-one dollars I went to
Happy Nails in the Kmart plaza at least twice a week for a fill. While
making the twenty-five-minute drive into town, I'd marvel at my
hands on the steering wheel. They'd always looked so shabby before. Now they rivaled Bonnie Crawley's. I tried new shades of
polish every time, Tahitian Twilight, Tinsel Town Taupe, Not So Innocent Pink.

I also began taking the cure for depression as it was most com-
monly dispensed in Prairie City. I went to a tanning salon. As winter began to seep through the cracks of autumn and the clocks were
set back and twilight came at 4:30 the citizens of Prairie City hit the
tanning capsules as though they were treadmills, the artificial UV
rays pumping serotonin into their bodies like hot Zoloft. It was
what they did instead of psychotherapy. The tanning beds were
their Freudian couches. But true to Prairie City form, you got so
much more bang for your buck. Just as a house that would have

sold for half a million dollars in the tristate area went for a mere eighty thousand dollars in Prairie City, eighteen minutes in a bed at Hollywood Tan on Prairie Boulevard would do more for one's general outlook and ability to cope than any fifty-minute hour in the office of an Upper East Side shrink. And as the temperature dropped, the epidermal hue of the average Prairie Cityite became a deeper and deeper shade of orange.

I myself tanned three or four times a week. Once I got started, it was hard to bring myself to let it fade even slightly. It was as if the tan, deep and shiny and scented with the brown-sugary smell of the Volcanic Tanning Mud lotion I'd purchased at the salon for thirty-five dollars, protected me from the mounting blankness of the days. Even when faced with the nothingness of the morning, the flatness of the land, the ranch-house-flanked highway that led to County Road F, I could bring my forearm to my face and smell my tan. I could look at my manicure, tap my plastic nails on my desk, throw my gym clothes in the washer, and feel a sense of, if not exactly ac-complishment, at least maintenance. Even as the days ran into each other, even as I left in the morning and returned six hours later af-ter going to the gym, the nail salon, the tanning salon, and then the Hinky Dinky to pick up the ingredients for one of my increasingly complicated dinners, I could at least rest on the notion that I was fit and well groomed. Even as Mason stormed through the door with a frozen TV dinner for Erin and prodded her into eating the mushy french fries before she could return to her video, I could distract myself with the preparation of veal cutlets with red wine sauce and scalloped potatoes. We went to bed earlier and earlier. First 9:30, then 9:00, then 8:30. Mason kept chocolates by the bed to stave off nighttime cravings and I allowed myself one or two in the mornings as an incentive to get out of bed and start the gym routine all over again.

It was during the preparation of shrimp with feta cheese, scal-lions, and two teaspoons of vermouth that Sue called and told me I had been elected to the board of directors for the Prairie City Coalition of Women.

"It's a fabulous group of women," she said. "I think you'll really like them. And Christine's going to be on the board, too."

"I'm honored," I said, licking a dab of vermouth off my finger.

"It's nice because everytime I try to organize a group of women at my house men end up coming," said Sue. "It starts with Leonard and then it just snowballs."

A shadow appeared outside the kitchen window, as if someone were standing outside. I looked up and gasped as a huge white object knocked itself against the glass, producing a tremendous thud. Lucky the horse was standing right outside the window, stamping his gigantic hooves and rearing on his hind legs.

"Oh my God," I said. "The horse escaped."

"What?" said Sue.

"The stallion. He got out."

"Don't go outside," Sue said. "Stay inside the house. He could be dangerous."

"But the puppy is outside," I said. "What if he steps on him?"

I ran to the back door and found Sam Shepard curled up on the stoop surrounded by shrapnellike pieces of a beer can that he must have pulled from the recycling bin and gnawed on until he became exhausted. I let him in and he toddled right to the oriental rug and urinated on it. I looked out the window and saw Lucky running in circles around the yard as if it were a show ring. He'd lost his bridle, so there was nothing to grab on to. I dialed the number of the grain elevator.

"Mason took the rest of the day off," Frank said.

"What do you mean he took the rest of the day off?" I said. "I need him right now. The horse escaped!"

"He said he had an appointment."

"Where?"

"I don't know, Lucinda," Frank said. "The important thing to do is think positively. Channel your energy in a positive direction. Try to imagine what the horse is thinking."

I hung up with Frank and dug up the number of Lucky's owner. The woman who answered told me he was at work at the Firestone plant. She said she wasn't getting involved with "no horse." A baby was crying in the background. Lucky was now prancing around in the prairie grass west of the house. All he'd need now was to get in the road and cause an accident. I called the landlord.

"He's out harvesting," said the landlord's wife. "I'll try him on his cell phone but sometimes he doesn't hear it ring."

I watched through the window as the horse wandered farther and farther into the pasture. I prayed he wouldn't get inside the other pasture, the one where the elderly, gelded Cupid stayed. Lucky would fight him to the death.

An hour passed and finally the landlord's truck came up the driveway. He gave a little wave with the hand that was missing a finger. Mason pulled up right behind him. I went into the house while they wrangled the horse, which involved not so much wrangling as luring him back to the corral with several ears of corn. From the kitchen window I watched them talk in the driveway. They were laughing, each resting a foot on the bumpers of their trucks. Congenial as pie. It had been fifty-three days since Mason kicked the meth, fifty days since getting Sam Shepard. I put the dog outside the front door and let him run around to the back so Mason wouldn't notice he'd been inside. Mason called the dog Sam. He was nearly too big for me to lift now and I watched Mason scoop him up like a baby, clutch him to his chest, and then hold him out to show the landlord. Mason's photo albums were filled with pictures of him holding his children in precisely that way, their tiny legs dangling at eye level, Mason's face seen in profile with a smile wider than he'd had occasion for since.

He came in a while later, the bottom of his plaid flannel shirt flapping in the wind. There'd been frost on the grass that morning but he still wore his flip-flops.

"It's getting cold out there," he said.

"How the hell did that happen?" I said.

"Oh, must be a little hole in the fence," he said. "I'll have to walk the fence line and see."

"That's it?" I said. "We could have been sued, you know. If that horse did any damage."

"Oh he just wanted to take a little stroll," Mason said. "Who'd blame him? Being cooped up in there."

"Where were you when I called Frank?"

"Just swung by to see a friend," he said.

"What would I have done if I couldn't get ahold of anyone?"

"Oh he would've come back eventually," Mason said. He came up behind me and pinched my butt. "It's no biggie, boots."

Mason spent the rest of the afternoon puttering around in the barn and fixing the hole in the fence. I wrote a memo to Faye Figaro pitching a segment called "Tanning Salons: Bad for the Skin But Good for the Soul." It was Mason's turn to prepare dinner so he made tuna helper and a salad and we sat down to eat at 5:30 and were in bed by 9:00. The coyotes shrieked all night. I got up twice to check on Sam Shepard. He'd chewed his dog house to bits in the first two weeks and now he slept in a horse stall in the barn. In my robe, flashlight in hand, I navigated through the darkness. At night, the flip of the light sent things scurrying into the hay bales. The swallows would stir in their nests. Lucky would shift his bulk in my direction. And Sam Shepard, growing gawkier and furrier by the day, would open his eyes without moving any other muscle of his body and, upon registering my face, leap from his straw bed and run to the gate. I couldn't keep myself from going into the stall to tuck him back in. The second time I checked him that night, when dawn was just a few hours away and the coyotes had seemed to stop howling the moment I stepped outside, I sat with the puppy on my lap for a good twenty minutes. He needed me. There would be no leaving now.

* * *

Board meetings for the Prairie City Coalition of Women were held at the home of its president, Brenda Schwan. Brenda's house was located in an expensive real estate development on the edge of Prairie City called Pioneer Hill, a neighborhood that wasn't so much a hill but about 50 acres of what had been natural prairie grasses until they had been cleared to make room for approximately 150 gigantic and nearly identical-looking houses designed to be reminiscent of medieval castles. The final product was a maze of winding streets and cul-de-sacs with names like Shamrock Court and Ophelia Drive, all lined with homes that looked like miniature versions of the Excelsior Hotel in Las Vegas. Every house had a two- or three-car garage and an SUV parked in the driveway. The only way I could find Brenda's house was by looking for her SUV, which had a Gore/ Lieberman campaign bumper sticker on it.

Brenda, like most members of the Prairie City Coalition of Women, was in her early fifties. Divorced some seven years earlier from a corporate lawyer with whom she had two grown children, Brenda had channeled most of her single-woman energy into home decor. A glass-enclosed, two-sided fireplace divided the cathedral-ceilinged, sunken living room and the wooden-raftered dining room. In the living room, where coalition meetings took place, a lime-green modular sofa snaked around a glass coffee table in a U shape. It sat twelve. Tall, cylindrical wicker baskets filled with cattails and peacock feathers sat in the corners of the room. White carpet covered every square inch of the house, even the three steps leading down to the living room; for this reason, only white wine was served. Chrome-framed prints by the graphic artist Patrick Nagel adorned three of the walls and over the glass fireplace, on the living-room side, hung a colossal oil portrait of Brenda's son and daughter in their preteen years. Smooth jazz played on the stereo.

"Lucinda, we are *so* glad to have you aboard," Brenda said, kissing me on the cheek. Smoke from a Virginia Slims 100 curled around her fingers, which, I noticed, were nicely manicured. I recognized the Wyatt Erple Purple polish. "I think your input is going to be really interesting for us."

Valdette Svoboda-Lipinsky, the board secretary, had already arrived. She blew me a kiss from across the sofa. The spread on the coffee table included deviled eggs, carrot sticks, pigs-in-blankets, and Rice Krispies treats. I sat down and took a deviled egg.

"So what kind of wine can I get you, Lucinda?" said Brenda. "White or white?"

"You know Christine's coming tonight, right?" Valdette said to me.

The other women began trailing in, all carrying bottles of white wine. It was November now, 36 degrees at noon that day. They wore parkas over their denim jumper dresses and corduroy pants, dangling earrings sticking out at odd angles under wool hats. One woman looked familiar. She wore an Indian print tent dress and had salt-and-pepper hair tied into two braids. Then I remembered. Estrogen Therapy. She was the guitar player, composer of "Jane at the Register." Her partner trailed behind her carrying a Tupperware container.

"M.J. and Dee Dee!" Valdette cried, giving no indication of who was whom.

"Greetings, radical women!" tent dress wearer said.

"I brought deviled eggs," said the other one.

"More deviled eggs!" I said.

"*These* are filled with tofu," said the one holding the Tupperware. "Less cholesterol. Who's got the booze?"

Sue arrived with Christine and immediately everyone swarmed around Christine as if she were a visitor from a remote Polynesian village, pawing her Brooks Brothers' overcoat and her Isotoner gloves.

"Gorgeous coat," one of the members of Estrogen Therapy said to her. "And I love your shoes. And your earrings. And your bag."

The first order of business at the board meeting was to approve the minutes of the last meeting. Only two people had brought the minutes of the last meeting with them. Valdette slipped a copy to me. It said:

Minutes for Coalition of Women (COW), 10/13/00, place: Brenda's house

- Brenda raised the issue of setting up a booth at next year's Steakfest to bring attention to poor conditions for meat packers, especially women
- Sue pointed out that it might be better to focus COW activities on political venues
- Valdette said she fears for future of reproductive rights
- Pat reached out to M.J. about her recent hysterectomy
- Sue raised concern that hysterectomies are performed more often than necessary because of insensitive male doctors
- Brenda thought COW could consider doing something about that
- Pat expressed ongoing frustration with the city council's ongoing refusal to include coalition on their official list of P.C. boards, she said council's opinion that there's too much overlap with the P.C. chapter of the National Organization for Women (NOW) is short-sighted and patriarchical
- M.J. suggested organizing a softball game between NOW and COW; members agreed to form subcommittee to discuss the idea and vote at a later date
- Gail reached out to Pat about her marital problems

- Sue reached out to Gail about her son's recent
  juvenile offense for marijuana possession
- Pat joked to Sue that "lesbians have it figured
  out"; Sue countered that enablers come in every
  size, shape, color, and sexual orientation
- Valdette's pad thai was deemed "killer"

"These only cover the first ten minutes!" the tent dress Estrogen Therapy member said, slapping her knee.

"It's hard to keep up with you, Dee Dee," said the apparent keeper of the minutes.

Finally, a positive I.D.—tent dress: Dee Dee, the other one: M.J.

"And hard to take notes when you get as shit-faced as we did!" said Sue. They erupted in laughter.

Brenda shuffled some papers in her lap and lit another cigarette with a leopard print lighter. "Okay," she said. "All those approving the minutes say 'Aye.'"

They said, "Aye." Dee Dee said, "Aye, caramba."

"And now I'd like to introduce our new board members," Brenda said. "Christine Robinson and Lucinda Trout."

Valdette clapped her hands lightly and let out a little "yay."

"Christine is a case worker at the P.C. Recovery Center for Women," Brenda continued. "She recently moved here from Des Moines, where she got her master's in clinical social work and mental health policy. She is a wonderful addition to the P.C. community and we're just thrilled to have her!"

"Welcome, sister!" Dee Dee said, raising her glass of Fetzer.

"And our other new member is Lucinda Trout," Brenda said. "Okay. First order of business. Did everyone see the article in the *Daily Dispatch* about the latest domestic violence figures? Last year the P.C. police answered over twelve hundred domestic disturbance calls. Three hundred women entered the battered women's shelter."

"Which begs the question, what happened to the other nine hundred?" Valdette said.

"I'm sure some of those calls were to the same house," I said, munching on my deviled egg.

The room fell silent. Everyone stared at me. This had been my first contribution to the Coalition of Women.

"Not that that diminishes the importance," I added. "Not that domestic violence isn't a serious thing."

"These statistics don't even reflect the women who don't reach out for help," Brenda said. "Which is most of them."

"It's an epidemic," said Valdette. "It really makes you want to start your own little Utopian colony."

"I hear ya," said Sue.

"Oh, let's do that!" Dee Dee said. "Let's start our own town!"

"I'd nominate Christine as mayor," Valdette said. "I've never seen someone so phenomenal at reaching out to people."

"I second the nomination!" Dee Dee said.

They dissolved into a din of chatter and giggles. Brenda brought out a new bottle of wine and refilled everyone's glass.

"Did you hear that Barb Podicek left her husband?" someone said.

"No!" Sue gasped.

"He always was such a dick head."

"I heard he slept with his nurse practitioners."

"I heard he slept with his patients."

"I heard he fondled Kathy Janssen while he was doing a Pap smear."

"Does that surprise anyone?" said Sue. "I mean, hello!"

"I can't understand why any woman would go to a male gynecologist anymore," said Dee Dee. "Someone should circulate a petition to keep medical schools from letting them enter the field."

I noticed that Christine wasn't saying anything. Nor was I, for that matter, though I was trying hard to think of something to say, mostly because this was the first social situation I'd been in for a long time, not counting Sunday afternoons at Susannah's when Mason and I dropped off Sebastian, and it had been ages since I'd heard the sound of my voice making a loud and trenchant point and everyone else saying "yes, Lucinda is absolutely right." Not that it had ever been that common an occurrence.

"What do you think, Christine?" Brenda said.

"What do I think about what?" Christine said. She was clutching a tissue that she used to wipe the lipstick off her glass everytime she took a sip.

"About the predominance of male gynecologists."

"I guess I think," Christine said softly, "that for me personally I'd rather go to a female doctor but often it's hard to find them. They're booked up or something."

"That's exactly right!" Valdette screamed. "Because there aren't enough of them. You've hit it right on the head."

"Actually," I said, "the latest figures on medical school enrollments show that there are actually more women than men attending med schools."

"But honey," Dee Dee said, "how many of them actually become doctors? It's very easy to fall back on statistics. But the fact is that many women are forced to leave the job force because of childcare responsibilities and male chauvinism. I'd like to know how many of those little premed students you're talking about actually finish their training and become doctors?"

"I have no reason to believe it's not proportional to the number of men who quit medical school," I said.

"What about you?" Dee Dee said. "Do you feel that you were pushed into a traditionally female role?"

"No. I'm a journalist."

"What do you do most of your reporting on?"

"Well, my aim is to move into public television," I said. She must have been looking at my nails. I'd just had them done in a shimmery opal color called Moon over Miami.

"But what kinds of stories has your boss forced you to do, your no doubt male boss?"

"My boss is a woman," I said. I'd never in my life wished more that Faye Figaro was in the room. She'd throw a cigarette into the wicker cattail basket and that would be the end of it.

"They make you report on shoes, on aerobics, on how to throw parties."

Was she angry that I hadn't invited her to the barn dance? That I hadn't asked Estrogen Therapy to perform? I tried frantically to recall my most recent loud and trenchant point, thinking perhaps I could recycle it here. The only one I could think of had to do with Pilates.

"Well," I said, "that is, unfortunately, how my profession works. You have to pay your dues. I have no doubt that if I wanted to be a doctor that no one would have stood in my way. Many women I went to college with are doctors."

"And where did you go to college?"

"I went to Smith!" I yelled. Surely that would shut them up.

"Where's that?" Christine asked.

Oh Jesus, I thought. As if being a folk singer isn't a traditionally female role.

"Hey, sister, I'm not trying to give you a hard time," Dee Dee said, leaning over and resting her elbows on her haunches. "I just like philosophical debate. Sorry, I'm a child of the sixties, I can't help it. Let me just ask you this, do you have a partner?"

"A business partner?"

"She has a boyfriend," Valdette said, emptying the last dribbles of Fetzer into her glass.

"Okay," Dee Dee said. "You have a partner. What does he do?"

"He's, uh, in the agricultural field," I said. "And an artist."

"And suppose he was a doctor," Dee Dee said. I was sure I heard someone snort. "Suppose he'd gone through medical school. And suppose you had, too. Who do you think would have received more encouragement, more approval, more funding, more patient contacts, you or him?"

"I'm having a very hard time making this imaginative leap," I said. I looked at my empty wineglass. Brenda leaped up for the kitchen.

"Well, it's not that much of a leap," Dee Dee said. "The truth is that until recently, medical schools had quotas for women. The men were privileged not only because they could get in but also because, once they were in, they had the benefit of a huge and powerful old boy network."

I imagined Mason at home right now, hiking around the farm with Sam Shepard, picking branches out of the fields and making a campfire behind the barn. I imagined him blasting Neil Young from the stereo and lighting a joint.

"A legacy of male privilege," Dee Dee continued. "That's what we have in this country and that's what we must fight against. Because until we do, women like you—and it's your generation I'm concerned about—will be sitting at home like little wifeys, getting paid seventy cents on his dollar, and changing diapers while he puts on a macho suit and goes to the office. Now how fucked up is that?"

It actually sounded like heaven. Except the diaper-changing part. And how could we get the seventy cents on his dollar if we were sitting at home? Her logic was eroding. This was the kind of argument that used to take place in "Intro to Women's Studies" at Smith and in "American History 101" and "Physics for Poets" and in the locker room of the field house for that matter. I suddenly recalled the slightly guilty relief I'd felt when I began my job at *Up Early*, where the women freely called each other cunts. Or at least Faye did.

Another bottle of wine had been opened. M.J. had reached over to Dee Dee and begun massaging her shoulder as if she had undergone an assault. She leaned over and kissed her on the cheek, then on the mouth. I saw Christine look away.

"All I'm trying to say, honey," Dee Dee continued, "is that you should do everything you can not to let a man keep you down. Their legacy is of patriarchical privilege. Ours is of submission. And we must fight against it every day."

"Can I just say something?" Christine asked.

Finally, some defense. Christine would cut through this reductive p.c. bullshit and the two of us would band together as the voice of Gen X reason. Perhaps we could then get together for drinks at a later date and make fun of everyone.

"I think," Christine continued, "that there are some Web sites that direct women to sources of funding for higher education. Personally, I had a small scholarship from Catholic Social Services."

Funny, I would have thought the Miss America Foundation. The United Vanessa Williams College Fund. Hee hee hee, I tittered to myself, refilling my wineglass. If I'd been with Daphne or Elena or even Mason I would have said that out loud. If I'd said that to Faye she would have said "That's racist—yet brilliant in terms of the social construct."

Instead I said, "That's interesting."

"That's a fabulous point, Christine," Sue said.

Despite the lack of real points made, despite the fact that Brenda's five-CD changer contained at least three Kenny G albums and M.J.'s tofu deviled eggs had more mayonnaise than tofu, I actually enjoyed myself at the Coalition of Women meeting. I'd always enjoyed arguing and since arguing with Mason wasn't really possible, as his favorite retort was "Whatever you say, bootsy, you're from New York so you must be right," I spent most of my time at home arguing with myself. Even then I usually lost the argument. I made a mental note to come to the next meeting armed with statistics and some prethought-out talking points. *Yogurt: what happened? It just went away?* I couldn't believe how my intellectual powers had atrophied.

"Is everyone reading *Clip My Wings and I'll Grow a New Pair?*" Brenda said. "We're going to get around to discussing it one of these days, I hope."

Apparently, they were a book club, too. No one had told me.

"Oh, it's fabulous," Sue said. "I just love Idabelle Sugar."

"Christine, I'm sure you've read *Clip My Wings and I'll Grow a New Pair,*" Brenda said. "You're probably way ahead of us on that one."

Presumably Brenda thought this because Idabelle Sugar, the prizewinning, grossly overrated author of several memoirs about her impoverished inner-city youth, was black.

"Actually, I haven't," Christine said.

You go, girl.

"I'll lend you my copy," Sue said.

"Lucinda, as a writer of sorts you've probably read Idabelle Sugar," Brenda said.

"Actually, no," I said. Solidarity with Christine. I tried to catch her eye.

"I'm reading *Harry Potter*," Christine offered.

I gulped down the rest of my wine. Any more and I wouldn't be able to drive. And what did Brenda mean "a writer of sorts"? I was a legitimate social analyst and thinker. I had once been seated next to Salman Rushdie at a dinner party and he'd laughed (I was pretty sure) at a joke I'd made about Cat Stevens (he'd asked for tea after the meal and I'd said "But not Tea for the Tillerman, eh?"). So what was I doing arguing with a lesbian in a tent dress in a faux medieval castle on Camelot Circle? At least I had lost the six pounds. Plus I was tan.

Mustn't think those thoughts, I thought while driving around the labyrinth of Pioneer Hill, trying to find Highway 36 so I could get home. Mustn't think about how deeply I'd screwed up my life. Must resist the urge to take my cell phone out of the glove compartment right now and call Elena to tell her the Vanessa Williams College Fund joke.

I was well aware that my blood alcohol level was most likely above the legal limit. But wasn't drunkenness, like craziness, not really in effect if you suspected yourself of it?

"And then she said 'I'm reading *Harry Potter*,'" I said into the phone two minutes later.

"I'm reading *Harry Potter,*" Elena said.

My head was spinning. The lights on Highway 36 were a blur. I felt like the evening had somehow pulled out a stitch and I was beginning to unravel, like a ratty sweater everyone makes fun of when you're not around.

Today's Word Is Glamoricious

To: Lucinda Trout
From: Faye Figaro
Subject: Are You Isnane?

The day Up Early does a piece on tanning salons is the day we start covrage on foreing policy in the middleeast. First of all they are totally unhealthy and b) they are totally trashy. Do you want to get cancre? Next thing you know youll be getting fake nails.

We're planning a special report on book clubs and want you to reprot on a book cbub in the mid-west. Samantha will call yo abouut it.

Also start hinking of Holiday ideas.

Like the water in the horse troughs, which froze every few hours and had to be broken with a hammer at regular intervals, the house sat like a block of ice on the hardened plain. Though we burned through ten dollars of propane a day, heat escaped through every windowpane, every gap in the shoddy insulation, every crack in the floor. In the time it took to open and close the back door, a gust of wind could dart like a burglar up the stairs and into the bed-

rooms, where the windows were frosted over and even a glass of water left by the bed would grow shards of ice by morning. Mason and
I dragged an electric space heater from room to room, tacking a note
by the back door reminding us to unplug it before leaving the house.
Save the trips to the gym and tanning and nail salons, I rarely left
the house anyway. The electric bill exceeded two hundred dollars a
month and when I asked Mason if he might be able to chip in, he
suggested we close off the second floor until spring.

"What!" I yelled.

He was preparing dinner. Meat loaf, at my request. I was sitting
at the kitchen table finishing off my second glass of wine. Though it
was just past five, the outside floodlight had kicked on and the sky,
other than the low-slung lights of Prairie City twenty miles to the
south, was already black.

"The insulation upstairs is shot," he said. "Obviously the people
who were here before didn't use the second floor. That's why there
was a bed in the den."

"Jesus."

"The house is too big to heat," he continued. "That's all there is
to it. Unless you want to put in a second furnace."

"We can't move everything downstairs!" I shouted. I pictured
my desk and computer crammed into the den, which would leave
no room for our bed. And where would the kids sleep? Erin had already announced that her room was too small; toys spilled from her
closet and covered every inch of the floor.

"Whatever," Mason said. "You're the one who's complaining
about the cold. I could sleep outside in this weather."

That night, I could have sworn we were sleeping outside. The
wind shrieked and flung itself on the windowpanes like a body
thrown against a car hood. Though we lay under four blankets and
I wore long underwear and two pairs of socks—Mason always slept
naked, even, he said, when he camped in the winter—the chill kept
me awake all night. In the morning, even after Mason had turned
the space heater back on (he refused to run it at night for fear of

starting a fire), I could see my breath. Mason got up to make coffee. When he came back, handing me a mug of coffee that was already lukewarm from the journey up the stairs and into the bedroom, he said we'd have to move downstairs.

"I can't have the kids sleeping up here," he said. "They'll get sick."

"There's no room!" I whined. Though the truth was that the first floor of the house was more than double the square footage of my apartment in New York.

"Look, it's winter," he said. "It's what you have to do some-times. The pioneers did it. They all slept in the same bed until spring. These houses weren't designed to be used fully all winter."

They were designed, I thought, to be used by people who could afford an extra furnace. Like Susannah. Besides, we were renters. We couldn't have installed a new furnace even if we'd happened to have one sitting around. I had come to understand why the rent was so low—eight hundred dollars a month for a house that would have gone for ten thousand dollars a month had it been situated in, say, Montclair, New Jersey. It was essentially not winterized. It was a summer cottage disguised as the set of a movie about struggling farmers. The shower also leaked through the bathroom floor and into the dining room, mostly because porcelain bathtubs were not designed for showers and therefore sent the water rolling over the curved sides of the tub. The towels I'd stuffed around the claw-foot legs, alternately soggy from the water and stiff from the soap, were rank and permanently discolored. A crack had formed in a wall of my office; every few days it seemed a fraction of an inch longer, a hair wider, as if our time in the house—or at least my residency in my office, where no fewer than twelve pieces of computer and stereo and video equipment were tangled into extension cords leading to a single electrical outlet—was as finite as the route of a plane.

We moved the bed and the TV into the dining room, the dining-room table into the living room, and my desk, the stereo, and Erin's toy boxes into the den. My office love seat, which folded out into a short, miserably lumpy bed, was squeezed between the wall and my desk. This was what Erin would sleep on. The boys would sleep on the living-room sofa and on the floor in a sleeping bag. This would be, according to Mason, "fun for them." The proximity of my desk to the back door, said Mason, would give me "incentive to get outside more often." He shut the upstairs doors and lined them with blankets and duct tape. He sealed off the door to the attic with a thick sheet of plastic. Of course we still had to go upstairs to use the bathroom, but Mason said I should really try to get more used to peeing outside, which he claimed was "invigorating and ultimately more satisfying" than using modern facilities.

Dear Miss Trout,

I am writing to tell you how much I have been enjoying your reports from Prairie City. It certainly sounds like you have found a new life for yourself! I especially enjoyed your report on how to throw a barn dance. My husband and I have a house with a barn in Bridgehampton and we plan to throw a similar event and incorporate some of your ideas. Anyway, kudos!

Delores and Hal Steingarten
New York, NY

Dear Lucinda Trout,

I used to watch you on *Up Early* and was always very tickled by your tongue-in-chic reports on things like the platform shoe craze and thong underwear. When they announced you were moving away to the Midwest I thought maybe it was just for a few months but it seems like you've been there for a while. I wonder how you like it.

My fiancé and I are considering buying a house in Rhinebeck, New York. It is 90 minutes from the city and, needless to say, the idea of being that isolated really scares me. I wonder if you might write back to me and tell me how you deal with being so far away from restaurants, Broadway shows, and culture in general. Maybe you just read a lot of good books, who knows? Have you read *Clip My Wings and I'll Grow a New Pair*? It's great. I highly recommend it. Your friend and diehard *Up Early* fan,

Jennifer Mengers
Brooklyn, NY

A week before Christmas, I received, like a crate of supplies dropped on a refugee camp, a package of letters from the *Up Early* administrative assistant. Some dated as far back as a year earlier. Why had they taken so long to forward them? Spreading them out among the scripts and VHS tapes and Barbies that cluttered my desk, I scanned the letters for praise, quickly turning over anything that imparted words like "condescending" and "hokey." There were at least five unequivocally positive letters. I'd save them and make sure Faye saw them. A few were critical, one or two downright nasty, and one was from a stalker type who wanted to "grab a coffee and talk transcendentalism next time you are in New York." All in all, not a bad ratio.

Most of the letters had been opened and marked STANDARD REPLY SENT by the administrative assistant. But there was one more, at the bottom of the stack, still sealed in the envelope. The return address said Chamomile Press.

Dear Ms. Trout,

I have been watching with interest and more than a little inspiration your Quality of Life reports on *Up Early*. As a Connecticut native who sought her fortune in New York many moons (and dress sizes) ago, I can relate to the serenity of country life and the spiritual benefits of waking up to sounds of birds rather than sirens. As a senior editor at Chamomile Press, a publishing company that specializes in high-resolution glossy coffee-table books, many of which

deal with spiritual subjects and their visual counterparts, I
wonder if you might be interested in writing a book about
your journey on America's Great Plains.

My vision for this project centers around the idea of
"inspirations from the heartland." Like most of our books,
this would be a series of photographs accompanied by your
text. I see it as part diary, part spiritual inquiry.

If you are interested in pursuing this, please call me at
the above number. In the meantime, I hope life in the Midwest is proving peaceful and purifying.
All best,

Sarah Vanderhorn
Senior Editor

Holy shit! A book deal! A book offer. A potential book deal or,
at the very least, interest in a book. I'd always wanted to write a
book, I'd just never been able to think of a topic aside from the ramifications of Chinese baby girls on the Upper West Side.

The letter was dated May 24. Six months ago. Those assholes at
Up Early!

I dialed the number on the Chamomile Press letterhead.

"Sarah Vanderhorn's office," a female voice said.

"Yes, this is Lucinda Trout calling for Sarah Vanderhorn."

"May I ask what this is in reference to?"

"I am a journalist," I said. "I am a writer. I am calling in response to a letter she sent me about writing a book."

"I'm afraid she's not in today."

"Well, could I leave a message?"

"Yes, but she's only in Tuesdays through Thursdays."

"So she can call me back on Tuesday?"

"Except she's on holiday right now," said the assistant, who did
not have a British accent but seemed to be trying to sound British.
"She's abroad. She won't be back until after the new year."

Perhaps Sarah Vanderhorn was out of the country meeting

with an author she had hired to write *Inspirations from the Côte d'Azur*. Perhaps she'd already contracted *Inspirations from the Heartland* with some writer living in a farmhouse with two furnaces—and an architect-husband. I left a message and agreed to call back in January.

Perhaps it is better this way, I told myself. I'll have plenty of time to organize my *Inspirations from the Heartland* thoughts before talking with Sarah Vanderhorn. But I had a very good feeling about this. Chamomile Press would solve my problems. I could quit that sell-out, exploita-job at *Up Early* and become a legitimate author. Plus I'd be rich.

Newly invigorated, I went to Hinky Dinky and bought a hundred dollars' worth of groceries for Christmas dinner. It would be just Mason and me—Susannah was taking Sebastian and her husband to her sister's house, Jill was taking Peter to her mother's, and Julie, who had requested that we keep Erin for an entire week in January so she could go to Cancún with some women she knew from Effie's Tavern, was doing whatever it was she usually did with Erin on Christmas. Mason had no real idea what holidays for Julie entailed and wasn't even sure of her religious background. He'd met Julie's family only once, at Erin's christening, where they'd mistaken him for a maintenance man because he'd arrived early and was wandering around the church in shorts and flip-flops.

At Hinky Dinky I bought an eight-pound ham, a can of pineapple slices, pumpkin pie filling, a bag of potatoes, and five bottles of Fetzer. I got in the checkout line and saw that my cashier was Clara, the one Dee Dee had written the song about, the one whom I fantasized about pulling aside and administering some counseling about college options. As I got closer in line, I noticed that Clara looked different. Her regulation blue shirt was untucked. Her Hinky Dinky apron puffed out in front of her and her face, once even toned and free of acne, was pocked with blemishes.

"Would you like to use your Hinky Dinky preferred customer card?" she said.

And then I saw she was pregnant. Her khaki pants, once pleated and pressed, were now at least three sizes bigger and she rested her hands on the backs of her hips while I fumbled through my purse. I gave her my card and when she handed it back to me I saw, on the bloated fourth finger of her left hand, a ring.

Was she seventeen? Eighteen? Was it a testament to my elitism, my know-it-all sanctimony, my strident, arrogant psuedo-liberal take on the world that I got upset? Or was I simply a run-of-the-mill busybody, a person so bored with her own catastrophes that she sought drama in everyone else's? I was not so much upset by Clara's new incarnation but *angry*, not even angry at her circumstances (and who knows what they were; maybe she wasn't so bright after all, maybe she'd never made the field hockey team) but angry at *her*. I watched her swipe the credit card through the machine, her manicured nails offset by the gaudiness of the ring. In my mind, a lecture poured forth, a supercilious, grotesque, utterly uncalled-for sermon. Clara, you stupid, self-sabotaging idiot! You terrorist of your own future, you sloth, you victim! Here you are, the classiest act in Hinky Dinky, the only one who bothers to tuck her shirt in, and you fuck it up! You let him go all the way in the car, you forgo the condom, you forget your birth control, whatever it was. And, then, what's more, you fuck up on top of the fuckup. You irreverse the reversible. You *marry* the guy. It's not so much that you got pregnant, not so much that you're probably now going to have to get your GED when you could have gone to Prairie City State College not to mention Smith, not so much that you chose to keep the baby rather than put it up for adoption, but that you're wearing the guy's Wal-Mart ring. That you're probably flipping through the bridal magazines during your breaks. That, priding yourself as you do on your strong work ethic, you're going to work right up until your due date and then probably, Lord knows, not come back for another year and a half, not come back until he's left you or been laid off from Firestone, not come back until you're sitting in your basement apartment in the slums of Prairie City watching the

House and Garden channel and thinking "well, at least at Hinky Dinky I was an employee/*owner.* Well, at least my mom can watch the kid for me." Fuck you, Clara!

"That comes to $101.63," said Clara. "Will that be cash or credit?"

"Credit."

That was the entirety of our exchange. A retarded guy carried my bags to the car. I got in and started the ignition, where I heard Peter Frampton's "Do You Feel Like We Do?" for the seventh time that week.

Heartland inspirations:
Christmas in the heartland comes wrapped like a present under a grandmother's tree. It was shopped for before the holiday rush, purchased at leisure before the last-minute shoppers flocked the stores.
As Gertrude Stein might have said, Christmas in the heart-land is more Christmassy than Christmas on any isthmus.

Three days before Christmas, as I put the finishing touches on my proposal for *Inspirations from the Heartland* (Sarah Vander-horn, astonished at its thoroughness, would surely hand me a check before she even finished reading it), Mason returned early from work and said he had a present for me.

"It's in the barn," he said. "It's a present that has to stay in the barn. At least for now."

Sam Shepard was barking at something in one of the horse stalls. Mason made me close my eyes and led me through the yard.

"Open your eyes," he said.

Mason had put it in one of the horse stalls. It stood on spindly legs that looked as if they could hardly bear its weight and its belly swung from side to side and nearly touched the ground. Its eyes were so deeply embedded in folds of fat that I could barely see them. The animal's most prominent feature was its nostrils, which sat on its nose like a pair of undulating headlights. It was a pig. A giant black pig, no fewer than 150 pounds.

"Oh my God!"

"Merry Christmas, bootsy," Mason said.

"Where did you get it?"

"At the humane society," he said. "It was in the paper. I wanted to get you something special."

"The humane society?"

"Yeah," he said. "Apparently she wandered onto a farm. Some farmer brought her in."

A stray pig! Imagine that. Mason didn't know how old she was or even exactly what kind of pig she was. He figured she was a cross between a Vietnamese potbellied pig and a regular sow.

"Irresponsible breeding," Mason said. "But she'll have a good home here."

"What does she eat?" I asked.

"They were feeding her dog food at the pound," he said. "But pigs will eat anything. We can give her our leftovers."

"She'll need a lot of them."

"We'll have to think of a name for her," he said. "Too bad Sam Shepard's taken."

Sam Shepard, in the meantime, was sitting outside the gate of the stall staring at the pig. Just four months old now, he was already seventy-five pounds. I hadn't yet introduced him to the leash. Lucky, suddenly aware of a new animal presence, bucked in his stall at the end of the barn. I felt like a mother whose children had suddenly grown larger than she. Our menagerie was bulking up around us like sea monkeys sprouting in a jar. Surely we couldn't just feed the pig leftovers. We hardly ever had leftovers.

"You can pet her," Mason said. "Go on inside the stall. You'll need to spend time with her, get her used to you."

I opened the stall and took a step inside. I held my hand to the pig's nose and her nostrils flared as if I were showing her a moldy sponge. Slowly, I stroked the bristly skin on her back, which was dimpled with folds of fat.

She let out a sound so shocking, so loud, so deathly that I jerked my hand away and stepped backward so fast that I turned my ankle in the straw and fell to the ground. The pig recoiled in the corner, a move that required her giant, practically spherical body to travel three feet in what had to have been record time for any pig. In doing so, she stepped on my hand, creating a sensation not unlike slamming it in a car door. Worse, she continued making the sound from the corner of the stall, a gruesome moaning sound that was somewhere between a horse whinny and the whistle on the Staten Island Ferry.

"Oh my God!" I screamed.

"Calm down," Mason said. He helped me out of the stall, which is to say he closed the stall door behind me when I got out.

"She's mean!"

"No she's not," he said. "She just has to get used to you."

"She stepped on my hand," I said.

"Ah hell," he said. "I once had a horse step on my face."

"Has she had all her shots?"

"Pigs don't need shots."

"How do you know?" I asked.

"Listen, I know about animals," he said. "She's fine."

I looked at the pig, poor thing, crouching in the corner. It was hard to see her in the darkness of the stall, a glint of late-afternoon sun came through the small window and cast a square of light on her giant rear. I realized then that she was taking a dump. I had a sudden flashback to the episode with Erin in the bathroom. My whole life revolved around shit.

"We'd better let her do her thing," Mason said.

"She's been traumatized," I said. I looked at Mason. His forehead was slightly wrinkled as if he were afraid I didn't like my present. I noticed he'd swept out the stall and put down a layer of straw

before putting her in. He'd obviously planned ahead. At least somewhat. He would have put her under the Christmas tree if he could
have. Looking at her, I had no idea how he'd gotten her out of the
truck.

"She's a great present," I said. "Thank you."

"No biggie, boots."

The kids came over on December twenty-third, tearing open their
presents simultaneously and, in Erin's case, disappointedly.

"I said I didn't want *Where the Wild Things Are!*" Erin whined.

"Erin!" Mason snapped.

"I wanted Diva Starz Alexa," she said.

Diva Starz Alexa was the latest release from whatever sadistic
company manufactured the Diva Starz dolls. Every evening on the
news there was a story about how the stores were sold out of them
and parents were driving ten hours to Toys R Uses in other cities because they'd heard the thing was in stock.

"Well, you can't always get what you want," Mason said.

"Mom said I was getting Diva Starz Alexa."

"But if you try sometimes," Mason said, "you just might find
you get what you need."

Had he actually said that? Mason was slumped back in the
rocking chair, which, due to the cramped quarters, could not be
rocked without hitting the dining table. He was drinking a Mountain Dew even though it had started to snow. We were getting a
white Christmas, perfect fodder for my *Inspirations from the Heartland* proposal. That morning, I'd thought of a new passage.

> *In the heartland, the heat is hotter and the cold is colder,
> but the white Christmases are even whiter—and that makes
> up for everything.*

"I wanted a new Diva Starz!"

"Go to your room!" Mason shouted.

Erin stomped into the den and slammed the door. I prayed she wouldn't touch the computer. Ever since I'd taught her how to type "Diva Starz" and "Pocahontas" she couldn't leave the thing alone.

Sebastian and Peter, like youngsters from another era, had received a baseball mitt and a wooden toboggan, respectively. They said polite thank yous. I went to the den to check on Erin, even though I felt like yanking her tangled hair out of her skull.

"Let's go outside and see the pig," I said. She was punching keys on my fax machine.

"It's too cold out," she said.

"I know it's cold but don't you want to wish the animals a merry Christmas?" I said. "We have to give Sam Shepard his present."

"What's his present?"

"Well," I said, "I figured since you didn't want *Where the Wild Things Are* I would just give it to him. He'd love it."

"What?"

I picked up the book. "This looks like a nice thing for him to chew on."

"No!" Erin wailed.

"You want it then?"

She started sobbing. Her little body, clad in tiny blue jeans and a red and green sweater that said HO HO HO, began to shake. Her face was turning red. A tantrum. I immediately feared for my computer.

And then I feared for the child. As if caught in the admonishing glance of a supermarket shopper, I suddenly saw the scope of my cruelty. This little girl who couldn't control her bowels, who had no room of her own, who made do with a father whose responsibilities had accumulated around him like blinding snowdrifts, was wanting of nothing more than a Diva Starz Alexa doll. And I had given her a book she didn't want. Not so much because I believed the book had greater cultural merit but because—and it was the first time I'd allowed myself to think this out loud—I didn't want one god-damned more pink plastic toy in my house. Because it would mess up the decor more than it was already messed up. Because after all the time spent in Prairie City, after all the ways that I'd felt I had overcome my shallowness and arrogance and bitterness over people like Haley Bopp owning prime downtown real estate, the truth was that not only was I still shallow and arrogant, I was also shallow and arrogant in a way that hurt people. I had proved nothing to myself other than that I could acquire a fake tan.

"You know what?" I said to Erin. "I have another present for you."

"You do?" She was trembling, trying to stave off the breakdown.

"We haven't named the pig yet," I said. "And I think you could give her a good name."

"She doesn't have a name?"

"Not yet. And getting a name from you will be her Christmas present."

We bundled up. Sweatpants on top of jeans, snow pants on top of sweatpants. Mittens that invariably fell off the coat pegs and landed in the mountain of boots by the door. Outside, the boys were on the toboggan. Mason was pushing them and Sam Shepard was chasing them. The snow was falling in soft chunks. A Currier and Ives print. Other than the Sunbird and Mason's truck, which were quickly becoming covered in white, there was no indication that it was the twentieth century.

Erin and I went to the pig's stall. She'd made herself a nest with the straw and was sleeping, snores emanating from her like an asthmatic tractor trailer.

"So what do you think?" I asked. "What's her name?"

"Diva Starz."

Allowing a pig to be named Diva Starz was, in my opinion, a charitable act. So was preparing an eight-pound ham, mashed potatoes, ambrosia, and a pumpkin pie while Mason was in the barn blasting Neil Young and staring into space. Holidays depressed him, he said. On Christmas Eve, Mason returned the kids to their mothers, a treacherous and snowy journey made worse by the traffic backed up for a mile in front of the Kmart plaza, then he retreated, with a six-pack of beer, into the tack room "to read." After taking a call from my parents, who wanted to know when I was going to bring my "friend" down to Florida for "some R&R and a serious tennis match with Dad" and another call from Faye, who wanted me to come up with ten ideas for *Up Early*'s "Brand-New You" package for January's Resolution Month—"What's the cosmetic surgery scene like in Prairie City?" she'd asked—I began making hot apple cider. I thought the scent might improve the atmosphere if and when Mason decided to come inside.

By 4:00, with the ham in the oven and the potatoes almost mashed, Mason came in the house and stood in the mudroom. He didn't remove his coat.

"I'm gonna take off," he said.

"What?"

"I just need to get away."

"What's the matter?" I said.

"Nothing," he said. "I just don't like holidays."

There was no way to fight this without its turning into the kind of scene that you remember for years and years, thinking, with each recollection, "Why didn't I just let him leave? Why didn't I just show some dignity?" There was no way to get him to stay without acting like a teenager just dumped by her boyfriend, clutching his coat and asking "Can we still go to the prom together?"

"Do whatever you need to do," I said.

It was, in fact, the very kind of thing I said even when I was a teenager, dumped or not. I'd been a low-maintenance girlfriend all my life and now, at age thirty, I was whipping potatoes with an electric mixer while my boyfriend abandoned me on Christmas Eve. I bit the inside of my cheek as he closed the door behind him and got in his truck. As he plowed down the driveway, I realized I didn't even feel like crying. I opened up a bottle of Fetzer. I finished the potatoes and started the pie. I got out the videotape of *Country* starring Jessica Lange and the human Sam Shepard that I'd purchased before moving to Prairie City and watched the whole thing over more wine. At the end of the movie, when Jessica Lange rallies the other farmers into boycotting the foreclosure auction, I cried.

Dark had come. The ham was done. I took it out of the oven and began cutting it into pieces. I found an aluminum pan and filled it with meat, mashed potatoes, pumpkin pie, even ambrosia. I put on my coat and hat and mittens and carried the pan outside, where Sam Shepard leaped up at the smell of the food and followed me to the barn. The wind burned on my cheeks, the snow crunched under my boots like gravel. Inside the barn, I turned on the light and the room jerked awake. The horse grunted at my presence. The pig, sentient now to the dinner bell, trundled to the front of her stall. I undid the latch and walked in slowly. Forgetting the origin of the meat, I held out a piece of ham and Diva Starz chomped it noisily and pointed her snout upward for more.

Sam Shepard had followed me into the stall and I fed him one piece at a time, sometimes holding up a slice and then taking a bite myself, a game that made him tremble with anticipation. Pretty soon, the cat (the one we'd kept after she'd proven herself unpregnant) jumped down from the rafters and there we all were, like some sentimental cartoon, eating Christmas dinner out of an aluminum pan. No longer fearing the pig, I sat down in the straw. Sam Shepard tried to crawl into my lap, though he was too big now, and the wind knocked against the side of the barn like a crazy man at the door. When I'd eaten enough ham and scooped mashed potatoes out of the pan with my fingers, I placed it on the ground where the animals rushed it, tearing the meat up like carrion, wolfing down the potatoes and ambrosia until even their ears were dabbed with food. And though I was cold, though I knew I had to break the ice in the horse tanks, I sat against the stall and closed my eyes, the effects of the wine descending from my head like a slow leak. At the end of the barn, Lucky stomped his mammoth hooves. The barn swallows, small as stones and far too delicate, it seemed, to survive the winter, rustled in their nests in the eaves. The shrieking wind drowned out even the coyotes. Every evening, darkness brought a cacophony to that farm. There was no such thing as a silent night on the prairie.

I had bought Mason a sixty-dollar rag wool fisherman's sweater from Banana Republic. He opened it on Christmas morning, where we sat by the tree like nothing had happened the night before. Though he was angry at me for giving all the food to the animals, he'd stopped himself just as he'd started to lecture me. He'd come home sometime after midnight. He said he'd gone out to the river and tried to get on the abandoned railroad trestle. He'd taken a few steps but the ties were icy, so he'd sat in his truck for a long time looking at the moon.

"Thanks, boots," he said, holding out the sweater.

"I know it's no pig."

"Not sure I have any formal occasions to wear this on," he said.

"It's a wool sweater," I said. "It's not formal."

"If you say so," he said.

"I'm going to New York next week," I told him.

I hadn't booked a ticket yet, but in the calamity of the previous night, I knew I had to get away. Other than a few short trips before we moved to the farm, where I'd stopped in at the *Up Early* offices and was treated like a former employee dropping by for a visit, I had barely spent any time in New York since coming to Prairie City. I had not, as it turned out, saved so much money that I could fly out to have drinks with Daphne every month at Bar Barella.

"When did you decide to do this?" Mason asked.

"You know I have to make regular trips," I said. "For work."

His eyes shifted sideways as though he were figuring out a math problem. He said nothing, just rocked slightly in the rocking chair, rubbing the dining-table leg as he did so. Then he sprang up and began collecting the ribbon and bits of torn wrapping paper. He went outside to check on the dog and, passing through the mudroom on his way back, picked up the dust mop as if it were a piece of candy in a bowl and he couldn't help himself. He sprayed Pledge

on the wood and, though there was barely any empty floor space—
nearly everything from upstairs had now been moved downstairs,
making the house look like a low-end antiques store—began to mop
the floor.

The flight to LaGuardia took two and a half hours. The cab ride
from the airport into Manhattan took two hours and forty-five minutes. Traffic sat motionless on the Triborough Bridge and acceler-
ated to only five-mile-per-hour lurches on the FDR Drive. I almost
threw up in the cab (this would not have been a first, only a first
while sober). It was nearly 5:00 by the time I reached midtown,
where Daphne, on whose couch I'd be sleeping, was illegally subletting a high-rise apartment from someone who was subletting it from
someone else. She'd left keys with the doorman and when I entered
the apartment there was a note by the door saying her temp agency
had called her for an overnight word-processing shift.

> Make yourself at home. Sheets and towels are on sofa. See
> you tomorrow. We'll go out for drinks and eats can't wait—
> xoxoxo, D. P.S. Can you believe this place?

The apartment bore no resemblance to any space ever inhabited, even for a month, even for a day, by Daphne. It was an alcove
studio; a Japanese screen separated the living area from a small re-
cess just big enough for a full-size bed. Kitchen counters and a stove
and refrigerator spanned the length of the wall closest to the door;
a freestanding counter with three stools demarcated the eating area
from the living area, which had parquet floors and an imitation Per-
sian rug I recognized from Pottery Barn. This was clearly an apartment that had never been occupied, at least for very long, by any
one person. The furnishings, while expensive, were almost aggres-
sively bland. Were it not for the Eames chair and a single bookshelf
of hardcover books—the most obvious kind, the best sellers of the
last year and a half plus a couple of art books from the MOMA gift

shop—it could have been a hotel suite; there were outdated copies of *Time* and *Newsweek* on the coffee table and even the remote control for the television, which was hidden in a varnished entertainment center (though Daphne had left the cabinet doors open), listed the names of the networks and their corresponding channels. The only sign of Daphne was a heap of boxes filled with paints and sketch pads and Alpaca sweaters and leather-bound journals that had fallen open to reveal dabs of watercolor and verses of poetry written in a sprawling, curling handwriting. She had lived in the apartment for only a few weeks. Her previous place, also a sublet of a sublet, had been suddenly reoccupied by some original owner. This place, if I'd understood her correctly, functioned more or less as a crash pad for a colleague of her father's, a businessman living in Europe who slept there only a few nights a year.

The main attraction, of course, was the view. The apartment was on the twenty-first floor and outside the windows, which ran from nearly floor to ceiling of one wall, the city tumbled forth like children's toys dumped out of a bucket. The Chrysler Building, with its gleaming Art Deco spire, stood several blocks down. Across the street, directly in my line of vision, was an office building with computers glowing from every window. Women in black pants and turtleneck sweaters sat at desks and glided from office to office—I could make out the occasional potted tree or a corner of a framed art poster; it was probably a publishing company of some kind. Stacks of papers were piled in front of windows as if the view had been sacrificed for filing space. A woman sipped coffee from a paper cup at her computer; I watched her swivel her chair and gaze absently at the street below, then she abruptly swung back and picked up the telephone. Even through the sealed windows, I could hear the car horns and the belching buses.

I was suddenly exhausted. I thought about calling Elena, who was busy at a trade show all weekend but had penciled me in for a postyoga coffee, but instead I called Mason. He was sullen and taciturn. I asked him how his day had been and he said it was like every other day. I could hear the sound of Erin's cartoons in the background. I knew he'd go to bed as soon as she did. Like the pioneers, we usually had no reason to stay up long past dark. And because I couldn't remember the last time since I'd stayed up even in time to watch the 10:00 news, because that morning I had risen at 5:30—not to catch my flight but because that's when we always got up—I felt my body retreat into itself. Though I was hungry, the task of taking the elevator back down to the street in search of food (which would naturally present too many options to ever allow for the proper decision) seemed insurmountable. I spread the sheets out on the sofa, brushed my teeth, and changed into my long underwear. Lying on the sofa, I reached for the remote control and then realized the moment before pressing the power button that I didn't want to watch TV. It wasn't even 6:00. It would be an hour or more before those women in the office across the street left for the evening (and given their commutes and gym workouts and after-work drink dates, more than two hours before they'd probably eat dinner) but I wanted only to sleep. In the morning I would go to the offices of *Up Early*, where I would tell Faye my ideas for upcoming "Quality of Life" segments. I lay there looking at the smoke alarm on the ceiling as the apartment slowly dimmed with the twilight.

I woke, unsurprisingly, before dawn. Perhaps it was the sound of Daphne's keys in the door. More likely I was just no longer capable of waking up at a usual adult time. Even on weekends, Mason and I were usually roused by Erin, who, by 6:30 or 7:00, would roll out of her fold-out love seat in the den that was now her bedroom and trot into the dining room that was now our bedroom. Because she'd want to watch cartoons—and because the television was by our bed—I'd have to drink coffee and read the newspaper in the kitchen while Mason went out to feed the animals. Now, in the gray apartment, I feigned sleep while Daphne tiptoed from the bathroom to the bed behind the Japanese screen. I gave her half an hour to fall asleep and then slinked off the sofa. I took a shower, pulled on some clothes in the steamy bathroom so as not to disturb her, and grabbed my coat and bag, which I assembled in the elevator. I had forgotten my scarf—the one hint of color in an otherwise all-black outerwear ensemble—but didn't want to go back for it. On the street, where the sun was rising over the East River, I found a coffee shop and ordered a four-dollar espresso. Already the place was packed with people on their way to work. There was only one empty seat, an overstuffed chair by the window, and I made a beeline for it, cutting off the path of a guy talking on a cell phone, who glared at me as I threw down my bag.

Up Early aired from 7:00 to 8:00 A.M. Faye, who claimed to watch the show at home, though I knew she didn't even get up until 10:00, wouldn't be in the office until after 11:00. I sat in the coffee shop for two hours. Since the *Up Early* office was downtown—a forty-five-minute walk at a good clip—I figured I would make the journey at a leisurely stroll. This turned out to be necessary for more reasons than just the killing of time; I'd drunk so much coffee that I needed to stop every few blocks to find a bathroom. This meant ducking into either a Starbucks or a Barnes and Noble and it was in the third Barnes and Noble—this one just a few blocks from *Up Early*'s converted warehouse office—that I noticed, on the "our staff recommends" table by the revolving glass doors a gleaming, oversize hardcover book by the formerly esoteric diarist Haley Bopp.

Though the Internet journal, long since relinquished to Time Warner, had been called "This Broad's Sheets," the book was entitled *A Broad and Her Sheets.* Pictured on the cover was Haley, nude. Her long black hair covered her breasts, which, for good measure, were also covered by her knees, which she clutched before her as though to suggest a dreamy girl sitting on her bed writing in her diary—except that this girl was naked and the bed in the photograph was a stark futon stripped of any covers other than a single white sheet and red velvet pillow. The text, printed in large courier font with occasional words crossed out and replaced with handwritten words, was formatted to look like a journal. Instead of dates, entries were marked with headings like "Monday, raining, feeling blue" and "April, midnight, a little dewy down there." Pen-and-ink sketches of a girl vaguely resembling Haley appeared every ten pages or so. In one, she walked alone in the park in a vintage zebra-print coat. In another, she sipped a martini in a bar, her Marlboro-smoking date shown only from the back. In still another, Haley was naked beneath her sheets, the shadow of her lover creeping over her shoulder as she stared into space. I read one of the entries.

> October, full moon, listening to Billie Holiday:
> C___ just left, said he couldn't handle it anymore, said I was too much, said I demanded too much. Funny how he didn't say that when he saw me that first night at Dragon Bar, that night when the music poured like honey over both of us as we talked at the bar, talked like there was no one else in the room, talked like we'd been at a monastery all our lives and had never talked, never said a word, never ~~fucked~~ *made love* until the moment we saw each other and knew that from then on everything we did would be like the first time we ever did it. Fuck him. He says I'm too much, too much like Simone de Beauvoir, too much of a daily reminder of his inadequacies, too much . . . I don't know. Well he is no Jean-Paul Sartre. That much is clear. And I will not rest until I find my Sartre, my brilliant lover who can fuck my mind instead of just fucking *with* my mind.

Though I desperately had to pee, I was so mesmerized by the book—less for its content than for the way it caused my mind to reel as to how much money she'd received for it—that I flipped to another page. The entry was accompanied by a drawing of Haley sitting on a mountaintop wearing a loose blouse and dangling earrings.

Thursday, rereading M____'s old letters, listening to Joni:
Can I just say I *so* relate to that song where
she's talking about all these guys who are
totally in love with her but she's not really
into them because she's made such a big point
of "being free"? At the end of the song you
realize that being free makes her totally un-
happy. That could *completely* be me.

Thoroughly repulsed, I threw the book down on the table and
bolted up the escalator to the rest room, where several women and
children with enormous shopping-bag-laden strollers were waiting
in line. How had Haley Bopp managed this, I wondered. How had
she conspired to turn her college-girl musings, her mundane and
largely lonely (albeit sluttish and loft-dwelling) existence into a book
that, I noticed on the back jacket, *New York Magazine* had deemed
"smut for smart people" and *US Weekly* had called "a razor-sharp
glimpse into the millennial heart." How was it that Haley Bopp was
actually getting rich and famous by sleeping (or not sleeping) with
dozens of hip New York guys who bought her martinis and I was
getting poorer and increasingly obscure living in a drafty house on
a wheat patch with a drug addict, a four-year-old, and a doll that
said *Today's word is glamoricious*?

But that would change, I thought as I finally got in and out of
the bathroom and fled the bookstore before I had a chance to stum-
ble upon another reminder of my professional failure. Haley Bopp,
I reasoned, might be enjoying the thirteenth minute of her soon-to-
expire fame but I, Lucinda Trout, modern pioneer and deep-
thinking appreciator of subtle landscapes and authentic living in
general, would be the next "it girl." Upon the publication of *Inspirations from the Heartland*, I, too, would appear on the staff rec-
ommendation table. And I would prove myself more worthy of
adulation and money than Haley because, instead of posing nude, I
would appear on the jacket of my book in a 1940s-style floral print

dress, my hair blowing in the prairie wind, my mind calm and contemplative, my soul clean and pure and good. And the book would be such a hit that I would become the host of my own Charles Kuralt kind of television show—not a local show, like *Up Early*, but a national show, maybe even a show on PBS—and I would make so much money (not from public television but from the book, which would inspire a line of gift cards and journals and coffee mugs) that I would be able to buy not only an extra furnace for the house but maybe also the house itself, wherein Mason, relieved of the financial pressures that drove him to drug abuse, would clean up his act or, if not, move away so that Sam Shepard (the man) could come live with me and Sam Shepard the dog.

Galvanized, I strode the remaining blocks to *Up Early*'s building and took the elevator to the office. I breezed past the receptionist and into Faye's office, where she was talking on her phone headset and smoking a cigarette. She gave me a once-over as I entered and it was only then, as I removed my coat that had no accompanying scarf, that I realized I was wearing a baggy pair of Levis, a ski sweater, and snow boots. In the precoffee haze of Daphne's steamy bathroom, I had forgotten that I was no longer in Prairie City.

Faye hung up the phone and, with the enthusiasm of a child being made to eat peas, climbed slowly out of her chair and kissed me on both cheeks.

"You're looking . . . comfortable," she said.

"Just thought I'd stop by," I said. I was mortified by my appearance. Had I been aware of its effect even two blocks before reaching the office, I would have stopped at a Banana Republic and bought an entire outfit.

"The barn dance segment got a high rating," said Faye. "God knows why."

"You should have been there," I said.

"I don't think so," she said.

"So I have some new ideas," I said.

"Let's not go into them right now," said Faye. "You're gonna do the book club, right? You have some fat housewives who read books. Since you contributed *nothing* to the holiday package."

"They're reading *Clip My Wings and I'll Grow a New Pair.*"

"Holy fucking Jesus," said Faye. "That's perfect, though. I want to shoot that in a few weeks. Will they have read it by then or do they have to take it a page a day?"

I had not actually broached the subject of taping the book discussion with the Coalition of Women. Though I had no doubt they'd be thrilled (hadn't Brenda even suggested this long ago?), I also knew that they considered themselves a political action group as well. They would surely try to use the occasion to express their views on women's issues. There was also a potential problem in the fact that many of them—in fact all of them other than M.J. and Dee Dee—had already appeared in the barn dance segment, although most of them, including Sue, had been edited out of the final version under orders of the stylist. As it was, I could not imagine that M.J. and Dee Dee—barring major liposuction and total makeovers— would make it into the final edit of the book club story, either. That left Brenda Schwan and her house as the major figures. Though there was always me.

"Have you gained weight?" Faye asked.

"No!" I yelped.

"It must be the clothes then."

"Oh yeah," I said, crossing and uncrossing my legs in an effort to hide the bagginess of the jeans. "You wouldn't believe it. The airline lost my luggage. I still don't have my suitcase. I wore this on the plane. Believe me, this is *not* what I usually look like. I mean, I haven't gone *that* downhill."

"The fake tan isn't helping, Lucinda," Faye said.

"What tan?" I said. "Oh, I don't go to a tanning salon. I was just pitching a story on it!"

"You look like you work at a Dairy King," she said.

"You mean Dairy Queen?"

"This is really getting boring, Lucinda."

*   *   *

Daphne, a vision in leather pants, a hand-knit sweater, and a very whorish-looking pair of high-heel leather boots she would later tell me she charged to Visa for four hundred dollars, greeted me at the door when I returned to her apartment that evening.

"You're so tan!" she said.

We decided to take the subway downtown to Bar Barella. Though Daphne was my favorite friend, though her almost mystical ability to live lightly—with just a handful of boxes, with more watercolors than oils, with no urge to forward her mail even if she was gone for months—gave me hope that I, too, could one day have a life that didn't press down so hard on me, we had only spoken a few times since I'd left the city. She had drifted to Cape Cod, then to Seattle, then, hearing of a sublet, back to New York, where she'd lived in the Village until she was again uprooted to the midtown high-rise. Though I'd seen her once amid our usual gaggle of friends on a previous trip back, we hadn't sat down together since the last time we'd gone to Bar Barella, the night I'd returned from the methamphetamine story.

We pushed past the crowd at the bar, settled on the Victorian sofa in the back, and ordered vodka and tonics. She drew out a cigarette—"off the wagon," she said—and, in solidarity, in intimacy, I took one, too. I'd changed into a black leather miniskirt and a lace camisole under a vintage beaded cardigan. We sat with our legs crossed blowing smoke into the air.

"So," she said, "I have a story for you."

"Tell."

"I spent a couple months playing for the other team," she said.

Daphne smiled and cocked her head to the side as if she were confessing to an embarrassing high school incident.

"A woman?" I asked, though there was no need for clarification. She hadn't been cryptic, merely coy.

"Yes," she said.

"When?"

"Until just recently," she said, exhaling a ring of smoke. "Until I moved to that crazy apartment. Lesbians don't do midtown. Which kind of made me glad."

Daphne began, as all women do, telling the story in unnecessarily minute detail. She had been temping at a small publishing company specializing in art books; the woman (slightly older, dyed-in-the-wool but not butch) worked there as a designer; they began eating lunch together at the sandwich shop down the block; at first they talked about painting, then relationships (after that they never discussed art again); interoffice e-mails compensated for that which they could not bring themselves to talk about face-to-face; the woman invited Daphne over for dinner; Daphne, knowing the deal but not admitting to herself that she knew the deal, came for dinner (in Brooklyn's Park Slope, naturally); the woman made a pass; Daphne was bored with her life in general and drunk at that specific moment and the woman had put on a very old Joan Armatrading album that made Daphne think of her prep school days (even back then it had been an old album); comforted by thoughts of Choate Rosemary Hall, where she had done so many things (cocaine, for instance) without repercussion, Daphne had let the woman kiss her, though, she hastened to add to me now, that was all they did that night.

"And then?" I asked.

"And then," said Daphne, "she decided she wanted to marry me. So at least I can say someone once wanted to marry me."

We sat for a minute, lighting more cigarettes and ordering more drinks.

"So how was it?" I asked.

"Good," she said. "But . . . too much."

"How long did it last?"

"Two months," she said. "Four if you count the breaking up."

"There was never any point when you thought you really had it in you?" I asked. "Because sometimes, you know, it's easy to think it might be easier that way. Easier being a lesbian. Than dealing with men over and over again."

"She never would have left me, that's for sure," Daphne said. "Although she always said it wasn't true what people say, about lesbians bringing a moving van to their second date. But that's not really what I mean."

The waitress brought our second round of vodka and tonics. She appeared to have overheard the last bit of conversation and smirked a little, as if she'd heard it a hundred times, probably on that very Victorian sofa.

"It was so crowded," Daphne continued. "I don't mean the sex. The sex was fine, interesting at the beginning, then less so, like with anyone. But then, it just seemed, I don't know, redundant."

"No space," I suggested.

"Totally," she said, which was one of the many nice things about Daphne. She gave you credit for summing up the point, even if you were off. But in this case I didn't think I was off.

"It's a crowded thing, being with another woman," I said.

"Because you did it, didn't you?"

"In the most cursory way," I said.

The five nights I had spent, during my sophomore year at Smith, sharing the bed (actually the mattress; it was customary among the more sophisticated students to remove the frames and box springs and sleep on the floor) of a senior international studies major were little more than a blur of intermittent kissing and lengthy discussions about the latest Suzanne Vega record. Upon the sixth day, the senior, choking back tears, had told me that she "couldn't handle the idea that I was just experimenting." A year after graduation she married a medical student named Rob Piscorelli and moved to the D.C. suburbs.

"I kept somehow thinking," Daphne said, "that there would be more dignity in it."

I recalled her encounter, more than a year ago, involving the Smurf sheets.

"I thought about what it would be like," Daphne continued, "to not have to wait for her to call. Because she always called. And I thought that maybe if I could just get rid of the variable—get rid of the man factor—I could be happy or at least satisfied and not have to go through the constant humiliation of competing. Because even if you're not trying to compete you always are. You're competing for the same handful of losers with women who are clearly so much smarter, so much prettier, so much more talented than those fuckers we have to choose from. And so I tried to convince myself that, since I already knew women were better, I could just be with a woman and call it a day. Because it was pleasant. I wasn't faking it. It was just—"

"Too much?"

"And not enough," she said. "There was no edge. Not that she, personally, didn't have any edge. Together we had no edge."

"Were you operating as a couple?" I asked. "Were you going out to places together?"

"Some, but mostly all we did was talk. Because I liked talking to her. But after a while I didn't feel like talking anymore. You know how with a guy someone can ask what you have in common and you can say 'Gee, I don't know'? That would never have been the case. We had everything in common, including a goddamned pussy!"

"That was always my argument," I said, "when people asked why I was going out with Dave, the pilot. We had zero in common, which made our being together sort of . . . original. I always thought, on some level, that that was the essence of heterosexuality. You mate with someone who's truly the opposite of you. Not a male version of yourself."

"Totally," she said.

"There's something sort of annoying about lesbians," I said. "They think that people—especially straight people—who go out with someone who seems 'inappropriate' are limiting themselves. But it seems obvious to me that going out with that kind of person— like Mason, for instance—is an unlimited experience. Because you have so much room to breathe. The person doesn't crowd you by always saying what you were just about to say. "

Daphne looked slightly perplexed. "Hmm," she said.

I took a drag off my cigarette and looked around the bar. A scrawny guy in a *TV Guide* T-shirt was holding court with three sleekly dressed women at the next table. Daphne stubbed out her cigarette and immediately lit another one.

"So how's that going?" she asked. "With Mason."

"Up and down," I said.

"I know I kind of gave you a hard time when you were dating the pilot guy," she said. "I shouldn't have."

"Everyone gave me a hard time about that," I said.

And then, because Daphne had never admitted that she had perhaps been too hard on Dave Davenport, who, the one time he'd met her, had referred to girls as "gals" and worn a yellow polo shirt *tucked in*to a pair of khakis, I decided to do something I had not, at that point, done in even the smallest way. I decided I would tell Daphne about Mason's drug problem, the money he'd blown, the weekly onslaught of kids, the thrice-weekly visitations of Erin, who had turned the den into little more than a toy closet that happened to house my desk. I thought, given Daphne's yarn about the lesbian affair, that she would find it, at the very least, interesting on a sociological level.

I had to begin, of course, by explaining the situation with the three mothers. Like my other friends, Daphne knew Mason had three kids but presumed they were the result of the same woman. And because explaining the number of mothers required telling not only the story of the marriage to Susannah and the "long relationship" with Jill but also the details of Mason's inebriated Halloween encounter with Julie and the cat costume and, subsequently, Mason's endearing but ultimately pathetic offer to be her Lamaze coach, it took a good ten minutes to get to the part about the ten thousand dollars spent on meth.

Daphne sat there with her mouth open, her cigarette ash an inch long. Despite my talents as a storyteller, she appeared confused.

"So wait," she said. "You only found out about the different mothers after you'd moved in with him?"

"No, I already knew about them."

"And when did he tell you about them?"

"On our first date."

"And have you, like, met the kids?"

"They're at our house all the time," I said. "Especially the girl."

"And you had no idea he'd become a drug addict?"

"None," I lied.

Daphne looked at me as if I'd told her I'd been raped. In the silence, her ash finally dropped. Then she used a quintessential Daphne word, though I'd never heard this particular one before.

"My mind," she said, "is reeling with . . . incredibilization."

"The thing is, though," I said, "he's kicked it. I think there's a good chance this was a one-time thing."

"He hasn't done it again?"

"I don't think so," I lied again. "I've seen no evidence of it."

"Are you happy with him?" she asked.

"A lot of the time, yes," I said. "I can't tell you how much I love the farm. We have animals. If he could just get his act together I think I could be happy."

That last line, I knew for sure, had in the past been uttered verbatim by both Susannah and Jill.

"Because I would say," said Daphne, "that if he starts doing it again you have to leave him. Period."

"Oh I know," I said, putting out my cigarette. "Totally."

The next day, from Daphne's apartment, I called the office of Sarah Vanderhorn at Chamomile Press for the third time.

"It's just that I happen to be in town," I told the assistant, "and I thought if she had a moment I might stop by."

"She is just now back from holiday," said the assistant, "and she's a bit knackered."

"I know that," I said. "It's just that I have a very hectic schedule. I am a journalist and she had written me, you see, about possibly writing a book. And I just happen to have written up some notes that she might want to, you know, take a look at."

In fact, I had written up more than just notes. I had compiled a twelve-page proposal, tentatively entitled *Inspirations from the Heartland: A Prairie Meditation*, wherein, in anticipation of accompanying Ansel Adams-style photographs, I had categorized the passages according to season. The first section, which I'd given the minimalist heading "Spring," began with this:

Sipping Coffee on a Suddenly Snowless Morning

Open your eyes. It's just the thing to do. It is now that the calves are born, now that the grass grows long and green, now that the snow, which, just yesterday, made this place look like the tundra, seeps into the ground for safekeeping.

Open your eyes. What do you see? Space. Space to run and keep running.

"Sarah does not accept unsolicited material," the assistant said.
"It's not unsolicited."
"Well, why don't you put in the post?" she said. "And I'll tell her you rang. Again."

The Guy in the Clouds

It was dark when I landed at Prairie City Municipal Airport. With so few lights from the town and the thick layer of snow that obscured even the rooftops and the few trees, it felt like we were descending into nothingness. The plane was late by more than three hours and yet the friends and families waiting by the gate registered no irritation. Children, allowed to stay up past their bedtime, ran to fathers who stopped in their tracks, dropped their bags, and scooped them high into the air. This slowed the deplaning process considerably. I brushed past the crowd in the terminal. My car was in the long-term parking lot. Mason, who had the kids that night, was not picking me up.

It took nearly twenty minutes to knock the snow off the Sunbird and defrost the windows. The roads were glazed with ice and I nearly skidded out on the ramp to Highway 36, where I remained in the far right lane, going twenty miles an hour as the occasional four-wheel-drive truck or SUV passed me, kicking dirt and snow onto my windshield. The access road to County Road F was barely plowed and I inched forward as my rear tires slid to the left and right. There was a small incline at the corner where I needed to turn and it was only at the last second, as I gunned the engine to get a running start up the hill, that I saw a snowbank on the left side of the road. The Sunbird plowed into it head-on, sending the back of the car sliding down into the gulch next to the shoulder. I hit the brakes, the cardinal sin of skidding, and the whole car slid sideways off the road into yet another snowbank.

Fuck, I said. I was shaking. The windows were fogging up. I rammed down the accelerator and spun the wheels until I could smell the rubber burning. Finally I put the car in neutral and climbed out. Other than the glare of my high beams, there was no light on the road; the moon was new and hidden by a layer of clouds. I walked around to the back of the car and attempted to kick the snow away, but I was wearing my lizard-skin mules—after the humiliating moment in Faye's office, I'd sworn off the snow boots for the duration of my trip—and now my feet were wet and freezing and I could barely stand. I got back in the car and attempted once more to drive it out of the ditch. It was a hopeless case. I took out my cell phone and called Mason. The line was busy.

It made no sense that the line was busy. It was 10:00 at night. There was no reason for him to be on the phone. He would, in fact, be in bed. I waited a few minutes and tried again. Perhaps there was something wrong with the telephone lines. The house was about five miles up the road. I considered getting my boots out of my suitcase and attempting to walk it. But the wind was blowing hard from the north. I would be fighting it all the way. I called information and asked for a tow truck company.

"Where are you?" the tow truck dispatcher said.

"Country Road F," I said. "About ten miles north of Prairie City."

"That far out of town and this time of night," the dispatcher said, "will run you about two hundred dollars. And cash only."

I had exactly seventeen dollars. I sat in the Sunbird, with the engine idling and Peter Frampton's "Do You Feel Like We Do?" playing on the radio, for another ten minutes hoping that someone with a truck would drive by and pull me out. When no one came I decided to call Sue and Teri's house. They lived in the country. Perhaps they knew how to handle this kind of thing.

"That's rural life for you, Little Ms. Pioneer!" Sue said. "Let me make some calls. We'll get you out of this."

I sat in the car for another forty-five minutes while 96.9 "The Edge" played Grand Funk Railroad's "American Band," George Thoroughgood's version of "One Bourbon, One Scotch, One Beer," Gary Wright's "Love Is Alive," Heart's "Magic Man," The Beatles' "Revolution," and, astonishingly, replayed Peter Frampton's "Do You Feel Like We Do?" (though it's possible I'd changed stations by then). When Wilson Phillips' "Hold On" came on I was very close to tears. It was then that I saw a pair of headlights coming up from behind. An SUV pulled past me and then turned around so its backside was facing the ditch. In my headlights I saw the bumper sticker: MY KID IS A SOCCER STAR AT MILTON ELEMENTARY.

Leonard Running Feather, bundled in a parka and a hat and thick gloves, jumped out and ran down the slope to my car. I rolled down the window.

"I've got a winch," he said. The wind had become worse. I could barely hear him. "I'm going to drive backward toward you a little bit so I can get close enough to put the chain on. It's in four-wheel drive so I won't slide. Don't be scared."

He got back in the SUV and inched it down the slope. Then he got out and attached a chain to the front of the Sunbird.

"Steer yourself out!" Leonard yelled. "Keep it in neutral and steer!"

I thought for sure the whole hood of the Sunbird would break off. The sound was that of some medieval torture session, a body being split in two. After several minutes of awful crunching and creaking and the sound of the chain rattling against the bottom of the Sunbird, Leonard dislodged me from the snow and pulled me back onto the road. I was sure the car was ruined. He jumped out of the SUV again, a cigarette dangling from his mouth.

"I'll drive ahead of you to your house," he said. "Stay in my tracks."

We drove gingerly up County Road F. I kept my eyes glued on the bumper sticker so as not to stray from his tire tracks. When we turned into the long driveway to the farm I almost got stuck again and Leonard stopped and waited while I negotiated the ice. The house was dark. I got out of the car and, in my mules, hobbled across the driveway to the SUV. Leonard gestured for me to climb in the passenger's side.

"Oh my God, thank you," I said.

"You might want to consider getting four-wheel drive," he said, stamping a cigarette out in the ashtray. "I mean, even Sue's Saab would have been better than that thing."

"I know."

"Is Mason not home?" he asked.

"There's something wrong with the phone."

Leonard looked down at my shoes. My ankles were turning blue.

"You're not exactly dressed for the weather," he said.

"I know," I said. I felt like I was about to cry. "I can't tell you how much I appreciate this."

"No big deal," he said. "I didn't have the kids tonight anyway. Next time I'll bring the garbage truck."

"I can't believe you came all this way," I said.

"Oh hell, it's nothing," he said. "*The Sopranos* was just ending anyway."

Leonard had the SUV in neutral and he was staring at the snow-covered barn. He seemed in no hurry to leave and although I knew the kids were sleeping in the house I asked him if he wanted to come in for a cup of tea. Not inviting him in seemed unthinkably rude. Besides, he wouldn't say yes.

"I'd love some tea," Leonard said.

Inside the house, Erin was sleeping in the den and the boys were camped out in the living room. Next to Erin, the telephone receiver was not only off the hook but smeared with peanut butter. I hung it back up and tiptoed into the kitchen where Leonard was standing in the dark.

"We have to whisper," I said. "I'll heat up the water in the microwave. The kettle would wake up the kids."

"Why aren't they in their rooms?" he asked.

"We can't heat the upstairs."

Instead of turning on the ceiling light, I lit a candle that was sitting on the kitchen table. It was a slablike, peach-scented aromatherapy candle I'd purchased at Pier One. The effect was one Leonard might have construed as romantic. Instead he seemed alarmed.

"You're not using the second floor?" he whispered.

"Not for a while."

"Doesn't Mason work at the elevator on Highway 36?"

"Yes, but propane is so expensive this year."

"Still," Leonard said, "you'd think he'd be able to heat his house."

The microwave timer started to beep and I jumped up to turn it off. I stuck a tea bag in the mug and handed it to Leonard.

"Do you want some milk in it?" I asked.

"If you have any."

I opened the refrigerator, the light illuminated Leonard's figure in the kitchen chair. He hadn't taken his coat off. I realized I hadn't, either. I opened the milk container and sniffed it. Even from his seat at the table, Leonard could smell that it was spoiled.

"Don't worry about it," he said.

"Sorry."

"I'm sorry," he said, "that you seem to be having such a hard time."

"Oh no," I said. "Everything's fine."

"Seems like you were doing a whole lot better when you first showed up around here," Leonard said, a little too loudly.

"We have to whisper," I whispered.

"Have you seen Sue lately?" he asked.

"I see her from time to time," I said. "Why?"

"Just wondering," he said. "I should probably get going. Doesn't seem like now is the time for visitors."

"Take your tea with you," I said. "You can keep that mug."

It was an *Up Early* mug, the kind that Bonnie and Samantha sipped from on the air.

"A brush with stardom," Leonard said, examining the mug.

He put his hat and gloves back on and trundled out the door into the snow.

"Thanks again for helping me," I said. "I don't know what I would have done."

"Take care of yourself, Lucinda," I heard Leonard say through the wind. "I mean it."

When I slid into bed next to Mason he stirred for a moment and rolled over with his back facing me. I stared at the ceiling for an hour, reeling with shame over what Leonard had seen of my life. When I finally slept, I dreamed of a plane crashing in a noiseless, slow descent into the pastures surrounding Prairie City Municipal. Just before impact, I was awakened by the violent jerk of Mason's leg.

It had come back. Like a tumor. I'd suspected it for weeks, but couldn't bring myself to ask. In the mornings, as the house tried to thaw out from the frozen night, I would hear the door to the tack room in the barn open and shut. Even inside with the windows closed I could hear that far-off rattle, like a child coughing in a distant room. He was like clockwork. It was a five-minute procedure; once first thing in the morning, then again before he took off. In the evenings, he'd steal into the barn four or five times. It was this relentlessness that I hung on to. Sitting at my desk, looking at the phone that now rang two, maybe three times a week, I concocted reasons to ignore the problem. I'd tell myself he couldn't possibly be smoking the stuff *every time*, with every single trip, so therefore maybe he wasn't doing it at all. In bed at night, he twitched. His leg would jerk spontaneously while I woke in and out of dreams about children left alone by the side of the road, puppies starving in the barn, planes plummeting through clouds to a ground that wasn't there. I dreamed of Elena's calling me to say she knew, of Faye Figaro's telling me my series was canceled, that New Yorkers no longer cared about the "Quality of Life Report" or any other report from someone whom people used to know—by face if not always by name—but had now, through her own volition, through her own indolence and cop-outs, been entirely forgotten.

Prairie City had been graced with mild winters for four years running, a welcome side effect of global warming that caused its citizens, whose well-cushioned bodies and closetfuls of down parkas inured them to the bracing elements, to don shorts everytime the temperature rose above 35. During my first winter in Prairie City, in that twelve-hundred-square-foot showplace whose utilities were paid by the landlord, only a few inches of snow fell on the sidewalk and, even then, a man came to shovel it at no expense. But the next year, the year on the farm, winter was like an alien force. Even the stoic Prairie Cityites complained about the cold and ice, the city's negligent plowing system, the outrageous cost of heating oil. They ran into gas stations to keep warm and buy Powerball tickets as they filled their SUVs. They talked about not seeing a winter this bad since the 1970s, that uncooked time before the greenhouse effect, that time that was now so long ago, though the radio still kept all the hits in heavy rotation. In January, ten feet of snow fell on Prairie City over a three-week period. Every few days, the temperature would warm to just above freezing, generate an inch or two of slush, and freeze hard again, turning the entire prairie into an ice rink.

The farm was barely visible. Frost covered every window; there was no seeing outside. Snowdrifts the size of buildings accumulated in the pasture. White lumps emerged in the yard where bushes had been. Cupid, barred from the barn by Lucky's unwieldy machismo, grew ice balls on his hooves. The barn, white except for its slate gray roof, now looked like an optical illusion. Only with the doors open could you be sure a barn was there. Somehow the animals inside survived. The dog and cat bedded down together in the straw. The pig slept the days away. The swallows crammed five and six to a nest. The horse stood and waited it out.

Only Mason came and went with any regularity. Even when the wind pushed in at fifty-five miles per hour, screaming through the night like a beast and straining the windowpanes so hard that I kept every inch of skin under the blankets in case glass shattered over the bed, Mason rose before dawn, put on long johns and a fur-lined parka Jill had given him years ago, and went outside. He took the long walk to retrieve the *Prairie City Daily Dispatch* at the foot of the driveway. He went to the barn and fed the animals. He broke the frozen water in Cupid's trough and then, as I made coffee and toast and the pink morning light came in from the east, he went in the tack room and got high. He was meticulous about it; the time he took to do it was the time it took to make a piece of toast. By 6:15 he was warming up the truck and back in the house, climbing out of his boots, pouring himself a cup of coffee, and unfolding the newspaper.

I clung to his normal moments, the relevant comments he made about the headlines, the times he elected to say "I love you" before leaving. And I avoided the tack room. Everytime I went to the barn to check the animals and break the trough water, I told myself to go inside. Just duck your head in the door and sniff, I told myself. Open a few drawers. Look behind the paintings stacked against the wall. But it was always too cold for that, too cold or too windy or I needed to get to the gym. There was always another day for that.

Who knows what made me do it the day I finally did it. It seemed an act of self-sabotage, given that with the wind chill the air was 45 degrees below zero and the hammer, after I'd slammed it against the layer of ice in Lucky's trough, shrank beneath a glaze of ice within seconds. Perhaps if I had picked a different day I would have made a different discovery. Perhaps if it had been any season other than winter, if Mason hadn't had to tow the Sunbird out of a snowbank in the driveway three times in the past month, I would have done something about what I did indeed discover. But then again, it wasn't a matter of discovering. It was a matter of confirming.

I put Sam Shepard in his stall and opened the door of the tack room. What did it mean that Mason hadn't bothered to lock it? Was it sheer cockiness or just confidence in my powers of denial? The room smelled only like cigar smoke and the regular mustiness of the barn. Mason's demonic heads stared down from the canvases. The books were toppling off the shelves: Edward Abbey, Ken Kesey, more Edward Abbey. A small wooden box where I'd seen him keep pot was sitting on the shelf. I took off my gloves and opened it. It was empty. I looked behind the books, behind cardboard boxes of bootlegged tapes of Grateful Dead concerts. There was nothing but cobwebs, hawk feathers, the occasional bird's nest he'd found in pieces and reassembled with glue. On an end table against the wall sat a framed photograph of Mason and me. It had been taken haphazardly by Sebastian a few months earlier after he'd received a camera for his birthday. It wasn't a particularly great picture but we looked happy in it—Mason had his hands around my waist and I was laughing about something. It was one of the few photos we had of both of us and Mason had bought a frame at the drugstore and slid the snapshot inside. When I picked it up to look at it more closely I noticed, sitting behind it, a plastic film canister. The canister rattled when I shook it. My fingers were going numb from the cold but I managed to pry the top off. Inside was a small rock, yellowish white. I poured it into my palm. It was instantly familiar. As a picture, a piece of granite in a palm, scrutinized like a mug shot, I'd seen it before. And now it was in the palm of my hand.

The word "fuck" issued forth under my breath. I felt like throwing up. What do you do with a pebble of meth? Do you flush it down the toilet? Like a suburban mom who finds pot in her son's pants while doing the laundry? I thought of sticking it back in the can with a little note—"gotcha" or "pack your bags." But the drama of that seemed trite. I put it back as it was and went outside. Even with all my layers of clothing, leggings under jeans under ac-

etate warm-up pants, a turtleneck under a wool sweater under a po-
lartech jacket under a now-torn cowhide jacket Mason had given
me, the cold pierced every inch of my flesh. The wind seemed to
pick up entire mounds of snow from the pasture and hurl them into
the yard. The Sunbird was almost completely buried. If I wanted to
leave the farm, even to get groceries, I'd need Mason to take me in
his truck.

Back in the house, I thought about who to call. Elena? Absolutely not. She'd send me a plane ticket to New York and refuse to
speak to me until I used it. Daphne, of course, had issued her de-
cree; if he started up again I was to walk. But she could not possibly
understand the depth of the snow. There was no way to elucidate, to
someone who floated from city to city with nothing more than a few
boxes, the particular feeling of entrapment that comes from windows too ice covered to see through, furniture too copious to move
without assistance, ice in the troughs that required, at least first
thing in the morning, a grown man of notable strength to break.
There would be no way to convince anyone that I couldn't, at least
for now, live here without Mason. Moreover, despite the degree to
which my fantasy had collapsed around me, there was no way I
could have convinced myself to leave the farm. Even if I hadn't been
almost completely out of money, even if I could have taken all the
animals and moved into town, even, I daresay, if I'd suddenly in-
herited a rent-controlled apartment on Gramercy Park, nothing
would have taken me off that farm. And though I wasn't exactly
sure why that was, I knew it had to do with more than just not being able to get out of the driveway.

"A Subaru Outback," said Elena on the phone later that afternoon. "That's the solution to your problems. See, crisis resolved."

I had done with Elena what I always did when I didn't want to
tell the whole truth. I'd told half the truth. I'd told her things
weren't going so well with Mason and I felt ensnared by the weather
and the farm. Although given the situation, "not going so well" was
more like a quarter of the truth and as the conversation went on the

white lies piled up until there was no truth left at all. She felt all-wheel drive was the answer.

"It kicks into four-wheel drive automatically when you need it," Elena continued. "It's like an SUV except you're not one of those horrible boomer assholes driving an SUV. You're more like a public radio tote-bagger type driving a Subaru. So go to the dealership, put down a little cash, trade in that Firebird or whatever it is you're driving, and get a finance deal for an Outback. Then you can get out of your driveway and live like a free and independent woman!"

"I don't have that kind of money," I said. Mason would be home any minute. I hadn't decided what to do and this conversation wasn't helping.

"Can't you borrow money from your parents?" Elena said.

I thought I heard Mason coming up the driveway, the sound of huge tires skidding through the drifts. Naturally he'd spend five minutes in the tack room before coming inside.

"God, now I want an Outback," Elena said. "And I don't even drive!"

I pulled some chicken breasts from the freezer and put them in the microwave to defrost. I took out a bottle of Fetzer and opened it with the corkscrew. Mason emerged through the back door and began peeling off his clothes in the mudroom.

"Hey, bootsy," he said.

He was in a good mood. I hated to ruin it. I stood there holding my wineglass (it was 4:50 P.M.) and watched him strip down to his boxer shorts. His clothes were always so dirty from the grain elevator that he threw them in the laundry basket in the mudroom and spent the rest of the evening in his long underwear. He kissed the back of my head and went upstairs to take a shower, where the wet towels underneath the bathtub had turned icy from the lack of heat. I boiled water for rice and listened for the shower to turn off. I took out the chicken breasts and poured tomato sauce on them and shoved them in the oven. I refilled my wineglass.

Mason came downstairs, flushed from his shower, took a bottle
of water out of the refrigerator, and sat down at the kitchen table.
He drank less beer now. He'd lost weight during the summer, during his first bout with the addiction. He'd attributed it to "cutting
down on the brewskies." And though he'd bulked up a little since
the fall, his clavicle was protruding from his chest again.

"How was your day?" I asked.

"Fine," he said. "Yours?"

"Fine."

"Those horses are going through hay like there's no tomorrow,"
Mason said. "I'll have to get some more this weekend."

I took a sip of wine and stared at Mason. I had to say something.
I'd rehearsed several versions and now I needed to choose one and
proceed. I could sound like a soap opera and say *Why are you destroying yourself like this?* I could say, with a menacing, resolute
calmness, *I know.* I could throw my wineglass across the room. But
that would have wasted wine.

Instead, I said—and this was what would seal my fate, this was
what would lead, like rivers emptying into an ocean, to not only
everything that happened later but also to the numb resignation,
the torpor, the even greater devotion to tanning that would charac-
terize the ensuing months of my life—"Be sure to call about getting
more propane."

"Oh right," said Mason. "I keep meaning to."

From there, I said nothing else. I tore up some lettuce for a
salad. Mason set the table and, when the chicken was done, I put it
in the Pier One Italian swirl-style ceramic bowl. We ate in silence.

"Not too talkative tonight, eh, boots?" Mason said finally.

"Guess not," I said, pouring more wine. "Maybe the cold makes
me groggy."

The cold had taken the very life out of me. It had also (though
who's to say extreme heat wouldn't have provided its own set of ra-
tionalizations?) left me so paralyzed in every aspect that all I could
think about at dinner was the road conditions and how many days

it would be until I could get the Sunbird out of the driveway and to the YMCA and the tanning and nail salons. After Mason cleared the table and I began washing the dishes in the sink, saving the leftover pieces of food for the animals, he put his coat on over his long johns, slipped into his boots without tying them, and went out to the barn. Though I wouldn't have believed it at the time, though I would have insisted that a confrontation with Mason was only a matter of the right circumstances—a little less snow, a new set of nails—the truth was that by *not* choosing to throw my glass against the wall or say *I know* I had in fact made a very clear choice to do nothing. Despite my belief that I'd simply postponed my choice, even a fool—and, in retrospect, certainly Mason—could have seen I had already made the choice and was, even as I placed the dishes in the wooden drainer, carrying it out in full force. He was destroying himself and I was complicit.

> To: Lucinda Trout
> From: Carol and Richard Trout
> Subject: Cruise?
>
> Does your friend (Marlon?) enjoy the sea? We are thinking of booking a week-long Carnival Cruise for next year and wondered if you two wanted to join.

Erin had taken to asking me questions, some of which I could answer ("Why is there ice underneath the bathtub?" "Why does the dog eat horse poop?") and some of which I felt unqualified to answer ("Why do Sebastian and Peter and I have different mommies?" "Why won't Dad let me come in the barn with him?"). One night, when I was reading her the bedtime story about the divaish little pig (she continued to love this book, both for the girlishness of the protagonist and for the coincidence of having a pig herself) she shushed me and said she wanted to ask me something.

"Is there a guy who lives in the clouds?" Erin asked.

"A guy who lives in the clouds?"

"Yeah," the girl said. "Like an old guy, in the sky."

A few months earlier, I would have suggested that she pose the question to her father. But Mason, though he made an exhaustive practice of educating his children in the ways of deer tracks, birds, and different kinds of wild-animal droppings, often responded to his children's intellectual curiosity with an exasperated "Don't worry about that right now." With Sebastian and Peter, whose mothers seemed eager and well equipped to pursue such lines of inquiry, Mason's disengagement was harmless enough. But Erin appeared to rely solely upon me to answer even the most prosaic of questions (such as "Why does poop get stuck?"). To my surprise, I had come to enjoy playing the role of all-knowing semistepmother. Though she still didn't ask questions like "Does the moon have dreams?," the "guy in the clouds" was a promising step.

"Do you mean 'a guy in the clouds' like a guy some people would call 'God?'" I asked.

"I guess so," she said.

"Well," I said, "some people think there's a guy in the clouds and some people don't."

"Do you think there is?"

"I don't know. Sometimes I do and sometimes I don't. What do you think?"

"I don't know, either."

"You know," I said to the five-year-old who had slid her thumb out of the storybook and was staring at the ceiling as if the guy in the clouds might have taken up residence on the frostbit second floor, "we don't know if it's even a guy who lives in the clouds. There might be a little girl in the clouds. Or just a spirit in the clouds."

"Like a ghost?"

"Like a friendly ghost," I said. "But it's up to you to decide whether or not you think there's a God. Some people think that God is not just in the clouds, but around us all the time."

"Mom said he's in the clouds."

"Then that's what she must believe."

"There's a little girl in the clouds, too?" Erin asked, slightly alarmed.

"I don't know," I said. "I'm just imagining that. We can't know for sure. There could be all sorts of spirits in the clouds."

"Are animals in the clouds?"

"Maybe," I said. "Maybe there's even a pig in the clouds."

I reached for the book in an effort to return to the story, but the girl was so pleased by the notion of a pig in the clouds that she began to convulse with giggles.

"There's a pig in the clouds?" she asked.

"Maybe."

"Like Diva Starz?"

"We can only hope."

"Is there a Barbie in the clouds?"

"No," I said. "There is not. There are only the spirits of living things in the clouds, and only if you decide that's what you want to think."

"I think Dad is in the clouds," said Erin.

Astonishing. The girl had become precocious, even prophetic, all thanks to me and my ability to unleash creative energy in those around me. Perhaps I could somehow incorporate this into *Inspirations from the Heartland*. I finally coaxed her back to the story and tucked her into the blankets on the fold-out love seat.

"Your dad will be in in a minute to say good night," I said.

"Okay."

Mason took more than a minute to return from the barn. He took half an hour. By then, the child had already fallen asleep, perhaps dreaming of things in the clouds that, if she was lucky, did not plunge to the ground like the fiery airplanes in my dreams.

There was no guy in the clouds that winter. Nor did there appear, most days, to be a sun behind the clouds. Winter hung in the air like a flu in the chest. Snow came and stayed. School-closing an-

nouncements ran across the bottom of the television screen at night.
Weather, like a manic-depressive, knew no moderation on that
land. In the summer, we'd been warned daily of tornadoes, of fun-
nels, and of rotator clouds whose paths could be tracked, like a wild
animal loose in a town, down to the individual street. But winter did
not come with alerts that expired. Instead it just sat there, a non-
perishable item in the fridge, and collected its own debris. The porch
steps eroded from salt. The mudroom towered with boots and wet
socks. The streets of Prairie City, grimy from blackened snow, sat
mute as citizens, too cold to stop and chat, scurried in and out of
their cars. They often kept their motors running as they ran into su-
permarkets and banks; in Prairie City this was a safe enough practice, though it choked parking lots with carbon monoxide and
turned the air the sallow color of the sky.

Because of the weather, only three members of the Prairie City
Coalition of Women were present at the January meeting. Prairie
Cityites, mindful of the importance of being home for the holidays and equally determined to flee town during the winter, often
took their vacations in January and February. Most went to places
like Mexico; the slightly more upscale to the Caribbean, and, in the
case of Joel Lipinsky, whose intellect required more stimulation
than could be afforded by the average beach resort, a week-long
guided tour (with meals and accommodations included) of the gal-
leries of Florence, Italy. It was for this reason that Valdette Svoboda-
Lipinsky held the Coalition of Women meeting at her house. Joel
had gone to Florence without her, leaving her free to work extra
hours at the rape crisis center and spend quality time with her
girlfriends.

Brenda Schwan, who usually hosted the meetings, had gone to
Aruba with her daughter. The members of Estrogen Therapy, according to Valdette, had a gig in Kansas City and the other members of the group were similarly indisposed, leaving just me and
Valdette and Sue. Wanting to keep things official, Valdette handed
us the minutes from the last meeting.

Minutes for Coalition of Women (COW), 11/15/00,
place: Brenda's house

- We welcomed our newest members, Christine
  Robinson and Lucinda Trout
- Brenda cited the latest domestic violence fig-
  ures as reported in the *Prairie City Daily Dispatch*
- COW members discussed how alarming the
  figures were and what we might do about it
- Sue suggested we start our own town (hear
  hear!)
- Pat mentioned that Barb Podicek left her hus-
  band
- COW members discussed gender inequalities
  in the medical profession
- Christine made an excellent point about the
  shortage of female gynecologists
- Dee Dee reached out to Lucinda about various
  issues
- COW members were reminded that the next
  book up for discussion is *Clip My Wings and I'll
  Grow a New Pair* by Idabelle Sugar (we looooove
  her!)

No meeting in December because of holidays: Merry
Christmas, Happy Hanukkah and Happy Kwanza to all!!

"M.J. and Dee," said Valdette, lighting a cigarette with the
flame igniter used for the fireplace, "are doing a benefit for a
spousal abuse prevention center. Working for free."

"It seems like they always work for free," I said.

"God bless 'em," Valdette said. " 'Give back,' " I say. " 'Give
back.' "

"Speaking of giving back," I began, even though what I was
about to say had nothing to do with giving back, "I have a proposition for you."

"Do we get to be on TV again?" asked Valdette.

"Actually yes," I said.

I could see Sue start to roll her eyes. She was no dummy.

"So they just want to get some footage of different book clubs throughout the country discussing different kinds of books," I said ("throughout the country," according to an e-mail from Samantha, was the Upper West Side of Manhattan, Short Hills, New Jersey, and Prairie City). "And since you're all so intelligent and interesting, I thought it would make a lovely segment."

"Do we get to have Idabelle Sugar come as a guest?" Valdette asked.

"Hey, that would be something!" said Sue.

"No guests, I'm afraid," I said. "Unless you count our trusty cameraman."

"He's still recovering from that horse," Sue snorted. "*I'm* still recovering from that horse!"

"There won't be any horses in this one," I said.

"We don't allow penises at coalition meetings," said Valdette. "Unless we hire them specifically!"

She burst into cackles and lit Sue's cigarette with the igniter.

"Speaking of penises," said Sue, "how are things with Mason?"

"What do you mean?" I asked. This seemed a bit crass for Sue. It was as if she'd decided to stop being polite about him. I reached for a cigarette. Since the evening with Daphne, I'd been indulging in the occasional smoke when Mason and I went to Effie's Tavern or even sometimes in the bathroom, where the window hadn't been sealed shut. Mason found this disgusting, which I found laughable.

"I mean, how are you two doing?" Sue asked with obviously contrived nonchalance. "Are you getting along okay?"

"Things are great," I said.

"He's quite a man of mystery," said Valdette.

"I didn't realize," said Sue, "that his kids are from two different mothers."

"Three," I corrected her. There seemed no point in lying. Everyone in Prairie City knew one another. She'd find out eventually.

"Oh!" Sue and Valdette said simultaneously.

"When did you start smoking?" Valdette asked, blowing two perfect columns of smoke through her nostrils.

"I didn't," I said. "I just felt like having one."

"Oh," said Sue.

"Normally I smoke crack," I said. This would have made Elena or Daphne laugh. Sue and Valdette sat there and nodded. I was starting to feel drunk.

Valdette finally leaped from her seat and scurried over to the enormous TV.

"Well," she said, "given the small attendance at our meeting today, I thought we'd take a break from serious discussion and watch a movie."

"Great idea!" said Sue.

"What's the movie?" I asked.

"Well," said Valdette, "since we are a women's group and, you know, committed to the advancement of women, I thought we'd watch one of my all-time favorites, *When Harry Met Sally*."

"I love that movie!" Sue shouted.

They made popcorn. I drank several glasses of water—it would be a long drive on icy roads back to the farm. Halfway through the movie, just before the part where Meg Ryan imitates the orgasm, I could no longer take their murmurs of "That's so true" and "Another cute outfit she has!" I said I had to leave.

"So soon?" said Sue.

"I need to get back," I said. "I need to stop at the supermarket."

"Is everything okay?" asked Sue.

"It's fine," I said. "I just need to . . . get some things."

"Okay then," she said. "See you at the next meeting, if not before. We need to get together more often."

"Yes, totally."

Valdette handed me the minutes from the last meeting and hugged me good-bye. As I walked to the Sunbird, which was parked across the street, a gust of wind knocked the paper out of my hand and blew it down the street.

It was just before 10:00 P.M. and looking like it could snow at any minute. Mason had all the kids that night; the boys would be sleeping in the living room by the time I got home. I needed to stop at Hinky Dinky, mostly because we were out of wine. When I entered the store Clara was at the first register, her belly distended and her face even more blemished than before.

Hinky Dinky, already a freak show during daytime hours, was transformed into a veritable house of deformities after dark. Every possible mutation was represented. A guy whose arm looked like it had been recently reattached—he held it in a sling and giant pins stuck out from both sides of his elbow, which had turned blue from bruising—stood zombified in the canned vegetable aisle. A blind woman tapped her cane down the length of a meat freezer, a man less than four feet tall held the hand of an obese woman in a Pizza Hut uniform. After I got the wine I went to the produce section to get a head of lettuce and noticed a small, redhaired woman fussing over tomatoes. She'd pick one up, inspect it, and then put it back. In her cart she had soy milk, bean sprouts, and a box of Cheerios.

"Jill?" I said.

She looked up, appeared startled for a moment, and then smiled. She had blue eyes like Mason's and Peter's but hers were brighter somehow; even through her glasses they were the first thing you noticed. She wore snow boots and a long heavy coat over jeans and a ski sweater.

"Lucinda!" she said. "Oh God, I know I look like a bag lady."

"No you don't," I said.

Though I saw her from time to time when I went with Mason to pick up Peter, most of my dealings with Jill took place over the phone. Unlike Susannah, whom Mason and I often had coffee with when we retrieved Sebastian, or Julie, who communicated mostly via notes left in Erin's Pocahontas knapsack, Jill made at least a once-a-week ritual of calling Mason to discuss Peter's school work, eating habits, mood shifts, and overall well-being. Because Mason spent so much time in the barn it was usually me who took those calls and while I didn't converse with Jill in the sense that she tried to discuss Peter's well-being with *me*, we had developed a tacit and almost bemused bond over the fact that Mason was so rarely in the house, even on the coldest days, and, once in the house, often neglected to call her back.

"It just seems that the only time I have to shop is late at night," Jill said.

"I know the feeling," I said, even though I had no day job and didn't know the feeling at all.

Jill shuffled her feet for a moment. She looked in her cart as if pretending to take stock of her items, though there were just three, and then turned to me with a rather pained expression.

"So how's everything going out there, Lucinda?" she asked me.

"Oh, I was out tonight," I said. "I'm sure Mason's watching a movie with the kids.

"I don't mean tonight, I mean in general."

"Everything's great."

"Because I was down at Effie's a few weeks ago and I ran into Julie," Jill said. "And Julie isn't exactly my favorite person in the world but we got to talking and she mentioned a few things."

"Like?"

"Well, like Mason sending Erin off to school with two different shoes on. And being late to pick her up from school a lot. I guess one time he never showed up at all and the school had to call Julie. No doubt he was at the bar . . . but, you know, stuff like that."

"Really?" I said. "When was that?"

"It sounded like a few weeks ago," she said. "I mean, is he drinking a lot?"

Jill looked down at the three bottles of Fetzer in my cart.

"He's actually drinking less," I said.

"Oh."

"I'm sure it was just an honest mistake that he forgot to pick Erin up," I said. "He gets confused sometimes with all the kids' schedules."

"Well, it's pretty straightforward, isn't it?"

"As for the shoes," I said. "You know Mason's sartorial powers can be a bit . . . lacking."

The conversation was making me extremely nervous; my heart was pounding. Nonetheless I took a certain delight in using the word "sartorial." Though Jill didn't appear to know what it meant, I thought my large vocabulary might suggest that there was no possible way anything could be amiss in our house.

"Well, I thought maybe I'd stop by sometime," Jill said.

"Yeah, you haven't seen the place since we redid the downstairs," I said, smirking like a witty cocktail party guest.

"You redid the downstairs?"

"We winterized the place," I said. I continued to smirk and arch my eyebrows and make little nodding motions with my head. I felt very clever. Jill looked vaguely bewildered. She told me she had to get going but that she would come by sometime, not necessarily right away, since there was so much snow and she didn't have four-wheel drive, but when it warmed up a little, which she didn't think would be too long from now.

"Make sure to wear a skirt when you come," I shouted as she walked away with her shopping cart. "Because Mason prefers that we pee outside!"

A few shoppers turned their heads, but this sort of statement was nothing out of the ordinary at Hinky Dinky. Jill, taking her place in line at Clara's register, looked back at me and issued a bland titter. I was still in the produce section, still smirking, still a bit foggy from the tipsiness of a few hours earlier and, though it would be months before I realized it, very close to being deranged.

To: Lucinda Trout
From: Faye Figaro
Re: Book Club

Are you geering up for the book club shoot? I hope so because its been along time and Upstairs is having questions about your out-put. You will here from a stylist about what the book clubbers should wear.

Also, New York Mgazine is doinf a story on Up Early so you might get a call form the repirter. Don't say anythng stupif!

The book club segment was postponed from February to March because, according to Sue, too many coalition members were still out of town and they wouldn't be having a February meeting. The month had slipped right by me, anyway. A week before the shoot, I was clearing Barbies and various unidentifiable pieces of broken pink plastic off my desk in preparation to write the script when the phone rang.

"Is this Lucinda?" a female voice said.

"Speaking," I said, hoping, as I did everytime the phone rang, that it was Sarah Vanderhorn from Chamomile Press.

"This is Julie."

She had never called before. Was it possible that Jill, despite Julie "not being her favorite person," had said something about our encounter at Hinky Dinky?

"Mason's not here right now," I said.

"There's something I want to talk to you about," she said.

"Something you want to talk to Mason about?" I asked. "He's at work. Do you have the number?"

"No, there's something I want to talk to *you* about." Her voice was edged with anger, the manufactured umbrage of a none too bright woman. It was not unlike the tone Dawn had taken with the cameraman during that first "Quality of Life" segment. I opened the desk drawer and pulled out a cigarette.

"Sure," I said.

"Why did you tell Erin that God was a pig?"

"What?"

"You know what, Lucinda?" Julie said. "You don't have kids, so maybe you don't understand how they think. What you told Erin really upset her. You told her that God was a filthy, disgusting animal. You offended not only my faith but the lessons that I am trying to teach her."

She was clearly reading from notes.

"Furthermore," she continued, "from what I hear your house is more fit for a pig than for people, especially little children. She says she's sleeping on the couch. Did you know that I can make one phone call and take away your custody? Did you know that it's a negligible act making a child sleep on a couch? She could fall off and break her head open. Not that you'd care."

I sat there tapping the cigarette on the desk. I had no ashtray, nor matches, so there was no way to buffer the conversation with nicotine. I was perplexed that she said "your custody," as if I were the child's parent. As for the house, Mason kept it spotless. It was just overrun with furniture, a condition Erin might have interpreted as messy.

"She sleeps on a fold-out couch," I said. "There's no way she can fall off. And in the spring she'll move back upstairs. To her own room."

"The spring is a ways away," said Julie. "And frankly I'm more concerned about these ideas you put in her head. No one gave you the right, *no one* gave you the right, to talk to her about God."

"Maybe you should talk about this with Mason."

"Mason," she said, "is useless."

That was it. I was furious. Not at her—though I was disgusted with her, more for her tone than for her moronic dogma—but at

Mason, not just for getting drunk and screwing Julie in her cat costume, but for trying to do the right thing when he so obviously couldn't, for establishing himself from the get-go (Lamaze coach? what had he been thinking? he'd probably been high) as a first-class chump, as someone who could be manipulated into a lifetime of babysitting and Christmas presents he couldn't afford and child support payments that, though they nearly broke him, amounted to so little in the grand scheme of things that his primary value was that of a nanny, a nanny who provided siblings and a farm, a nanny with a girlfriend who gave a damn, a nanny who loved the child far, far more than it sometimes appeared, and, were it not for that child, might have actually maintained a level of sanity that precluded the taking of illegal drugs and allowed him to heat the upstairs of his house. Though that was a cheap shot. Even with no kids, Mason wouldn't have heated the upstairs of his house. As it was, he still hadn't arranged to get more propane so we could keep heating the downstairs. If he had his druthers, he'd have lived his whole life outside. It was only women who forced him indoors. And I was number four.

"Maybe we should talk about this in person," I said to Julie.

"Look, I'm really, really busy," she said. "I work two jobs. I don't have time to talk about this in person."

"You're working two jobs?"

"Yes, Lucinda, I have a daughter to support."

"Well, I just want you to know that Erin is very well cared for here," I said. "And you're welcome to come out to the place anytime you like."

"I doubt I'll have time but it's kind of you to offer."

"Anytime."

"And Lucinda," Julie continued, "I think you should know that people are talking about you. This isn't a big town."

"What are they saying?"

"Things. Just things. A lot of people think you have an attitude."

"An attitude?"

"And it's not that attractive," she said. "Maybe that's how people are in Boston, but here it's really not cool to tell little children that God is a pig."

"I'm from New York."

"Congratulations," she said. "And if I hear that you've been talking to Erin that way again you're gonna hear from my lawyer."

Then Julie hung up. She was so much like a bullying high school girl that I found it hard to believe Mason could have sustained enough dialogue with her, even drunk, to make it back to her condo and into her bed on that fateful Halloween night. I didn't know whether to tell Mason about the phone call. Surely he should know about the "custody" threat (although given Julie's regular patronage of Effie's, where Mason suspected she went every night we had Erin at our place, it was unlikely she'd give up her free babysitter) but I also had the sinking sense that my offer for Julie to come by the farm was one I shouldn't have made. I could imagine him reacting as though I'd given her the keys to the house. Still, she seemed too uninterested to actually follow through; she didn't even know where the house was.

"The only people who talk about their lawyers are the ones who don't have a lawyer," Mason said when I told him about Julie's phone call but *not* that I had invited her to come by the house.

"Well, you might, you know, want to talk to Erin about things like guys who live in the clouds," I said. "Unless you want her to become a Seventh-day Adventist."

We were eating tuna helper out of the Pier One swirl-style ceramic bowl. Erin, having finished her TV dinner, was watching cartoons in our bedroom. The rooms seemed suddenly very cold, even the food was getting cold on our plates. I got up from the table to get a sweater.

"Did you have the door open earlier or something?" Mason asked. "Were you smoking again?"

"No," I said.

"The goddamn heat isn't on," Mason said. He got up and put his hand in front of the vent. "There's nothing coming out of here."

The thermostat read 50 degrees. I turned it up to 80 and the blower kicked on. The air coming through the vents was ice cold.

"It's fucking broken!" Mason yelled, wincing when he realized he'd cursed in earshot of his daughter.

"Did you check the propane?" I asked. "Maybe we ran out."

"We didn't run out," he said. "There's plenty in there."

"Are you sure?"

"Yes, I'm sure."

"Why don't you check?"

"It's not the propane, it's the damn furnace. We'll have to call the landlord."

"Why don't you check the propane tank first?"

"All right, Jesus."

Mason jerked on his coat and hat and boots and tromped through the yard to the propane tank. Rubbing a spot through the frost in the window, I saw him look at the gauge, kick the side of the tank, and walk into the barn and then the tack room. Five minutes later he came back inside.

"We're out of propane," he mumbled.

I just stood there and nodded. There was nothing to say that wasn't completely obvious and unoriginal. I'd told him at least seven times to check the propane level.

"I'm sorry, bootsy," Mason said. "I screwed up."

I called the propane co-op and got a recording saying that if you needed an emergency refill after hours or on weekends there would be a $100 house call fee, a $75 penalty charge for letting the pilot light go out, and a minimum refill order of two hundred gallons. Considering the price of heating oil and that it was Friday, that put the cost at somewhere around $500. I had roughly $275 in my checking account.

"What?" Mason yelled.

"That's what they said."

"We'll have to figure out something else," he said.

"Some other way to get propane?" I asked. "You happen to have some lying around?"

"Well, I don't have five hundred dollars."

"So we're not going to call?" I asked. "We're going to stay here all night and freeze to death because you forgot to check the tank?"

"Just stop!" Mason yelled. "I said I'm sorry."

Erin came into the kitchen, scooting along the floor in her socks, and announced that she was cold. Mason told her to get into her pajamas.

"And then put a sweater on top of your pajamas," he added.

Half an hour later, we could already see our breath. Mason made another trip to the barn and back.

"I guess we'll have to all sleep in the same bed," I said when he returned. "Like the pioneers."

And then, though I did not even remotely expect it—as sarcasm constituted such a large portion of Mason's and my dealings—Mason picked up the Pier One Italian swirl-style ceramic bowl, which had been left on the counter for washing, and in a single, lightning fast motion threw it on the kitchen floor.

Being ceramic, it broke into four or five pieces rather than shattering. The incident knocked some of the wind out of me, but I managed to turn around and leave him standing in the kitchen, where he immediately got the broom and began sweeping up the pieces and, while he was at it, the rest of the floor.

I went into the bedroom where Erin was watching *World's Funniest Car Chases.* I was afraid I'd cry if I spoke, but the house in its one-story incarnation afforded no hiding places. There were no doors between the downstairs rooms, just the eggplant-colored sheer panel between the living room and what was now the bedroom. The den was separated from the living room only by a wide archway.

"What broke?" she asked.

"Just the bowl."

"You broke it?"

"It fell off the counter."

"Can you fix it?" she asked.

"I don't think so," I said. "But we have other bowls."

The back door slammed and then I heard Mason's truck start up. The light from his high beams slid across the walls as he plowed down the driveway.

"Where's Dad going?" Erin asked.

"I don't know," I said. "Out for a while, I guess."

On the television, a police car slammed into a giant Ronald McDonald statue in a fast-food parking lot.

"This show is stupid," said Erin. The little girl's breath was as visible as smoke.

"Yes, it is."

The phone rang in the den. I feared, momentarily, that it was Julie. I walked to my desk and debated whether or not to answer. On the sixth ring, I picked up.

It was Daphne.

"Just wanted to see how you were doing," she said. "Is this a bad time?"

"No," I said, though hearing the sound of her voice, I had to bite the inside of my cheek to keep from crying.

"So how are you doing?"

"Fine."

"Really fine?"

"Yes," I snapped. "What do you mean?"

I couldn't believe I was getting mad at Daphne. Everything about her ran so counter to inciting anger. It was like being mad at a deer.

"I don't know," she said. "I've just been sensing something in your voice lately."

"You haven't heard my voice lately."

"Well, then I've been sensing something in your lack of voice."

"Is that supposed to be a metaphor?"

"You sound angry," Daphne said. "I'm asking one more time: is everything okay?"

"No," I said. My jaw grew heavy with tears. I whispered to hide the crying. "He's doing it again."

"Are you kidding?"

"No."

"What an asshole," she said.

"It's not that bad, really," I said.

"It's very bad."

"No," I said, "it's hard to explain."

"Lucinda—" Daphne began, but she was cut off by Erin, who had suddenly appeared by the desk, Diva Starz Nikki in tow, and was tapping my arm.

"It's too cold in here," said the child.

"I know," I said. "We're gonna warm up."

"The other thing I have to tell you," said Daphne over the phone, "is that I'm back with the Park Slope woman."

Today's word is "glamoricious," said Erin's doll.

"I think maybe I was being too hard on her," Daphne continued. "I mean, compared to all the asshole guys I've put up with . . . and she has a really nice apartment."

"Uh huh," I said.

"I mean, maybe you should consider getting involved with a woman," she said. "For real this time. Maybe all this bullshit you put up with with Mason is just masking your true impulses."

"What?" I asked.

Silly willy I look like a noodlehead, said the doll.

"What was that sound?" asked Daphne.

"I gotta go," I said to Daphne. "I'm fine. I'll take all that into consideration."

Daphne started to say something else but I hung up. Erin, as though she sensed the presence of some crisis that required sudden maturity, was trying to unfold the love seat in preparation for her bedtime. But it was far too cold for either of us to sleep without the space heater.

"You know what?" I said. "How about we both sleep in the big bed tonight?"

"In your bed?"

"Yes?"

"With Dad, too?"

"When he comes home, yes."

"Can we watch more TV?"

"Sure," I said. "For a while."

I had her put another sweater on top of the sweater that was already over her Little Mermaid pajamas. I moved the space heater closer to the bed and, in a sudden burst of pioneer spirit (and, in retrospect, an unconscious concern that Julie would catch wind that I had shared a bed with Erin and we'd all end up on *60 Minutes*), opened the back door and let the dog in.

Mason didn't like having dogs in the house, but I often let Sam Shepard in during the day. He lay on the love seat in the den and, after a few painful lessons, was now housebroken, though Mason didn't know it and regularly referred to Sam as "strictly an outdoor dog." Now, partly to spite Mason and partly because, frankly, we needed the extra heat, I patted the bed and invited him up. Erin, having no grasp of the origins of the dog's name, called him Samsha Perd.

"Is Samsha Perd going to sleep with us?" she asked. He was so big it was as if I'd let a pony in the house.

"I think he will," I said. "Just for a special treat."

"But what if he poops?"

"He won't."

Erin, however, *did* poop. Though Mason had forgotten to check the propane level, he had not, for once, neglected to give Erin the children's Ex-Lax that Julie had packed in the Pocahontas knapsack. Hours later, after we had all fallen asleep, Erin in her pajamas and sweaters, me in my neoprene jersey and running tights, the dog dutifully at the foot of the bed, Erin's bowels released themselves. Even in sleep, which had only come after three glasses of wine and a round of tears that had me biting the blanket so as not to wake the child, I smelled the stench. The dog, of course, had been way ahead of me on that.

It was 4:30 A.M. Mason hadn't come home. In half sleep, I reasoned that it was better not to move her, so I got up and led the dog into the kitchen, where I turned on the oven and sat by it, with the door open, for an hour until the sky cracked into pink streaks outside the frosted windows. I made coffee and sat at the kitchen table reading *The New Yorker*. It was only after the second cup of coffee that I realized how much the scene in my house resembled notes in a caseworker file.

I gagged when I pulled the blankets off Erin and she began crying when she awakened, a jag that mounted into hysterics when I took her upstairs and began running a bath. It had only occurred to me after the third cup of coffee that the water heater was electric and we would therefore have hot water. And while a real mother would have thought to begin running the bath *before* waking the child I led her to a bathroom that was like a meat locker. She stood there, barefoot and bawling, on the freezing tile. The backs of her legs were soiled and I wiped them off with toilet paper and wrapped her in my robe. Her face had turned red from sobbing, though it could also have been from the cold. With the hot water running, the collision of steam and cold air was so pronounced I wondered if we might actually produce thunder.

"Why why why why?" Erin bawled. She was crazed and nonsensical. My socks were soaked from the melting ice on the towels underneath the bathtub.

"Just get in the tub," I said. "It'll be okay."

"No!" she shrieked.

"Get in the tub, Erin."

"It's too hot!"

"It's *not* too hot!" I snapped.

I lifted her up, still in the bathrobe, and placed her in the few inches of water that had amassed in the tub. For the most fleeting of moments, a span of time with room for only the vaguest of perceptions, I congratulated myself for taking the initiative and putting her in the bath. It was an adult thing to do, a good-person thing to do. It was a thing I never would have thought to do in my previous life. But of course the water was too hot. She screamed again—a piercing, terrifying shriek—and I lifted her back out. Her ankles and feet were red.

"I'm sorry!" I said. "I'm sorry. I'm sorry."

"You don't even know how to give a bath!" Erin screamed. "You don't know how to do anything!"

I heard the back door slam downstairs, then a muffled curse as the door opened and shut again and Mason let the dog out. His footsteps creaked up the stairs. As he opened the bathroom door, steam spilled into the freezing hallway.

"What the hell is going on?" he said.

Erin, shivering in the wet robe and still sobbing, ran to him and clutched his legs.

"Daddy!"

There was nothing he could say. At first, Mason assumed the dog had soiled the bed, but as soon as he removed the sheets he stopped and sat down on the mattress, rubbing his temples and looking like he might cry, though judging from his eyes he already appeared to have cried a great deal.

"Lucinda," he said, and then said nothing else. It was the first time I could remember him actually calling me by name.

Erin, who now splashed contentedly in a bath of more moderate temperature that Mason had drawn for her, was singing the Pokémon theme music. The redness in her feet and ankles had quickly receded, taking with it my fears that Child Protective Services would be arriving by noon. The Diva Starz Nikki doll lay on the bedroom floor and when I accidentally kicked her she announced *Silly willy I look like a noodlehead.*

"Why couldn't you have broken this doll?" I said to Mason.

He continued to sit on the bed with his head in his hands. Then he carried the sheets into the mudroom and put them in a garbage bag. We had only one other set of sheets. He poured a cup of coffee and sat at the table near the open oven.

"I just can't stand living with someone who hates me," Mason said.

"Who hates *you?*"

"Everytime I walk in the door you look at me like I'm a criminal," he said. "If you're so miserable why don't you just leave? Are you waiting for the snow to melt?"

"Where did you go last night?"

"I slept at the elevator."

"Why couldn't we all have slept at the elevator?"

This was an unfair question. The grain elevator, which was packed seven stories high with corn and wheat, was infested with rodents. The one time Mason had given me a tour, two rats had scurried across the floor of the basement storage room and I'd screamed so loudly that Frank Fussell came down because he thought someone was injured. I would have slept in the barn before sleeping in the elevator, although it, too, had mice.

"I just needed to get away," Mason said. "I'm sorry. I'll never do it again."

"What is it about your life that makes it so unbearable?" I asked.

"What is it about your life that makes you have to pretend it's some stupid movie?" Mason asked. "Why do you have to turn everything into a damn Christmas card? Why do you have to throw a barn dance and pretend I don't even live here?"

"I wasn't pretending that to the people *here.* It was just for the segment. I told you, it needs to seem like I live here alone."

"You could never live here alone!"

"I know," I said.

"Which is why you stay with me," he said. "Otherwise I'd be gone already. You could have your stupid women's meetings here and all your pals could come from New York and be impressed at how independent you are. And Sam Shepard himself could come and live here with you and maybe you could have him jump into the freezing river for your TV show, although he's so old he'd probably have a heart attack."

"Are you mad about that?" I asked. "The bathing in the river thing?"

"Do you know what idiots you people from New York are?"

"It's not like that . . ."

"Do you know what an idiot I look like, what a total ass people think I am living out here with some girl from New York who dresses me up in costumes and films me bathing in the river? With a fucking scrub brush that I'd *never* use!"

"I'm sorry . . ."

"You think Jill's a nag?" Mason said. He took the filter from the coffeepot and dropped it in the garbage can. "You think Julie screwed me backward and forward? They got nothing on you, sister."

"You're a drug addict!" I hissed. "You are a fuckup. All your life, you get close to having it good, and then you just screw up and screw up and screw up!"

"At least I know I'm a fuckup," he whispered. Upstairs, Erin had stopped singing. "At least I know what I am. What are you? An artist? Some kind of TV star?"

"I'm just trying to live my life."

"Bullshit! You're trying to make your life into some kind of project. You're trying to sell your life. *I'm* trying to live my life."

"What kind of life is that?"

"I work in a grain elevator. I have kids. I hike around. I do a little more drugs than I should probably do. That's it."

"That's pathetic."

"Fuck you!" he said. "And the horse you rode in on."

"Daaaad!" Erin called from the bathtub. Mason got up and headed for the stairs. It was not yet 8:00 A.M.

"That's a real life," he said as he climbed the stairs. "I know it's not really your style. I'm sorry I couldn't have been a better sub-ject . . . and the propane guy is on his way."

Embrace, Empathize, Empower

To: Lucinda Trout
From: *Up Early* Clothing and Accessories Department
Re: wardrobe suggestions for book club shoot

Lucinda, in keeping with the warm, sisterly nature of book clubs we'd like to stick with as many earth tones as possible with a few accents of color thrown in (red but not green and a deeper red rather than a brighter red). We would ask that the participants keep their hairstyles as simple as possible and that the more heavyset members try to position themselves in either oversized chairs or at the end of a sofa so as to minimize figure flaws. Below are some further suggestions:

- Turtleneck sweaters are good; please encourage two or three women to wear turtleneck sweaters, preferably in teal, burnt sienna, or charcoal (but no two people in the same color, obviously)
- No plaids or animal prints, subtle prints are fine so long as not green

- Earrings and accessories should be small and tasteful, no dangling earrings or large bangles, jewelry should be platinum or silver (no gold!)
- No smoking on camera

Also Faye says to please send the exact street address of the location of the book club as she needs it on file for legal purposes. Have a blast!

I was chastened by what Mason had said. Perhaps it had been wrong to ask him to bathe in the freezing river, though more than a year had passed since then and I thought he'd more or less forgotten about it. The barn dance segment, it was true, had omitted the fact that he lived on the farm at all—that he meticulously maintained the barn, that the animals that inhabited it could not have survived without his care—but considering that the event had coincided with the peak of his first bout of drug addiction, I had questioned neither my ethics nor my manners.

In the end, we had been without heat for only about sixteen hours. Mason had called the propane co-op from the grain elevator and by the time Erin got out of the bathtub, a guy had come with a gas truck and relit the pilot light and put in two hundred gallons of heating oil. Mason paid him five hundred dollars cash. When I asked where he got the money he just said, "I got it, okay?" and then he looked at me and said, "I'm finished with the meth. That was the end of it" and because I was too tired to do anything else, I'd gone out and bought him two bags of Hershey's kisses, most of which Erin and I ate.

Meanwhile, Faye called to say that the *Up Early* executives were putting pressure on her to improve the "Quality of Life" series and that unless the book club segment went really well—"Like someone having a sudden flashback to being molested as a child," she said— my job would be in serious jeopardy.

"That's not the kind of thing I can guarantee," I told Faye.

"Can't you maybe ask one of them to say something like that?" she asked.

"You're disgusting."

"Lucinda, Upstairs is threatening to make me come out there and direct the segment myself," Faye said. "And God knows that's the last fucking place on earth I want to go."

"You're gonna come out here?"

"No, but they're making me call that guy, Joel Lipschitz or whatever his name is, and make sure he knows how crucial it is that this turns out right."

"I have no reason to think it won't go smoothly," I said. "These women are very passionate about Idabelle Sugar."

"Well, Upstairs is very passionate about not getting beat in the ratings by *A.M. Style*, which is on goddamned *cable*," Faye said. "And we've got a reporter following us around all week for the *New York Magazine* story and since that tart Bonnie already pronounced Bosnia like 'bonsai' live on the air yesterday we can't afford another fuckup."

"Bonnie didn't know what Bosnia was?"

"That girl couldn't find Africa if she was screwing Queasy Mfume on a relief map," said Faye.

"*Kweisi* Mfume," I said. "And I wasn't aware he had much to do with Bosnia."

"Don't be fresh!" Faye yelled into the phone. "Just remember, I want some serious repressed memory syndrome at that book club or we're both going to be updating our résumés. If you have to, tell them you were fondled by your gynecologist."

Three days later, I reported for duty at Brenda Schwan's house.

"Nothing's better than good friends, good food, and good conversation," I said in front of the camera. "And more and more, people are throwing something new into the mix—good books! Today we're visiting a book club in the midwestern town of Prairie City, where women of all different ages and backgrounds have come together as they do once a month to talk not only about the world they share but also about how a special book can bond them together in ways they never imagined. This month's selection: *Clip My Wings and I'll Grow a New Pair*, by renowned poet and novelist Idabelle Sugar."

Jeb, crouching behind his tripod in Brenda Schwan's snow white, sunken living room, motioned for me to stop. Sue and Valdette had burst through Brenda's door as I was finishing my intro, thereby ruining the take. I put down my microphone and waited as they wiped their shoes on the mat. They each carried grocery bags filled with wine.

"It's the big night!" Valdette cooed. "I'm so nervous!"

Sue looked at me uneasily. "Are you going to be filming the whole time?" she asked. "Because we kind of have an issue we want to discuss after the book part."

No doubt the issue was the softball match against the Prairie City chapter of NOW.

"Jeb will be here for only an hour or so," I said. "We won't even get through two bottles of wine before he's done."

"Actually," said Jeb to me, "Lipinsky told me to take more time on this one. Apparently your boss has a lot riding on this."

"Oh, that's just Joel being a perfectionist!" said Valdette.

"No, Joel's pretty lax," said Jeb. "It's the TV show that's squeezing our balls. I guess he talked to Lucinda's boss. He seemed pretty shaken up."

Jeb had Sue and Valdette sit down while he ran the microphone cord underneath their blouses, which were green and zebra print, respectively. I noticed that Sue had worn her beaded African necklace. In the middle of this act, M.J. and Dee Dee barreled through the front door. Dee Dee, who was wearing a turtleneck *under* an Estrogen Therapy T-shirt (which featured a guitar whose neck formed the yoni sign), clucked when she saw Jeb.

"Didn't know we were being frisked," Dee Dee said.

M.J., when she took off her coat, revealed a teal turtleneck sweater and a beaded African necklace. Her earrings hung nearly to her shoulders.

I wondered if either of them had been molested as children and whether or not *Clip My Wings and I'll Grow a New Pair* might elicit some memories. With any luck it would be M.J., as she was the slimmer of the two.

The rest of the Coalition of Women arrived en masse, including Christine, who, other than her gold watch, had adhered flawlessly to the wardrobe requirements. As Jeb pawed them with the microphone cords, Brenda dispensed white wine and laid the food out on the chrome coffee table. There were deviled eggs, Rice Krispies treats, Fritos, cold cuts of ham and turkey, M&Ms, string cheese, pizza rolls, and four bottles of Fetzer. Six women were seated on Brenda's lime green modular sofa. I suggested that Dee Dee move to the overstuffed chair.

"Okay, you guys," I said. "Don't do anything different than you normally do. We're just going to shoot the meeting in its natural state and edit it later."

"We're rolling," said Jeb.

Valdette and Brenda immediately lit up cigarettes.

"Okay," Brenda said, exhaling a plume of smoke. "As president of this coalition, or, I should say 'club,' I guess I'll just remind everyone that the first thing we do is go around the room and let everyone share with the group the passage from the book that was most meaningful to her."

"I'll go first," said Dee Dee, who was sitting with her enormous thighs spread open in the overstuffed chair. "Because I feel—being a veteran of the civil rights movement—that I need to set the tone."

"Before you do that," Brenda interrupted her, "let's just all be clear on what this book is about—because I know sometimes some of us get a little, ahem, behind in our reading."

Brenda held up the book and looked right into the camera.

"*Clip My Wings and I'll Grow a New Pair* tells the story of a young African American girl growing up in the projects of the South

Side of Chicago," she recited, paraphrasing from the back of the book jacket. "She lives in a two-room apartment with ten brothers and sisters, a few of whom are the result of her mother's being raped by the building superintendent, who, of course, can turn off the heat if he feels like it so she has to submit to him. The girl grows up in these absolutely awful conditions, surrounded by racism and sexism and terrible abuse from men, and eventually discovers that she has enormous gifts as a painter. So she gets out of the projects and becomes a famous artist who eventually goes back to the projects and founds a battered women's shelter that's also an art school."

"But that's after she's raped by her art teacher," Dee Dee interrupted. "Who makes her pose nude."

"Right," said Brenda.

"And don't forget the back-alley abortion," said Valdette. "Which still goes on today."

I made a mental note to ask if any of them had undergone a back-alley abortion.

"Right," Brenda said again, finally putting the book down. "But the point is that she uses her gift—her gift of painting—and her experience with all these struggles to give back to the community she came from. And that final scene, that image of all the women's paintings on the wall of the shelter, with the terrifying images they depict, I just found it so powerful."

"Well, now that she's described the whole book—" Sue began.

"More wine!" Valdette shouted. A few other women clapped.

"Seriously," Dee Dee said. "I'd like to read the passage I found most meaningful. Because I think it just, well, it cuts right to the bone."

"Go ahead," said Brenda.

"*The foul breath of the morning caressed my face like fruit gone bad,*" Dee Dee read. "*Mama had already gone, to the first of her three jobs, this one cleaning house for a white lady who called her 'the girl,' though in my mind I couldn't imagine Mama ever being a girl. We didn't see no white folks where we lived, just on the TV, until Mr. Dawson pulled it out of the wall with his beasty hands and tossed it out the window one night when he was drunk. Mama said to pay him no mind. But I paid him mind. I paid him mind when I drew pictures. I drew pictures of Mr. Dawson looking like a beast, his teeth fangy and his black skin darker than the meanest black dog. Years later, when I'd become famous and was showing my paintings in Paris, white folks would tell me my work was haunting. But compared to those pictures of Mr. Dawson, which I hid in the closet where Mama couldn't find 'em, everything else I did was as bright as the sun shining on the Chicago River, all lit up like a ribbon wrapped right around heaven hallelujah amen."*

The room was silent. M.J. reached over to Dee Dee in the overstuffed chair and put her hand on her knee. A few women nodded and murmured.

"That was very powerful," Sue said finally.

I looked at Christine. She'd been following along in the book. Now she was staring into her wineglass.

"I'm curious," I said to Dee Dee, knowing that she was far too fat to ever make it into the segment and I could therefore veer off the topic, "as to how this connects to what you were saying about being a veteran of the civil rights movement."

"I think that's pretty clear," said Dee Dee.

"How, specifically?"

"Well, for one thing," said Dee Dee, resting her elbows on her spread-eagle knees, "this is a very powerful and candid exploration of race."

"Uh huh."

"And for another thing," she continued, "she rises above her circumstances by using her circumstances. She doesn't want to become white. She loves blackness. She paints blackness."

"So beautifully," Valdette chimed in. "Even though you don't see her paintings you can tell she's a genius."

"So tell me," I asked Dee Dee, "a little bit about your civil rights activities. I'm interested."

"Oh honey," Dee Dee said, waving her hand. "We don't have time. Let's just say I was very active in the sixties."

"In Prairie City?"

"In P.C., in Des Moines, in Sioux Falls, you name it. Let's put it this way, you know the strip mall on Prairie Boulevard?"

I did know it as it was the location of Hollywood Tan.

"That land," she continued, "was once an open field. And we had a benefit concert there like you wouldn't believe."

"I remember it," said Sue.

"It was intense," said Dee Dee. "It was freakin' Yasgur's farm."

"And now there's a Payless Shoes and a Weight Watchers there," said M.J.

"What are you gonna do," said Dee Dee. "'They paved paradise, put up a parking lot.'"

Jeb had taken the camera off the tripod and was snaking around the modular sofa trying to get a closeup of Dee Dee, which was a colossal waste of time. Brenda lit another cigarette.

"Moving right along," Brenda said. "Who wants to be the next person to share a passage that touched her?"

"I'll go," Valdette said. She stamped out her cigarette and put on her reading glasses. "This is from page 274."

"Everyone find it?" asked Brenda. "Go ahead, Valdette."

"'Get your black ass out of this place,' the beastylike fangy-fanged toothed Mr. Gallery owner, Mr. Black-girls-can't-paint-but-they-sho-can-pose art expert extraordinaire shouted at me," Valdette read. "'Your kind wasn't made for painting. Throw some paint on the floor and wipe it off,' he said. 'That's what you're good at.' But he was wrong. Even as the hot sun soaked the loft like Mama's oven had come alive and taken over the world, I knew that he was wrong. I knew that I could paint and paint better and with more heart and soul and godly godliness than most white folks, except maybe

Michelangelo, ever had. Even then, after the fangy-fanged gallery owner had tried to rip off my dress, even after he'd clipped my wings so I couldn't fly, I felt new ones a'sproutin'. He'd clipped my wings and I'd done gone grew a new pair. He'd clipped my wings, but I had some to spare."

Valdette was weeping. M.J. handed her a tissue.

"Intense stuff," said Dee Dee.

"I just relate to that so much," Valdette sniffed. "I thought about becoming an artist. But I didn't think I was good enough."

"They tried to keep you down," Dee Dee said.

"I've never told anyone that before," said Valdette. She dabbed her eyes and lit another cigarette.

"This is a safe haven," said Brenda, refilling the empty wineglasses. "This is a place where you can say anything."

"Is there anything else you want to say?" I asked Valdette. "About people trying to keep you down?"

"Like what?" she asked.

"You know," I said, "any way in which you were oppressed? Battered? Exploited?"

I was hating myself, and hating Faye even more.

"Well, for starters," Valdette said, "my seventh-grade art teacher mistook my self-portrait for a drawing of Minnie Mouse."

"That must have been very painful," said Dee Dee.

Sue squirmed uncomfortably. "Did you get enough, Lucinda? Or should we go on?"

"We haven't heard from Christine yet," said Brenda.

"Christine is so smart," said Valdette. "Her analysis is going to put us all to shame."

Christine, in her gray cashmere turtleneck sweater, slim wool pants, and tiny pearl earrings, shifted in her seat in the other overstuffed chair. Even her shoes were perfect, delicate flats worn with opaque knee-high stockings. Her shimmery lips highlighted her smooth, light brown skin. I held my breath as she thumbed through the book. Whatever she said was guaranteed to wind up in the segment and would probably constitute most of it. She was the only one who looked good enough.

"I have to say," she began. Jeb squatted in front of her and pointed the camera right in her face. "That I didn't actually have a chance to read the book."

Shit! I thought.

"Oh!" said Brenda.

"Don't worry about it!" cried Valdette. "I know how it is. Not enough hours in the day!"

I thought, for a moment, that Christine might have neglected to read the book on principle. Clearly by now she'd have "gotten hip" (as Sue might have said) to the efforts of certain Prairie Cityites to infuse into their daily lives a multicultural spirit that would lift them to a higher plain than the flat, snow-covered expanse on which most residents were more than happy to sit. Surely she recognized that her induction into the Coalition of Women, which had been celebrated with considerably more gusto than my own, was less a matter of her intellectual contributions at meetings (she had, according to my count, opened her mouth exactly once) than with the guileless way she mesmerized Prairie City's more liberal citizens with her particular blend of dark(ish) skin and correct English, a combination that Idabelle Sugar, for instance, knew better than to show to the general public (and this was why Idabelle Sugar would go on, the following year, to win another prestigious literary prize and it would take Christine more than fifteen years—although she would eventually win by a large margin—to be elected to a seat in the state legislature).

Christine, still with the camera inches from her face, fidgeted with her wineglass and crossed and uncrossed her long, slender legs.

"It's just," she said, "that I'm still reading *Harry Potter and the Goblet of Fire.*"

I was panicking. This segment was a disaster. In desperation, I clapped my hands and yelled "Folks, folks, there's an issue I've

been wanting to raise, something I thought might have some reso-
nance in conjunction with this very powerful novel."

"Speak, woman," said Dee Dee.

"Has anyone here ever been fondled by her gynecologist?" I
asked.

"Are you talking about Barb Podicek's husband?" Valdette
gasped.

"No names, please, ladies," said Jeb from behind the camera.

"Honey, why in the world don't you go to the P.C. Women's
Wellness Center?" Dee Dee asked me. "It's totally holistic, they accept most insurance plans—"

Dee Dee was interrupted by the doorbell, which played a very
long, chiming version of "Moon River." This must have been the
reason that everyone else just came in without ringing the bell.

Brenda shouted that the door was open and from where I sat I
saw only Brenda's bewildered expression as whoever it was entered
the house.

"Can I help you?" Brenda asked.

"Where's Lucinda?" a voice asked.

I turned around and, there, in the doorway, stood Faye Figaro.
A short guy in a bomber jacket pushed in behind her. He wore a
knapsack and was carrying a notebook and was so unassuming that
Faye's austere presence seemed to eclipse him totally.

Like a hallucination, Faye stood on the steps leading to the
sunken living room, a black leather coat wrapped around her skele-
tal body, high-heel boots tracking snow onto the carpet. Her head
was covered (as if to protect her from the weather) with a filmy silk
scarf. In the whiteness of Brenda's living room, Faye's dark, attenu-
ated figure, combined with the pallid face that even beneath the
kerchief conveyed her horror at Brenda's design sense, lent her the
appearance of a phantom who couldn't bear the decor of her haunt.

The Prairie City Coalition of Women must have surely believed
they were looking at a ghost. Valdette jerked in her seat as though
an icy breath—perhaps one similar to "the foul breath of the morn-

ing"—had grazed the back of her neck. Faye scanned the crowd, registering greater disgust with each coalition member she surveyed, until she spotted me.

"There you are," she said.

"Faye!" I gasped.

Jeb still had the camera rolling. I motioned for him to stop but he shook his head and motioned toward Faye. "I can't," he mouthed.

"Can I help you?" Brenda asked again.

"This is my boss, Faye Figaro," I said to the coalition.

"Oh!" The coalition sighed. They began talking among themselves excitedly. Valdette got her coat, a down parka with a fake leopard collar, and offered it to Faye.

"We're just now doing the filming," Valdette said. "We didn't know you were coming, otherwise we would have waited for you."

Faye surveyed the women again, as if to catalog the particular atrocities of each of their outfits, and began shaking her head. Dee Dee hoisted herself from the overstuffed chair, ambled up to the entrance way (from which Faye, no doubt fearing the sunken living room, had not ventured), and stuck out her hand.

"I'm Dee Dee," she said.

Faye looked not at Dee Dee's face but at her Estrogen Therapy T-shirt, the letters of which were partially obscured by the folds of her stomach.

"Estrogen Rape?" Faye asked.

"Estrogen Therapy," Dee Dee said. "We're a folk vocal duo. That's my partner, M.J."

"Holy Jesus," Faye said.

"Is this your partner?" Dee Dee asked, looking at the guy in the bomber jacket.

"Oh God no," Faye said.

"I'm Randy Abrams from *New York Magazine*," the guy said. "I'm doing a story on *Up Early*. Faye came out here to supervise the shoot and I thought I'd tag along."

"You're kidding!" I yelled.

"How wonderful!" Valdette cooed.

"Well, have a seat," Brenda said. "I'll get you some wine. I guess it's a multimedia event!"

"Stop the tape!" Faye barked at Jeb. "Lucinda, I want to speak with you privately for a moment."

Faye walked with me to Brenda's kitchen and as soon as she got out of Randy Abrams's line of vision she grabbed me by the elbow and dragged me into the bathroom. It was done entirely in pastel pinks and had a beach theme. Seashells and pieces of coral lined the counter and the toilet seat was covered with a padded turquoise cushion. Faye pushed me down on the toilet seat, causing air to seep from the cushion in a slow hiss.

"What the hell is the matter with you?" Faye yelled.

"What are you doing here?" I asked.

"Is this the book club?"

"What do you think it is?"

Faye slammed her fist on the counter, flinging a seashell onto the floor.

"They're all fat!" she screamed. "What do I keep telling you about shooting fat people?"

"You expect me to hire actors?" I asked.

"When the people look like that, yes!" she yelled. "And maybe a set designer while you're at it. What is with that sofa?"

"You only came here to impress that reporter, didn't you?" I asked.

"He has halitosis," Faye whispered. "I keep offering him Altoids but he's not catching on."

"Did you offer him cash, too? To not write about what a freak you are?"

"Lucinda," Faye said, her giant hands pressed against my shoulders, "we are in serious trouble. Upstairs says you have to get this segment right! Otherwise they're going to, like, make structural changes."

"They're going to fire you?"

"Oh God no," she said, her mouth curling. "They just might, like, kill your series. And then you'd be stuck out here, exhaled from New York. Like a fugitive. I don't want that to happen to you."

"Do you mean exiled?"

"Plus," she whispered, her face contorting like she'd tasted something rotten, "they're threatening to make me have sensitivity training, with role playing and falling backward and having someone catch you and all this other bullshit. That is just so profoundly uninteresting to me."

"Faye," I said, "those are good women out there. They've been really nice to me and they really care about the book. So we need to go out and do the segment."

I was surprised by how much truth there was to that. They were good women. Maybe it was only in seeing them in the same room with Faye that I had finally realized it. This was pathetic, I knew.

"You mean you're, like, *friends* with them?" Faye asked.

"Please don't embarrass me in front of them," I said.

Faye looked at me as though I'd just drooled all over myself.

I left her to pick up the shells in the bathroom, one of which had broken, and returned to Brenda's living room. Randy Abrams was holding court with the Coalition of Women, telling them about his recent interview with Bruce Willis.

"Moving right along!" I said. "We're very lucky to have Faye here to guide us in our discussion."

"It's wonderful to see a woman in a position of authority," Dee Dee said. "You're lucky to have her for a role model, Lucinda."

Jeb turned the camera back on and pointed it at Dee Dee. She stared into it, flustered, and finally said, "M.J. and I could sing a song!"

"Oh yes!" Valdette shouted.

Faye came back into the room and surveyed the group until she fixed on Christine, who was twirling a piece of her straightened hair between her nails. I could see Faye's eyes growing wild with excitement. She whispered something to Jeb and he shifted the camera toward Christine.

"You," she said, pointing at Christine. "I want to hear what you think of the book."

"Well, unfortunately," Christine said meekly, "I haven't had a chance to read the book."

"She's reading *Harry Potter*," Valdette said.

"So what do you think of *Harry Potter*?" Faye asked.

"It's good," Christine said.

"What else?" asked Faye.

"I don't know," Christine said. "It's entertaining. It's suspenseful."

"What else?"

"I don't know," Christine said. "It's just . . . cute!"

Faye was nodding and obviously hoping that Christine's adjectives about *Harry Potter* could be spliced into the segment so that they appeared to be about *Clip My Wings and I'll Grow a New Pair*, not that there was anything terribly "cute" about Idabelle Sugar's work.

"One of the reasons book club is so special here," I said, "is that the book often opens the door to other topics of discussion. For instance, I thought we might pick up on that thread about feeling like we're being kept down."

"Excellent idea," said Sue.

"Were you really fondled by your gynecologist?" asked Dee Dee. I saw Faye's eyebrow arch.

"No, I was just throwing that out as a topic," I said.

"Well, I can't say I've been," said Brenda.

"Me neither," said Sue. "Though I suppose we're all vulnerable."

"Any other issues anyone wants to raise, then?" I asked.

"Especially you," Faye said, pointing at Christine.

"Not really," Christine said.

"There is something we wanted to get to," Sue said, "but we

wanted to do it when we were done filming. So if you're done, maybe these guys can take off and we can, you know, get to it."

"We're shooting everything," Faye said. "Just pretend like we're not here."

"Yeah, but it's kind of personal," Sue said.

"That's fine!" I shouted. "The more personal the better. As long as you're comfortable with it."

"It's more like if *you're* comfortable with it," Sue said.

"Of course I am!" I said. "That's what we want! Is it the NOW versus COW softball game?"

In an effort to make herself less conspicuous—though it was Randy Abrams, stealth reporter that he was, who had managed to disappear into the corner, where he was furiously scribbling in his notebook—Faye had begun pacing around the living room and now stood mesmerized by the portrait of Brenda's children above the fireplace. Her cigarette ashes were falling on the carpet.

"It's not the softball game," Sue said. She shifted in her seat on the sofa and looked at Brenda. "What do you think, Brenda? Should we do this?"

"I'm not sure this is the time," Brenda said, glancing at the camera, which was still pointed on Christine.

"Please," I said. "Go ahead! Nothing's off limits."

"Okay, Lucinda," said Sue. "For lack of a better word, this is an intervention."

Faye whipped around, the remainder of her cigarette ashes cascading through the air like a disseminating dandelion tuft. I sat there, holding my wineglass to my lips, afraid to take a sip. The entire Coalition of Women stared at me somberly. Their drunkenness seemed to have emptied out of them. Valdette had her "concerned" face on; her head was cocked to the side and her mouth was spread into a half smile as if she had discovered an abandoned puppy on the road. Dee Dee reached over and put her hand on my knee.

"It seems like you're having a hard time," Sue said.

I looked at Jeb. Inexplicably, he still had the camera poised on Christine. I motioned for him to stop the tape.

"Maybe this isn't the best time for this," I said.

"*No!*" Faye thundered. "Keep going!"

"Faye," I said, "this is totally off topic."

"Thank God for that," she said.

"I do feel a little uncomfortable reaching out to Lucinda with the camera on," said Sue. "It doesn't make for a very safe space."

Faye had taken a position right behind Jeb. She had her hand on his back as if she would dig her nails into him if he stopped the camera. She paused for a moment, studying each coalition member once again and then set her gaze on me. My hand was shaking, so much so that the wine was almost sloshing out of my glass. I took a gulp and tried to set the glass down on the coffee table, knocking Valdette's leopard print lighter onto the floor.

"The truth is," Faye said slowly, glancing over at Randy Abrams, "that I have been concerned about Lucinda myself. That's actually why I came. I care deeply about my employees and when I feel like one of them is in trouble I do everything I can to help them."

The members of the Coalition of Women looked like they would cry. They buzzed among themselves, whispering words like "sisterhood" and "real support system." Valdette offered me a cigarette, which, although the camera was still rolling, I took from her and lit with the leopard print lighter.

"What bullshit, Faye," I managed to say, coughing through the smoke. "How patently untrue!"

"Don't be defensive, Lucinda," Faye said. "I've been very worried about you. I'm here not as your boss but as your friend."

"Did you join The Forum or something?" I asked.

"It's very natural to feel defensive in this kind of situation," said Sue. "But we really feel that you're in an unhealthy situation at home. In fact, we all discussed it at the February meeting. And we took a vote and decided we had to intervene."

"You had a meeting in February?" I asked. "I thought it was canceled."

"The usual order of business was canceled," said Brenda. "We decided we needed to talk about you . . . and Jason."

"Mason," said Sue.

"I mean Mason," said Brenda.

"Is he physically abusing you?" Dee Dee asked.

"Wait!" Faye screamed.

"Yeah, wait," I said. "He's not abusing—"

"Stop!" Faye interrupted. She moved from her place behind the camera and grabbed Christine's arm and pulled her from the over-stuffed chair.

"I want this one to sit next to Lucinda on the couch," Faye said. "You two, with the earrings, get off the couch."

"Jesus, Faye," I said.

"Shut up!" Faye yelled at me. Then she softened. "We're just trying to help you."

Faye made Jeb, who seemed utterly terrified of her, stop the camera as she moved Sue and Valdette off the couch and positioned Christine next to me. Then she got her purse, took out her compact, and began rubbing foundation on my face.

The Coalition of Women seemed terrified of Faye, too. She had managed to herd all of them but Christine to one side of the modular sofa, where they sat like patients in a waiting room. Dee Dee muttered something under her breath about "exploitation" and Faye, without missing a beat, turned to her and gave her a shy smile.

"When we're done I'd like to hear you sing," Faye said to Dee Dee. "We're always looking for new musical acts to book on *Up Early*."

"Really?" said Dee Dee.

"We had on Ani, what's her name, Frankendyke," said Faye.

"Ani DiFranco," I said.

"Whatever," continued Faye. "But I thought she was too socially constructed. We need something fresh."

"Really!" said Dee Dee.

"But let's focus on Lucinda and her needs right now," Faye said.

"I'm still not sure this is something we should do with the camera on," Sue said. She was squeezed on the left side of the sofa between Brenda and Valdette. "It seems a little unfair."

"Let me tell you something about Lucinda," Faye said. She smeared lipstick on me and stood in the middle of the room. "She is the kind of person who thinks nothing is worth doing unless it's a public event. It's either on TV or it doesn't count. This is a common malady of our media-saturated culture. It's quite sad really. But she's kind of like Madonna in that sense. I've known Lucinda for years. And I know that to really reach her you have to meet her on her level."

"I see," said Valdette.

"Well, whatever works," said Sue.

Faye knelt down and whispered something in my ear that I couldn't entirely understand, though I did hear the words "or your career will be over." She resumed her position behind Jeb and nudged him to turn the camera on. No one was in the shot except me and Christine.

"Okay," said Faye. "One of you was saying that Lucinda is being beaten up by that Unabomber of a boyfriend she has. Anyone care to elaborate?"

The room was silent. Christine was tapping her nails on her wineglass. Finally Sue cleared her throat and spoke.

"It just seems to me," she said, "that you're in a situation that you're refusing to get out of. Or maybe you feel like you can't get out of it. And we just want to tell you that you can get out of it."

A surge of nausea rose from my stomach and seemed to well up in the bottom of my throat in the form of tears that I immediately vowed not to shed until I was out of Brenda Schwan's house. I tried to concentrate on how to respond. The challenge, of course, was to figure out what exactly, in their minds, constituted "the situation" without revealing any more about it than they already knew. Did they know about the drugs? The heat going off? Erin sleeping in her own fecal matter? Weighed on their own, did any of those misfortunes warrant an intervention? I looked at Faye for some kind of cue, but her attention had wandered and she was examining a tiny glass giraffe on Brenda's fireplace mantel, turning it around in her hands and cringing as if it were a piece of debris from a car crash.

"Has Mason hit you?" Sue asked.

I snorted out a little laugh. "No!" I said. "Oh God no."

"Has he threatened you?" asked Valdette. "Does he hurt his children?"

"Never," I said. "Is this what the intervention is about?"

"Sometimes," said Sue. "You don't know what the intervention is about until you actually do it."

"Okay, stop right there!" Faye yelled, dropping the giraffe back down on the mantel and causing Brenda to wince. "Can you say that?"

"Me?" I asked.

"Not *you*, the one next to you," said Faye. "What's your name?"

"Christine," Christine said.

"Christine," said Faye. "I want you to say exactly what she just said. The thing about not knowing what the intervention is about until you actually do it."

"You want *me* to say that?"

"Yes."

"Why?" asked Christine.

Because everyone else is too ugly and you're the only one who's going to wind up in the segment, you idiot, I thought to myself. I couldn't believe Faye was being so completely unethical right in front of a reporter from *New York Magazine*. This was a new low, unmatched even by the time she made Samantha Frank go undercover as a phone sex operator as a way of testing the job's effect on one's libido. I turned around and looked at Randy Abrams. He was sitting in the corner by the coatrack with his mouth hanging open.

And then Christine, like Helen Keller learning the sign for water, lit up suddenly. She smoothed out her already-smooth hair and sat up even straighter.

"Oh!" she said. "You mean, you want me to act as a sort of moderator?"

"Precisely," said Faye.

"Christine is brilliant at that," Valdette said.

"I'm very glad to hear it," said Faye. She poked Jeb in the back again. "Okay, we're rolling."

"Lucinda"—Christine said, turning to me and gazing into my eyes as if she'd suddenly become another person—"sometimes you don't know what the intervention is about until you actually do the intervention. Maybe you could describe briefly your situation at home with your partner."

"What do you mean?" I asked.

"I mean, you do feel like your situation is a bit . . . out of control?"

"Not really," I said.

Perhaps Christine had beamed her former personality into my body.

"You have so much going for you," Christine said. "We just can't understand why you'd choose to be with someone so . . . I don't know . . ."

"Limited," said Sue off camera.

And right there, with the wisdom of a thousand interventions she'd no doubt overseen at the P.C. Recovery Center for Women, Sue had managed to hit me where I lived.

"He's not limited!" I exploded. "He's a meth addict!"

The room fell silent, as if someone had dimmed the lights. The Coalition of Women gawked at me like I'd stripped naked on the median of Highway 36. Faye was salivating. Randy Abrams was scribbling again.

"And more important," I continued, addressing the whole group, "he's not my partner, he's my boyfriend. And most important of all, Idabelle Sugar is a hackneyed, self-exploitive thief of

bleeding liberal hearts. Her book is execrable, as are her twenty-
three other books, and if you continue to treat Christine as your
own personal pet of color I'm going to buy you a dog house that she
can lie in when she's here because she obviously has nothing to say
to you anyway!"

They said nothing, just sipped from their wineglasses without
putting them down. Somehow I had failed to intimidate them.

"Let's try to stay on the topic," Christine said.

Faye was bouncing on her toes and silently clapping her hands
together.

"A meth addict?" Brenda said finally. "Didn't you come here to
report on methamphetamine in the first place?"

"And now she's an addict herself," Faye said. "Christine, ask
her how she got addicted."

"I'm not a meth addict!" I yelled.

"It's okay, Lucinda," Sue said. "We're here for you."

Jeb started to pan the camera around to Sue but Faye slapped
him and made him go back to Christine.

"How long has this been going on?" Brenda asked.

"Has what been going on?" I asked.

"The addiction," said Christine. She put her hand on my knee.

"I don't know," I said. My lip was suddenly trembling. My head
was spinning. I must have had three glasses of wine without eating.
I tried to speak but couldn't get any words out.

"Just let it out," said Sue. "There are no judgments here."

"Bullshit!" I screamed, though I was crying now, which made
me furious at myself. Tears were streaming down my face. Faye's
makeup was dripping onto my lap. "All you do is judge me!"

Why had I said that? My eyes were so cloudy now that I could
barely see the Coalition of Women, only Faye's dark figure gestur-
ing for me to keep going. Valdette handed Christine a tissue to hand
to me.

"Why do you think you're being judged?" Christine asked.

"Never mind," I said.

"No, tell us," Sue said.

"I don't think that," I said.

"Fucking tell them!" Faye screamed. "Don't be unprofessional!"

"Because," I began, though I had no idea what I was saying, "not everyone can have your perfect lives! Not everyone can be empowered and not need men and reach out to people all the time. Not everyone can get out of their driveways without someone helping them, even if he does happen to be a meth addict! And so what if he's a meth addict? He makes good meat loaf. All I wanted to do was see what would happen if I left New York. All I wanted was to improve my quality of life! I didn't think any of this would happen!"

For the next five minutes, I cried harder than I ever had in my life, harder than I had for those seventeen minutes in my old apartment the night before I left New York, harder than I had on that freezing evening in bed with Erin and the dog. On the lime green sofa, I held my face in my hands and bawled like a bereaved mother. Jeb got every second on tape. Faye pushed him into me so that the camera was practically in my lap. The camera rolled as each member of the Coalition of Women hugged me and put their hands on my shoulders. Faye made sure Christine's light brown, perfectly manicured hand was on top. Then she finally yelled "Cut."

"That was genius," she said.

"Fuck you," I blubbered.

"I've gotta say," said Randy Abrams, who had finally abandoned his post in the corner, "that was a pretty damn good intervention."

"Just doing my job," said Faye. "I like to be very hands-on. Lucinda, we'll meet tomorrow at your house to discuss editing."

I sat on the sofa, blowing my nose and watching them incredulously. The Coalition of Women seemed too impressed with Faye and Christine to bother being offended by what I'd said about Idabelle Sugar, a speech I'd rehearsed many times while driving alone in the Sunbird, never imagining it would ever find an audience. Now that it had found an audience, it seemed ridiculous and I wanted to take it all back. I noticed that Sue was glaring at Faye.

"I guess that's show biz, huh Faye," said Sue.

"It's times like these that I remember why I got into this business," said Faye.

I grabbed my coat and bag and ran for the door. Sue held it open for me and followed me outside, where I saw that Faye had kept a taxi waiting.

"I can see why you left New York," Sue said gently.

I turned to her, my face swollen and my nose still running, and suddenly I felt more affection for Sue than I'd felt for anyone in months. I wanted to hug her, and before I could make a move she reached out her arms and hugged me.

"I'm sorry for what I said about Christine," I said.

"Leonard said the same thing about her," Sue said. "But you have to remember, Lucinda, that being interesting isn't the most important thing in the world. And not everybody can be as interesting as you."

I had never in my life felt less interesting. Still, this was one of the nicer things I'd heard in a long time, even if she hadn't exactly meant it as a compliment. I vowed to never be angry with Sue again. She had, after all, been loyal to me. She could have stayed in the house with the others but instead she'd come outside with me. She'd seen through Faye and subsequently understood what I had fled from, what had informed my decision making, what kind of depraved moral context had shaped my frail psyche. Maybe she now saw that Mason wasn't so bad. At least compared to Faye. Maybe now she was on my side. Maybe she'd even start inviting him to her parties.

"You are going to leave Mason, aren't you?" Sue said. "Or at least take some kind of action step?"

And then the only thing I could think of was how much I wanted to reach out and strangle Sue with her beaded African necklace.

*   *   *

It was after midnight when I got back to the farm. Mason was sleeping and by the time he woke in the morning Faye had already called and said she was stopping by the farm on her way to the airport.

"Randy would like to get a quote from you for his article," she said. "He would have asked you last night but he didn't want to intrude."

Remarkably, Mason was hardly nonplussed when I explained that Faye was on her way out to the farm. We had woken to a winter morning that felt on the verge of giving way to spring. For the first time in months, the water in the horse troughs had not frozen during the night. The snow was melting in patches, lending to the farm a sense of muddy optimism, a promise of warmth in the not too distant future, a traction in the driveway that I'd all but forgotten about.

"So how did the filming go?" Mason asked over breakfast. He'd decided not to go to work (it was soap opera season at the grain elevator anyway) and made scrambled eggs and sausage.

"They staged an intervention," I said bluntly. "They accused me of being a meth addict and I had to explain that *you* were the meth addict."

"What?"

"Does that upset you?" I asked.

"No."

"How could it not?" I asked.

"Because I'm not a meth addict anymore," he said.

It was always so simple for him. He hadn't done meth yesterday or the day before and was therefore no longer an addict. It made me sad to think that he didn't even care if the whole world knew. I remembered what he'd said long ago about having a reputation as a good father. *It's better than being known as a drunk or a pervert.* Was being a drug addict better than that, too?

"How did your boss think it went?" Mason asked.

"She loved it."

"Well, I guess it worked out," Mason said.

A taxicab crunched up the driveway outside. Through the window I saw Faye, still in the leather coat and head scarf, climb out with Randy Abrams. Sam Shepard sprinted toward them and tried to chew Faye's coat. She kicked him out of the way.

Mason got up and opened the back door. Faye stumbled into the mudroom, tripping on the shoes and boots piled on the floor.

"You're the guy who bathes in the river!" Faye said.

Seeing Faye in my house brought me back to the gravity of the situation, as if she'd pinched me. It was the reverse of waking from a nightmare of having to tell yourself it was just a dream.

"You're not going to air that segment, are you?" I asked Faye. I realized I was still in my bathrobe. Mason was wearing his long underwear.

"That's up to Upstairs," she said. "Personally, I thought it was your best one yet."

"I assume that was your way of firing me."

Faye started to say something but then glanced at Randy Abrams and stopped herself.

"You know I care about you deeply, Lucinda," she said finally. "I truly did come out here because I was concerned about you. It's just lucky that we could combine my concern with a really powerful and groundbreaking segment."

"Faye really has impressed me," said Randy Abrams. "In fact, this article is turning into more of a profile of her. So I'd love a quote from you about what it's like working with Faye."

"After all that you need a quote?" I asked.

"Coffee?" Mason asked them.

"No, thanks," said Faye. She lit up a cigarette and Mason made a face.

"Do you feel she saved your life?" Randy Abrams asked.

"Faye saves lives every day," I said facetiously. "That's what being a television producer is all about."

Faye was characteristically revolted by the disarray of the house—"It suits you," she said within earshot of Randy Abrams—though, like any New Yorker would be, she was impressed with its size.

"There's an upstairs, too," I said.

"Really?" said Faye. Apparently she hadn't noticed from the outside.

"I'll show you the barn, if you want," Mason said.

My stomach tightened. Showing the barn and especially Mason's paintings to Randy Abrams and especially Faye struck me as a very, very bad idea.

"Let's see the barn," Randy Abrams said.

"It better not be gross," Faye said.

We tracked through the melting snow to the barn. Randy Abrams tried to engage Mason in a discussion about the architecture of the house and the septic system and the types of pesticides used in the area—he claimed to know a lot about these subjects. Mason opened the sliding door to the barn and we gathered around the stall that housed the pig. She was lying in the straw inches away from her own shit.

"That's Diva Starz," I said.

"That is absolutely disgusting," said Faye, stamping out her cigarette.

"Is that a peccary pig or a North American sow?" asked Randy Abrams.

Lucky the horse grunted in his stall and kicked his hooves. Mason steered us in the other direction.

"And you can see the tack room if you'd like," he said. "This is where I paint."

No no no no no, I thought.

Mason opened the door of the tack room. The air was musty, but it also smelled like paint. Light from the small windows cast narrow beams onto his canvases. The figures, misshapen and contorted and screaming like feral asylum inmates, seemed to leap off the walls and into the room. The horse painting—the one Mason had started to redo the night of the barn dance—had been restored somewhat; now the horse head was dabbed with vague images of feathers and bones. Polka dots appeared only faintly in one corner. I shifted my feet and held my breath, waiting for Faye to say something obnoxious.

Instead, Faye got up close to one of the paintings and studied the brush strokes.

"Are these yours?" she asked.

"Yupper," said Mason.

"These are quite conceptually aware. Where do you show?"

"Show what?"

"The paintings!" said Faye. "Where is your gallery?"

"Here, I guess."

"Where did you study?"

"Oh, I took some classes at P.C. State College for a while," Mason said. "But I was never much for school."

Faye stood back as far as she could without hitting the opposite wall, which was covered with horse harnesses and circle saws.

"These are fucking brilliant," said Faye. "Don't you think so, Randy?"

"They remind me of de Kooning," Randy Abrams said.

"They're a bit like Cecily Brown, minus the scatological exhibitionism," Faye said. "The social construction is contextualized, yet not overly so."

Mason looked at the floor, shuffling his feet.

"Do you have a catalog?" Randy Abrams asked.

"Oh fuck," said Faye. "The only catalog this guy has is an L. L. Bean catalog. Lucinda, take some photos of these and send them to me."

"Really?" I asked. I was so stunned I couldn't even look at Mason.

"Our cab is waiting," said Faye. "God knows how long it's going to take to get home from this shit hole. Lucinda, I'll call you about the segment. And get me the number of that black girl. Upstairs would slobber all the way into the basement if they saw her."

We marched back through the yard, where the taxi, with the meter running, was still in the driveway. The driver was leaning against the car smoking a cigarette. Mason, who knew him from Effie's, slapped him on the back.

"Not bad for a meth addict," Randy Abrams mumbled as Faye kissed me on both cheeks.

"Grow up," Faye said. "All artists are drug addicts."

The Margin Widens

I knew I needed to take an action step. The problem was that no actions I could think of seemed particularly appealing. As much as the Coalition of Women had been right about Mason, they did not seem to understand the love I felt for the farm. And since Mason was as much a part of the farm as the house and barn themselves, since in fact he was, despite his troubles, more or less the very foundation of the farm (as I was certain I couldn't have lasted longer than a week there by myself) I continued to love him almost as if by association.

Besides, the prolonged crisis of winter had finally lifted. If the intervention had failed to affect me the way the Coalition of Women would have liked, it did manage to break the cold spell. As though a warm front had come through and kicked Faye out of town, the land began to thaw as soon as she left. Mason and I moved the beds back up to the second floor. We unpeeled the duct tape from the doorways and I reassembled my office and, one by one, Erin's toys were retrieved from the sofa cushions and the mudroom and the dusty corners where they had rolled and put back in her bedroom upstairs. It was as if the house had exhaled, as if our lives, which had become constricted and mangled and even delirious from the cold, sprawled into our reacquired space and finally gave us room to walk around. For the first time in nearly half a year, it was now possible for Mason to read a book in the living room while I talked on the phone in my office. Erin's cartoons, while still audible from the upstairs bedroom, no longer saturated our dinner conversation. Even her loathsome Diva Starz Nikki doll could be heard only faintly behind the closed door of Erin's room. I had insisted she confine the doll to her room lest the dog eat it. Alarmed, she kept it in her bed, where she'd roll on it in her sleep and be awakened by *Today's word is "bodalicious."*

Mason did not make as many trips to the barn. Now that the frost was gone, I could easily observe him through the windows. From Sebastian and Peter's room I could see his every move in the yard. I watched him mow the lawn and plant more flowers. I watched him brush the horse and trim his hooves. Mason's leg no longer jerked at night and the tack room, which I inspected weekly, then monthly, contained not even a single lighter. Instead, the place was lined with canvases. Spurred by Faye's enthusiasm, although reluctant to send her photos of his work, Mason had begun to paint with a fervor I had never once applied to the writing of television scripts or even the ill-fated *Inspirations from the Heartland* (Sarah Vanderhorn had never called). Though he would not, as I suggested, attend Narcotics Anonymous meetings, he seemed to have replaced his addiction with the creation of increasingly disciplined works of "conceptual awareness." The faces were no less demonic, but they were rendered with a confidence I hadn't before seen in either Mason or his work. It was as if he had recognized the barrier between the artist and the art; as the faces became scarier, he became less so.

Even Lucky the horse seemed more benign. Though I was still afraid to ride, Mason showed me how to snap a rope onto Lucky's bridle and walk him to the prairie grass west of the house. There I could tie him to a tree so he could eat the grass. This cut down on his hay consumption and, Mason said, gave the animal a much-needed change of scene. "How would you like to be confined to a corral all day?" Mason asked. "You'd whack off on people at a party, too." Indeed, Lucky's face seemed to have retained a hazy smirk since the barn dance. Now, everytime he brought out his staggering organ he did so with the brazen showmanship of a porn star. Not even the bitter winter had compromised his virility and now that it was spring, his masculinity was sprouting with the plants. He greeted me pendulously when he saw me walk toward the corral, stomping his feet as I opened the gate and swallowing my apples in one bite. Because one stud on a farm was more than enough, Mason finally got a vasectomy. The regulars at Effie's threatened to throw him a retirement party.

The Coalition of Women, ever respectful of the female voice, be-grudgingly accepted, if not my opinion on Idabelle Sugar, my right to have one. Though they did not accept my insistence that Mason's bout with addiction had run its course—twice, Sue had sent me notes on the EMBRACE, EMPATHIZE, EMPOWER stationery saying "We always have a spare room," and "Your options are limited only by your fears"—Christine, who had repeatedly had to tell Faye on the phone that she had no interest in a television career, finally got us back to the business of the NOW versus COW softball game. I agreed to play shortstop. Sue offered to bring wine coolers.

Though I didn't catch on at first, Faye had done more than re-lieve Mason's self-esteem problems. She had indeed relieved me of my job. I learned of my dismissal a few weeks later in Randy Abrams's *New York Magazine* article.

> "Faye saves lives every day," says Trout, whose 'Quality of Life' series was recently kiboshed when *Up Early* signed a generous deal with best-selling author Haley Bopp. "That's what being a television producer is all about."

Though I gasped when I read that line, my shock had less to do with "kiboshed" than with Haley Bopp's being a "best-selling au-thor" and, moreover, the idea that Randy Abrams could have wit-nessed my intervention from such excruciating proximity and yet omit it from his article. Since I no longer subscribed to *New York Magazine*, I read the article standing by the rack at the bookstore in the Homestead Mall. And since *New York Magazine* arrived at the bookstore at least a week late, if at all, the article would have already been on the stands in New York for several days, making me roughly the three millionth person to learn that I'd been fired.

I did not, however, throw the magazine down in disgust. Nor did I run to the nearest pay phone to call Faye or Daphne or Elena or even Mason at the grain elevator. Instead, relief rushed through me. Even though I had run through my savings, even though I had spent more on rent and heating bills in six months than Mason had spent on meth during the entire period of his addiction, the idea of never again having to do another "Quality of Life Report" filled me with such bliss that I strode through the mall to the food court, where I bought myself an Orange Julius and, though I'd never in my adult life actually sat down in a food court, found a table and took a seat to enjoy my drink.

In groups of twos and threes, mostly young women with their babies and their mothers, the Prairie Cityites ambled through the mall. They carried shopping bags and diaper bags. They wore sweatpants with sandals and appeared so unhurried, so serene, so unbothered by what I still believed to be an ungodly distance between Dillard's and Sears, that I suddenly realized that quality of life was not about barn dances or bathing in the river or even sipping coffee in the prairie grass, but simply about being able to go to the mall. It was about being able to not only buy something at the mall but also buy *several things*—shoes and accessories and maybe even an egg roll at Egg Roll Express—without having a complete crisis of purpose and identity, without worrying that everyone else was buying the same things, without thinking endlessly about *what it meant* to be a person—one of many people, one of millions of people all over the damn United States—who bought those things. That was where I had failed. I had thought much too much about being or not being *one of those people.* And in the end I was as much one of them as I'd always been. I was in a food court drinking an Orange Julius. I was astonished at how good it tasted.

In the silver glow of the mall corridor I spotted Joel Lipinsky walking past the Sunglass Hut stand. He was in his customary black suit but he wore running shoes and carried an Eddie Bauer shopping bag in one hand and a plastic Barnes and Noble bag in the other. My first inclination was to hide from him, but then, as if the mall had broken down the last vestiges of my resistance to common pleasantries, I eyeballed Joel until he noticed me in the food court. A look of embarrassment crossed his face as he approached me.

"I never come here," he said.

"Have a seat," I said, as it suddenly occurred to me that perhaps I could convince him to give me a job on *Parent Talk* with Loni Heibel-Budicek. "I only come here for the Orange Juliuses."

"I make those at home," he said. "With vodka."

Joel sat down, but it seemed more out of a desire to put down his shopping bag, which was so full it had started to rip, than to actually converse with me.

"I was sorry to hear *Up Early* let you go," he said.

"When did you hear that?"

"A few weeks ago," he said. "I got an e-mail saying they wouldn't need to coproduce with us anymore. I just hope it wasn't my fault."

"Why would it be your fault?"

"Because I wouldn't release that footage that Jeb shot at Brenda's house," he said.

"What?"

"I know I should have talked to you about it," said Joel. "But as it turned out, *my boss* looked at it and said there was no way we could send that out into the world. It doesn't give a very good impression of our community. I mean, meth! Come on, Lucinda. We get enough bad press from *Cops.*"

"You never sent *Up Early* the footage?"

"Your boss hassled me over it for weeks," he said. "But I just couldn't do it. Besides, Valdette was all bent out of shape about not being on camera. She's got some competitive thing with Christine.

Everyone was on my case. So I just said screw it. I destroyed the tape."

Suddenly I loved Joel. Sort of, anyway.

"Can I buy you lunch?" I asked. "Do you want an egg roll or anything? A funnel cake?"

"No thanks," Joel said. "Although, I gotta say, I wish I'd destroyed that barn dance footage, too. In all my years in television I've never gotten horse semen on my pants. You might want to consider a career as a producer in the porn industry."

I figured that statement pretty much shot down my chances of getting hired on *Parent Talk*.

"You know, Lucinda," Joel continued, "you remind me a lot of the way I was when I first came out here. When I left New York, I had big plans to turn this part of the country into a major market. I was going to revolutionize public television. I was going to make Prairie City known for high-end, original public programming the way Seattle was known for coffee. Granted, that was before Seattle became known for coffee. But you know what I mean. Man, I was a fireball of ambition. I tried to create a roundtable news show, like *The McLaughlin Group*. I tried to develop a documentary series about barns that had been converted into architectural award-winning homes. I tried to make a fucking kids show! It was a kind of *Zoom* meets *Barney*, only edgier because it had kids learning to speak different languages. And I'm not just talking about Spanish. I'm talking about Vietnamese, Arabic, Czech, *sign language*, for Christ's sake. I thought I was going to change the world and be all the more impressive because I changed it from *here*, because I didn't sit in some office in midtown Manhattan making lunch appointments but actually did the shit from Prairie City. I mean, I'd love to see Ted Turner try to do his business from some godforsaken place like this."

"He kind of does, doesn't he?" I said.

"Okay, bad example," said Joel. "But you know what I'm saying. And what I want to tell you, Lucinda, is that, in the end, I

stopped caring. No one wanted to do *The McLaughlin Group* thing.
I'd called it *Lipinsky and Significant Others,* which, admittedly,
wasn't the sexiest title. No one wanted to do the barn documentary
series. No one wanted to do the kids foreign language show. So we
kept making *Parent Talk.* We kept churning out local news stories
about ethanol production. And suddenly, that was my life. I was a
guy who produced local programming in a third-tier market. End
of story."

That would be me in a few years, I thought. If I never left
Prairie City I would be sitting in the mall waxing despondent over
my unrealized dreams, my still-unsold proposal for *Inspirations
from the Heartland,* the brilliant New York career that I threw away
because I stupidly thought I could achieve success on my own
terms. If I stayed here long enough I'd probably listen to *The Buena
Vista Social Club* soundtrack until I was fluent in Spanish, or at
least knew all the words to "Amor de Loca Juventud," the first line
of which, if I wasn't mistaken, translated to "Lost are the dreams of
my deluded youth." By then Faye could be the president of NBC.
Bonnie Crawley would be anchoring the nightly news. Maybe Joel
had the right idea. Maybe the third tier was the place to be. Maybe
there was an inherent morality there that compensated for its lack
of glamour. Who knew? I was exhausted from trying to make sense
of it all.

"You should be proud of the work you do," I said lamely and
utterly disingenuously.

"You bet your ass I'm proud of it," Joel said. "This is what I'm
trying to tell you. Let it go! Accept the life you've walked into. Enjoy the sunny days. Spend the rainy days inside the house making
love. Hey, man, there's more to life than bagels and lox. As Frank
Fussell told me that night at your farm, 'I'm a wild seed, let the
wind carry me.' I say 'Right on' to that."

"I think that's a Joni Mitchell lyric," I said.

Joel stared at me.

"Well, there's nothing new under the sun," he said. "Shake-speare said that."

The diamond stud in Joel's ear caught a glint from the fluorescent lights of the food court. He rose from his chair and picked up his shopping bag. In the Barnes and Noble bag, through the semi-transparent plastic, I noticed the unmistakable dust jacket of Haley Bopp's *A Broad and Her Sheets*.

When I arrived back at the farm, there was a note stuck in the back door. Written in the bubble handwriting of a teenage girl, it said: "Had the day off so I stopped by. Very interesting.—Julie."

I couldn't imagine why she had come by without calling first, nor did I know how she'd gotten directions, unless Jill had told her. I assumed that by "interesting" she was referring to the mural that Mason had begun painting on the side of the house. In his new ambition, and his dwindling supply of canvases, he'd embarked on an abstract expressionist rendering of Lucky the horse. Since he was using the exterior paint left over from doing the trim the previous summer, the mural had the added benefit of actually matching the house. Even the landlord liked it. Mason hoped it would serve as an advertisement for the horse-boarding operation.

It was still midday; Mason wouldn't be home for a few more hours. I e-mailed Daphne and left a message for Elena. I was pulling up my résumé on the computer when I heard a loud knocking on the door downstairs. Looking outside the window, I saw a sheriff's car in the driveway.

"Ma'am, did you lose a horse?" the sheriff asked when I opened the door. He was tall and gaunt and looked to be near sixty, the kind of sheriff who looks more like an actor playing a sheriff than an actual one.

"No," I said.

"Are you sure about that?"

"Yes," I said. I slipped into my clogs and stepped outside. Cupid was in the pasture. I couldn't see Lucky in his corral; surely he was in the barn.

"How many horses you got out here?" the sheriff asked. The name on his badge said T. Gastinov.

"We have two horses," I said. "The other one must be in the barn."

"Who else lives out here? Your husband?"

"My boyfriend."

"Your roommate?" the sheriff asked, his eyes narrowing a bit as though he were measuring our sleaze factor. "Is your boyfriend your roommate?

"Yes," I said. "But he's at work now."

"We got a complaint from someone a couple miles down the road about a horse that's gotten himself in their pasture," the sheriff said. "Why don't you and I take a walk back to the barn and make sure your horse is in there?"

"Okay, sure."

We walked through the yard to the barn, the dog trailing behind us. The sheriff, pausing briefly to look at the mural, said, "Well that sure is interesting."

Lucky was not in his stall. Moreover, the gate to his corral was open. I'd taken him out in the pasture that morning. Was it possible that I had not shut the gate all the way when I brought him back?

"Oh my God," I said.

"Was that a white horse?" the sheriff asked. "A stud?"

"Yes, actually."

"Because you got some folks down the road who are pretty angry right about now. It seems they have a mare in heat and your horse here got in and, according to them, mounted her several times."

"Oh my God!"

"You gotta keep a stud locked up real good, ma'am."

"I know," I said. "I just . . . maybe I left the gate open. I'm from New York."

"I'm gonna need to take some information," he said. "They've secured the animal."

"Is he okay?"

"From the sound of things, he had a real good day."

I laughed. This was a sheriff with a sense of humor. This was no big deal, just another wacky day on the farm. It would have made a good segment for *Up Early*. The sheriff was petting Sam Shepard. He pulled a dog treat from his pocket and gave it to him.

"Are we going to get a citation or anything?" I asked, now confident that the sheriff had distinguished me from the usual scumbags and would be impressed with my level of cooperation.

"Not unless there was any damage to the property, which it doesn't sound like there was," he said. "As for the condition of the mare, that'll be between you and your neighbors. I suggest you talk to them when you retrieve the animal."

"Of course," I said.

We walked back through the barn. Passing the tack room, the sheriff glanced through the glass door and saw Mason's paintings.

"You've got quite a museum in there," he said.

"Mason's a painter," I said.

"Mind if I take a peek inside?" he asked.

"I guess not," I said.

Then, in the stupidest thing I had done since not only coming to Prairie City but since being born (this is no exaggeration, I had a lot of time to think about it and came up with nothing even close), I failed to consider my rights to refuse him entry into the tack room and, as if the sheriff were an art dealer, opened the door and led him inside.

The place was ransacked. Paint brushes were flung on the floor, cans of water spilled over, bones and birds' nests and tools thrown everywhere. A few of the canvases had been knocked over and books and framed pictures had fallen off the shelves.

"Must be quite the angry artist," the sheriff said.

"I don't know what happened here," I said.

Mason would never have left the tack room in that condition. I wondered if the wind had somehow blown the door open. Or maybe an animal had gotten in. Then I saw a note on the table. It was written on the back of one of the horse-boarding flyers in Julie's idiotic handwriting. Before I could read it I saw something else on the table. A small white rock next to an empty film canister. The sheriff closed in on the table. As he picked up the rock, I picked up the note. It was one word long. Even then, it was misspelled.

Gotchya, it read.

"Ma'am," the sheriff said, "I'm gonna ask you to come with me."

There's nothing much to say about riding in the back of a sheriff's car that hasn't already been said by people far wittier and more experienced with run-ins with the law than I was on that spring day. After being read my Miranda rights I'd been handcuffed. "It's for your protection as well as mine," the sheriff had said. "If you stay still they won't cut you." As he spoke into his radio, saying "We got white female, age thirty-one, in possession of an eighth of an ounce of methamphetamine," I sat in the car with my hands in my lap, silently cursing Mason while wanting nothing more than to call him, to hear his voice, to have him pull into the driveway right then and there, although I figured he'd be arrested, too.

I would like to say that I continued to joke with the sheriff as we drove down the gravel road and made our way to Prairie City. I wished I could have been the kind of person who said things like "Not your everyday runaway horse call, eh?" or "Guess I really am between a rock and a hard, uh, *thing*." But I said nothing during the forty-five-minute trip to the sheriff's department, a trip during which Sheriff T. Gastinov never exceeded forty miles per hour and took us right through downtown Prairie City. We passed the library and the Thirteenth Street TGI Friday's. We passed the main post office and the YMCA and the Prairie City Recovery Center for Women, where an EMBRACE, EMPATHIZE, EMPOWER banner was hanging in the front window.

The sheriff's department was tiny, the size of a couple of double-wide trailers; even the walls were paneled with fake wood like the inside of a mobile home. A receptionist sat at the front desk below a Thoroughbred horse-of-the-month calendar.

"Come this way," T. Gastinov said, leading me into a small, un-occupied office where there was a desk, a phone, and an empty cof-fee mug that said I HATE MONDAYS. "Use this phone and make your call."

He stood beside me while I dialed the grain elevator. Frank Fussell answered.

"Frank," I said, "It's Lucinda. I was arrested at the farm."

"Try some circular breathing," Frank said.

It apparently didn't matter much what Mason had done. It was my farm—my name alone was on the lease—and since everything that occurred on it was my responsibility, Mason was not charged with the possession of the eighth of an ounce of meth that, as he later in-sisted, was the first meth he'd touched since the night the propane went out. I knew from my research that most meth addicts relapse at least three times before kicking for good; even then, most never kick it for good. The meth had again been in the film canister be-hind the framed photograph of Mason and me. Julie, who had in-deed been tipped off by Jill ("but I never thought the bitch would do *that*," Jill said later), had rummaged through the tack room un-til she found it. Leaving it out in the open with the note, she later said, was an attempt to get back at us for "scalding" her daughter's ankles that morning when I'd put Erin in the too-hot bathwater. Julie also claimed to have been suffering from PMS, though in the end none of it mattered. She was never charged with illegal entry. And though she hadn't known it at the time, she was also pregnant by another guy from Effie's Tavern.

As Frank Fussell told it, Mason had broken down in tears in the grain elevator when Frank went to get him after my phone call. He had been loading corn from last year's harvest onto a train car and Frank, shouting to him under the din of the grain pouring from the huge elevator bin, had pulled Mason into the office and told him he needed to send a lawyer to the sheriff's department rather than going to get me himself. Mason knew a lawyer from Effie's Tavern. Though he couldn't remember the guy's name, they'd smoked pot together in the early 1980s and Mason got in his truck and drove to Effie's to ask the bartender how to reach him.

It was four hours before anyone came. I was put in a jail cell—the "women's cell"—as T. Gastinov called it, which presumably distinguished itself as a feminine space by virtue of its cushioned bunk beds. For four hours I sat in it alone, crying softly and intermittently, not so much out of fear but out of grief over the apparent inevitability of losing the farm. To me, that meant losing everything. Even after recovering from the coma of winter, after believing Mason had kicked the meth for good and thinking, like a fool, that he might actually lift himself out of the error margin and become a serious painter or, at the very least, cease to be a liability to everything he touched, I had once again looked the other way while he blithely fucked up both of our lives. And naïveté no longer worked as an excuse. Now it was just plain laziness and denial, which was far less charming than naïveté. That, right there, was what finally shook me awake. The horror of being judged was nothing compared to the fear of being dull, of being less than endearing, of being written off as a loser. Even after all that had happened, even after I'd fallen through more cracks than I'd ever even stepped over on the sidewalks of New York, I'd managed to hang on to my belief that I was not, despite my obnoxiousness, without my charms. But now it was clear that there was nothing charming about me. I was as boring as the problems I was refusing to face. And though it shamed me to admit it, being uninteresting was the last straw. In the Lucinda Trout universe, this was simply an unacceptable condition.

A sheriff—not T. Gastinov but another one—came and told me that someone was sending a lawyer for me. He asked if I wanted coffee and just to make things feel a little less dire I said yes. Ten minutes later I had to pee.

The lawyer, whom I recognized from Effie's, sat outside the holding cell and told me the case would probably be thrown out. From what he'd gathered from the sheriff and from Mason, it sounded like an illegal search and seizure. And given the evidence of a break-in (although it hadn't really been a break-in; technically I'd invited Julie to the farm, and the tack room hadn't been locked) it was doubtful anyone could press charges of any kind. The lawyer had a ponytail and a goatee. He made me sign documents agreeing to his representation. He said I'd have to stay for a few more hours, that there was a mountain of paperwork, though it was strictly routine.

"How much do you charge?" I asked.

"We'll work it out," the lawyer said. He had reading glasses on a string around his neck and he pushed them down on his nose and looked at me as if he were about to say something profound, or perhaps scold me. I could hear a commotion outside in the office, the ringing of phones, the static from radios.

"I've known Mason forever," he said. "These things happen."

He put his papers in his briefcase and the guard escorted him back into the office. A few minutes passed and a woman in orange jail garb walked in the door, followed by the same female guard who'd brought me in.

"You've got some company now," the guard said, opening the gate to the cell.

It was Dawn, my downstairs neighbor from the house in town. Her tangle of hair covered her face, but as she passed me and sat down on the opposite bunk bed, I recognized her round face, her green eyes, and patchy skin. Her extra-large scrub pants were pulled flat across her hips. She looked like she had been crying. I gasped. I turned away so she wouldn't see me. But after a few seconds, because I was desperate to talk, because even my embarrassment couldn't override my urge to explain myself, I stared at her until she caught me eye.

"Dawn?" I said.

"How do you know my name?" she asked.

"I used to live upstairs from you."

"When?"

"About a year ago."

She smoothed out her hair and studied me from across the cell. Her jaw dropped slightly.

"Holy shit," she said. "Melinda, right?"

"Lucinda."

"Lucinda!" she said. "Oh honey, I'm sorry I forgot your name."

"What are you in for?" I asked with a smirk, though she of course took me literally. She looked at the wall and shook her head.

"My husband, of course, got loaded last night."

"He's out of prison?"

"Oh he got out awhile ago," she said. "He was clean. He stayed clean for six months. And then, boom, he's back at it. Fucking crack. It makes him crazy."

She had a bruise on her arm, a big green blotch under her wrist.

"Did he hit you?" I asked.

"Oh no," she said. "He wouldn't dare."

"So what happened?"

"I told him last week that he if got loaded again I'd slash him from asshole to elbow, that's what happened. And he went and got loaded. And of course he's selling it to the whole goddamn town, which is what got him locked up before. So I did it. I took a kitchen knife and carved one in him. The shit. He didn't feel a thing."

I stared at her. I didn't know whether to admire her or fear her. I recalled suddenly the image of her key chain on my kitchen table: I'M NOT A BITCH, I'M *THE* BITCH.

"The people upstairs called the cops," she said. "The people in the apartment where you lived. There have been at least four different people moving in and out since you left. The rent's so expensive."

"Is he okay?" I asked.

"Oh yeah."

"Do you have a lawyer?"

"Honey," she said, "I don't need a lawyer. That asshole was so fucked up they're not going to do anything to me. Besides, a woman in this town wouldn't be prosecuted on an abuse charge if she cut a guy's balls off."

She was certainly familiar with the Prairie City legal system. I would have liked to hear her contributions to a Coalition of Women meeting.

"Don't let them give you coffee," Dawn said. "It'll only make you have to pee."

"Do you want to know why I'm here?" I asked.

"You probably got a DWI," she said. "Someone like you, that's the only reason you'd wind up here."

"Guess again," I said. And then, even though she didn't ask, I told Dawn the whole story. I told her about Mason's three kids by three different women. I told her about Julie's yelling at me about the pig remark. I told her about the farm and the meth and Mason's paintings and Lucky the horse and how I had neglected to properly secure the corral gate and how I had been so sure that Mason was clean that I'd invited the sheriff in to look at the paintings—"because they're actually really good, because he's actually quite talented, a member of the New York art community even said so." I explained how the maniac Julie had broken into the tack room and left the meth on the table and how she had left a note that was not only unoriginal and overdramatic but also *misspelled*—"because that's how stupid she is and she takes his money and buys the kid Barbies for Christ's sake." And when I got to the end, adding that I had just, that very day, found out I'd been fired from my job, though now it seemed like weeks ago, Dawn looked at me and rolled her eyes. I waited for her to tell me to get off the farm. I waited for her to say, like Daphne had said that night at Bar Barella, that I had to leave him. Period.

"Man," Dawn said. "That sucks that you got fired."

One Year Later

To: Lucinda Trout
From: Sarah Vanderhorn
Re: Chamomile Press submission

First of all, mea culpa for taking so long to respond to your delightful book proposal *Inspirations from the Heartland: A Prairie Meditation.* Between my travel schedule and a slew of manuscripts the months just got away from me. Eighteen months to be precise, ooh a million apologies! At any rate, I'm afraid I signed another writer to the heartland book before I had a chance to read your manuscript. However, there has been some interest in our office in a book on the topic of *Almost Amish.* It seems there's a national trend toward "plain" living as exemplified through sobriety, celibacy (for singles), and lack of reliance on technology. As someone who has been living the simple life for a while now, perhaps this is a subject you're familiar with. I envision this volume including high-resolution photos of sparsely furnished homes with Shaker furniture (I know the Shakers are different from the Amish, but you know what I mean). Let me know if you'd like to kick around some ideas. In the meantime, happy simplicity!

To: Sarah Vanderhorn
From: Lucinda Trout
Re: Re: Chamomile Press submission

Fuck you and the horse you rode in on.

True emancipation on the prairie is simply not possible without four-wheel drive. If it hadn't been for Sue, who sold me her Isuzu Trooper when she decided to buy a Subaru Outback, I would have been forced to leave the farm. I know that sounds reductive, but sometimes you have to reduce things to their bare essentials—and in this case it was the winter conditions of County Road F—to fully understand what you need to survive. I needed better traction. Mason needed a spiritual guide.

In the weeks following my arrest, Mason, who hadn't been charged with drug possession given the odd circumstances of the break-in, took his few belongings out of the house and moved back to his cabin, which was really Frank Fussell's cabin, and embarked on a meditational journey that commenced with a complete rereading of the works of Emerson and Thoreau and concluded, several months later, with the inclusion of two of his paintings in a group show for local artists at the gallery adjacent to the Heidi Vidlak Memorial Film Theater. In a write-up in the *Prairie City Daily Dispatch*, Loni Heibel-Budicek (who occasionally doubled as an art critic) called the work "weird and slightly disturbed but also fun, mostly due to its quirky devotion to the local landscape." Mason cut out the review and nailed it to the door of the cabin. "This way people will know what they're getting into," he said.

I spent most of my days alone, talking on the phone with Daphne and Elena and trying to convince them to move to Prairie

City and start an artists' colony (or even a publicity firm—I was open to anything) at the farm. I'd tried to be angry at Mason for what he had done, but in the end, I found it hard to be mad. At dusk, the light hit the tall grass in the west pasture with such a breathtaking yellow glow that I could only feel gratitude toward anyone who could have brought me to such a place. Though Mason had cried when he'd moved out, he'd also said he felt like he was leaving a movie set. "It's just you and the pig and Sam Shepard now," he'd told me. "But I'll still mow your lawn."

I learned to mow the lawn myself, though. Teri gave me her tractor mower when she decided to hire a professional landscaper and, when it broke, Leonard came over to fix it. As much as I cringed at the knowledge that the Coalition of Women had, to a large extent, been right all along about Mason, I was so grateful for their help that when it came my turn to select the book club title I chose Idabelle Sugar's *Ain't No Mountain Too Steep for Me and My Girl Posse* and dedicated it to "the friendship and sisterhood shown to me by all of you" (though I did not read it). I hosted all-women dinner parties and served tofu steaks from the health-food store. I let Teri practice acupuncture on me after I twisted my ankle when climbing out of the Isuzu Trooper. In the end, none of that was really necessary. Everyone understood that everyone screwed up once in a while. "Don't be so hard on yourself," Sue said to me. "I once dated a woman who'd voted for Barry Goldwater. Talk about lowering your standards!"

I took it upon myself to learn how to be alone on the farm. I cleaned out the pig's stall and kept track of the propane level and knocked the cobwebs out of the barn rafters. Though I sent the horses packing when I asked Mason to leave, a trough of frozen water no longer seemed beyond the realm of my coping ability. I also got a proper job. I taught journalism at Prairie City State College. I sent students out to cover church fairs and antique shows. I taught them how to interview people so that they forgot they were being interviewed. "Tell them your problems so they'll tell you theirs," I said. "Confess your worst sin. Make it up." Even at nineteen, they had sins. They didn't need to invent them. A few told me they wanted to go to New York. They wanted to live in the Village. They wanted to go to cafés and foreign movies and date artists. I told them to go immediately, to go before they made a mistake that would keep them here forever. Most never went. They stayed. Like the westbound homesteaders a hundred years earlier, the ease of staying was matched only by the difficulty of leaving. The wind blew too hard to take a step forward. A person couldn't make it to age twenty without succumbing to prairie madness. I was afflicted now, too. The fever of complacency lulled me to sleep at night in that big, creaking house. The sheer size of the place still felt like a marvel. I was addicted to all the space. There would be no going back to my old life.

The next spring, a colt was born, the result of Lucky's afternoon excursion on that day I got hauled away. Mason paid the neighbor's veterinary bills. Like a dutiful Lamaze coach, he visited the mare as she swelled like a wound. He wanted to adopt the colt when it got old enough and keep it at my farm. It had been so long since he'd had one, he said. He felt it was time for another, plus Erin wanted a horse and I, if I had any sense, would want one, too.

I was hesitant about the colt idea, but all summer long, as the tornado warnings came in and out like the afternoons themselves, I would drive down the road on the way to town to see the little animal tearing around his pasture like a wild thing. He fell so many times you'd have thought he'd damage himself forever. But, always, he got up like nothing had happened. In all that space, under all that sky, there was no form of recklessness the homesteaders hadn't already tried. There was no mess that the wind couldn't blow away.